NORTH - EASTERN EDUCATION AND LIBRARY BOARD

BOOKS are issued for 21 days but may be renewed on request
F if not required by other readers. Please quote date due
O and details in Box A above.
R

YOU are requested to take care of the stock and to notify
the staff if any book has been in contact with an
infectious disease.

Library Headquarters: BALLYMENA. Tel: 41531/2

LOUISE BRINDLEY
THE SMOKE SCREEN

BANTAM PRESS

LONDON · NEW YORK · TORONTO · SYDNEY · AUCKLAND

TRANSWORLD PUBLISHERS LTD
61–63 Uxbridge Road, London W5 5SA

TRANSWORLD PUBLISHERS (AUSTRALIA) PTY LTD
15–23 Helles Avenue, Moorebank, NSW 2170

TRANSWORLD PUBLISHERS (NZ) LTD
3 William Pickering Drive,
Albany, Auckland

Published 1992 by Bantam Press
a division of Transworld Publishers Ltd

A catalogue record for this book is available
from the British Library

ISBN 0 593 02463 X

Printed and bound in Great Britain by
Biddles Ltd, Guildford and King's Lynn

Julian and Brandon;
for the good times.

THE SMOKE SCREEN

Prologue

Paris in November. A thin rain had fallen throughout that weekend, Suki remembered. Not that she had minded. Apart from shopping, they had spent most of the time in the hotel overlooking The Champs Elysées. The waiters who had brought food and champagne to the suite had called her 'Madame', and she had flaunted the wedding ring – borrowed for the occasion – and the magnificent solitaire diamond Faulkner had given her, revelling in the luxury of it all, the gilded Empire sofas and chairs, soft carpets, apricot silk-shaded lamps, the great white jardinières of long-stemmed roses. At dusk, the view of the floodlit Arc de Triomphe from the balcony windows. She had not even disliked the sexual aspects of the affair which she had accepted as the price one paid for the privilege of rich living. Nor had it crossed her mind to feel guilty . . .

London in February. Snow falling from a leaden sky yellowed by the glow of neon lights. Homeward bound office workers scurrying beneath a multitude of black umbrellas.

Looking out of her office window, Suki saw Faulkner's secretary crossing the slush-filmed carpark, hurrying, head bent, towards her pale blue Citröen.

The coast clear, Suki went along the corridor to

Faulkner's office. Not bothering to knock, she entered to find him shuffling papers into his briefcase. Smiling, she perched becomingly on the edge of his desk, crossing her legs. He seemed preoccupied. The employer not the lover. What curious creatures men were. One might almost suppose that the weekend in Paris had never happened. A sudden image of him standing shuffling papers in his underwear presented itself. Pompous idiot!

'In a hurry?' she asked, tapping her heels against the desk.

He gave her his busy, put-out look, 'I'm late as it is, and the roads are bound to be bad with this damned snow. Is it important?'

'The reason I'm here? Well, yes, you could say that.' Her smile deepened. She sighed. 'You see, I'm going to have your child.'

Chapter One

Faulkner was later than usual. Almost eight o'clock, and still no sign of him. Glancing out of the kitchen window, Sarah saw that it had stopped snowing. Still, the roads must be bad, traffic out of London almost at a standstill. Thank goodness she had decided on a casserole, not chops, for the evening meal, she thought, turning down the oven temperature.

He drove out of London on the M4, cursing the lumbering pantechnicons and goods vehicles, the flung spray hitting the windscreen, stunned by the news that Suki was going to have his child.

He had, at first, refused to believe her, assuming that she would have taken the necessary precautions. Why hadn't she? Bemused, sensing a trap, angry. 'What the hell do you expect me to do about it?'

'It's quite simple really, darling. You have a choice to make.' Getting up from the desk, placing her hands on his shoulders, looking up at him with those devastatingly lovely blue eyes of hers, she said, 'You must ask your wife to divorce you.'

'But that's impossible! Out of the question!'

'Why? I know you're not in love with her. You told me so, in Paris. Remember?'

'Even so . . .'

'Shall I tell you the alternative?' Suki's smile resembled

that of the Mona Lisa. 'If you don't tell her tonight that you want your freedom, I shall either have an abortion, go to New York, and you'll never see me again – or I might just decide to have the child, name you as the father, and claim maintenance. But no, forget I said that. You see, darling, I'm so terribly in love with you!' The violet blue eyes swam suddenly with tears. And, Oh, Christ, he thought, spitted on the horns of a dilemma, knowing that he wanted Suki as he had never before wanted a woman.

'Promise me you'll tell her tonight? Tomorrow may be too late.' He had sensed then the closing of the trap; albeit a velvet trap.

Driving west, Faulkner wondered how he would break it to his wife that he wanted his freedom to marry a girl scarcely older than his daughter.

Quitting the motorway, nosing the Mercedes through Marlborough, passing beneath the 'bridge of sighs' as the college students called it, he turned left at Fyfield, four miles out of Marlborough, swept the car through a series of hamlets; then signalling right, he entered his driveway, eased the car into the garage, and switched off the ignition.

Sarah knew, from long experience of her husband's philandering, when this latest affair had begun. Not the name of the woman, although she could hazard a guess. The signs had been umistakable – his restlessness and underlying excitement; traces of perfume on his clothing, that November 'business' trip to Paris from which he had returned in evasive mood, unwilling to discuss even the broad outline of his visit. And so, in a sense, she was half prepared for the outburst that would shatter her life.

She knew by his face when he came into the house that

something was wrong. Not that he was ever communicative, but it struck her as odd that he made no reference to his lateness or the state of the weather. Standing in the hall, she watched him take off his outdoor things and go through to the drawing room, walking unsteadily, she thought, as though he had been drinking. He seemed not to have noticed her, like a blind man, or one so deeply enmeshed in his own thoughts that he remained unaware of his actions; oblivious of the fact that he had not even spoken to her.

Following, she saw him switch on the lights, bringing the room into focus, illuminating the Lowry painting over the mantelpiece (a picture she had never cared for), watched silently as he went over to the drinks cabinet and poured himself a stiff whisky. No ice. She thought how his waist had thickened throughout the years. He had been slim as a young man. Now he relied on his tailor to minimize the toll of rich living.

She said, 'Dinner's ready when you are.'

'I'm not hungry.'

'What's wrong, Faulkner?'

'Everything's wrong.' Downing his first glass of whisky at a gulp, he poured himself another, and stood nursing the glass, his back towards her. She sensed that this was deliberate.

'Would you care to explain?' She stood quite still. Waiting.

'I want you to divorce me.'

Puzzled by his wife's silence, he turned, glass in hand. 'Did you hear what I said?'

'I heard.' It had happened at last, this thing she had been half expecting all along. She felt relieved, almost, that the waiting was over.

13

'Then why don't you say something?' He was on the defensive now.

'What do you expect me to say? Are you so blind as to believe that I knew nothing of your love affairs? The times you have been unfaithful to me?'

'I don't know what you mean.' His mouth sagged open in surprise. 'What the hell are you talking about?'

'The word is adultery, which you have committed time and time again during the past years. Oh, don't bother to deny it. It started when the children were little. Her name was Carmen Longstaff, that journalist who wrote an article about you for a Sunday newspaper.'

'Carmen Longstaff?' The name meant less than nothing to him now.

'Don't tell me you've forgotten? After all, you did sleep with her in our bed!'

This was a Sarah he had never seen before, a quietly angry woman thrusting unpalatable truths down his throat. 'If you have forgotten her, I haven't. We were on holiday in Dorset at the time, when you received that mysterious phone call from London. You left the children and me to finish the holiday alone. They cried when they knew you had gone away without bothering to say goodbye to them. I told them what you told me, that you had an urgent business appointment. They didn't understand. How could they?'

'Oh yes, that bloody holiday in Dorset,' he said scathingly, 'when you left me alone with the children to poke around Lawrence's cottage?'

'And how do you suppose I felt, trying to explain that "Mummy" had taken it into her head to swan off by herself for the day?'

'It's no use, Faulkner. You are not pinning the blame

14

for what you did, on me. You destroyed our marriage as deliberately as if you had taken an axe to it!' Sarah's anger was rising now.

'You are imagining things,' he blustered. 'But then, you always did have an overfertile imagination!'

'To the extent of imagining the initialled handkerchief I found under my pillow when the children and I came back from Dorset? But *why*? Why did you do it?'

'You really want to know? Well, I suggest that you take a look at yourself in the mirror. Tell me if the woman you see there bears the slightest resemblance to the girl I married.' Swallowing his second drink, 'Very well then, I admit it! I *have* made love to other women. The reason why I leave to your imagination. You are fat, Sarah, a fat, dowdy woman who never cared tuppence about my friends, my career. Any other woman would have given her eyeteeth to possess half I've given you – this house, a car, plenty of money . . . '

'Money, which has always been your god,' Sarah said bitterly, 'but what about decency and honour? What about the children? Tell me, Faulkner, why this sudden, urgent need of freedom? Could it be that the woman you took to Paris is pregnant?' Sarah knew, by her husband's expression, that she had hit the nail on the head. 'Well, are you going to tell me her name, or shall I make another educated guess?'

Badly shaken, Faulkner said, 'Her name is Suki Mitford, my public relations officer. I happen to be in love with her.'

'Love? I doubt if you know the meaning of the word.' Sarah turned her head away, hating the scene of their confrontation – the modernistically furnished drawing room with windows at the far end overlooking the patio and the swimming pool, which reminded her of the set of a West End play, or one of those upmarket TV sit-coms at which audiences rocked with laughter. 'By the way, how old is this woman you're in love with? Twenty-two? Twenty-three?'

'What the hell has Suki's age got to do with it?'

'A great deal, I imagine, from the children's point of view! Has it never occurred to you to wonder how they'll feel when they find out that you intend marrying a girl half your age?'

'It is none of their business!'

'That's where you are wrong. It is very much their business. You might have got away with an older woman, but this . . . ' Suddenly Sarah's anger evaporated. Looking at her husband, she saw him, momentarily, not as the man he was now, but the man he used to be.

'Can't we be adult about this?' Faulkner refilled his glass. 'Couldn't we leave Suki out of this for the time being? Tell them that we have agreed to end our marriage on friendly terms?'

'No, Faulkner, I'm sorry. I refuse to lie to them any more. I am tired of lying on your behalf. All these years – covering up for you! Daddy has gone to Vienna, Rome, Paris, Madrid, New York, or wherever, on a business trip. No, Faulkner, the ball is in your court now. I'm leaving.'

'*Leaving?* What do you mean, *leaving?*'

'I thought you wanted your freedom? Well, now it's all yours! Take it, and be thankful!'

'But you can't simply walk out on me like this!'

'Can't I? Just watch me!'

'Christ, Sarah, you are putting me in a hell of a position!'

'*I* am putting *you?*'

16

Faulkner said disbelievingly, 'You can't leave at this time of night.'

'Nine o'clock is scarcely the witching hour.'

'But we haven't discussed the divorce.'

Oh God, she thought, what had happened to all the love and laughter they had once shared?

'Just tell me what you want done, and I'll do it.' Sarah spoke very quietly, drained of emotion. No longer angry. Just tired.

'Well, obviously I wish to marry Suki as soon as possible . . .'

'Till the End of Time', that romantic song sung by Della Reece. Why should she think of that now? Perhaps because time seemed to have run out.

' . . . Don't worry, I'll take care of you financially: make you a generous allowance, and you can keep the car.' Making plans. Pleased now that he had brought the matter to a head, had not prevaricated when it came to telling his wife that he wanted his freedom, ruthless in all things, Faulkner Vale knew that he usually got what he wanted in the end.

Sarah looked at him as if she had never really seen him before. 'I don't want the car, or your money. I am not a servant to be pensioned off with a golden handshake. All I want is what is mine by right, my books, pictures and furniture. Now I'm going upstairs to pack.'

She was emptying drawers, folding clothes into a suitcase when he followed her to her room. 'This is utterly ridiculous and childish,' he said thickly, swaying slightly on his feet.

'But then I *am* ridiculous. You have made me so.' Sarah closed the case.

17

'But we haven't settled about the divorce yet. We have to talk.'

'What is there left to talk about?' she asked quietly. 'We have said everything that needed to be said. Things we might have said to each other a long time ago, not harshly but gently.'

Picking up the case, taking a final glance round the room, 'I'll go down and ring for a taxi now, if you'll allow me to pass.'

He was standing in the doorway, a powerfully built man, glossed over with success, hair greying at the temples, the picture of a self-made tycoon whose business acumen had brought him to the top of the ladder, a far cry from the eager, questing man she had married twenty years ago.

'About the divorce,' he persisted, wanting everything cut and dried.

'I'll ring my solicitor first thing tomorrow morning. Don't worry, Faulkner. I want this divorce just as much as you do!'

Brushing past him, Sarah hurried downstairs, rang for a taxi, put on her outdoor things, and stood near the front door, waiting, praying the driver would hurry, feeling like a lost soul, faced with the realization that her decision to leave this house would mean not simply the end of her marriage but the loss of security; the loss of a familiar if not an ideal way of life.

Tension mounting minute by minute, Sarah saw the sweep of headlights as the taxi entered the drive, and heard the crunch of its tyres on the snow. Opening the front door, she walked out into the darkness, aware that Faulkner was standing on the stairs, watching.

'The Castle and Ball Hotel,' she told the driver.

As the car moved forward, the headlights illuminated

briefly the bushes flanking the driveway, the ice-filmed fishpond, the gateposts. Turning her head to look back, she saw, for the last time, the house in which she had spent the past ten years of her life, and glimpsed, through undrawn curtains, the drawing room where the saddest decision of her life had been made. The only possible decision in a no-win situation such as this.

She could not have borne to remain in the house a moment longer: to pick over the bones of a failed marriage.

The taxi driver idled his engine at the Fyfield turn off, a dangerous crossing even in daylight. Then, when the road was clear, signalling right, he accelerated and drove quickly towards their destination.

As Sarah had anticipated, the hotel was half empty, Marlborough a ghost town.

Asking for a single room, she booked in, and was shown up to it by a fresh-faced girl who wanted to know if she would require dinner. It was then Sarah remembered that she had left her husband's dinner in the oven. Would he eat it or leave it to burn? Strange to think that what Faulkner did, from now on, need not concern her.

She said she was not hungry, and, when the girl had closed the door, Sarah looked out of the window at the snow-filmed High Street. Nothing would have induced her to stay another night under the roof of that oversized house built by Faulkner more as a status symbol than a home. Chilled by the memory of the final confrontation, feeling lost and forlorn, she remembered the hurtful things they had said to each other; that searing moment when she knew she must go away. And yet she knew that her hastily spoken words, 'I want this divorce as much as you do,' were not strictly true, in face of the years she had spent trying to hold the marriage together for the sake of the children.

Why hadn't she tackled Faulkner about his relationship with Carmen Longstaff at the time of his first affair? Why hadn't she mentioned the handkerchief she had found under her pillow? Cowardice? Perhaps. But that episode had marked the end of their own relationship. Faulkner had made some excuse to sleep in the spare room, and the practice had continued. They had never gone on holiday together again. Following the Dorset disaster, she had taken the children to Gloucestershire to stay with their grandparents, making the excuse that Faulkner was too busy to come with them.

This, at any rate, had been partially true. Faulkner had entered the field of user computers at exactly the right time, and if her parents thought it odd that their son-in-law had not put in an appearance apart from driving his family to and from the old vicarage, and noticed the coolness which had sprung up between their daughter and her husband, they were too wise to make an issue of it, although Sarah's mother had taken her aside one day and asked if things were all right at home. And, 'Of course, Mum,' Sarah replied brightly. 'Faulkner really is up to his eyes in work at the moment.'

'You would tell me if anything was wrong?'

'Nothing's wrong, honestly.' She had felt guilty, uttering an untruth, but how could she possibly have burdened two gentle people, who believed in the sanctity of marriage, with Faulkner's infidelity?

'I just wanted to be sure.'

Sarah had wept, later, when the children were asleep, remembering the way she had felt on her wedding day – so much in love that she couldn't see clouds for stardust.

Their first home, a terraced house in Swindon, had seemed like heaven to her. She had been engaged in secretarial work at the time, whilst Faulkner, struggling to gain a foothold on the ladder of success, had attended evening classes in computer technology, advanced mathematics, French, German, and Italian.

He had not been overjoyed, Sarah realized, when she told him she was pregnant. 'Oh, Christ,' he groaned, running his fingers through his hair, 'this would have to happen now, when we need every penny we can lay hands on!'

'I thought you'd be pleased.' The first niggling seed of doubt had entered her mind. 'You *are* pleased, aren't you?'

'Yes, of course.' But she knew that he wasn't. Not really, when, ruffling her hair, he added, 'Never mind, as soon as the baby's born, you'll be able to start work again.'

'Are you suggesting that we should – farm out our child?'

'Darling, there are such things as nursery schools!'

'I daresay, at a price. And I don't mean money!'

The thought of dumping her baby in a crèche for some other woman to take care of had seemed horrendous to Sarah, but Faulkner had been unwilling to discuss the matter further. That was the first time she had come up against the driving force of his ambition, his overriding love of money.

In the event, Sarah had never gone back to work. Eleven months after the birth of her son, Richard, she had produced a daughter, to Faulkner's displeasure – who appeared to hold his wife responsible for the short time lapse between her confinements.

Then she had been faced with the endless routine of nappy changing, getting up at the crack of dawn to either breast or bottle feed the infants, never knowing which one to attend to first, whilst Faulkner, the uninterested father, closing his ears to their wailing, had remained in bed, his head jammed against the pillows.

It seemed odd on the face of it, Sarah thought, turning away from the hotel window, that Faulkner, who did not care for children, was now prepared to rush into a second marriage with the certainty of becoming a father yet again. But, with money no object, this time he would engage a nanny, and Suki Mitford, whom Faulkner had described as, 'Tall, blonde. Very bright and efficient', when she joined the firm, would raise no objection to that arrangement.

Undressing, Sarah got into bed. The sheets felt chilly. Hailstones cracked against the window. Unable to sleep, she dreaded the thought of tomorrow, of seeing her solicitor; setting the wheels of the divorce in motion. Above all, she worried about the children, thinking she had, perhaps, been too harsh in putting that particular ball squarely into Faulkner's court. She was, after all, their mother, and too many hurtful, cruel things had already been said and done.

Mr Lumsden, who had acted on Sarah's behalf in various small disputes connected with her writing career, had his offices in Swindon.

Telephoning from the Castle and Ball after an early breakfast, she made an appointment to see him at eleven o'clock, packed her case, paid her bill, and caught a bus to Swindon from the High Street.

George Lumsden was delighted to see her. 'What is it this time?' he enquired jovially, asking his receptionist to bring in some coffee and biscuits, 'Another publishing firm in arrears with their royalties?'

'More serious than that, I'm afraid.'

'My dear girl, this is shocking news,' he said, when she told him what had happened, thinking that Faulkner Vale, despite his business acumen, must be lacking in native intelligence to even consider making an honest woman of a girl, half his age, daft, or shrewd enough to have allowed herself to become pregnant by him in a Paris hotel bedroom.

'You will act on my behalf?' Sarah, shivering with cold, beseeched him.

'But of course, my dear! Now, please drink your coffee. You look half frozen.'

'The bus wasn't very warm.'

'The – *bus?*' Lumsden appeared even more shocked. 'But, surely, you have a car?'

'*Had* a car.' Sarah attempted a smile. 'I left it behind, last night, after the row. I told my husband I didn't want the car, or his money, and I meant it. All I want are my personal belongings, and his written assurance that he will look after the children, financially, until they are old enough to fend for themselves – Verity in particular.'

'But this is a nonsense! Forgive me, but your husband is a very rich man who has responsibilities towards you as well as his children. Maintenance is not to be sniffed at. You will need money – a great deal of money . . . I *am* right in thinking that your husband will not expect you to leave the family home?'

'I have already done so, Mr Lumsden,' Sarah said quietly.

'In the heat of the moment, perhaps. But you will go back there eventually?'

'No. I shall never go back.'

Lumsden drummed the desk anxiously with his finger-tips, deciding how best to tackle this curious situation, faced, as he was, with a client whom he greatly liked and admired, who, nevertheless, was not acting in her own best interests.

Coming to a decision, he said, 'I understand your feelings but, as your friend as well as your solicitor, I must advise you to consider your position. Your husband can well afford to pay the price of his indiscretion. Indeed, in my view, he should be made to do so.'

'No, Mr Lumsden. I am grateful to you, but I should feel like a "kept" woman. Besides, perhaps it is time I learned to stand on my own feet.'

'But how will you manage? Where will you go? What will you do?'

'I haven't the faintest idea. Possibly I shall move away from this area entirely.'

'But, surely, my dear, you will want to make a home for your children when the dust of this affair has settled?'

'I'm not sure they'd appreciate that, Mr Lumsden.' Sarah set down her coffee cup and saucer. 'I realize, of course, that I still think of them as children, but they have been living their own lives for some time now; sharing flats with their fellow students. The last thing they need is a mother flapping her wings over them, making them feel guilty if they failed to turn up every weekend to visit me. They would hate that kind of commitment.'

Facing the stone wall of Sarah's resistance, drawing in a deep breath, Lumsden tried a new tack. Treading on eggshells, 'This is a very personal question,' he said, 'but how are you placed financially at the moment?'

'Frankly,' she admitted, 'I'm not very well off right now, but my Public Lending Rights' earnings are due at the end of the month, and there are bound to be royalties in March or April from *Lawrence*; *Swan Song* – you know, the novel I wrote based on the life of Anna Pavlova? From *The Visionary*, and *Faery Lands Forlorn*.'

'Would that your books had earned the recognition they deserved,' Lumsden said stalwartly. 'I have read all of them, and they are in a class of their own. Every one of them a potential bestseller.'

'I didn't write them to make money,' Sarah said gently. 'I wrote them for the sheer, possibly the selfish pleasure of the research involved, to take my mind off . . . ' She stopped speaking abruptly.

'I think I understand, my dear. You mean that your husband's affair, with Miss Mitford, was not the first?'

'No. But the children never knew, and they mustn't be told.'

Glancing at her watch, rising quickly to her feet, 'Well, I'd better be going.'

'Where to?'

'To London, to see the children: tell them what has happened.'

'Then where will you go?' Lumsden enquired anxiously.

'I don't know.'

'But you will keep in touch? I shall need to know what to do about your furniture, your personal belongings.'

'I wonder, would it be possible to have them put in store for the time being, until I decide what to do with them?'

'Yes, of course. I know a good firm in Marlborough. Meanwhile, I shall write to your husband saying that I am acting on your behalf.' Lumsden smiled sadly. 'Cold comfort, perhaps, but since Mr Vale has admitted his adultery with Miss Mitford, the proceedings should be quite straightforward. Even more straightforward since you are not seeking maintenance – although you know my feelings on that score.'

'Please don't be angry with me.'

'As if I could. But there is such a thing as fair play, and, in my opinion, you have not had a fair crack of the whip.'

She caught a train from Swindon to Paddington, where she treated herself to a ham sandwich and a cup of coffee before going in search of a telephone booth, from which she dialled the number of Verity's school of art.

'My name is Sarah Vale,' she told the voice on the other end of the line. 'May I speak to my daughter, Verity? It is rather urgent.'

'Hang on a sec. I'll find out.'

Nervousness chewed at Sarah as she waited.

'Hello, Mummy? Why are you ringing? Is anything the matter? Where are you?' Verity sounded faintly hostile, Sarah thought, cradling the receiver.

'I'm here, in London, darling. The thing is, I'd like to see you and Richard as soon as possible. Could you meet me somewhere?'

'Richard's not here. He's gone off somewhere on a computer course.' A pause. 'Look, Mummy, what is all this? You sound terribly uptight. Daddy's not ill, is he?'

'No, he's perfectly well.'

'Then why all the mystery? It isn't terribly convenient, you know, dragging me away from my life class like this.'

'I'll explain later. Where can we meet?' Sarah felt like a delinquent child about to face a bad-tempered headmistress.

'Oh, very well, then. The Cedar Cafe in Kensington High Street. I'll be there around four thirty.' The line went dead. Verity had hung up in her usual, abrupt manner.

Awaiting Verity, Sarah rehearsed what she would say to her. But how to begin a conversation leading to a betrayal?

Watching the door which opened frequently to admit students from the nearby colleges, listening to their chatter, she worried about their inadequate clothing. But they were young, Sarah thought. Young, strong and unafraid of catching cold. Unafraid of life. Sitting alone, waiting, Sarah felt old by comparison, out of place. Then Verity walked in, wearing stone-washed jeans and a faded blue anorak, long blonde hair whipped by the wind, clutching a portfolio, a bulging Italian leather bag slung over her left shoulder.

'I've saved you a seat.' Sarah smiled.

'So I see.' Verity did not return her mother's smile; made no attempt to kiss her. Putting down the portfolio, unhitching the bag, 'Well, let's have it,' she said. 'Daddy *is* ill, isn't he?'

'No, I told you.'

'Oh, come on, Mummy. You're as transparent as a pane of glass. You didn't come to London to drink coffee. You hate London.'

In one sense, Verity's attitude came as a relief to Sarah. The girl had obviously geared her mind to receive bad news. Even so, words were difficult to formulate. She said haltingly, 'The fact is, your father wants his freedom. I have agreed to a divorce.'

A moment's stunned silence, then Verity said mutinously, 'I might have guessed this would happen. My God, Mummy, but how could you have let it?'

'You don't understand . . . '

'Of course I bloody well understand! I'm not a child.'

'You talk as if I wanted this to happen.' Sarah felt suddenly bewildered.

'Didn't you? Oh, don't look so shocked. Poor Daddy! How he has put up with you all this time, I can't imagine.'

'*Verity!*'

'If only you had bothered to dress decently, had your hair done; worn at least some makeup. But no, you didn't care tuppence what Daddy's friends said about you behind your back. All you cared about was sitting at that blasted typewriter hammering out stupid books that nobody wanted to read anyway! Richard agrees with me. Know what he calls you? "Sloppy Sally!" Well, I don't blame Daddy for wanting rid of you. I just hope he finds someone . . . '

'He already has,' Sarah said quietly, feeling as though her world had collapsed about her. Tears were close to the surface. Cut to the heart by her daughter's cruelty, the words, 'He already has,' came in almost a whisper. But she must not cry. How could a mere child be expected to understand the stresses of the adult world? The girl had spoken in anger because she had been hurt. Verity, like her father, had always needed a whipping boy.

'What do you mean?'

'Her name is Mitford. Suki Mitford.'

Verity's eyes widened in horror. 'You *are* joking? Not that ghastly blonde bimbo I met one day in his office?'

28

'No, darling, I am not joking.'

'Then damn you both to hell!' Hastily gathering her belongings, Verity rose swiftly to her feet. 'If Daddy imagines . . . You can tell him this from me. If he marries that – that . . . ' Words failed her.

'Verity! Come back!'

But the girl had already gone. Flinging down a pound coin to pay for the coffee she had not touched, Sarah hurried after her.

Standing on the windswept pavement, seeing the uncaring faces of strangers hurrying by, a feeling of desolation swept over Sarah. Slowly, she began walking towards the nearest tube station. Where she would go from there, she had no idea. But she must go somewhere. Impossible to roam the streets of London like a bag lady.

What price her pride and good intentions now? Where did she really belong? Nothing would induce her to return to Marlborough. Her parents were dead, and she had no other living relatives.

Butting her way against a sea of strangers, facing the stinging February wind, wearing slacks, boots, thick-knit sweater, and a green anorak, carrying her case, her mane of gold-brown hair whipping about her face, thinking about her parents brought back memories of the old Gloucestershire vicarage, apple trees in blossom, daisied lawns; the tucked away lane leading to the church of which her father had been the rector. If only memories, like that lane sloping down to the church, might lead to some haven of peace, of physical sanctuary.

Suddenly, there she was, standing near the entrance of High Street Kensington tube station, not knowing where to go, what to do next, gripped with a terrifying fear, like a lost child, desperately in need of help.

At that moment, despite the roar of the traffic, the pulsing noise and confusion of the city, came a curious feeling of calm, a still, small voice, as though her father had spoken to her, implanting the seed of an idea. It was then she remembered the City of York, the happy times she had spent there when her father had been called upon to attend ecumenical meetings at the Archbishop's palace. York, such a lovely, gracious city.

Stepping into the mêlée of strangers thronging the entrance of the tube station – hurrying, grim-faced men and women intent on their own lives, their own problems – filled with a new sense of purpose, Sarah bought a ticket to King's Cross.

The time was ten to six, the York train due to depart at six o'clock. The hands of the station clock had inched forward five minutes by the time she reached the barrier.

Flinging herself and her suitcase into the nearest compartment, she managed to find herself a seat.

What she would do when she arrived in York, she had not the remotest idea, apart from finding cheap accommodation for the night. Then what?

'Sufficient unto the day . . . ' Leaning her head against the window, watching the lights of London slipping away through the enveloping darkness of a winter night – all those glaring neon lights searing the sky above the world's greatest city with its multitude of lost and lonely people – Sarah saw, when the neon city had been left far behind; across invisible fields, the little, winking lights of scattered homesteads in which ordinary people, like herself, lived and had their being.

The thought occurred that, somewhere, there must be a place for her; peace of mind. Perhaps running away wasn't the answer. It was, however, the only answer that made sense at this stage of her life, this distancing from all that had gone before. Her marriage to Faulkner, in which she had witnessed the changes success had wrought in him, so that she no longer recognized the man who had once been all the world to her.

She could have forgiven his first affair if he had come to her and told her the truth. What she could not forgive, that he had allowed the pursuit of money and success to coarsen his spirit. Nor could she forget the way in which lying had become second nature, so that she had lost faith in him. Just as terrifyingly, she had lost faith in herself as a wife. The greater Faulkner's success, the more ineffectual she had been, incapable of understanding the purpose of it all, when success had, seemingly, meant the end of happiness. Or perhaps Faulkner did not see things that way and had grown impatient with her because of her lack of enthusiasm for the trappings of wealth, her inability to shine among his new-found coterie of friends and business associates, her refusal to join the flower-arranging groups and the women's luncheon clubs to which his friends' wives belonged.

And so she had turned inward upon herself, finding solace in the written word, losing herself in the research she loved, blotting out the present in the vital, to her, the living world of the past.

Chapter Two

The Perivale Guest House was both cheap and depressing, but beggars could not be choosers.

Sarah's narrow room was, at least, clean, the food adequate if not inspirational. She disliked eggs cooked in oil, the yolks unbloomed, warmed through meat and soggy vegetables.

Thankfully, her Public Lending Rights' cheque would soon be paid into her bank account – a little under six hundred pounds – which proved that some people must be borrowing her books from their local libraries. Still, she had a long way to go before hitting the maximum six thousand pounds available to bestselling authors.

Sarah had spent her first week at the Perivale writing change of address letters to Mr Lumsden, her agent, Freya Soboil, her bank manager and her children. Freya had written back, on pink notepaper, wanting to know what the hell was going on? Why on earth she had decided to stick herself away in the 'wilds' of Yorkshire, and had she any new book in the pipeline? Reading that letter, Sarah smiled, conjuring up a vision of her unorthodox agent, sitting at her desk, filling the page with that childishly looped handwriting of hers.

The reply from Mr Lumsden, on the other hand, typed on headed notepaper, was businesslike in the extreme. 'I write to inform you that Mr Faulkner Vale is now acquainted with your intention to institute divorce proceedings against him on the grounds of his adultery with Miss Susan Mitford. Mr Vale has, furthermore, agreed to the removal of your personal belongings from your former home, to be placed, pro-tem, in Hindle's repository in Marlborough, awaiting your further instructions. Yours, etc.,'.

Typically, Mr Lumsden had added a personal P.S. 'My dear Sarah, How are you coping? Anxiously awaiting news. Yours sincerely, George Lumsden.'

Sarah wrote back immediately: 'Dear Mr Lumsden, the Perivale Guest House is not my idea of paradise, but it will do well enough until I find somewhere permanent to live, to which end I have literally haunted the local estate agents, most of whom have started hiding when they see me coming.

'They cannot, apparently, understand that I do not want a couple of furnished rooms with use of kitchen and toilet facilities, but a self-contained, unfurnished flat, preferably within walking distance of the city centre. I realize, of course, that I am asking for the moon, that coming across a Ming vase on a junk stall would be marginally easier than finding an unfurnished flat to rent in this day and age. But I shall keep on trying.

'York, at any rate, has not proved a disappointment. The more I see of it, the more I love it. How to explain? It's as though history lies encapsulated within these grey city walls.

'At the moment, I am casting around for the theme of a new novel, and I think, possibly, that I have found one . . .'

Laying down her pen, Sarah recalled that coach trip to the Hutton-le-Hole folk museum. Looking out of the coach window, she had regretted, momentarily, the loss of her red Mini. How enchanting it would have been to explore this green and pleasant countryside alone, stopping when and where she chose: making discoveries along the way, instead of which she had found herself lumbered with an elderly spinster in the next seat – a Miss Prynne – who had obviously visited the folk museum many times before, and would insist on telling Sarah all about it beforehand.

'But, to my way of thinking,' Miss Prynne said, 'the glass furnace is the most interesting of all the exhibits.'

'In what way?' Sarah's natural good manners forbade the turning of a deaf ear.

'Because, my dear, it is unique. Proof positive of those unknown glassworkers of Elizabethan times, who came and went, in Rosedale, leaving hardly a trace behind them.'

'Tell me more.' Suddenly, Sarah's interest in Miss Prynne had ceased to be that of politeness. 'You mean those Elizabethan glassworkers came to this area, built the furnaces, then simply disappeared as if they had never existed?'

'Yes, that is exactly what I mean! Strange, isn't it? Most of them, I imagine, arrived from France both before and after the last quarter of the sixteenth century to escape religious persecution. You see, my dear, years before the massacre of the Huguenots on St Bartholomew's Day in 1572, hundreds of Protestant Frenchmen and their families had sought refuge in England, and the glassworkers were among them.'

The coach had arrived at its destination shortly after Miss Prynne's dissertation on the history of the glassblowers, and they had clambered down to enter the grounds of the museum. Enchanted, Sarah saw a wide expanse of green, dotted about with exact replicas of artisan dwellings throughout the ages, rooms furnished with the artefacts true to every generation of those who had passed this way before, from the humble cottager to the lord of the manor.

Coming, at last, to the Rosedale furnace, housed in the shed built to contain and protect it, Sarah experienced an unaccountable feeling of sadness: an image of strangers, in a strange land, building and working that furnace. So, where had they gone to, what had happened to all those Frenchmen who had come to a foreign country to escape religious persecution? Who were they? What were their names? Why had they simply disappeared, leaving no trace?

Sarah remained in the furnace shed long after her companions had departed, attempting to come to grips with the seed of an idea formulating in her writer's mind, staring at the crumbling stones which had once formed the central chamber where the crucibles had been placed prior to the annealing process, seeing, in her mind's eye, the sweating figures of the men whose task it was to bring wood for the fuelling of the furnace. Seeing them, not as ghosts, but as flesh and blood human beings forced, by circumstance, to face the heat, the roar of the flames, rather than face the bigotry of their own countrymen.

Then she had felt a tug at her sleeve, and Miss Prynne was there beside her, saying the coach was waiting to take the party to Lastingham, for lunch at the Grange.

After lunch, the insistent Miss Prynne had tugged, once more, at Sarah's sleeve. 'Come with me, my dear,' she hissed. 'I have something interesting to show you.'

Unearthing a document from her capacious leather handbag, she said, 'I have here a copy of the Lastingham Church records, which show clearly that, between 1570 and 1600, there was an influx of strangers into the Parish, many of which have a foreign sound – Agaret, for example, Hogonet, Roulland, and Ballaine. And yet no mention of glassblowing occurs in the existing records, apart from one which records the death of the wife of Amabie, the Glassman, in 1593, whose grave I discovered on a previous visit.'

'Where is the grave? Would you show it to me?'

'I hoped you'd ask. I felt sure you'd be interested.' Miss Prynne beamed. 'Come with me, my dear. The grave is tucked away in a neglected corner of the cemetery. Take care, the ground is rather slippery.' Miss Prynne, tall and angular, led the way. 'There are other graves, too, but the stones are indecipherable. One imagines these foreigners were thought little of, the poor things; simply put under the ground and forgotten.'

The air, resinous and moist, smelt of autumn rather than spring, as if the rain and snow of five hundred years had permeated the earth, creating a strange miasma, a sorrowful exhalation of buried grief, of loneliness and pain. Tenderly, Sarah pulled aside the trailing fronds of ivy clambering about the headstone, which she touched gently with sensitive fingertips, tracing the blurred and ancient lettering, as though her touch might bring comfort to the wife of Amabie, the Glassman, who had died so long ago – a stranger in a strange land. But who was Amabie? From where had he come, and why? Strange to think that, almost five hundred years ago, he must have stood where she was standing now, head bowed, watching the interment of his wife's coffin, filled with the pain of loss – a fugitive from his own country, embittered, perhaps, but proud, and strong, unvanquished, unconquerable.

It was then Sarah knew she had the theme of her

next novel, that her time, from now on, would be spent in finding out all she could about glassblowing, reading every book she could lay hands on that was relevant to the massacre of the Huguenots.

Other members of the coach party entered the church-yard at that moment, laughing and talking, casting curious glances at the two silent figures standing in a far corner of the cemetery, 'Whose grave is that you are looking at?' one of the women, a fat blonde, elderly, wearing slacks and trainers, sang out. 'Anyone famous?'

'No, far from.' Sarah managed a smile. Walking forward, knowing she could not bear it if the fat blonde came to look at the grave of Amabie's wife, effectively blocking the way. 'Miss Prynne and I were just saying that this corner could do with a bit of tidying up, weren't we, Miss Prynne?'

'Yes, it's a disgrace.' Miss Prynne reacted magnificently.

'That was very kind, very clever of you,' Miss Prynne said mistily when they boarded the coach for the return journey to York. 'I realized, of course, that you were a kindred spirit the moment I saw you, and I was not mistaken.' She smiled, and the smile lit up her thin, intelligent face. 'It has been a lovely day out. I always try to fit in a visit to Hutton-le-Hole before going home. I taught history, you see, before my retirement. The subject fascinated me.'

'Where do you live?'

'At Lytham St Anne's, near Blackpool, in sheltered accommodation. And you?'

Sarah laughed. 'I am living in a form of "sheltered accommodation" too – the Perivale Guest House in Coppergate, until I find a place of my own.'

'Then I wish you every success, my dear. May you

soon come across that place of your own you are searching for.'

Two days later, walking along Stonegate towards the Minster, Sarah noticed a discreet brass plate bearing the inscription, 'Trumble and Allpress, Estate Agents, established 1906'.

Imbued with a sudden feeling of hope, she walked up two flights of rickety stairs to an office in which time appeared to have stood still, where, having briefly explained the purpose of her visit to an elderly reception-ist, she was ushered along a narrow corridor to the inner sanctum of Mr Eustace Trumble, who rose to his feet as she entered.

'A Mrs Vale to see you.' The receptionist smiled, closed the door and departed.

'Ah yes. Mrs Vale. Please, sit down.' Mr Trumble rubbed his hands together in a washing movement. 'Now, how can I help you?'

Here goes, Sarah thought, smiling to soften the blow. 'I'm looking for an unfurnished flat, to rent. Somewhere quiet, because of my work. I'm a writer, you see, of his-torical novels.' She threw in that item of information to establish her credentials, knowing that most people were impressed by writers, or at least the 'mystique' of their profession. 'A Georgian house would be nice, a spare bedroom an advantage, if and when my children came to visit.'

Catching Mr Trumble's slightly pained expression, 'Not that they would come very often, and they are not children, but young adults. Responsible young adults,' she added quickly, lest Mr Trumble imagined an invasion of rowdy teenagers who would do nasty things to the paintwork.

'Both are at college, in London. My son, Richard, going on twenty, is about to sit his finals in computer technology; his sister, Verity, a year younger, is into her second year at the Kensington School of Art.'

'You specified a Georgian house. May I ask why?'

'It's quite simple, really. You see, my father was a Church of England minister. The house we lived in – the Old Parsonage at Brampton, in Gloucestershire – was a Georgian gem: spacious, elegant, a bit draughty, too, as I recall.' She smiled wistfully, 'But there was a sense of timelessness, and space, and I think that I am probably in need of space at the moment.'

'I see.'

'Oh. I realize that I am asking for the moon, but, as Robert Browning wrote, "A man's reach should exceed his grasp, or what's a heaven for?" I really am desperately in need of a home, Mr Trumble. You will try to help me?'

'Yes, of course. Unfortunately, I have nothing on offer at the moment. You do realize that self-contained flats to rent are practically impossible to come across nowadays? But if you would care to leave your address and telephone number, I will contact you immediately if something suitable turns up.'

'Thank you, Mr Trumble.' Sarah gathered together her belongings, ancient leather shoulder-bag and woollen gloves, 'I'm staying at the Perivale Guest House, in Coppergate. The 'phone number is 419 double O.'

Trumble made a note on his desk pad.

'Don't bother to see me out,' Sarah said, turning at the door, 'I can find my own way. You have been very kind, very patient.' And yet she felt, reaching the street, that her visit to Mr Trumble's office had been a waste of her time and his.

39

*   *   *

Ten days later, on her way down to the dining room, the proprietress told her there had been a phone call from a Mr Trumble. Urgent, by the sound of it, and would she call him back as soon as possible?

Would she?

An appointment to view the property he had in mind had been fixed for ten o'clock the following morning, Eustace Trumble told Sarah. 'I'll meet you outside the south-west door of the Minster, if that is convenient. Yes, the entrance with all the scaffolding. The flat is not very far from there.'

Sarah scarcely slept that night, filled with a sense of predestination, a churning excitement – déjà vu in reverse. In time to come, she would convince herself that she had known exactly what to expect beforehand, as though she had glimpsed, in some former life, the cobbled lane near the house, and the house itself with a narrow path leading to the front door, two patches of grass, iron railings, and wooden tubs filled with early spring flowers.

The day had started sunny, then the sky had begun to cloud over, threatening rain. Taking her umbrella, Sarah sallied forth after breakfast, and walked quickly towards the Minster to await the arrival of Mr Trumble, knowing she was far too early.

Standing near the south-west door, beneath the scaffolding and its adornment of heavy duty dust sheets, dwarfed by the Minster's towering façade of intricately carved stonework, overwhelmed by its beauty and historical significance, she thought about the small miracle that had led her there, that still, small voice beyond the noise and confusion of a busy London street, telling her what to do next, and of that other miracle which had prompted her to take that coach trip to Hutton-le-Hole, the happy chance of her meeting with Miss Prynne, the blinding moment of certainty when she knew she had found the theme of her next book. Now, all she needed was one more miracle, a place of her own in which to write that book.

Mr Trumble, also carrying an umbrella, and armed with a briefcase, arrived at five minutes to ten. 'Good morning, Mrs Vale. About this flat,' he said, without further pre-amble. 'Shall we start walking? I'll explain as we go along.'

Obediently, Sarah fell into step beside him. 'The property,' Mr Trumble continued, as the first drops of rain began to fall, 'belongs to a consortium of archaeologists concerned with the practical field education of students on a world wide basis.

'The main building is, in short, an academy-cum-hostel. There is, however, an annexe comprising two self-contained flats which the administrators are prepared to let to carefully selected tenants.' He paused momentarily to catch his breath. 'Their requirements are nat-urally, somewhat stringent. No pets, no children, and no smoking. You don't smoke, do you?'

'No,' Sarah said firmly, thinking that even if she wanted to, she couldn't afford it.

Apparently relieved, Mr Trumble continued, 'The lower flat of the annexe is occupied by a single gentleman who looks after the garden. There is quite a large and charming garden to the rear of the property for the private use of the tenants. Well, here we are.'

Sarah regarded thoughtfully the kind of house she had pictured in her dreams. Late Georgian in design, with a fanlight-embellished front door, iron bootscrapers, and a brightly polished brass letterbox, set back a little way from the cobbled cul-de-sac leading to the Minster's private car-park, with two patches of grass flanking the path, the iron railings and the tubs of spring flowers she had imagined.

The annexe, set at an oblique angle to the main build-ing, had been added at a later date, but the style of the original had been faithfully copied, with tall windows and a similar front door. In a dreamlike state of enchantment, she noticed, above the high, russet brick wall abutting the black railings of the carpark, the nodding branches of lilac and laburnum; yellow, purple and white buds already forming in anticipation of the coming Maytime.

'Oh, how lovely,' Sarah murmured ecstatically as Mr Trumble preceded her along the path; catching the scent of cool, damp springtime in the air.

Inserting a key in the lock, 'As you see, you would share the entrance with your downstairs' neighbour,' he explained, 'but the two flats are entirely self-contained.'

The hall was narrow, half-panelled, as she had sus-pected, hoped it would be, with a door to the right which, she imagined, would lead to the single gentleman's domain.

'Now, this would be your entrance.' Mr Trumble unlocked a second door at the end of the hall, which he opened to reveal a curving, iron-spindled flight of stairs, leading upwards.

At that precise moment, the door of the ground floor flat opened suddenly to the emergence of a tall, thin man, of scholarly appearance, wearing gold-rimmed glasses, cor-duroy slacks and a disreputable sweater, carrying a pair of garden shears, who stared bemusedly at the elderly estate agent and his companion.

'I am most f-frightfully sorry,' the man said, 'I didn't hear you come in. As you see, I am about to engage in a little g-grass trimming. The front lawns s-scarcely warrant the use of the Flymo. My name is Foster, by the way. Ralph Foster.'

'In case you hadn't noticed, it has started to rain quite heavily,' Sarah said politely.

'Oh, has it? Thanks for telling me. In that c-case, no use tearing it up by the r-roots.' Smiling amiably, he backed away, raised the shears in a kind of salute, turned and closed the door behind him.

Amused by the encounter, Sarah followed Mr Trumble up the curving staircase, her heart beating fast with excitement.

There was a landing with doors leading to the sitting room and the bathroom. The sitting room was spacious, with half-panelled walls, a handsome fireplace, and two tall windows overlooking the front garden, the cobbled lane, the rain-swept carpark, and the great buttresses of honey-coloured stone upon which rested the mighty weight of York Minster.

Standing at one of the windows, looking out, Sarah could see the carpark attendant saluting the clergy as they arrived. The dark-robed clergymen, hurrying to get out of the rain, brought back memories of her father, the Reverend Oliver Constantine, striding down the lane to his church to start matins, saying mildly to his wife, 'No need of an umbrella, my dear, I shan't get very wet.' Her mother's teasing reply: 'I suppose that you will run between the raindrops?'

Memories. So many memories . . .

Watching her closely, curiously moved by her silence, Mr Trumble thought that Sarah belonged here – inexplicably, that she had been here before, in another time, another age, perhaps.

'Oh, I'm sorry.' Turning with a smile, 'I mustn't waste your time.' And yet he noticed, despite the smile, that her eyes were bright with tears.

'No hurry, my dear.'

'This is a charming room. Where does that door lead to?'

'The kitchen and the bedrooms. As you can see,' opening the door, 'there is another hallway . . . '

'So many doors.'

'This is the master bedroom. The former occupant – an elderly lady who lived here for a number of years – believed in fitted cupboards rather than wardrobes, and she had a telephone plug installed so that she could carry the 'phone through with her when she came to bed. A wise precaution.'

'What happened to her?' Sarah opened a cupboard door, saw there a long rail and shoe-racks.

'Mrs Hunt? She moved, recently, to Norwich, to be with her daughter.'

'I see.' Sarah closed the cupboard door, thinking how useful all that hanging space would be, sparing her the necessity of buying a wardrobe. The heavier furniture from the old vicarage had been sold at auction, everything apart from the smaller items she could not have borne to part with. But she hadn't got a bed, and beds cost money.

'The second bedroom is rather small,' Mr Trumble said, 'but the wallpaper is pretty, and there's a view of the rear garden.'

Looking out, Sarah saw an extensive lawn, herbaceous borders, a trellis with climbing roses coming into leaf; drifts of daffodils and narcissus, a high, sheltering wall with an arched gate, a bird-bath: cushions of rock-plants. Apparently, Mr Ralph Foster took his gardening duties seriously.

44

'On the other hand, the kitchen is quite spacious. The Trust had it modernized some time ago. The colour scheme, blue and white, is quite pleasing, don't you think? And Mrs Hunt was kind enough to leave her electric cooker for the use of the next occupant. The bathroom has also been modernized, a rather nice coloured suite. Avocado, I believe it is called. I suppose it might have been handier had the bathroom been placed near the main bedroom. Doubtless there were reasons why that would have been impractical.'

Sarah did not mind where the bathroom was, as long as she had the sole use of it. When she had admired the avocado suite they returned to the living room. There were dark and polished patches on the floor, the unpolished areas where Mrs Hunt's rugs had been strewn. Thank heaven no one had thought to modernize this room, Sarah thought gratefully, gazing at the age-blurred panelling and the Regency green paintwork above, that lovely dull green between a moss and lovat green; the deep skirting boards, and the folded back shutters to the windows, the pristine white paintwork, high mantelpiece, and the two twelve-paned windows.

It was all so lovely, so right, and yet . . . Her heart sank. 'Tell me truthfully, Mr Trumble, have I the remotest chance of living here?'

'Oh yes, Mrs Vale. The flat is yours, if you want it.'

'*Want* it? Oh, Mr Trumble, I think I want it more than I have wanted anything in my life before. But . . . '

Then came the admission which he might have expected from a woman of her calibre, 'I am rather poor, at the moment, and I would not want to lumber you with an unsatisfactory tenant.'

Trumble smiled, well satisfied. 'The only unsatisfactory tenants, in my experience, are those who have no intention of honouring their contracts. I feel certain that you will honour yours.'

'Thank you, but that rather depends on the rent, and so on. Frankly, I'm scared of biting off more than I can chew.'

Eustace Trumble regarded her kindly. An acute assessor of human beings, he had liked this plump, somewhat untidy lady from the moment of their meeting. There was something about her eyes – very direct, grey blue in colour – her smile, her demeanour, and her obvious longing for a home, which had prompted him to give her the first refusal of this particular flat. Moreover, engaging in a little detective work, reading her books, he had ascertained that Sarah Vale was, indeed, a writer. A very fine writer, in his opinion, whose talent had, possibly, so far, been underrated. Smiling, opening his briefcase, 'In that case, I had better tell you what you would be letting yourself in for. Shall we sit on the top step?'

'Yes. Why not?' Mr Trumble, Sarah decided, was a dear little man, not at all stuffy, despite his age, and the few remaining strands of hair plastered to his scalp from a low side parting.

First of all he wanted to know how much the Perivale Guest House was costing her per week. When Sarah told him, he did little sums on a piece of paper: told her, solemnly, that the rent of the flat would amount to no more than twenty pounds a month extra.

'Yes, but my rent at the Perivale is inclusive of food, the use of lighting; laundry, lavatory paper, and so on,' Sarah reminded him.

'And is the food very good?' Trumble enquired mildly.

'No. As a matter of fact, it's ghastly,' she admitted.

'In short, you would be able to feed yourself more adequately on your own?'

'You bet I could! Mr Trumble, I'd live on boiled eggs, toast and coffee for the rest of my days, if only . . . ' She sighed deeply. 'But what about electricity?'

'That depends on how much electricity you would use to boil your eggs,' he replied, with a twinkle. 'Now, have you any furniture, carpets, curtains?'

'Oh, yes,' she said, clasping her hands, 'I have practically the entire contents of my parents' home. Except, I think, curtains to fit the living-room windows. The ones from the vicarage were so shabby, so threadbare, they fell apart when I attempted to wash them. It was the sunlight, you see – all those years of sunlight streaming in through the windows.' Her voice caught on a sob of remembrance for all that was past, over and done with for ever, those happy years of her youth and childhood when sunshine had been a living, lovely thing, and no-one had cared tuppence that sunshine faded carpets, curtains and furniture alike, as long as doors and windows were flung open, from spring to autumn, to admit the benison of daylight: the sounds of lowing cattle in the buttercupped fields beyond the hawthorn hedge bordering the vicarage garden: Sunday church bells flooding the air as her father's stalwart team of bellringers went into action. So many taken-for-granted sounds and impressions, half forgotten or pushed to the back of her mind during the sunless days of her marriage to Faulkner Vale.

Faulkner, who had relegated most of her belongings to a series of crates stacked in a garden shed, except her mother's rose-coloured settee, and various other items she had gathered together, beyond his jurisdiction, in that one room of the house, her so-called 'study', which had been her only escape route to happiness, albeit a tentative kind of happiness, the door of which she kept locked, as she had kept her mind locked against his power to destroy her pleasure in her research, her reading. Above all, her writing.

Touching her hand, Mr Trumble said quietly, consolingly, 'You mustn't be worried or upset, Mrs Vale. The Archaeological Trust are not monsters. Rest assured that whatever assessment I give them of the worth of a potential tenant, will be accepted without question. I have faith in you. Now you must have faith in yourself.'

Rising unsteadily to her feet, Sarah knew that the third miracle had happened. Strung between laughter and tears, she knew that she had come home at last. Knew that, in this place, with the adrenalin flowing, the spectre of failure acting as a burr beneath her writing saddle, she would, God willing, write the story of Amabie as she had never written before. It seemed as though, having served her apprenticeship as a creative writer, she now stood poised on the brink of conjuring up, from her vivid imagination, a love story, linked inescapably with truth, set against the turbulent background of the St Bartholomew's Day Massacre, as deeply moving and compelling as Heathcliff's and Cathy Earnshaw's had been.

She would entitle her book *Amabie*, would begin the story with Amabie and his wife standing on the deck of a ship, setting sail from France, seeing the shores of England rising up from the mist. Amabie, tall and proud, standing there, dark hair whipped by the sea-wind, a comforting arm about his wife's shoulders, aware of the hardships confronting them, the prejudice awaiting them as foreigners in a strange land.

48

'What are you thinking?'

'Oh, sorry, Mr Trumble, I was miles away.' Sarah smiled. Stepping into the street, she put up her umbrella. 'I simply don't know what to say, how to thank you for your kindness.'

'Not at all, my dear.' Putting up his own umbrella. 'Now, would you care to come to my office today, or tomorrow, to sign the contract?'

'Tomorrow, if you don't mind. Right now, there is something else I need to do.'

'Ah yes. Quite so. I understand.'

They parted company near the Minster's south-west door where they had met an hour earlier. Across the road, turning to look back, Mr Trumble saw that Sarah had lowered her umbrella preparatory to entering the Minster.

Naturally, he thought, a woman of her sensitivity would wish to give thanks where it was due.

Kneeling, hands clasped, looking at the deep purple altar cloth indicative of Lent – Christ's forty days in the Wilderness – Sarah prayed for one thing more, necessary to her happiness and peace of mind – that her children would come to understand why she had taken this brave, perhaps foolish step into an unknown future.

Chapter Three

Nicholas Tierney had slept throughout the journey from King's Cross to York. Now, hearing the guard's announcement over the tannoy, he got up, eased his aching neck muscles, and reached up for his flight bag.

As the train slid alongside Platform 14, he noticed that the station was chock-a-block with holidaymakers. Inevitably so. The Easter weather forecast, mainly warm and dry, had obviously acted as a spur.

Slipping on a pair of dark glasses, when the train stopped he strode quickly past the barrier to the taxi rank, pausing briefly to breathe in fresh air, head thrown back, dark hair brushing the collar of his supple leather coat. Then, opening the door of the first taxi, throwing his Pan-Am bag on the back seat, 'Hotel Carillon,' he told the driver.

Adjusting his driving mirror, the man glanced curiously at his passenger, wondering where he had seen him before. An avid watcher of sport on television, it occurred to him that his back-seat passenger bore more than a passing resemblance to the cricketer, Imran Khan.

Arriving at the Carillon, paying the driver, telling him to keep the change, Tierney hurried up the steps. 'Good to see you back, Mr Nicholas,' the uniformed commissionaire said.

'Thanks, Jennings.'

Entering the private elevator which would sweep him to

the penthouse apartment he shared with his Aunt Sophia, Nicholas knew that she would not question him about the funeral.

He could not, in any event, bear to speak of it. Not yet. His memories of the past few days were still too sharp, too cruel. Memories that would haunt him for the rest of his life.

Entering the shrouded drawing room of the house in the Rue St Hélène, he had seen his mother's body lying in state, the coffin surrounded with steadily burning candles, and hot-house flowers.

Drawing closer, he saw that her face was lightly veiled, her dead fingers entwined in a gold and pearl rosary.

Anger had welled up in him then. Hatred of his father who had allowed this to happen, who had not even told him that Madeleine was dying until it was too late to say goodbye to her.

Standing beside her coffin, looking down at her lifeless form, he had wanted her to wake up, to smile at him with those deliciously curved lips of hers. Heart overburdened with grief, he could not believe that she was dead. People like Madeleine, full of life and laughter, could not simply pass into oblivion, as if they had never existed.

By the light of the tall candles, a sudden dancing of the flames, caught in the draught from the open door as a servant entered the room to say that Sir Clive wished to see him in his study, Nicholas thought, for one heart stopping moment, that Madeleine had stirred. But when the servant had gone away, closing the door behind him, nothing had changed. The candles continued to burn, the scent of massed white roses and gardenias to cloy the air with their sickly sweet fragrance.

Gardenias, his mother's favourite flowers. A clear cut

memory of Madeleine standing serenely on the threshold of the embassy ballroom, welcoming guests, invaded his mind at that moment. Wearing a simple white jersey silk dress, with gardenias tucked into her upswept hairstyle, Madeleine, chic, slim, supremely elegant, had made every other woman seem overdressed.

Gardenias had been her hall-mark. A bowl of fresh white gardenias had been brought to her bedroom each morning at the same time as her breakfast tray.

As a small boy, he had been allowed to carry the flowers to her bedside table all by himself, taking great care not to spill the water.

Then, rewarded by her brilliant smile, he would cuddle up beside her to share her coffee and croissants while Madeleine, propped up against white satin pillows, wearing a frothy lace negligee, made her early morning phone calls; ringing her hairdresser, her dressmaker, and her most intimate friends; flicking over the pages of her leather-bound diary; fitting the long Russian cigarettes she preferred into a jade holder; pausing now and then to kiss him; making him feel important; unaware of the dangerous game she was playing – a mother flirting outrageously with her own son, sowing the seeds of jealousy of anyone – his father in particular – who drew her attention away from him for even a second.

Closing the gates of the elevator, Nicholas went along the corridor to Sophia's drawing room.

Seated in her favourite chair, listening to music, she smiled when he entered and held out her hands to him. But how tired he looked. Appalled at his appearance, 'You must try to rest before dinner,' she said. 'Or would you prefer not to come down to the dining room tonight?'

'Thank you.' Kissing her hands, 'But I'd sooner dine

with you. I'll feel better when I've bathed, and got rid of this.' He rubbed his fingers over the dark stubble of beard. 'See you at half past seven?'

'Yes, of course.' When he had gone, what had happened, Sophia wondered, apart from the funeral? Grief over the death of a beloved person was one thing, despair another. And she had read despair in her nephew's eyes.

In his own suite further along the corridor, slowly Nicholas undressed and lay on the bed he had bought one summer, in New York, during an Oxford vacation. How Madeleine had laughed when he presented her with the bills for the bed and the cost of its transport to England. He recalled her lighthearted remark, 'But Nicky, darling, why a bed? A tester no less! Whatever made you want such a thing?'

'Because the shopkeeper said George Washington had slept in it before Gettysburg.'

'*George Washington?* You mean Abraham Lincoln! Oh, my poor darling, that antiques' dealer must have rubbed his hands with glee when he saw you coming!'

Even so, Madeleine had paid for the bed. Money had never meant much to her, possibly because she had never known the lack of it. It was she who had sponsored her son's vacations in Greece, Italy, America, and Africa; who had paid for his clothes; had fostered his appreciation of the good things in life.

And yet she had left the house in the Rue St Hélène, and the bulk of her fortune to his father.

Sleep overcame him. When he awoke, the afternoon had darkened to evening, and his room lay in shadows, pierced by the distant glow of lights from the A19.

Getting up to bathe and shave, he felt the stirring of

53

the hotel as a heartbeat – the distant whirring of the lift to the floor below; muted laughter, the slamming of car doors heralding the arrival of late guests.

Lifting his face to the needle sharp spray on his eyelids, he wished that the water might wash away the memory of the procession of sleek limousines to the cemetery at l'église St Germaine; his mother's coffin piled high with flowers, the black-robed priests; glimmering candles; the tormented Christ figure above the altar of the church where Madeleine had worshipped as a girl; his father's handsome, ascetic face betraying no sign of emotion as his wife's casket was carried in and the solemn ritual of the Mass began: his own grief, the feeling he'd always had that his mother's religion stood as a barrier between them.

Stepping out of the shower, his lean, muscular body beaded with water, slipping into a towelling bathrobe, looking at himself in the mirror, he saw his face as that of a stranger, ruffianly with its dark growth of beard. Ashamed, now, that he had not shaved before the funeral, and had drunk too much wine the night before, he hoped that Madeleine would understand that he could not have faced the day cold sober. Certainly his father had not understood.

At least the charade was now over and done with. God willing, he need never set eyes on his father again, Nicholas thought bitterly, picking up his razor.

Shaving, he wondered why Madeleine, lovely and light of heart, had married a man as coldly withdrawn as his father. She must have known, must have realized that the marriage of a devout Catholic to an uncompromisingly stern Anglican, stood little or no chance of success.

Had she been attracted to Clive Tierney by his undeniably good looks; seduced by the idea of becoming an ambassador's wife; visions of dazzling balls, champagne luncheons, the glamour of meeting and entertaining world famous names? Wealthy in her own right as the widow of Philippe Joubert, director of the Joubert Steel Corporation, Madeleine might have married anyone. So why had she chosen to marry his father?

Bathed and shaved, Nicholas slid open the doors of his wardrobe and selected his evening clothes. Shrugging on his dinner jacket, he experienced a frisson of pleasure. In dressing so meticulously he felt that he had slipped back into his own skin; remembered Madeleine's pride in his appearance, the way she would tuck her hand in his arm at those embassy dinners; 'Let us stop the show, tonight, Bobo', she would whisper, using her pet name for him, to his father's annoyance, or, 'You could charm the birds from the trees, my Bobo. See how the women envy me my handsome escort.' This he had felt to be true. In his mother's presence, the glow of her luminous personality, he saw himself as she saw him, debonair, supremely self confident of his ability to turn women's heads longingly in his direction.

With a final glance in the mirror, he knew that Madeleine would approve his appearance tonight, the cut and fit of his evening suit, the monogrammed silk shirt, gold cufflinks; clean-shaven face, the fragrance of Givenchy aftershave lotion: deftly arranged bow tie. He wondered if she would also approve the way he had stood up to his father after the reading of the will.

But he must not think of that now. Later would come the memory of that final confrontation in his father's study. Now he owed allegiance to his father's sister, Sophia, who had been his friend, ally, and confidante ever since the day an unhappy, bewildered twelve-year-old boy had arrived on her doorstep prior to beginning his boarding school education, in what had been to him, at the time, a foreign country.

Gazing out of her drawing-room window, catching glimpses of fast moving traffic on the A19 beyond the boundary wall of the Carillon, streams of diamonds and rubies glimmering beneath amber-tinted neon, Sophia wondered how Nicholas would cope with the death of his mother.

She knew him so well, every facet of his odd, at times frightening personality, those moods of his which could switch, in a matter of minutes, from deep despair to a buoyant self confidence – a Gemini personality, as though two separate identities were contained within the same body, and one never knew which one would come uppermost.

His unkempt appearance when he came, earlier, to her room, had shocked her. Madeleine's funeral had taken place yesterday. Nicky's growth of beard suggested that he had not shaved beforehand – possibly not since he had left the hotel to catch the evening flight to Paris from Heathrow. But the wisdom of age had taught her never to pry, simply to be there when he needed her, as he had done that autumn day, twenty-five years ago, when her brother had brought his son to England to begin his adult education.

Although Sophia closely resembled her sibling, she had never cared for him deeply. Even though they had played together as children, sharing the same nursery, later the same schoolroom, they had never been as close as twins were supposed to be. Clive had been a coldly withdrawn little boy, unwilling to share his toys, jealous of his own possessions; far cleverer than she was, destined to follow in his father's footsteps, to make the diplomatic service his career.

And yet, after the horrifying death of their parents, he had been kind in inviting her to close the London house and share his pied-à-terre, in Paris, for the time being. Gratefully, she had accepted. Not that she had seen much of him – apart from his off-duty days when he would turn up, unexpectedly, to snatch a few hours relaxation.

Soon, Sophia had discovered that Paris could not compensate for the death of her parents; that one river looked very much like another, at dusk, with necklaces of light reflected in swiftly flowing water; that one could feel equally bereft in London or Paris.

To fill her lonely hours between Clive's infrequent visits to the apartment, Sophia had begun visiting the street markets; going out early each morning to watch the vendors setting their stalls with mouthwateringly fresh produce – melons and grapes bloomed by the warmth of the Italian sun; fish sent post-haste from Marseilles, Dover and Ostend – squid, monkfish, giant prawns, plaice, turbot and halibut, packed in splintered ice, eyes and scales still gleaming; Jerusalem artichokes, celery, asparagus, juicy red tomatoes; fresh herbs; tarragon, rosemary and thyme.

All these things, this bounty of land and sea, she had perceived as a lifeline in a confusing world of loneliness and self doubt. There was something so basic and satisfying about food.

Soon, her visits to the markets had imbued her with a strong desire to learn to cook the way that French women cooked, with flair and imagination, and so she had enrolled at a privately run school of haute cuisine.

The only English person on the register, she had felt out of place at first among the German, French, Italian and Swiss hoteliers and restaurateurs there to add to their already considerable knowledge of cookery. But, she had quickly discovered, the preparation of food, food itself, spoke a universal language all its own. No-one thought it odd that an English spinster wished to learn how to cook to Cordon Bleu standard. She had seldom been happier, and one friend she had made there, a small, bad-tempered Frenchman, Michel Arnot, was destined to play an important role in her life.

Then, as her skill increased, Sophia began to dream of opening an hotel, of putting her new-found expertise to good use, of selling the London house, willed to her by her parents, to underwrite the venture. Clive had pooh-poohed the idea, 'Pie in the sky' he called it, nursing a grudge against his parents because they had left the house to his sister. 'What do you know about business? Hotel management?' And, 'Nothing at all,' she'd said, 'but I am willing to learn.'

Returning to England to see her solicitor about putting the Cheyne Walk house on the market, and to place advertisements in *The Lady*, *Country Life* and *The Dalesman* for a suitable property, she had returned to Paris to Clive's shattering announcement that he had become engaged to marry a widow, Madeleine Joubert, whom he had met at an embassy dinner.

Awaiting the arrival of her nephew, memory drew Sophia back to the first time she had ever seen Madeleine. The news of her brother's engagement had come as a shock to Sophia, who had seen him as a dyed-in-the-wool bachelor.

What Clive's fiancée would be like, Sophia could not imagine, as she prepared a celebratory dinner for the three of them – chilled Spanish gazpacho, Chicken Marengo, and chocolate soufflé, whilst Clive, as nervous as a kitten, had fussed about the wine before setting off to escort Madame Joubert to the apartment.

When the bell rang, Sophia opened the door, expecting to see a plump, middle-aged matron. Shock waves ran through her when she saw a beautiful woman, holding a sheaf of red roses, dressed stunningly in a plain black dress, her long blonde hair drawn back from her Madonna-like face, wearing no make-up, apart from pale pink lipstick, no accessories apart from the corsage of white gardenias pinned to the neckline of her dress.

Smiling, 'I am Madeleine Joubert,' the vision said in halting English overlaid with a charming French accent. 'And you must be Sophia. Thank you so much for inviting me to dinner. These roses are for you.' Offering the flowers, 'Oh, what a charming apartment! Clive is parking the car, but I could not wait to see you. Mon Dieu, but how alike you are!' Wrinkling her brow, 'I hope that I shall not come between you and your brother, that you and I will be good friends. Ah, here is Clive now.'

During dinner, Sophia could not help wondering if a marriage between two such widely differing personalities could possibly work. They looked wonderful together, of course, Clive, tall, handsome, gravely formal in speech and manner, providing the perfect foil for Madeleine's effervescent charm and beauty; her occasional difficulty with the English language, when she had burst into a torrent of French, using her hands expressively to emphasize her meaning. But would Clive, a stickler for correctness, continue to find Madeleine's insouciance amusing? How long would it be before Clive's uncompromising outlook on life began to depress the bubbling, extrovert Madeleine?

And had they given due thought and consideration to their widely disparate religious beliefs? Clive, Sophia knew, brought up to embrace the Church of England, would never allow children born of the marriage to be raised as Catholics.

Possibly she was being too pessimistic. Perhaps Madeleine's warmth and charm would melt the innate coldness of Clive's persona. At any rate, they had seemed perfectly at ease with each other that evening, and Sophia had discovered, to her relief, that her future sister-in-law was widely read, intelligent, with a mind of her own.

The meal over, when they were sitting together drinking Napoleon brandy from lightweight bubbles of exquisitely fashioned Murano glass, Sophia had imparted the news that she intended returning to England, after the wedding, to search for the kind of property she had in mind – preferably an old house, in need of modernization, which she would turn into a first-class hotel.

Turning away from the window, smiling as her nephew entered the room, pushing aside her memories of the past, 'Ah, now you look more like yourself,' Sophia said.

His personality change was typical of his Gemini birthsign, she thought as they entered the lift. To look at him now, one could not imagine that, a matter of a few hours ago, his face, the droop of his shoulders, had betrayed so much weariness, so much pain. Now it seemed as though he had drawn down a mental shutter, had flicked on some inner switch to dispel the horror of Madeleine's death.

Sophia's heart went out to him. She knew how much he had suffered when the briefly worded telex from Paris had arrived with the message that Madeleine was seriously ill; had seen the colour drain away from his face: watched him walk to the reception desk like a man in a trance, to make the necessary travel arrangements.

Gripped with a sense of foreboding, Sophia had felt in her bones that he would arrive in Paris too late to see his mother alive, and she had been right. Telephoning her brother after Nicholas had left the Carillon on his way to Heathrow, her fears had been confirmed when Clive told her, quite calmly, that Madeleine had died of a massive heart attack in the early hours of the morning.

So Madeleine was already dead at the time her brother had sent the telex. But why that impersonal message? Why had not Clive telephoned from the medical centre, in Paris, where Madeleine had died?

Dressed all in black, which had become Sophia's hall-mark, as gardenias were Madeleine's, Sophia entered the dining room on her nephew's arm, her keen eyes taking in everything from the flower arrangements to the personal appearance of the waiters moving deftly between the circular tables, savouring the stir their entry had caused.

Diamonds sparkling at throat and wrists, she walked slowly the length of the room to her table overlooking the floodlit garden, filled with a sense of pride in the achievement of a long cherished dream, despite the uphill struggle to make that dream come true.

Escorting Sophia, Nicholas experienced a sense of déjà vu. For one brief moment, he saw another dining

61

room, in another city, a beautiful woman in white, with gardenias in her hair: knew now, as he had then, the heady sensation of walking in the limelight of some brightly lit stage.

But all that was over and done with now. Madeleine was dead: that chapter of his life – Paris, the house in the Rue St Hélène – closed for ever. His father, Clive Tierney, had made that abundantly clear when, after the reading of the will, he had told his son that his presence in the house was no longer desirable.

'In other words, Nicholas, the sooner you pack your belongings and leave, the better.'

'You need not worry, Father. God willing I shall never set foot in this house, nor ever set eyes on you again. Just one thing, before I leave, how will you live with your conscience?'

Chapter Four

Sarah had breakfasted for the last time at the Perivale, humped her luggage downstairs, paid her bill, rung for a taxi, and set forth joyously to the flat to await the arrival of the furniture van.

No more burnt toast and soggy cornflakes. No more shepherd's pie smothered in lukewarm gravy. As the taxi sped through the rain-washed city streets, with a pale sun struggling through the clouds, she felt as if she had been released from prison.

Ralph Foster, about to leave the house as the taxi arrived, insisted on helping her in with her cases, making small talk, blinking rapidly behind his gold-rimmed glasses, stammering slightly, wearing a raincoat that had seen better days, his tie askew, as though he had dressed in a hurry.

'Really, Mr Foster, you mustn't let me keep you,' Sarah insisted. 'I wouldn't want you to be late for work – or whatever – on my account.' In no mood for small talk, she wished he would go away and leave her to cope with her own belongings.

'Not at all,' he said cheerfully, 'I am practically on the doorstep. I teach l-literature at St William's C-college, just round the corner.'

At that moment, preoccupied with thoughts of her removal, Sarah could not have cared less if he taught Urdu to Spaniards.

The van arrived at the precise moment Ralph had finished heaving her cases upstairs. 'L-look, Mrs Vale,' he said impulsively, recalling the chaos of his own removal day, two years ago, 'why not take my key? There's coffee and milk in the kitchen, plenty of sugar and biscuits.'

'That's very kind of you, but I couldn't possibly . . . '

'N-nonsense,' he interrupted, 'you'll need elevenses. It's the least I can do. 'W-what are neighbours for?'

Despite her protestations, he handed her the front door key to his flat, and hurried down the path, the April breeze ruffling his thinning fair hair, uplifted by the thought that he had done something positive for a change.

Entering the college, he formulated the daring idea of inviting Mrs Vale to have supper with him. A lonely man since the death of his mother, whom he had nursed devotedly during her last illness, he missed having someone to take care of. Not that he felt entirely at ease with women, certainly not the sophisticated type in whose company he felt totally inadequate. But Mrs Vale seemed a sensible person, capable of accepting a gesture of friendship at face value.

Possibly she was lonely too, he thought, shedding his raincoat and donning his gown for his first tutorial of the day. Hurrying along the corridor to his study, he made a mental shopping list. Soup. He would give her Baxter's game soup for starters, buy a ready cooked chicken from the delicatessen in Goodramgate; Waldorf salad, garlic bread, a selection of cheeses, freshly ground coffee, and fruit, he decided.

Catching, as he sailed along, gown flapping, the intermingled fragrances of beeswax polish and food from the refectory, he trod, happily, the lozenges of spring sunlight streaming in through the high windows.

Sarah disliked the idea of poking into strange drawers and cupboards to find coffee, spoons, and mugs.

The neatness of Mr Foster's kitchen surprised her. Single men, she supposed, might live in a muddle. Obviously he did not. His breakfast things had been washed and stacked on the draining board to dry. Waiting for the kettle to boil, she wondered why he had not married, if he was not 'as other men' – a term used delicately by a member of her father's church choir with reference to the effeminate young organist who had worn his hair too long for her liking – a term which Sarah had not understood as a child, and which no-one had seemed willing to explain to her. Besides which, she had liked that young organist, who had seemed to her far nicer than the old tabby cat whose unfriendly attitude towards him had finally ousted him from their midst.

Later, in her student days at college, she had met many such misfits. Gentle, introspective creatures on the whole, and kind – very kind. Far worse, in her view, were the full blooded men who made a mockery of their wedding vows.

But why rake over old embers? The past was over and done with, and yet she could not help remembering her wedding day; a woman in love for the first, possibly the last, time in her life.

Carrying the tray upstairs, she thought that first love, with its indefinable magic, innocence and trust, could never be recaptured or reprised.

When the workmen had gone, leaving her standing amid a sea of packing cases, she went down to Foster's flat to return the coffee things. Tired, hungry and dusty, she longed for a hot bath, a meal however makeshift, and an early night.

When the postman had called earlier, bringing her first ever mail to her new address, she had flicked through it in the hope that the children might have sent welcome cards. They hadn't.

The mail consisted of bills and circulars.

She was standing at the sink washing the coffee mugs when the back door opened and Ralph Foster walked in with his bag of groceries.

'Oh.' He seemed pleased to see her. 'Is it all over? I noticed the removal van had gone.' Screwing up his courage, he blurted, 'I've been shopping. I thought you might care to have s-supper with me.'

Sarah watched as he emptied the contents of the carrier on to the kitchen table; noticed that his hands were shaking slightly. Touched by his kindness, thinking how churlish it would be to refuse his invitation, she smiled, and accepted.

He had set the table in the sitting room; arranged a vase of daffodils as a centrepiece. The room felt warm, lived in, welcoming, with deep-red velvet curtains, wing chairs flanking the fireplace, long bookshelves; a bow-fronted Georgian sideboard on which stood a gadrooned silver tray with a cut-glass sherry decanter.

The thought occurred, as he handed Sarah a glass of pale amber liquid, that he might have tidied his desk a little more, neatened the pile of folders and reference books.

'Are you a writer?' Sarah asked the question diffidently, not wanting to pry.

'Not really. Well, not in the accepted s-sense. A bit of a dabbler, that's all.'

'Are you writing anything at the moment?'

Encouraged by her interest, 'Well, yes, for an A-American newspaper – about the Yorvik Viking Centre, the Minster, and so on.' He paused. 'S-sorry. Am I boring you?'

'No, not at all. Please go on.'

He had bought expensive new potatoes which he had boiled in their skins, to accompany the chicken and the Waldorf salad. Seated at the table, Sarah noticed that the tablecloth was edged with handmade lace, the willow pattern plates crazed slightly with age.

Eating hungrily, unworried by her personal appearance – pushed back hair, slacks, and bulky sweater – she felt surprisingly at ease with Ralph Foster. If, as she suspected, Ralph was not interested in women, he would not care tuppence about her appearance anyway – unlike Faulkner, with whom she had never felt at ease, knowing his preference for slim, sophisticated women; the type of women she could never hope to emulate in appearance or self-possession.

Sarah's interest in his writing had brought a flush of pleasure to Ralph's cheeks, a feeling of self-confidence; reducing his inclination to stammer and to blink his eyes – nervous mannerisms which he abhorred, intensified by his deep-seated lack of confidence and natural reticence: feelings he had nurtured since childhood; his schooldays, when he had suffered from weak eyesight, lack of physical stature, and his bloody nervous stammer, so that the rest of the kids had dubbed him 'Stuffy Foster' – a boy incapable of playing rugby or swimming for the school team. A misfit.

Now, in Sarah's company, he felt suddenly taller, more alive, able to speak freely; intelligently: unaware of his obvious physical defects which she appeared not to have noticed, revelling in the feeling that he had not been weighed in the balance and found wanting.

After supper, at his suggestion, they moved to chairs near the fire, and he put on a record of Elgar's 'Enigma Variations'.

Intrigued by her air of stillness and concentration, he saw that she was a very lovely woman indeed, with good bone structure, a milk and honey complexion, warmly curving lips, and blue-grey eyes: slim hands and feet despite the lumpiness of her body: golden glints in her mass of untidily pushed back hair. Also that she wore a wedding ring, although she appeared to be alone in the world. It was then he realized he knew nothing about her personal circumstances, if she was married, widowed, or divorced, but this was part of her charm. Most women with whom he came into contact – mainly the wives of his colleagues – spilled the beans regarding their health, home and children, within half an hour. More irritatingly, they had tried their hand at matchmaking, as though bachelorhood were a disease in need of a cure.

The music ended; he experienced a stab of disappointment when Sarah stood up. 'S-so – soon?'

'I'm afraid so. You see, my children might ring up, and worry about me if I didn't answer.'

'Of c-course. I quite understand.'

'This has been a lovely evening.' She spoke warmly, truthfully. 'You must have supper with me, when I'm settled.'

'Yes. T-thank you. I should like that.'

'Goodnight, Mr Foster.'

'Goodnight, Mrs Vale.'

She had switched on the immersion heater before going downstairs. The water should be hot enough for a bath, now, Sarah considered, and she desperately wanted a bath – to lie supine in deep, scented water – to soak away the stresses and strains of the past months; a kind of baptism to wash away the sins of the world, from which she might emerge cleansed and relaxed, the re-born Sarah Vale, the independent woman writer trying to make sense of her new life from the disappointing lumber of the old.

But what if the telephone rang while she was in the bathroom? She might not be able to hear it. Strung on the horns of her dilemma, she tried moving the phone closer to the bathroom but quickly realized that the cord would not reach far enough. And so she undressed, slipped into bed, switched on the radio, and lay rigid beneath the flower-sprigged duvet, willing the phone to ring.

But the phone did not ring.

When, at last, she fell asleep from sheer exhaustion, the radio was still playing . . .

Next morning she was up early, emptying the tea-chests, stacking china in the kitchen cupboards, hanging pictures, each item conjuring up memories of her parents, especially her mother, after whose death these treasures had been packed into containers and relegated to that garden shed.

A battle of wills had ensued on that occasion. Quietly but firmly Sarah had made the point that the way she furnished her own room had no bearing on the rest of the house. Overcrowded it may be, but it was hers – a bedroom overlooking the swimming pool, in which she had hammered out her first novel, *Lawrence*.

Arranging her books, Sarah recalled that Faulkner had accused her of not caring tuppence about his friends, his career. Even worse, Verity had said much the same thing. But was that really true? Hadn't she cared enough?

Sitting back on her heels, looking into the past, nothing was ever that cut and dried, she thought. She had done her best to be a good wife and mother, would have done anything in the world for her husband and children. Then, slowly but surely had come the realization that none of them needed her any more, that she was expendable. Verity and Richard had floated off to London, their father to Paris, New York, or wherever, with his latest conquest in tow, leaving her stranded.

Then Faulkner had given her a car, a red Mini, as a status symbol, because his colleagues' wives all possessed their own means of transport.

The gift had come as manna from heaven. Sarah had felt liberated, then, free, when her work was done, to meander through the countryside in search of tucked away villages, to eat, when she felt hungry, in country pubs where she would order a ploughman's lunch and chat to the landlord and his wife; storing up memories, as a squirrel stores nuts, against the coming winter of profound emotional hunger and heartbreak.

Not that Faulkner had taken the trouble to ask her where she had been to in the red Mini after he had left the house for his suite of offices in the Marylebone Road. For all he knew, she might have been to town to meet a woman friend, even a lover: to a theatre matinee, or the cinema.

Arranging the last of her books, seeing, with pleasure, the familiar titles, Flora Thompson's *Lark Rise to Candleford*, Winifred Holtby's *South Riding*, and Emily Brontë's *Wuthering Heights*, Sarah wondered if she had made too much of the children to the detriment of her marriage and her personal appearance. But fussing with her hair and face, dieting, and spending money on clothes had never come high on her list of priorities. In any event, in the early days of their marriage, she and Faulkner had been as poor as church mice.

Two babies later had come his first carping criticism of her appearance when, tired out with all the cooking, cleaning, washing and shopping she had done, not to mention coping with two lively infants, she had come to the dining table in the clothes she had worn all day.

'Really, Sarah, must you sit down to eat looking like a farm labourer?' he said irritably.

Suitably chastened, the next evening she had changed into a wool dress she had worn on their honeymoon, washed her face and brushed her hair, wanting to please him, thinking he might compliment her on her appearance. All he said was 'My God, Sarah, you've put on some weight.' And she knew that what he said was true. The dress which had fitted her to perfection when she was married now felt skimpy; looked far too revealing. She *had* put on weight, partly a result of childbirth, mainly because she lunched on hastily cut sandwiches, pork pies, or tins of soup. But weight, like unhappiness, came on swift and silent feet.

She remembered her father asking, on the eve of her wedding, if she was marrying the right man. Not that he had put his question as bluntly as that. But he must have realized that she and Faulkner had nothing in common, apart from a basic physical attraction destined to fade when the first, fine careless rapture was over; that the husband she had chosen cared more about becoming rich and powerful than the gentler things of life – art, music, books, religious beliefs. But she had seen none

71

of the pitfalls ahead. Faulkner, strong and masterful, had made the other men she had met at church socials and at college seem vapid and lacklustre, nor had she paused to consider that a romantically minded girl like herself might prove incapable of satisfying Faulkner's lust for life. She had simply listened spellbound when he talked about the future, seeing him in the role of a knight at arms battling to make his way in the world of high-powered business enterprise, herself as his companion at arms, the helpmeet of whom he would one day say, 'I could not have achieved all this without the support of my wife.'

So much for dreams.

Chapter Five

At last the moment had arrived. Sitting at her typewriter, Sarah rolled into it a sheet of top quality A4 backed with carbons and copy paper: typed 'Amabie', Page One, Chapter One.

But the strangeness of her surroundings slowed her mind and fingers to some extent. Inured to working at a window overlooking neatly mown grass and a swimming pool, the new scenery – ancient stonework, cathedral carpark, the coming and going of the clergy and the official guides – the new found space and freedom took some getting used to.

The furniture from the old vicarage blended in here as it had never done in the Marlborough house. Her study there had felt cramped to say the least, with tables and chairs standing cheek-by-jowl.

'You might at least have had that shabby settee recovered,' Faulkner had said disapprovingly when the removal men carried it upstairs. 'Better still, have got rid of it, along with the rest of your junk.'

The thought occurred that Faulkner had always been far too eager for concealment, the covering up of unpalatable truths.

Looking out of the window, Sarah remembered how, when the Marlborough house had been built to his specifications, he had himself chosen the furniture and fittings – the long leather settee and armchairs, the tables and chairs, the low, wall-length fitting for the hi-fi equipment. He had selected everything from carpets to curtains, table lamps, and pictures, not troubling to consult her, so that when all the rooms, except one, had been furnished according to his wishes, she had felt like a voyager on the 'Star Ship Enterprise', totally at odds with her surroundings, apart from that one room in which she had gathered together the 'junk' that her husband had so despised.

But the rose velvet settee had been a part of her life long before Faulkner had swum into her line of vision, recalling a slower, infinitely happier way of life.

She could almost see Faulkner, now, plunging into the swimming pool, his once slim, exciting body larded with fat, the thick mat of hair on his chest faded to the colour of ashes.

At eleven o'clock, a page and a half of writing completed, Sarah went to the kitchen to make herself a cup of coffee – the powdered, instant variety – and thought about Ralph Foster whom she had promised to invite to supper one evening. But not just yet. In a week or so, perhaps, when she had settled down more and felt equal to coping with a guest. She liked Ralph, but he overwhelmed her slightly with his fussiness – rather like a nice old dog wagging its tail in anticipation of a bone.

Returning to her typewriter, coffee mug in hand, by an effort of will, Sarah buckled down to work.

At four o'clock, drained and exhausted, the first draft chapter of her novel completed, she dragged herself away from her desk, put on her outdoor things, and went in search of food: a loaf of bread, eggs, baked beans; remembering the times when she had gone into Waitrose, in Marlborough High Street, to pack her trolley with food enough to feed an army – legs of lamb, shoulders of pork, corn-fed chickens: vegetables, gateaux, and the out of season fruits she had once purchased for the dinner parties Faulkner had insisted on throwing for his heads of department and their wives.

How she had hated those dinner parties: Faulkner's friends crowding into the dining room to partake of a meal which she herself had prepared and cooked, rather than have her kitchen overrun with a firm of caterers.

She thought she had managed quite well on the whole, with the help of Mrs Packard, her daily woman, who had washed up for her between courses. But Faulkner had not seen it that way.

'Christ Almighty, Sarah,' he'd said bitterly after one dinner party in particular, 'are you trying, deliberately, to make a fool of me?'

'I'm sorry, Faulkner, I don't understand. I thought it went quite well.'

'That just goes to show . . . '

'Show, *what*?'

'That you couldn't care less about my friends.'

'We have nothing in common.'

'Not surprising, since you prefer to behave like a servant.'

'I happen to like cooking.'

'That's beside the point.'

'What *is* the point?'

'God give me strength! The point is, your behaviour reflects badly on me.' He had turned to the whisky decanter for solace. 'My friends are important people interested in the future development of the Company. When they come to my house, I expect them to be received as such. I expect you to act as their hostess, not as head

75

cook and bottle washer!' Swallowing his drink, 'Why are you laughing?'

Sarah could not have explained, at the time, to her irate husband, that the ludicrousness of the situation had struck her amidships. What did it matter how she behaved, what his so-called friends thought of her, knowing that Faulkner had embarked on yet another of his clandestine affairs with the wife of one of those friends?

Dusting Faulkner's study one day, when the phone rang, she had picked up the receiver. 'Faulkner, darling, is that you? Marguerite here!'

'I'm sorry, you must have dialled the wrong number,' Sarah said firmly, hanging up on her, resisting the temptation of saying, 'I'm sorry, Mrs Fenton, my husband isn't here at the moment.'

The Fentons, Marguerite and her husband, Claude, had been guests at her dinner table that same evening. And so, Sarah thought, what difference would it have made had she greeted Faulkner's guests wearing black velvet and diamonds? He would not even have noticed.

Now, because she had put the past behind her, had chosen her own lifestyle, and refused to accept alimony, Sarah knew that she would live on boiled eggs, toast and beans for the rest of her life, if necessary.

She might even lose weight, she thought wryly, standing at the checkout.

But to what end, what purpose? Who cared a tuppenny damn about her anyway? Certainly not Faulkner, nor apparently her children.

And yet as she left the supermarket and trod the streets of the fascinating city she now thought of as home, then went upstairs to her flat and switched on the lamps, she experienced a deep satisfaction that she was here, alive and independent, and this was the way Amabie must have felt in helping to create the Rosedale furnace.

As a matter of self esteem, she set the polished dining table with her mother's best cutlery, a place mat and a damask serviette, and changed into her housecoat to eat her frugal supper of baked beans on toast, before washing up and settling down to watch television. Soon, sickened by the violence of the film, she switched off the set and tucked herself into bed to listen to a play on Radio 4.

The play over, she found herself thinking about Amabie. Unable to sleep, she got up in the early hours of the morning to sit at her typewriter, so engrossed in her work that she scarcely noticed the filtering of a new day between the closed curtains.

Reading the second chapter, Sarah knew that the words rang true, as if she had entered the mind of Amabie, as though the man himself stood at her elbow. Then, exhausted, but strangely fulfilled, she went back to bed and slept until the late afternoon.

In her dreams, the man came to her, a dark-haired man, young, strong and handsome, and held out his hands to her, smiling, begging her to follow where he led. And she climbed with him to high cliffs overlooking the sea, and stood there, feeling the strong, warm clasp of his hands, and looked down at the foam-flecked water stretching to a misty horizon, her hair blowing in the wind, the rain, like tears, upon her face, knowing that she loved this man as she had never loved before, with no regret for the past, strangely, no hope for the future, as though time had ceased to exist, and they were destined to stand together on that wind-swept cliff top until the universe disintegrated and the stars ceased to shine.

★ ★ ★

The letter from Verity was on the mat next morning. Sarah would have known anywhere that backward slanting handwriting. Breathless with excitement, she hurried upstairs to read it. Sinking down on the settee, tucking up her legs, she opened the envelope.

Verity's scrawl read: 'Well, Mummy, I hope you are satisfied.' Just that. Nothing more. What on earth could she mean? And then Sarah's shaking fingers discovered the cutting her daughter had sent, roughly clipped from a Sunday newspaper supplement. The caption above a photograph of Faulkner and Suki Mitford read: 'Tycoon to wed Girl Friday'. The blurb beneath: 'Cornered by our reporter at the Bradley-Oliphant engagement party, wealthy computer tycoon, Faulkner Vale, admitted his intention to marry his glamorous public relations officer, Suki Mitford, when his divorce from women's fiction writer, Sarah Vale, becomes final. The happy couple are now living together in Vale's house, near Marlborough, in which, according to the delicious Miss Mitford, there will be room enough for a nursery.'

How could Verity have done such a thing? Sarah stared briefly at the cutting before crumpling it up in her hand. Chilled by her daughter's maliciousness, she began to cry – fruitless tears welling up from the pent-up emotion of the past months.

Verity had been hurt, but was that reason enough to hurt other people?

Sarah had not cried like this since the death of her mother. But those tears were different, born of grief for the passing of someone dear to her. The tears she now shed were harsher, engendered by her daughter's lack of understanding, of sympathy and love.

78

When she felt calmer, drying her tears, Sarah bathed and dressed quickly, and hastened downstairs.

Entering the Minster by the south door, above which the Rose Window glowed with the colours of a rainbow, she thought, looking up at it, of the infinite patience of the craftsmen who had restored that window from a mass of shattered fragments after the fire, six years ago, which, sweeping the south transept, had brought it crashing down amid the heat and roar of the flames. That the Rose Window had been restored to its former glory was nothing short of a miracle – and one needed miracles to restore one's faith in humanity.

Dwarfed by the immensity of the Minster, a feeling of calm invaded her. Slowly, deep in thought, she crossed the transept and made her way to the All Saints' Chapel with its crimson altar cloth, and stood near the iron railings, looking at the gold cross; deriving comfort from the air about her – a musky scent of age and incense, as though every candle ever burned within the building, the fragrance of every flower arranged in the tall iron brackets flanking the fan-shaped, red carpeted steps leading to the high altar, had been drawn up high among the great, carved rafters of the building to linger there.

She would write to Verity, a loving letter, begging her not to allow bitterness to spoil her young life, inviting her to come to the flat, hopefully to break down the barrier which had sprung up between them.

Planning what she would say in that letter, Sarah sensed that she was not alone, that someone was standing close to her.

Glancing sideways, she saw a dark-haired man, wearing a black leather coat, staring intently into the chapel – a man so closely resembling her mental picture of Amabie, she

79

felt that the man she had conjured from the mists of time had become a reality. But figments of the imagination did not appear wearing black leather and smelling of Givenchy aftershave.

The building was chock-a-block with tourists at this time of year; Japanese, Americans, Swedes, Australians, Indians, Ghanaians – every nation under the sun following the guides on shuffling feet, keeping their voices down, enthralled by the majesty of York Minster. But this man appeared to be a loner, whose nationality Sarah could not guess, although his dark hair and tanned complexion suggested that he might be Italian. Certainly his coat was Italian. This much she knew because her son, Richard, had purchased a similar coat, in Italy, two years ago, and there was no mistaking the quality and cut of that soft, pliable leather.

What interested her most about the man was not his clothing but his stillness, the feeling she had that he was looking, not at the chapel, but into some private hell of the mind.

Moving away, gripped by a feeling of pity, Sarah walked back the way she had come, past the memorial sculptures of medieval lords and their ladies, and the wall tablets commemorating the lives of young officers and men who had died in the First World War. Turning to look back, she saw that the man she thought of as Amabie was still standing there, quite motionless, and wondered who he was, and what he was thinking.

Nicholas had entered the Minster on an impulse, drawn by the need of absolution from the bitter-sweet memories crowding his mind, as though, in some holy place, he might balance the scales of his dual personality.

Loving Madeleine, he had wished to share her faith in Mary, the Mother of God, the observance of the Saints' Days, her belief in Purgatory; he had watched her, during the impressionable days of his childhood, slip away from the house to attend Mass, a lonely figure, sombrely dressed, carrying her Bible and her rosary and had longed to go with her, to share the mysterious calling of her church with its glimmering candles, black-robed priests, and quiet-faced Madonnas; and those latticed confessionals.

Forced by his father to accept a less vital religion in which, apparently, the road to heaven was paved with tea-urns and cast-off clothing, Nicholas had bitterly resented the erection of an intangible barrier between himself and Madeleine, his feeling of ostracism from so important a facet of her life. In the same way, he had resented being denied access to his mother's bedroom until his father had left for the embassy. Many a time, as a child, he had cowered on the landing outside the closed door of Madeleine's room, wanting, needing desperately to see her, to ask for a drink of water, a story, or to cuddle up beside her and fall asleep in her arms instead of which he had been dragged back to his own room by his scolding nanny who had tongue-lashed him soundly for being such a naughty boy as to dream of disturbing his parents, who were probably fast asleep at that hour of the night.

Slowly had dawned the realization that his father's presence in the house in the Rue St Hélène meant that he, Nicholas, was less important to Madeleine than his father.

Gradually, over the years, had been sown the seeds of umbrage against the man whose air of detachment and lack of response to his son's need of affection and understanding had come to a head after his mother's funeral.

Awaiting the arrival of Madeleine's attorney, 'My God, have you no respect?' Clive had said scathingly.

'For you, Father? None whatever.' The moment of truth had arrived.

'That is perfectly obvious. You might at least have shown some for your mother. To attend a funeral unshaven and the worse for drink, is unforgivable.' The air between the two men was electric with anger.

Eyes blazing, Nicholas said, 'I loved my mother. Can you, in all conscience say the same? You made her life a misery with your coldness and jealousy. You hadn't even the humanity to warn me of her illness in time to say goodbye to her.'

'For heaven's sake, pull yourself together! You are behaving like a spoilt child. I blame Madeleine for that, for the softness and weakness she fostered in you, the way she indulged your every whim.'

At that moment, Simenon, the manservant, had knocked to announce the arrival of M. Renay, a dapper little man carrying a briefcase, who shook hands with both men.

Sensing the atmosphere, when Clive had invited him to sit at his desk, the attorney eased his collar. This was something he had always hated – the reading of a client's last will and testament. But the formalities must be observed, the servants, Madame Simenon, the housekeeper, her husband, and old Henri Fontaine, the gardener-cum-handyman, called into the study to receive word of their bequests, the generous sums of money that Madeleine had bestowed on each of them.

Claudette Simenon, who had served Madeleine since the

death of her first husband, Philippe Joubert, wept inconsolably, murmuring between sobs, 'Madame Tierney was a saint. All those years, and never a cross word. God rest her sweet soul,' as she was led from the room by her husband.

When the servants had gone, Renay had turned his attention to Madeleine's bequest to Sophia: four paintings which her sister-in-law had particularly admired for their simplicity and colouring – the colours of springtime which Madeleine had reflected in the creamy gold curtains and the moss green carpet of her private boudoir.

Indeed, the whole house reflected Madeleine's preference for bright, clear colours, simplicity, uncluttered lines, plus her unfailing instinct in choosing antique furniture to blend in perfectly with the plain, background colours of the walls: soft eggshell blues, misty greens, and gold.

She had also been clever enough to add dramatic touches here and there; she had spot-lit the shelves and niches displaying her fabulous collection of Famille Rose, Rockingham and Chelsea porcelain, and placed, strategically, the flower arrangements for which she was famous – great jardinières filled with double white lilac, blood-red peonies, long-stemmed American Beauty roses, or flaunting yellow daffodils, according to the season of the year, apart from the shallow crystal bowls containing her favourite flowers, heady scented gardenias, which had spiced the air with their haunting, lingering perfume, whatever the season.

Rue St Hélène 21 had been bought by Madeleine after the death of Philippe Joubert. On her marriage to Clive Tierney, she had invited him to regard the house as his home.

There were times when some important state function had necessitated their occupation of Clive's private apartment at the embassy, when Madeleine would play to perfection her role as the ambassador's lady, supervising the food and the flower arrangements, appearing, stunningly, by her husband's side to welcome guests; to dance untiringly with visiting heads of state.

Clive had fallen into the routine of staying overnight in the Rue St Hélène if there were no pressing diplomatic issues on hand, knowing his staff could reach him if his presence was urgently required.

Growing up, home from Oxford on vacation, Nicholas had sometimes accompanied his parents to embassy balls and dinner parties, to his father's displeasure, whose jealousy of his son had, by that time, become even more obvious.

Aware of the charged atmosphere between father and son, Renay continued: 'To my beloved son, Nicholas, I bequeath the contents of my safe, along with my undying affection.'

Glancing at the two men seated near the French windows, Renay wondered how the fair-haired Clive and Madeleine Tierney had produced so dark a son.

Casting his mind back, Renay remembered Madeleine Tierney as he had last seen her, sitting up in bed, smiling, a drift of lace about her shoulders, hair beautifully coiffed, a withered hand extended in greeting. Truly a woman worth remembering.

'Please continue, M. Renay.' Clive's cool, unemotional voice had cut into the *avocat*'s reverie. And, 'Oh yes, of course, I beg your pardon,' Renay flustered, adjusting his gold-rimmed spectacles.

Sick at heart, Nicholas realized that Madeleine had left the bulk of her estate to his father.

He knew, of course, that his mother's jewellery would

be worth a small fortune, but Madeleine had hated jewellery: the rings, necklaces, earrings, and brooches left to her by her first husband: everything except the diamond and sapphire brooch which his mother had told him came from a secret admirer: the strings of pearls she had worn with cashmere sweaters because they had made her feel so 'English'.

If only she had bequeathed to him something she had really loved.

After the will had been read, and M. Renay had departed, when Clive Tierney told his son that his presence in the house was no longer welcome or desirable, going up to his room to pack his belongings, Nicholas remembered how much he and Madeleine had meant to each other.

Walking slowly along the landing to her bedroom, he had seen her leather-bound diary on the bedside table, her gold pen: her green enamelled clock, its hands stilled by the death of the beautiful woman to whom every day, every minute of her life had been an exciting adventure.

Later, on the night flight from Paris to Heathrow, Nicholas remembered walking with Madeleine beneath the chestnut trees in the Tuilleries gardens, on his eighteenth birthday, when she had dared to ask him a question that only a mother would have dared to ask her son.

'Tell me, Nicky, have you ever slept with a woman?'

The question had shocked him, it was so unexpected.

'The reason I ask, because I could not bear it if I thought that I had spoilt you for other women.'

How lovely she had looked that day, wearing a pink Chanel suit and a matching wide-brimmed straw hat.

'That's nonsense,' he'd replied brusquely to hide his embarrassment.

'Is it?' Smiling sadly, taking his arm, she said, 'I hope

so. We have always been so close, you and I. Perhaps too close. You have never had to stand on your own feet. I blame myself for that.'

'I don't know what you mean.'

'Please, don't be angry.' She had stopped walking to face him. 'How can I explain? You seem so uncertain of your future, your motivation in life. You are eighteen, my darling, on the brink of manhood, and yet you have never mentioned that future, never expressed an interest in girls.'

'Because I've never met anyone that appealed to me. No-one who could hold a candle to you.'

'But that's exactly what I meant. Listen, my darling, when you return to Oxford, I want you to give some thought to your future. Find yourself a nice English girl to fall in love with. Forget about your foolish Maman. You see, the day will come when you will need someone to fill my place in your heart.'

And so, returning to university, he had done his best to fall in love – to no avail. The pretty girls he had invited out to the cinema, or to dinner, had proved empty headed and flirtatious, the less pretty, too intense, attempting to read some deep meaning into their relationship.

Then, one evening in York, staying with his Aunt Sophia, he had gone to the theatre to see *The Cherry Orchard* and had met Anna Stravinska – lovely, dark-haired Anna, in whose eyes he had read a message older than time. Her glance had told him as clearly as if she had spoken aloud that they would meet later, and alone.

And so he had waited for her, in the pouring rain, at the stage door of the Theatre Royal.

Chapter Six

Sarah discovered the public library set back a little way from Museum Street, a stone's throw away from the river. It was rather like one of those solid Victorian town halls of the West Riding, she thought, making her way up the wide staircase to the reference room.

The time had come when she needed more background information on fifteenth-century York, and glassblowing in particular. But she preferred working this way, researching as she went along rather than doing it all in one fell swoop at the beginning of a book. This way one came upon nuggets of information which fitted into the pattern as the work progressed – like digging for gold and finding it.

Approaching the reception desk, she saw that a tall, slim woman, grey haired, immaculate in a heather tweed suit and matching sweater, was conversing with an elderly gentleman wanting information about a cholera epidemic, of all things. A somewhat tetchy old man, Sarah thought, waiting her turn, whom the librarian handled with charm and tact.

Smiling, Helen Grayson turned to Sarah when the old man had departed clutching a folder of newspaper clippings. 'Sorry about that,' she said apologetically. 'The colonel does tend to get a little hot under the collar at times. He has been writing a monograph on the York cholera epidemic for the past ten years, to my knowledge.'

87

'I didn't realize there had been an epidemic,' Sarah confessed, her writer's curiosity aroused.

'Oh yes. In 1832 if my memory serves me correctly. The victims were buried in that little graveyard near the station. It's a sad story. Some of the victims were thrown into the street to die. Apparently the hell-fire evangelists saw the epidemic as God's punishment for everything from cockfighting to Catholic emancipation.'

'Really? How interesting.'

'Yes. Now, how can I help you?'

Books about medieval York were not hard to find in one of the towering glass-fronted cases. Glassblowing proved more of a challenge.

'I'll need time to check round the area,' Helen said, 'meanwhile, if you'd care to fill in this card, I'll contact you when I've found what you're looking for.'

Obediently, Sarah wrote her name, address, and telephone number. Glancing at the card, Helen frowned slightly. 'Sarah Vale?' she said disbelievingly. '*You* are Sarah Vale?'

'Yes, I . . . Why? Don't tell me you have heard of me?'

'Heard of you? I'm a fan of yours. The way you write, so imaginatively, in such detail. The amount of research required to write so knowledgeably boggles the mind.'

'I find my own mind boggling at times,' Sarah admitted.

'I had no idea you lived in York.'

'I haven't been here very long. A matter of a few weeks.'

'It isn't often that one comes across a real live author. My name is Helen Grayson, by the way. Wait till I tell Alec, he's a fan of yours, too.'

'Alec? Your husband?'

'No, Alec's my brother. We live together. I'm not married.'

The tetchy colonel came back at that moment. Helen said impulsively to Sarah, 'I wonder, would it be possible for us to meet one morning for coffee? I'm free on Thursdays. My day off.'

'Yes, of course. Where?'

'Do you know Betty's Café?' Sarah nodded. 'Then shall we say Thursday at eleven?'

What a nice woman, Sarah thought, settling down to her research.

Leaving the library, stepping into the sunshine of a mild, spring afternoon, Sarah walked towards Lendal Bridge, where she stood for a little while watching the river traffic, thinking about Helen Grayson, the colonel, and the cholera epidemic, feeling happy about her research, remembering that, returning home, Amabie would be there, awaiting her homecoming.

Betty's Café, situated in the bustling heart of the city, was much busier now than in the old days, Sarah thought. Apart from which, it had scarcely changed at all. The same delicious coffee aroma permeated the air, intermingled with the scent of freshly baked bread from the adjoining bakery. The church across the way was still there and the Theatre Royal. Possibly even the cane chairs were the same, but she couldn't be sure. Memory played tricks after so many years. Thank goodness the place hadn't been modernized beyond recognition. Glancing at the cash-desk, she could almost see her mother standing there, paying her bill, a sturdy figure wearing a brown coat and a plain felt hat.

Helen, who had arrived earlier, waved to Sarah across the crowded room. Gripped with a feeling of nostalgia, threading her way between the tables, Sarah felt suddenly disorientated in this bright, slightly unreal atmosphere – the penalty one paid for living too close to the past, perhaps. Curiously, Amabie seemed more real to her than the people sitting at the tables drinking coffee. But one owed allegiance to the living as well as the dead. 'Hello, Helen,' she said, 'how nice of you to have found a window table.'

A deeply sensitive person, Helen thought that Sarah looked strained, as though she had scarcely slept the night before. Alec constantly reminded her that she acted too impulsively at times, and perhaps he was right, Helen thought guiltily, when he pointed out that a creative writer might not want to be dragged away from her typewriter to drink coffee with a stranger. She said ruefully, as Sarah sat down, 'It was selfish of me to suggest a meeting. My only excuse, I lead a rather dull, prosaic life. I thought how marvellous it would be to talk to someone interesting for a change.'

'Interesting?' Sarah raised her eyebrows and laughed. 'Hardly that. I lead a pretty ordinary kind of life myself. Apart from writing, which I love, I shop, clean up, cook – the kind of things every woman does, I imagine.'

'*Ordinary* women perhaps! But you have a special gift. *Lawrence* should have been a bestseller, in my opinion. The way you got under his skin was nothing short of remarkable. As if you knew exactly how he felt at finding himself an outcast, divorced from all the fame and glory that had gone before. But how could you possibly have known?'

Sarah conjured a mental picture of a warm summer day in Dorset, the day she had felt herself to be an outcast from her husband's affection. 'That's a difficult question to answer,' she said. 'And *Lawrence* flopped rather dismally, I'm afraid. But perhaps I'm not writing the kind of books that hit the bestseller lists. I might have been better off financially writing about sex, violence, and drug abuse.'

She spoke tongue in cheek, but Helen seemed shocked. 'Stuff and nonsense. Decent readers need decent writers!' She smiled shamefacedly, 'I'm sorry, I tend to get a bit hot under the collar myself sometimes. Are you married, by the way?'

When Sarah explained the situation, 'Oh, Lord,' Helen said, 'every time I open my mouth I put my foot in it. Alec is always telling me to think before I speak.'

Anxious to change the subject, 'Tell me about your brother,' Sarah suggested. 'Is he a career man?'

'He was. Not now, I'm afraid. He made the Army his career until . . . ' Helen bit her lip. 'I'm afraid the Falklands' conflict put paid to that.'

'Please don't say any more. I didn't mean to pry.' Averting her eyes, Sarah noticed the dark-haired man she had seen in York Minster, deep in conversation with a girl wearing jeans and a baggy white sweater, whose hair, bleached to the brittleness of straw, hung wispily about her heavily made-up face. He was laughing as though he hadn't a care in the world.

So much for imagination, she thought. And yet that day in the Minster, Sarah could have sworn that the man she thought of as Amabie was deeply unhappy – the 'Hound of Heaven' at his heels.

Ralph Foster received his dinner invitation, at Sarah's flat, with mixed feelings of joy and nervous tension. What if he stuttered and stammered throughout the meal?

Drawing twenty pounds from her building society account, Sarah had gone to town on a fillet of lamb, frozen prawns, a bottle of reasonably priced wine, vegetables, and a carton of Wall's Vienetta.

Hunger had reared its ugly head. Feverishly she filled her supermarket trolley. Ralph, who had been kind to her, should be repaid for his kindness. Or was this simply an excuse for her spending spree? She had read somewhere that over-eating was a sure sign of some emotional disorder. Possibly starvation might also contribute to emotional instability, she thought wryly, adding mayonnaise, a selection of cheeses, freshly ground coffee, butter, and a loaf of wholemeal bread. Her bill came to a little over sixteen pounds. She did not care. Time to push aside her guilt feelings, her children's rejection. Her sense of euphoria might not last very long, but she viewed her spending spree in the light of a rearguard action fought against poverty and self denial, a spur to her writing ambitions. She *must* believe that *Amabie* would be successful, that she would one day leap the poverty barrier.

Cocking a further snook at life, on the way home she bought two bunches of freesia, tightly budded, wickedly perfumed, a sheer, blissful waste of money.

Ralph came up to her flat carrying a sheaf of mimosa in a cone of striped florist's paper, which he presented to her, willing himself not to stammer, remembering the advice his speech therapist had given him – to draw in deep breaths before speaking. Above all, to keep calm.

For the first time since he had known her, Sarah was wearing a dress, pale green in colour, with a frilled collar and cuffs, which made her look older, more matronly; a stranger. He much preferred her in slacks and a sweater, and he couldn't give a damn that she was overweight. She was Sarah, his friend and neighbour, intelligent and unassuming.

'Please come in. Oh, the flowers are lovely. Thank you. I'll put them in water.'

Entering the drawing room he noticed her typewriter, a stone jar filled with pens, pencils, Stabilo Boss; boxes of paper and carbons, a stack of folders and reference books. 'Are you a – writer?' he asked, perplexed.

'Well, yes,' Sarah admitted.

'Why didn't you tell me?' He felt hurt.

'I did not think it important, since you had obviously never heard of me from a literary point of view. You're not angry, are you?'

'Angry? My d-dear girl, why should I be angry? I'm delighted, just a little ashamed, that's all.'

'Because you had never heard of me?' Sarah laughed. 'Don't worry, neither has half the population of the British Isles. Make that seven eighths! Frankly, I'm a non-starter in the literary stakes. But let's not talk about that. Come and uncork the wine. There's a corkscrew somewhere in the kitchen.'

As Ralph struggled manfully with the cork, Sarah unearthed a plastic bucket which she filled with water, gently immersing the mimosa stalks, thinking that the blossoms reminded her of snow by winter lamplight, when the flakes drifted together.

'About your w-writing,' Ralph said, as the cork came out with a plop.

'What about it?' Opening the oven door, Sarah took

93

out the joint and turned the roast potatoes, feeling over-dressed, unnatural in her green dress, wishing she had stuck to her usual slacks and sweater.

'I'd like to hear more.'

'There's nothing much to tell.' Closing the oven door, turning her attention to the prawns sitting atop strands of lettuce: spooning on mayonnaise, 'I write what is known as "faction" – a blend of fact and fiction; historical novels which no one apparently cares tuppence about. After all, why should they, when the bookshops are chock-a-block with thrillers, spy stories and murder mysteries?'

'I know,' Ralph said, laying the cork on a work surface, 'there's a g-glut of that kind of rubbish these days.'

'I'm sorry, Ralph, I don't agree with you. It isn't all rubbish. Take Ruth Rendell, P.D. James, or Stephen King, for example. I admire their work enormously.' Leading the way to the dining table, carrying the melba glasses, 'Let's begin, shall we?'

Halfway through the meal, 'Forgive me, Ralph,' Sarah said, 'do you mind if I change? Frankly, I hate this dress I'm wearing. I feel so hot and uncomfortable. I much prefer slacks and a sweater.'

Ralph realized afterwards, that this was the moment he had fallen in love with Sarah, who had brought an added dimension of joy to his celibate and lonely life.

The trouble was, he scarcely knew how to express his feeling of pleasure in her company, tethered as he was to his deep-seated sense of inadequacy and inferiority, prompted by his speech impediment, his age, weak eye-sight, and rapidly thinning hair. He simply prayed that, in time to come, she would begin to realize that a shy, at times inarticulate, schoolmaster was not all he appeared to be on the surface. So few people were. There was always that baffling smokescreen to contend with, behind which human beings sought refuge against the discovery of their true identities.

After dinner, Sarah wanted nothing more than to sit in front of the fire, sipping coffee, listening to music. To talk, perhaps, about the ordinary things they had in common – crossword puzzles, the city in which they lived, the theatre, their favourite films, favourite flowers, recipes, food – anything which would not touch upon their private lives too succinctly. She liked Ralph, but not to the extent that she wished to bare her soul to him, or vice versa.

But Ralph, intrigued by her writing, would not rest until he had seen her books, and so she found herself kneeling, with him, in front of the shelves, explaining how each of them had come to be written, what had triggered off her ideas, how and where she had done her research, until Ralph said, admiringly, 'What a m-marvellous achievement.'

And yes, perhaps it was, Sarah considered. A far greater achievement than she had realized, to have written her way through times of unhappiness and self doubt. On the other hand, had she cared less about writing and more about her personal appearance, had she been prepared to starve physically as well as emotionally, she might have saved her marriage. But would physical and mental starvation have made any difference in the long run?

Men like Faulkner were seldom satisfied with what they had. Buried deep in their natures lay the lust for more money, more success, more women, more love affairs to shore up their ego, whilst she, by reason of her upbringing, had wanted nothing more than a husband, a home, and children.

But no. She was wrong, terribly wrong. There *had* been something more she had wanted from life – to write, to set down on paper her instinctive feeling for the past, to bring that past to life, however ineptly. To follow her own star.

That her star and Faulkner's lay far apart had become increasingly obvious as time went by, and yet they would always be responsible for the children they had brought into the world.

Sensing her tiredness, her withdrawal, feeling that he was somehow to blame, Ralph said quietly, 'I-I'd better be going now. T-thank you for a lovely evening, a s-splendid meal.'

Standing on the threshold of the room, his hand on the doorknob, he wondered what her reaction would be if, for once in his life, he dared to emerge from his smoke-screen of self-effacement as the passionate, caring human being he knew himself to be deep inside.

Smiling, Sarah said, 'Thank you for your company – and the mimosa.'

'Sure you wouldn't l-like me to g-give you a hand with the w-washing up?' he asked hopefully.

'No, really. Goodnight, Ralph.'

Hearing his footsteps on the stairs, she drew in a breath of relief that the evening was over, and thought, as she went through to the kitchen to make a start on the mountain of pots and pans, that despite all the food she had bought, cooked, and eaten, she would be hungry again tomorrow.

Chapter Seven

Converting a dilapidated Victorian mansion into a functional hotel had been Sophia's greatest challenge and most thrilling experience.

Tall and purposeful, wearing a tailored Donegal tweed suit, typically English despite the years she had spent in Paris, she had toured the house with the estate agent, seeing it not as it was but as it might be in time to come, wishing the man would go away and leave her to wander the rooms alone, to make her own assessment of its potential. She had not needed a stranger to point out its obvious charm or its equally obvious disadvantages, nor could she have told a stranger the thoughts that flitted through her mind when, standing in the hall, looking up at the oriel window beaming sunlight on to the broad, branching staircase with its massive mahogany newels and gracefully curved banisters, she knew that she had come home at last.

Built in the heyday of Victorian wealth and influence, the Cedars as it was then known, reflected the Victorian love of ostentation, solidity and space. Entering the rooms one by one, Sophia imagined the balls and soirees of a bygone age; ballads played on candled pianofortes, the swish of skirts and bustles, the strains of a palm court orchestra from the huge conservatory beyond the impressive dining room, the style and elegance of the house as it would have looked a hundred years ago, when the faded crimson and gold wallpapers were new and unstained with damp patches, the brass doorknobs brightly polished, the fireplaces radiating heat and comfort.

But visual enchantment and sentimentality had not blinded her to the present day problems – the cost of a central heating system to begin with; plumbing, re-wiring; having the antiquated Victorian kitchen made functional, more hygienic by the removal of the stone sinks, wooden draining boards, and the rusty iron range with its plethora of side ovens, dampers, and fire-grate. But this would be Michel's province, it would be up to him to plan the kitchen to his own requirements, if she decided to go in at the deep end.

By no means a rich woman, despite the sale of the Cheyne Walk house, Sophia knew that she would need, apart from the comfortable sum of money deposited to her account at Coutts, a sizeable overdraft, plus all her powers of persuasion to convince her bank manager that she was not throwing good money after bad.

Even so, she had gone ahead with the purchase of the Cedars, a lonely, idealistic Englishwoman forced, by circumstance, to stand on her own two feet, a woman of considerable resourcefulness and courage who, despite all the obstacles, had achieved her goal in the end, with the help and support of her friend Michel Arnot.

Michel.

The curious friendship between the fiery tempered Breton and the cool, calm Englishwoman, Sophia knew, had caused raised eyebrows, gossip, snide remarks, a certain amount of laughter among their fellow students at l'école de cuisine, but their friendship had endured. Both had been hurt by life. As time went by, Sophia had come to rely on Michel, he on her – especially during those early days at the Carillon when guests were thin on the ground and food went to waste because so few people had turned up to eat it.

When Madeleine gave birth to a son, Sophia had scraped together enough money to attend the christening. The house in the Rue St Hélène had seemed uncompromisingly plain and uninteresting at first glance – a square villa surrounded with a high wall and a plantation of trees to screen it from prying eyes; the windows with folded back shutters; nothing of architectural importance to commend it – until, crossing the threshold, Sophia had fallen under the spell of the light airiness of its interior, the glowing colours and charming flower arrangements – an atmosphere in which Clive had seemed strangely ill at ease, an awkward father embarrassed by his progeny, as if aware that fatherhood sat oddly on a man of his age and temperament.

Clearly, he was jealous of the child, his jealousy inflamed by Madeleine's obvious adoration of the baby: jealous, too, of the visitors who came to pay homage, upsetting his usual, well-ordered routine to the extent that he had begun to stay more often in his suite of rooms at the embassy; to avoid the guests whom Madeleine invited to stay to dinner, or for the weekend, if they felt so inclined.

Obviously, Sophia thought worriedly, the child had become a bone of contention between her brother and his wife. But if Clive's indifference had hurt Madeleine, she gave no outward sign, even to Sophia, in whose affairs she was deeply interested, wanting to know all about the newly launched Carillon.

When Sophia confessed, one afternoon in the drawing room, that despite all her hard work, the hotel had not taken off as she had hoped it would, and that her partner, Michel Arnot, and she were staring bankruptcy in the face, Madeleine's response had been immediate: 'But my darling Sophia, you must let me help!'

'I was afraid you'd say that. Thank you, dear, but no!'

'Why not?' The trace of a frown between those exquisitely fashioned eyebrows.

'A matter of pride, I suppose.'

'Mon Dieu! You drowned in the wool English!'

'Dyed in the wool, not drowned,' Sophia explained, smiling.

'Dyed – drowned – what the hell? I shall never – nevair – understand this English pride which makes life so difficult for everyone. What is the use of money—' She pronounced the word 'merney' —'if it is not put to good use?'

How lovely she looked, Sophia thought, in her soft blue wool afternoon dress, sitting on a gilt-framed Louis Quinze sofa, her forehead puckered into a frown of concentration, as slim as she had been before the birth of her baby, racking her brains to find a solution to the problem.

Suddenly, 'Have you tried – how you say – making known la Carillon?'

'Advertising, you mean? Yes, of course, I've placed adverts in all the local papers, *The Dalesman*, and *The Lady*.'

'Local papairs?' Madeleine looked startled. 'But you merst spread wider the net! Catch many more fishes! Rich American fishes. French, Spanish, Belgian fishes! Make them all swim together towards la Carillon for the so good cuisine.' Clasping her hands together, 'Also, you merst have the – what you call – gimmick! Together we merst create for you the new image.' She laughed delightedly.

'Of course! Black, that is the answer! You shall become the so eccentric mademoiselle de cuisine. Tomorrow, we will go shopping, buy lots and lots of black clothes: shoes, jewellery, accessories!'

'Stop it, Madeleine! That is out of the question,' Sophia said firmly, interrupting her sister-in-law's flow, 'I can't possibly afford to go shopping.'

'But this would be my loving gift to you,' Madeleine said persuasively. 'Surely you will not deny me that pleasure? First you turn down my offer of money, now this.' Her lips trembled appealingly.

Sophia laughed. 'You should have been an actress. You almost had me fooled for a minute.'

'An actress?' Madeleine sighed. 'Yes, I think I should have liked that. The limelight, the applause, pretending to be someone else . . . ' As if, Sophia thought, she disliked being the wife of a cold-blooded English diplomat.

The day that followed would remain in Sophia's memory as the most exhausting she had ever spent in Paris, and the most rewarding.

First Madeleine had taken her to a small but fashionable couturière in the Place Vendôme – the walls mirrored to reflect the pale mushroom carpet, swagged silk draperies, black leather chairs, and crystal chandeliers, where she had sat in judgement on the various black evening gowns Sophia had tried on until satisfied that the low cut dress with diaphanous chiffon sleeves caught into gold embroidered cuffs, and the less revealing garment flowing to a dramatically heavy, circular skirt, were exactly right for her. Then, with unerring good taste, Madeleine had selected a black velvet cape, silk-lined in deep midnight blue, to complement both dresses.

Afterwards, they had stopped for coffee close to Madeleine's next ports of call; tucked away boutiques specializing in exquisite lingerie, handmade leather shoes, belts and handbags. 'You really mustn't spend any more on me,' Sophia protested, but Madeleine simply laughed and said they hadn't even begun yet. Sophia would need at least six day dresses, blouses, skirts, sweaters. And a coat. She knew just the shop, a place nearby where the 'little man' who owned it had been clever enough to invent fabrics that looked exactly like fur, so that one could scarcely tell the difference, except, of course, by the price.

'Madeleine! This has to stop!'

'I agree, cherie. We must have lunch. Come, we will take a taxi to the Champs Elysées – to Bouvrier's. Emile will find us a table, of that I am certain.' With boundless energy and enthusiasm, Madeleine had flagged down a cruising taxi.

In years to come, Sophia would realize the source of her nephew's charm and vitality, his effect on the opposite sex. In the same way, men had turned their heads to look whenever Madeleine entered a room, bowled over by her loveliness, warmed by her charm and spontaneity, her bubbling personality linked to her supreme elegance and instinctive good taste.

'Now, isn't this nice?' Madeline glowed at the Poirot-like figure of Emile who, hurrying forward to greet her, expressed his delight at seeing her again, and hastened to assure her that he had indeed a table in one of the booths at the far side of the room. A table for two with a blue linen cloth, a centrepiece of white marguerites, in a curving, interspaced banque of deep blue velvet.

Gratefully, Sophia leaned back to study the menu.

When they had ordered – steak, pas bien cuit, salade, and a full bodied red wine, bemused and more than a little embarrassed by her sister-in-law's generosity, she remonstrated gently that she could not possibly accept more gifts – the coat, for instance, and certainly not the jewellery Madeleine had set her heart on purchasing after lunch.

'No, please darling, do not spoil my pleasure in giving,' Madeleine said softly, her eyes brimming with tears. And this time Sophia knew that she was not play-acting.

'What is it? What's wrong?' Leaning forward, Sophia touched Madeleine's hand. 'You can trust me.'

Madeleine shook her head, blinking away the tears. 'It is not important. I am a little tired, that is all.'

Sophia said compassionately, 'It's the christening, isn't it? You hoped that Clive would change his mind about the christening. But you must have known, when you married him, that he would never consent to a child of his being baptized in a Catholic church.'

'I knew,' Madeleine said, 'but I had not realized how deeply I would care.'

'I'm so sorry, my dear.' Sophia wished, at that moment, she could take Clive by the shoulders and shake some sense into him. Then, miraculously, Madeleine was smiling once more, holding out her hands to a handsome, dark-haired man threading his way between the tables of the main concourse of diners. A man who, approaching their table, seized her hands, both of which he kissed lovingly, lingeringly, brushing the tender skin with his neatly clipped moustache.

'Madeleine, ma chérie,' he murmured, 'it is so good to see you again. I thought . . . '

Was she being fanciful, Sophia wondered, in imagining

a liaison dangereuse between Madeleine and the handsome stranger? A look of warning in Madeleine's eyes as she made the introduction: 'Jules, I do not think that you have met my sister-in-law, Mademoiselle Tierney. Sophia, this is Jules Dinard, my late husband's partner and friend, who was so kind to me when Philippe died.'

'Enchanté, Mademoiselle Tierney.' Dinard bowed his head formally and lightly kissed her hand, but Sophia sensed the man's disappointment that Madeleine was not lunching alone.

When he had drifted away to join friends at another table, Sophia asked Madeleine, simply and directly, 'Are you in love with him?'

The colour drained suddenly from Madeleine's cheeks, her fingers tightened on the stem of her wine glass. 'In love with Jules? No, of course not! I told you, he was Philippe's friend. Surely you cannot believe that . . . ' Then, casting aside all pretence, looking like a frightened little girl caught stealing apples, 'Well yes, if you must know. Or I thought so – and then I met Clive.'

Sighing, Sophia said patiently, 'Then for God's sake why did you marry my brother? Oh, I know all his good points, believe me – his sense of honour, dedication to his job, his intellect, his looks, his physique. But was that really enough?'

'Perhaps not,' Madeleine admitted. 'But Jules, also, is a Catholic. Married. And our religion forbids divorce. We put aside our feelings for the sake of his wife and children. I married Clive in the mistaken belief that our marriage would somehow blot out the past for me.'

'Madeleine, my dear . . . '

'No, you must not feel sorry for me,' Madeleine said proudly. 'I have made my bed, now I must lie in it.'

Pouring more wine, a splash of red overspilled on to the blue tablecloth, betraying her emotion. 'You see, I have my son to love and take care of now. My Nicholas.'

In later years, during her flying visits to Paris – no longer a financial hardship since the Carillon had begun to make money at last – watching Nicholas grow up, the niggling seed of doubt that he was really her brother's child, had come uppermost in Sophia's mind. And, if Clive suspected that Nicholas was not his son, might that not account for his all too apparent dislike of the boy?

Now that the weather had turned warmer, Ralph Foster spent much of his spare time in the long, walled garden, which appealed to his love of beauty, order, and good husbandry.

Gardening had become a hobby of his when his mother was alive, working outdoors a means of escape from the faint odour, not of sanctity but sickness.

Illness possessed a peculiar, unmistakable smell all its own: a sad smell of decay, like damp November leaves. And the sick person filled the house with a feeling of hopelessness, especially when that person was old and dying.

During his mother's protracted, final illness, every room had contained reminders of her chronic disabilities – the cork seat in the bath, the bathroom cabinet chock-a-block with bottles of pills and antiseptic lotions to ease her suffering, the wheelchair parked in the dining room, the hall-stand containing a clutter of disused walking sticks, a long forsaken aluminium walking frame in the sitting room; kitchen cupboards containing packets of invalid foods, and a white china feeding cup. In her bedroom, a commode, plus a lavender scented aerosol on the mantelpiece and a rubber sheet in the top drawer of her dressing table in readiness for the district nurse who came in on Mondays, Wednesdays, and Fridays, to give Mrs Foster a bed-bath and to gently rub antiseptic ointment on to her bed-sores.

Taking care of his mother had seemed to Ralph the decent, humane thing to do. Never a strong woman physically, and less so mentally as time went by, he could not have borne putting her into a nursing home, although that would have been the sensible thing to do. But she cried so easily, those moist, speedwell blue eyes of hers dominating the creased linen of her face, her hands, tiny and wrinkled, like veined autumn leaves about to flutter down from the trees, moving him to an overwhelming feeling of pity when he remembered all the cooking, cleaning, washing, sewing and knitting those hands had done on his behalf.

The decision made, he had tendered his resignation from the small, private school at which he had taught history and English literature since leaving university, preferring the cloistered atmosphere of a prep school to the cut and thrust of a modern comprehensive.

He realized, of course, that his first class honours degree might have taken him to the top of the academic ladder via a headmastership: possibly a much prized fellowship at Oxford or Cambridge, had he cared to pursue either course, instead of which, an embryo 'Mr Chips', he had settled for anonymity, an atmosphere in which he felt happily at home, thankfully relieved of the hassle of high academic achievement.

Reasonably well off financially, happy in an uneventful kind of way, at ease with his colleagues – particularly his headmaster – never had Ralph felt himself capable of anything more demanding than inculcating small classes of little boys into the mysterious world of the Shakespeare sonnets, Robert Browning's superb 'Paracelsus', Wordsworth's 'Epitaphs and Elegiac Poems', Rudyard Kipling's 'If'; of chalking up, on the blackboard, the dates of the Battle of Hastings, Agincourt; the reign of Henry VIII, the succession to the throne of England of the first Elizabeth, the execution of Charles the First, and so on . . .

That his headmaster, Cornelius Swift, had invited him to dinner one evening for the purpose of making his deputy head teacher change his mind about resigning, had made not one iota of difference to Ralph's clear-cut decision to nurse his mother through her final illness. 'You s-see, Headmaster, I feel that I owe my mother at least a little dignity after all she has done for me,' Ralph explained over a pre-dinner glass of sherry in Swift's study.

'Naturally, my dear fellow, I appreciate your point of view, but have you considered that, if I accept your resignation, I shall have no other alternative than to replace you?'

'Yes. I could hardly expect you to do otherwise.'

'Very well, then, if your mind is made up, all I can possibly do is wish you the best of luck.'

'Thank you, Headmaster.'

'But have you thought this thing through Foster? What I mean is, have you thought what you will do . . . ' A pregnant pause, 'when the worst happens? Bearing in mind that I cannot guarantee your return here?'

'Thanks again, Headmaster, but when the worst happens, I shall move away from this area entirely. Apply for a part-time teaching post elsewhere.'

And so, after the death of his mother, and the ritual of her funeral, Ralph had put the house on the market and begun applying for part-time posts the length and breadth of the British Isles, not caring where he ended up – in Norfolk, Oxfordshire, Devon, Cornwall, or the outer Hebrides, as long as he felt reasonably happy in his new surroundings.

Called for an interview at St William's College the following April, he had known the minute he walked out of the station to see the swathes of golden daffodils blowing against the ramparts of the grey city walls, that here was a place in which he would be happy. *Would* – not *could* – for he had known, with an inner certainty, that he would be offered the job. He was not mistaken.

His furniture in store temporarily, he had started looking for somewhere to live, to put down new roots. The flat in the Georgian house, a stone's throw away from the college, had come to him through the auspices of the Principal of St William's, who knew the director of the Archaeological Trust.

So had begun a new life for Ralph Foster, untinged with regret of the old, apart from that chilling moment he had seen his mother's coffin disappear behind the curtains of the Gladesbrook Crematorium, and listened to the piped music of Psalm 23, 'The Lord is my Shepherd'. Regret that he no longer had anyone to care for.

Mowing the grass one warm, edging-towards-summer day, in the garden of the York flat, he felt happier than he had done in the fifty-odd years of his life, knowing that Sarah would come down later for a cup of tea with him, and to wander round the garden admiring his handiwork, exclaiming with pleasure at the scent of the newly mown grass and the amount of buds on the thickly clustered roses.

The warmth of their friendship had brightened Ralph's

life. Looking forward was something he had seldom done before. Now, each day held the probability of talking to Sarah on the telephone, or seeing her, however briefly. They had taken to ringing each other each evening to say goodnight, if they had not met that day, to ask how the day had gone, or to make plans for tomorrow.

These phone calls seemed to Ralph an umbilical cord of friendship, a precious link between two lonely people, imparting a wealth of direction and purpose to his life, so that when he mowed the grass, weeded the herbaceous borders, staked the lupins, delphiniums, and peonies, he felt that he was doing all these things not for the Archaeological Trust nor himself, but for her, to give her pleasure.

Enjoying the smooth action of the Flymo, he planned what they would have for dinner. Awaiting Sarah's arrival, he opened the windows to let in air. She looked tired, he thought, when she came down: weary and preoccupied.

Sensitive to her mood, he did not question her about *Amabie*, understanding the impossibility of switching from a state of deep concentration to sociability in a matter of minutes.

After coffee, she asked Ralph if he would walk with her to the river, and they went out into the warm spring evening, along College Street into Deangate, stopping now and then to look in shop windows, aware of the beauty of the city by night.

Standing beside him on Lendal Bridge, looking down at the water swimming with a myriad reflected shore lights, what price friendship without honesty, Sarah thought. She had not burdened Ralph with her personal affairs, but the letter from her solicitor saying that her divorce had reached the stage of finalization was burning a hole in her pocket.

She needed to tell someone, and Ralph, who demanded nothing of her save friendship was the obvious choice.

Hesitantly, she began to speak, staring down at the water, telling him of the rift between herself and her children, not looking up, aware of his sympathy, unaware of the thudding of his heart, his longing to hold her in his arms.

The time had come to tell Sophia about the funeral, the reading of Madeleine's will.

Nicholas broached the subject after dinner, in her drawing room, over their customary nightcap, after which he would go down to the bar to act as host; to dance with the women guests.

Handing him a whisky and soda, sitting down, Sophia waited, knowing there was something on his mind.

Standing near the fireplace, cradling the glass, absentmindedly tilting the contents, Nicholas said, 'You will, I imagine, receive word from Madeleine's attorney in a day or so.'

'Really? What makes you think that?'

'Because she left you those paintings you admired. The ones that hung in her boudoir. I expect my father will make arrangements with Renay to have them crated and sent to you as soon as possible.'

'How generous of Madeleine. How kind.' Sophia's eyes filled with tears.

'She was equally generous to the Simenons, the gardener, and my father.' Nicholas laughed mirthlessly. 'He came out of it all rather well on the whole. Madeleine left him the house and the bulk of her money.'

'And you?' Looking at her nephew, Sophia realized that the dark side of his Gemini nature was uppermost now, and felt shocked by the bitterness she read in his eyes.

'Madeleine left me that which she valued least of all, her jewellery.'

'But surely, that jewellery is worth a great deal?' As soon as the words were uttered, Sophia knew she had said the wrong thing; wished to heaven she had held her tongue.

'I thought that you, above all people, would understand that money doesn't enter into it! I would far rather she had left me her bedside clock, her last year's diary, her crystal bowl, the smallest of things she had treasured during her lifetime!'

'I know, Nicky darling. Believe me, I understand what you are going through . . . '

Interrupting, '*Do* you?' he said gruffly, 'I doubt if anyone could understand how I feel right now. How I felt when my father closed the door in my face!'

Gulping his drink, setting down the glass, Nicholas turned to grip the edge of the mantelpiece, his knuckles showing white. 'Frankly, he couldn't wait to get rid of me!'

Torn between love of her nephew and loyalty to her brother, Sophia said wearily, 'Have you any idea what life has been like for *me* these past few days? You must know how much it grieved me not to attend your mother's funeral. But I was needed here, at the Carillon.'

Standing up, she continued, 'I realize, of course, that there is no love lost between yourself and my brother, but he *is* your father.' As she uttered the words, Sophia wondered if they were true. But, true or not, she must speak her mind.

'Never before have I said this, Nicholas, but the time

has come for you to decide what to do with the rest of your life, unless you intend to float through it like the rolling stone that gathers no moss.

'No, please don't interrupt! The truth is, I have spoilt you in allowing you to drift into hotel life in a dilettante way, when I should have pinned you down to the realities of the job. If you really intended to make a career of hotel management, I should have made you sweat it out in the heat of the kitchen, polish silver, wash up in the stillroom, wait at table, study accountancy.

'The trouble is, growing up in an affluent atmosphere with money no object, you have never known what it is to be poor. Now, here you are feeling sorry for yourself because you have been left a fortune in jewellery.'

Drawing back her shoulders, standing tall and proud: 'Remember when you left university? You wanted to be an actor. Fair enough. But when you realized that acting was not simply a matter of walking on-stage in a blaze of glory, but one entailing a great deal of hard work at a drama school, you didn't want to know.'

She continued more gently, 'But even rich men must have some sense of purpose, some ambition, if they are not to become parasites. The wealthiest men I have met during my lifetime have been masters of good husbandry, knowledgeable about farming, afforestation, livestock, or horseflesh.

'Such men I admired, those who spoke quietly, who took an interest in their estates; who upheld certain traditions, cared deeply about religion and politics.'

'I must have been a damned disappointment to you then,' Nicholas said bitterly. 'And I thought you loved me.'

Sophia said, compassionately, 'It is because I love you

that I want you to face up to life. Not to waste it, as I have wasted mine.'

'Wasted? But I thought that your whole life centred about the Carillon, the success you have made of it.'

Sophia smiled sadly. 'Yes, you are quite right. But have you ever stopped to consider that I have missed out on the real values? Marriage, children – a love to call my own? Now, if you'll excuse me, I am rather tired.'

Turning at the door, 'Promise me one thing, that you will stay here with me, at the Carillon, for at least one more year.'

'I'm sorry, Aunt. I can't promise anything at the moment,' Nicholas said slowly, running his fingers through his hair. 'Please, don't misunderstand. I owe you so much, more than I can ever repay.' He brushed a hand across his forehead, like a child, Sophia thought, filled with pity for him, this man, as dear to her as a son, who had so much and yet so little, whose lack of motivation in life had led him from one abortive love affair to the next, as though, applying Madeleine's yardstick to every woman he came in contact with, none had measured up to his ideal of perfection.

He went on, 'Remember the first time I ever came here? The day my father brought me to England to begin boarding school?'

Sophia nodded. How could she forget? Nicky had been twelve years old at the time, a thin, handsome little boy, ill at ease with his father whose bullying, 'for God's sake be a man' attitude had robbed him, almost, of speech. There had simply been two enormous, dark eyes in the pale mask of the child's face, a trembling mouth, pipestem legs, a crackling, brand new school uniform which seemed to dwarf him, a cap which seemed too big for his head.

'Remember that you took me by the hand and asked if I was hungry?'

'Yes.' Sophia smiled.

'Father was furious. I knew he wanted to catch the next train to London, that he wanted to hustle me off to St Peter's as quickly as possible, dump me, and wash his hands of me, having delivered me, rather like a parcel. But you weren't having that. I'll never forget the way you looked at him and said I must be given something to eat first. Then you took me through to the kitchen and gave me a chicken sandwich, a glass of milk, and strawberry shortcake.' Nicky's eyes kindled with remembrance. 'It was then I knew that you were my friend, my ally. I had been uncertain beforehand. You looked so much like my father, I thought you would *be* like him. Madeleine had done her best to reassure me, but I thought . . .' He smiled ruefully, recalling the pain of that first ever separation from his mother, ' . . . well, I was wrong, that's all.'

He continued, 'You and Madeleine were always first in my heart. The Carillon became my second home. After university, what my father called my "wasted years", I knew that to live under the same roof with him was impossible. I would have stayed on in Paris, for Madeleine's sake, had I believed for one moment that my being there would have made her happy; balanced the scales for her. But I could see all too clearly that the tension was unbearable.' Nicky's voice roughened. 'To have stayed in Paris, to subject my mother to a tight-rope existence, strung, as she was, between her love for me and her loyalty to my father, would have been cruel. And so I came to England, to the Carillon. To you, Tante Sophia.'

'And now?'

114

'I don't know.' Nicholas bowed his head. 'I honestly don't know.' He looked up then, his face a mask of despair. 'I only wish I did. Everything you said was true. The time *has* come to decide what to do with my life. The truth is, I'm – lost! Since Madeleine died, there is no foreseeable future. It's as though I were faced with a gaping hole in my life, a thick, black void, like a tunnel, with no ray of light at the end of it.'

'Oh, my dear!' Turning away from the door, Sophia swept forward to take her nephew's hands in hers, distressed that she had not understood the depth of his isolation and despair. 'I'm so sorry, please forgive me. I had no right to speak as I did.'

'You had every right.' Attempting a smile, Nicholas pressed her hands to his lips. 'Don't worry. Nothing you could ever do or say would stop my loving you, trying my best to please you. All I ask is a little time, a little – space. Now,' glancing at his watch, 'it's time I was on duty downstairs.'

'You need not go, for my sake,' Sophia said huskily.

'Perhaps not. But, for my own sake, I must, if that makes sense.' Briefly, Nicholas pressed the slim, elderly figure of his aunt to his heart before quitting the room, shoulders squared, a Don Quixote tilting at the churning windmills of the mind, those endlessly churning windmills whose sails flapped wearily, continuously, against a host of memories best forgotten, or laid to rest if he hoped to gain any kind of strength or peace of mind to carry him through to an uncertain future.

Not ringing for the elevator, he stood awhile near a window at the far end of the corridor, staring into the past, remembering Madeleine, and Paris; how the tightly budded trees had overflowed like green fountains, when spring arrived, spilling shade on to sun-washed pavements. That magnificent city had been Madeleine's setting, the filigree which had held the jewel of her fun-loving personality: an atmosphere in which she had shone and sparkled like the bubbles in a glass of champagne. The pavement cafés, restaurants, theatres, shops, the churches and museums, all had been hers in the effervescent days of her youth and beauty. The great boulevards had echoed to her lightly tripping footsteps, the striped awnings of the pavement cafés had given her shade: the parks and gardens had shared her laughter; the Tuilleries in particular . . .

Caught in memory's web, Nicholas remembered that June day, almost twenty years ago, when Madeleine had begged him to think of his future, to find himself a nice English girl to fall in love with; his subsequent meeting with Anna Stravinska, in the pouring rain, at the stage door of York's Theatre Royal: his thickly beating heart as Anna had stepped out to greet him. How lovely she had looked, how desirable, the fur collar of her coat framing her piquant, heart-shaped face.

Eighteen years old at the time, Anna had appeared to him as a goddess of infinite wisdom and maturity, a mystic, fairytale creature in whose arms he might discover the meaning of love, of physical passion and release.

How old was she? Thirty? Thirty-five? Forty? Impossible to say. She had seemed a mere child on-stage with her petite figure and cloud of dark hair. In any case, what difference did age make to the way one felt? He had escorted her to a waiting taxi, and she had told the driver to take them to an address in Walmgate, an apartment she had rented for her stay in York.

Preceding him up the rickety stairs, laughing, 'You must forgive the muddle,' she said, unlocking the door,

'I am not the tidiest of mortals,' uttered in the fascinating Russian/English accent which had charmed the public and critics when she had first appeared as Hedda Gabler, at Drury Lane.

Watching her tidying away piles of newspapers and magazines, clearing away empty coffee cups, attempting to create order from chaos, marvelling at her beauty, he had scarcely known why he was there at all, except that she had, miraculously, told him by a look, a smile, a certain expression in her eyes, that she found him attractive, and wished to be alone with him.

The clearing up done, she shrugged off her coat. Standing close to him, placing her hands on his shoulders, smiling teasingly into his eyes, 'Tell me, is this your first time? But of course it is! How exciting!' Turning away, glancing over her shoulder, 'There's a bottle of wine in the kitchen; glasses. I'll be back in a whisper.'

Finding the glasses, uncorking the wine, he could scarcely restrain the trembling of his hands. His throat had felt restricted, his palms were clammy with perspiration. Taking the wine through to the other room, he wished that Anna had not asked if this was his 'first time'. Was it so obvious?

Waiting at the stage door, he had felt strong and purposeful, all male, deeply conscious of his need to prove his manhood. Now he felt more like a schoolboy, ashamed of his lack of experience.

When she returned, wearing the filmiest of negligees, her hair spilling about her shoulders, smelling divinely of some exotic perfume, he gave her a glass of wine, as dumbstruck as a calf, not knowing what to say to her.

Sitting down on the sofa, nestling against the cushions, her feet tucked beneath her, she regarded him playfully.

'Well, don't just stand there. Come, sit beside me. I am not going to bite you.' Amused by his discomfort, she said, 'Aren't you going to kiss me?'

Putting down the glass, she held out her arms to him. Mesmerized by her warmth, beauty, her perfume, her gently beckoning fingertips, sliding down beside her, finding her lips, he felt that he was swimming in a sea of scented water; sucked down by unsuspected currents, fighting for breath . . . drowning.

Eyes closed, tightening his arms about her, feeling her softness through the thin robe, he moved his lips like a goldfish in a bowl, half mad with desire to suck in that tantalising, flickering tongue of hers, until, pulling away from him, laughing, she said, 'I asked you to kiss me, not devour me! Now, give me a cigarette.'

'A – *cigarette*?'

'There, on the table.'

Silently, he complied, resentful of her laughter. Kissing her, holding her, he had felt the hardening of his flesh, the compulsion to drive that hard, pulsating rod of flesh deep inside her body. Now, holding a light to her cigarette, the drive, the impulse to make love to her was gone. Humiliated by her laughter, her withdrawal at the peak of his desire, he stood up, smoothing his hair, straightening his tie.

'Where are you going?'

'Does it matter? I'm sorry I came.'

Tilting her head against the cushions, smiling, 'Why did you?' she asked mockingly.

'You know why. Because you invited me.'

'Did I?' Arching her eyebrows into question marks. 'I don't remember.'

'You didn't have to say it. I knew.'

Anna sighed, stubbing out the cigarette. 'Stop behaving like a petulant schoolboy. Take off that ridiculous tie and jacket. How can I make love with a penguin?' Rising lazily to her feet, stretching slender arms above her head, as relaxed as a cat, she swayed towards the bedroom. 'Come to me when you are ready.' She smiled, narrowing her eyes. 'Then I will teach you how to make love.'

Slowly, he began to undress, hands trembling – awkwardly – like a nervous schoolboy undressing for the first time in a boarding school dormitory, aware of the crudity of this preparation for the act of love, the removal of his clothing; socks and shoes, the unzipping of his trousers.

Naked, he felt vulnerable, ridiculous even, acutely aware of his genitalia.

She was lying on the bed, dark hair spread about her on the pillows, the bright oriflamme of her nipples startlingly red against the ivory whiteness of her skin, the triangle of her pubic hair as black as jet.

'Ah, that is better. Much better.' A hint of excitement in her voice. 'Come here.'

Entranced, overwhelmed by her beauty, his first encounter with a naked woman, he moved slowly towards her, knowing his moment of truth had arrived at last, experiencing, once more, that glorious upsurge of power between his loins.

Forgetful of his youth, his inexperience, motivated by his natural male instinct of possession, eagerly, clumsily mounting her, a shuddering cry escaped him as he felt the warm seepage of semen on Anna's body.

He had not known, not realized before, that such humiliation was possible, that making love was not necessarily the culmination of a man's desire.

'Hand me a tissue,' Anna said calmly. 'There's a box on the bedside table. Not to worry,' treating him as a child, not a man, 'it will be different next time.'

'Next time?'

Stumbling through to the other room, shaking like a leaf, sick with shame, thrusting his legs into his trousers, pulling on his shirt, socks, and shoes, his body soaked in perspiration, his mind a kaleidoscope of shifting images overlaid with his failure to prove himself a man, Nicholas Tierney determined that there would never be a 'next time' for him.

Leaving Anna's apartment, the devil on his shoulder, he had started to walk in the rain, not caring in which direction, trudging the city like a sleepwalker.

At two o'clock in the morning, he had found himself on Lendal Bridge, staring down at the glassy, rain-spattered water beneath.

'Need any help, son?' The police car had drawn up silently, unnoticed.

'No, I'm fine. A bit damp, that's all,' hating the connotation of the word, 'son'.

'Far to go?'

'Not very. The Hotel Carillon.'

'Best get in. We'll give you a lift home.'

And so Nicholas Tierney had driven away from the dark river with its bewildering pattern of shore lights, but not from the humiliation of his brief encounter with Anna Stravinska.

Chapter Eight

Peter Tierney, the father of Clive and Sophia, had entered the diplomatic service with the enthusiasm of a latter day St George about to attack the dragon of beleaguered innocence.

His love of England, Home and Beauty, had come uppermost until, one pre-war day at Wimbledon, eating strawberries and drinking champagne in the V.I.P. enclosure, he had been introduced to the beautiful Adelaide Harkness, with whom he had fallen in love at first sight, and whom he had married, at St Margaret's, Westminster, the following spring. Truly a love affair to remember.

When war came, Peter had joined the intelligence service, and had, when the war ended, resumed his career with the diplomatic corps, first as a general aide-de-camp to Lord Louis Mountbatten at the crucial time of the partition of India, later as a senior member of staff at the British Legation, in London.

Being blessed with a father in the higher echelons of the diplomatic service had fostered Clive's career to a great extent, although the son had possessed none of the father's easy charm and affability – a fact that had worried Peter initially.

And yet the boy was athletic, handsome, extremely well mannered – above all, academically brilliant. So why the feeling that Clive was a square peg in a round hole? That, although the boy might one day rise to the height of his chosen profession, his cold persona would never inspire feelings of affection in the breasts of his colleagues, although his brilliance may well inspire confidence in his handling of foreign affairs.

Sophia, on the other hand, had not been blessed with her twin brother's brilliance. And yet it was Sophia that Peter loved best – a sensible, loyal girl, not pretty, but handsome. The kind of girl that young men ran a mile to avoid – and she knew it.

When Peter Tierney knew that he was dying from an inoperable cancer of the liver, it was his wife and daughter he worried about, not his son, who stood in line for promotion to an ambassadorship in Paris or Rome, with a knighthood in the offing.

Peter had not meant to worry his wife with the specialist's diagnosis, the fact that his life was drawing, inescapably, to its close. But they had always been so close, so inseparable, that Adelaide had guessed the truth.

'This means that we must leave Cheyne Walk, the contents of the house, to Sophia,' Adelaide had suggested gently, holding her husband's hand. 'Clive will make his own way in the world. Sophia will need all the help we can give her, after we are gone.'

'*We?*'

'But of course, my darling.' Adelaide smiled. 'You don't imagine that you are going anywhere without me?' Snuggling her head against his shoulder, 'Remember *The Petrified Forest*? "This is the end for which we twain are met"? We'll drive down to Cornwall next weekend, stay at a quiet hotel, walk together on the beach, look at the moon, sleep together side by side, make love, eat a perfectly splendid English breakfast, and then . . . You see, Peter my love, I wouldn't want to go on living without you.

'After breakfast, we'll drive to the cliffs, open a bottle of champagne, raise a toast to the glory of life, salute death, then you'll release the brake, hold me tightly in your arms, and . . .'

Their cremation in the burnt-out wreckage of their car had been their final act of love.

In his office at the embassy, laying down his pen, forgetful of the papers he had been about to sign, Clive Tierney stared into the past, conjuring up memories of Madeleine; remembering a hotel bedroom overlooking Lake Como, billowing curtains at a balcony window, the sound of music wafted on a breeze fragrant with the scent of bougainvillea; entering that room to find Madeleine awaiting his coming, wearing a chiffon nightdress, her long blonde hair loose about her shoulders.

Driven mad by his desire to possess her, he had done so forcibly, making her wince and cry out with the force of his entry, as though she were a virgin, not a widow, he a rapist, not her lawfully wedded husband, he thought bitterly, recalling the way she had turned her head away, in disgust, when he had done with her, and lain with her back to him afterwards.

Next morning, waking early from a troubled sleep, he had found a note on the bedside table, saying she had gone out sailing and would not return until late that evening, that she wished to spend the day alone, to swim, read, or relax, as her fancy dictated.

She did not say, in that hastily scribbled note, that she wished to be alone because he had disgusted her with the wanton misuse of her body the night before, but this he knew to be the truth of the matter.

Later, they had dined together on the terrace, as strangers, the weight of their wedding night standing between them like a stone barrier, robbing them of the easy going camaraderie one might have expected of a bride and groom on their honeymoon – the hand holding, the laughter, the anticipation of the coming night in each other's arms.

Never had it occurred to Clive to say, 'I'm sorry, my darling. Please forgive me.' He preferred to stand on his dignity as a misunderstood bridegroom deserted by his wife, left alone to fritter away time doing crossword puzzles in the hotel foyer whilst his bride went sailing.

Much later would come one blinding moment of joy when he knew that Madeleine was pregnant, a fierce feeling of achievement when he realized that, on their wedding night, he had accomplished more by his savage invasion of her body than her former husband had achieved during ten years of marriage to the same woman.

Still later would come the realization that the child he had fathered was far less important to him than having set his seal upon Madeleine; forcing her to bend to his will. Watching the thickening of her body as the child he had created grew inside her womb, he had grown more solicitous of his wife, attendant upon her every wish: smothering her, almost, with his good intentions, yet, curiously, never coming as close to her as he would have wished, never quite understanding why the mother of his child held him so charmingly at arm's length, but at arm's length, nevertheless.

Then, when the baby was born, jealousy had come uppermost, making him feel expendable, shut out, in no way relevant to Madeleine's adoration of the child, as though he, Clive, had had nothing whatever to do with its conception.

Swamped with memories, staring back even further into the past, Clive Tierney re-lived the day when he had come home from boarding school to find his beloved dog, Caesar, a black labrador, missing from its kennel, how he had raced madly round the garden calling its name: 'Caesar, Caesar, where are you?'

His father had come into the garden then. 'I'm sorry, old chap,' he said gently, 'Caesar's not here, I'm afraid.'

'Then where is he?' A truculent small boy facing the first real tragedy of his hitherto sheltered life.

'Well, you see, old chap, Caesar was very old, and in pain, and so . . . '

'You had him killed, didn't you?' The boy's voice harshly accusing. 'You killed my dog without telling me?'

'Believe me, old man, it seemed the kindest thing to do in the circumstances. He was old, deaf, half blind, in pain. Mummy and I talked it over with the vet. We all agreed . . . You *do* understand, don't you?'

'Oh, yes,' uttered carelessly, hands clenched into fists in his blazer pockets. 'He was a rotten old dog anyway!' Pretending not to care, keeping a stiff upper lip lest his father thought him a coward.

Tears had come later, in the privacy of his bedroom, when, struggling to come to terms with his grief, he had also, unwittingly, begun to build up a shell of indifference to the world in general, based on the belief that seeming not to care at all was the only antidote to caring too much, so that the stiff-necked pride of a hurt child had hardened, imperceptibly, into a lifelong mistrust of human motives.

Later on, the conventions of his chosen profession, the detachment necessary to decision making, the formality of state occasions, would suit to perfection his coldly intellectual qualities. He knew protocol like the back of his hand. The decisions he made were invariably right. Although not well liked, he elicited the respect, if not the affection, of his colleagues.

The embassies in which he had served had seemed to him oases, detached and remote from real life, standing for the altruistic ideals of a different age, different generations, long gone. That 'little corner of a foreign field that is forever England' – in a different context from Brooke's, perhaps, but consistent with his belief in the principles of democratic government, law and order.

Soon, these well ordered oases in which he had felt himself to be the captain of his soul, master of his fate, would peter out like a series of stepping stones across a river in spate, leaving him stranded in the non eventful world of his retirement.

There would be presentations, of course, speeches eulogizing his achievements, and then what? England, home and beauty? Clive Tierney thought not. The 'sceptred isle' of Shakespeare's *Henry V*, seemed more foreign to him now than the soil of France.

Picking up his pen, forcing his mind back to realities, Clive knew that, when the accolades, the speeches, the presentations in London were over, he would return to the house in the Rue St Hélène to end his days, to ponder on the past. Above all, to remember Madeleine.

Chapter Nine

Born within the sound of Bow Bells, Freya Soboil had succeeded in creating a new image for herself of which she was intensely, fiercely proud, including an upmarket, Mayfair accent – an invaluable asset when it came to dealing with the elite of the publishing world. Just as easy, she had decided, to breathe, 'Oh, *hello*, dahling,' as to holler, 'Hi, ducks!' or 'Wotcher, me old cock sparrer!'

'If you can't beat 'em, join 'em,' was Freya's maxim.

Dressing the part, being considered slightly eccentric, being noticed, had never hurt anyone either, in Freya's opinion. And a literary agent without clout might just as well join the nearest dole queue.

Her greatest achievement so far, the £100,000 she had earned via a client's series of bestselling novels with film and television rights thrown in, which had made possible the purchase of a small terraced house in Queen Victoria Street, the front room of which she had turned into an office complete with filing cabinets, word processor, a mahogany desk, fitted bookshelves, a plethora of telephones, and an answering machine.

In more reflective moments, Freya deeply regretted her two failed marriages, never having had a child, but never for one moment had she regretted becoming a literary agent – via a succession of jobs in publishers' offices; first as a tea-girl, eventually as a copy editor, learning the ropes, keeping her eyes and ears open, shrewdly assessing her own potential as a force to be reckoned with, realizing there was money to be earned from her uncanny ability to suss out a potentially successful manuscript from an also-ran, in promoting authors who, without a shrewd cookie like herself to represent and advise them, might have been swallowed up or rejected by the more powerful publishing companies.

Not that the succession of new clients who arrived at her office clutching their manuscripts to their bosoms were all potential Booker Prize winners. Goody for her if they were. She simply did her job to the best of her ability, fought hard for those whose work showed promise, and consoled the no-chancers with kindly worded letters wishing them better luck next time.

Freya enjoyed attending literary luncheons and dinner parties, keeping her ear to the ground, flying to Frankfurt for the annual Book Fair, jetting to New York to visit her American colleagues, driving round Central Park in a horse-drawn carriage, wearing outlandish clothes – ankle length skirts, hand woven ponchos, black boots with tucked in trousers. It was all such fun. But despite her recently acquired Mayfair accent, Freya remained a shrewd Cockney at heart, lacking the ability to take herself too seriously.

One morning, feeling frail after a celebratory dinner with one of her more successful male clients, Freya came downstairs light-headedly to pick up the post – a fan-shaped scattering of bills, letters, and manuscripts, which she flumped on the desk.

Pushing aside the bills which her secretary would deal with later, Freya noticed a bulky A4 envelope with a York postmark.

York rang a bell. Yes, of course, Sarah Vale was

living there now. A nice woman, Sarah, and a darned good writer. Slitting the envelope, Freya read Sarah's covering letter explaining that she had been working on the enclosed ten chapters of this new novel and would like Freya's opinion.

The letter went on, 'I realize that a book about a glassblower who died 500 years ago might not be everyone's cup of tea, but there's an interesting twist to the story. Amabie and his compatriots died in mysterious circumstances. They were not well thought of, those Frenchmen who came to a strange country to escape religious persecution. Imagine the bitterness of the natives of a small, enclosed Yorkshire community towards those foreigners who arrived to take the bread from their mouths.

'Then, one day in the York Library, I came across a startling piece of information – the trial, for witchcraft, of a young Jewish girl accused of liaisons with persons of French extraction, in a place called Rosedale, "with whom she had conspired to bewitch one Henry Capstick, a glassblower, whose right hand she had withered by a series of wicked spells and incantations uttered in a vile, foreign tongue".

'The poor girl, called Miriam, was found guilty and condemned to death. Mysteriously, on the eve of her execution, she escaped from her cell, and was never seen or heard of again.

'Following her escape, the name Amabie was found scratched on the wall of her prison, and, according to the sworn testimony of several of the local inhabitants, a pure white dove had been seen hovering above the prison at the time of her escape.

'Following this curious episode, began the mysterious

deaths of the Frenchmen, their wives and children. My own guess is that they were murdered, deliberately, one by one, in cold blood. And so, Freya, love, I plan to weave a bit of mystery and intrigue into the plot. A departure from the usual, perhaps, but I think it will work. The thing is, I can see it all so vividly in my mind's eye that I scarcely know where facts end and fiction begins.'

An hour later, when Mrs Blunt, the secretary, arrived, Freya, to her surprise, seemed not to have noticed the opening of the outer door. Sitting at her desk, chin cupped in her hands, a faraway look on her smooth, olive-skinned face, Freya, indeed, seemed not to have noticed her presence at all.

Mrs Blunt coughed discreetly. 'Good morning, Freya,' she said, 'is anything the matter?'

Freya replied, enigmatically, 'I think she has done it at last!'

'I'm sorry, I'm not with you. Who has done what?' Mrs Blunt uncovered the word processor.

'Sarah Vale! Find her number! Ring her right away! If this new book of hers isn't a bestseller, I'll . . . Oh well, never mind! Just find her number, OK? God, I'm not even dressed yet! When you get hold of her, tell her to hang on! Switch the call to the upstairs phone! I need coffee!'

Freya raced upstairs to her apartment, holding on to the first ten chapters of *Amabie* as if she was clutching a bag of gold.

Sarah worked harder than ever before, tapping away at her typewriter from daybreak to dusk, pausing only to shop, tidy the flat, cook frugal meals, and make herself endless cups of black coffee, inspired by Freya's enthusiastic phone call adjuring her to get on and finish the novel as quickly as possible.

Meanwhile, worried by Sarah's lack of a proper diet, Ralph felt it incumbent on himself to feed her, each weekend, steak and chips, rich cream gateaux, or whatever else he felt expedient to keep the flesh on her bones. Not that she seemed interested in food, or did justice to his cooking.

Intuitively, he guessed that financial worry lay at the heart of her feverish desire to finish *Amabie* to a self-imposed deadline, and longed to offer her money to help her through the crisis. He also knew that the offer of financial help would seem demeaning to a woman of her calibre.

And so he did what he could, in a quiet, unobtrusive way, leaving small gifts of fruit and flowers outside her door – a punnet of strawberries, perhaps, along with a carton of cream, or a few roses from the garden: occasionally a couple of currant teacakes, or a Danish pastry.

When she told him that it was high time he came up to her for a meal, he made the excuse that he had bought a new cook book, and wanted to try out some of the recipes.

If Sarah saw through his deception, she made no comment. It was good to leave her typewriter once in a while, to relax in Ralph's undemanding company – a man whom she still thought of as asexual, not attracted to women in the physical sense, nor to his own gender. A lonely man fulfilling his destiny in showing kindness to others, grateful for kindness in return. A gentle man, unpretentious and unassuming, who understood the problems of her precarious profession.

Even so, Freya's well meaning telephone calls wanting to know how the book was proceeding, and when it would be finished, pressurized Sarah to the extent that, one day, sitting at her typewriter, her mind had suddenly gone blank.

Never before had she experienced a writer's block. Never known what if felt like to face a blank sheet of paper which might remain blank for ever if no new ideas came to break the dreadful hiatus of an equally blank imagination.

In a panic of nervous tension, she had dialled Ralph's number; asked if she might come down for a few minutes to talk to him. Thank God this was Saturday, so he was sure to be home, either indoors, or pottering about in the garden.

Over coffee, Ralph said quietly, remembering to breathe deeply before speaking, 'You are driving yourself t-too hard. Why not take t-tomorrow off? We could take a river trip to Acaster Malbis; lunch at the Ship Inn.'

He went on enthusiastically to describe the seventeenth-century inn with its river frontage, near a row of ancient cottages used as munition stores during the Battle of Marsden Moor, saying they could eat outdoors if the weather was fine.

His invitation made sense to Sarah. The thought of a river trip appealed to her. Never, since her dramatic exit from the Marlborough house, had she experienced such an urgent need of escape. It would be heavenly, she thought, to watch sunlight glancing on the water.

Early next morning, she awoke to the sound of steadily falling rain; the kind of downpour destined to last the whole of the day. She heard its chuckling descent down the drainpipe beyond her bedroom window. Drawing back the living-room curtains, she saw that the puddles in the car park were inches deep in water; the arriving clergy tucking up their cassocks to prevent their getting soaking wet as they hurried, beneath the shelter of hastily unfurled umbrellas, to the sanctuary of the Minster's rear entrance.

Ten minutes later, Ralph rang up to ask if she would rather cancel the trip to Acaster Malbis.

'Because of the rain, you mean?'

'Well, yes.' Ralph sounded apologetic, as though it were his fault that the sun was not shining.

'No, not at all. I rather like rain.' Sarah reassured him.

Stepping aboard *The Empress*, hawsered to the landing stage near Skelderdale Bridge, Sarah saw, with delight, rain plopping into the river and the blurred outline of houses seen vaguely through a mist of rain.

Despite the inclement weather, the vessel was packed from stem to stern with holidaymakers: women wearing plastic mackintoshes and concertina rain-hoods, children in colourful macs and sou'westers, men in anoraks, with hopeful cameras slung round their necks.

Bareheaded, Sarah stood, with Ralph, near the stern railing, watching the crew casting off the shackles, drawing up the gangplank, filled with a thrilling sense of adventure – the way she had felt driving her red Mini, about to make discoveries.

Happy because she was happy, Ralph thought, as the vessel swung round and the engine throbbed into life, how lovely she looked with the rain on her face and that faraway look in her eyes.

If only he dare tell her he loved her; ask her to marry him. Yet never had she betrayed by a look or a word that she regarded him as more than a friend. Better, he decided, to leave well enough alone for the time being.

The rain eased off a little as *The Empress* nosed towards the Ship Inn's landing stage. Even so, Ralph realized that to eat outdoors would be impossible, the grass would be far too wet. But the last thing he had envisaged was lunching in a room full of chattering people, sharing a table with strangers.

Joining the queue in the bar-parlour, he ordered sirloin sandwiches, salad and a carafe of red wine.

Returning to the table near the window, he saw that it had been invaded by a middle-aged couple – the man with a beer-belly overhanging his trousers, a camera resting on his paunch, and a thin, worried looking woman with blonde hair, dark at the roots, with whom Sarah was chatting quite animatedly, as if enjoying their company.

'Just saying to your missis, a bugger, this weather, ain't it?' the man said, in a strong West Riding accent as Ralph sat down. 'Might just as well not have humped this thing along,' pointing in the direction of his stomach.

'No need to keep harping on about it, Ron,' the woman advised him. 'Happen you'll be able to take some nice snaps after us dinners.'

Sarah smiled conspiratorially at Ralph, warming his heart with a sudden feeling of camaraderie. Then, just as suddenly, her smile faded, and the faraway look was back in her eyes, making him feel expendable, shut away from her.

Following her gaze, he wondered why she was looking so intently at a couple seated near the bar – a dark-haired man talking to a stunningly beautiful redhead – who had not been aboard *The Empress*. Of this Ralph felt certain, otherwise he would have noticed them, for the simple reason that a couple like that would have been impossible not to notice.

Sarah thought, wherever she went, he was there, like a dream, a forgotten man of the past come to haunt her, as though her life was bound up with that of a stranger – a man she had never met, might never meet. Then why this powerful sense of recognition, of destiny, even?

Sleep did not come easily that night. Thoughts and impressions of the day were too strong, too vital to allow Sarah peace of mind. In a mood of restless energy, in the early hours of the morning, she returned to her typewriter.

Dawn was breaking when, too tired to write any more, she stumbled back to bed.

Sinking down to rest, she thanked God that the writer's block she had suffered, that curious stultification of her senses, her imagination, had been dissipated because of a river trip in the pouring rain.

Turning her cheek to the pillow, she remembered the outline of houses seen through rain, like phantom buildings possessing no substance, seen, perhaps, through the mists of time itself. For what, really, separated the past from the here and now? Perhaps time itself was an illusion.

Her last conscious thought, before sleeping, was of the man she thought of as Amabie. That dark-haired stranger who had somehow invaded her life as surely as he had invaded her dreams.

Chapter Ten

Freya had hustled the first ten chapters of *Amabie* to Sarah's publishers without delay, adding her own comments and commendation. She had also telephoned Sarah's editor, Carl Prince, saying how excited she had been reading the work so far. But no snap decision was likely to be made, Freya told Sarah. Publishers had their own deadlines to meet, budgets to consider; they had to plan ahead, find slots for manuscripts already commissioned. 'Just take my advice, darling, get on with the book, and don't worry. I'll let you know the moment there's any news.'

The trouble was, Sarah's bank balance was now practically non-existent. Every penny for rent, food, and household necessities had to be drawn from capital. Now she needed money – desperately needed money – in order to survive.

Night after night she lay tossing and turning in bed, imagining the worst – losing her home, having to admit to herself, and the children, that she had failed in her attempt to make a new life for herself; had failed miserably as a writer, a wife and mother.

Possibly she had been wrong in turning down alimony. George Lumsden had warned her about that, and she had been too proud, too pig-headed to heed that warning. But no. Even in her precarious financial state, she knew that nothing on earth would have persuaded her to accept

Faulkner's conscience money. Nor would she go cap in hand to him now, begging a loan to tide her over. So what was the answer?

Waking early one morning from a troubled sleep, she *knew*! If she could not live by writing, she must find herself a job. But where? How? Jobs were at a premium during this time of recession. Unemployment figures rising. But there must be an opening for a reasonably intelligent woman willing to work. A temporary, part-time job would do, just as long as she could earn enough to keep the cart on the wheels.

Wasting no time, getting up, she began scribbling a list of possibilities, beginning with housekeeping, cooking, and child-minding; adding waitressing, and filling supermarket shelves. But how to make a start? Should she go to the labour exchange – job centres they called them nowadays – or simply look in newsagents' windows at those numerous help wanted ads on display?

With Verity's birthday fast approaching, she would need money to buy the girl a decent present, something in keeping with her passion for design, some article of jewellery perhaps, a brooch or a necklace to complement her off-beat style of dressing – usually in jeans or colourful Indian cotton skirts worn with turtle neck sweaters, or men's open neck shirts cinched at the waist with a broad leather belt.

The thought occurred that Verity would probably throw aside the gift unopened. And what if she, Sarah, could not find a job? What if Foremost Books turned down *Amabie*? If, if, *if*! Oh, for heaven's sake, woman, she told herself severely, go out and look for a job.

Walking towards Coppergate, she paused to look at adverts

in a newsagent's window, most of which offered electrical appliances, perambulators, and wedding dresses for sale. And then, 'Temporary help wanted', she read. 'Capable teenager required to make sandwiches. Apply Alf's Cafe, Market Street'. Her heart sank. She did not even qualify as a sandwich maker at a second rate cafe.

Walking on, she came to a boutique, and went in, catching the fragrance of Eastern spices – turmeric, ginger, coriander and sesame, overlaid with the softer, sweeter smell of lavender, rosemary and thyme.

A large lady seated behind the counter looked up as Sarah entered. She was dressed bizarrely, wearing a great deal of makeup, her plump face framed with a mass of dyed auburn hair; she was smoking a cigarette fixed in a long jade holder. 'Can I help, or are you browsing?' she asked in a throaty, smoker's voice.

'Just browsing.' Sarah turned her attention to a show-case containing hand-beaten jewellery. One piece in par-ticular caught her eye, a medallion of intricately woven silver threads, rather like a spider's web, at the heart of which lay a tiny ammonite – a curled up reminder of an ancient, lost land, a forgotten race of people, of Biblical times. A mysterious thing set at the centre of a radiant web of delicately fashioned silver. The price tag read £25.

The woman behind the counter watched as Sarah turned away from the showcase and bent to examine an Ali-Baba basket containing a mass of colourful silk scarves, think-ing that her customer's face seemed familiar although she could not think where she had seen her before. Then, damnation, she thought, her plaster was giving her hell this morning. Easing her leg, trust that darned assistant not to turn up when she was needed. The second time this week, and this a busy time of year with tourists arriving by the coachload. Idle young monkey! A nice fix she'd be in when the shop began to fill up, with her blasted broken leg encased in plaster.

Feeling more than slightly irritable, Philippa Paget saw that her customer was now looking at the racks of herbs and spices, the le Creuset casseroles, ramekins and soufflé dishes in the cookery section. A nice-looking woman, Philippa decided, with a soft, mobile mouth, but why the hell didn't she do something about her clothes? And what a pity to scrape back that feral mass of gold brown hair when, with a little patience, she might achieve an intricately woven plait or a smooth French pleat. What a waste of a potentially beautiful woman, wearing not a scrap of makeup, not even moisturizing lotion, Philippa suspected, on that dry skin of hers.

A group of Americans entered the shop at that moment, filling the space with their presence. Philippa groaned. There they were, stuffing their hands with postcards of York to mail to their families back home in the States; with altar candles, lavender sachets, and hand-carved wooden toys; riffling through the silk scarves. And, she might have guessed, wanting to look at the hand-beaten jewellery, which meant unlocking the showcase. She'd sack that bloody assistant of hers, she really would – leaving her in a hole like this!

Getting up, Philippa hobbled towards the showcase, key in hand, holding on to her walking stick. Meanwhile, deep in thought about the medallion, Sarah edged her way towards the door, past the people near the counter. 'Hey, honey, would you mind wrapping these things for us? We're in kind of a hurry,' an American lady said, handing Sarah several silk scarves.

139

'Oh, I'm sorry, I'm not . . . '

'Well, can you beat that? I guess they don't want our custom. Let's go!'

'No, just a minute. It's just that we're a bit short staffed this morning.' Catching Philippa's nod of approval, Sarah slipped the scarves into a colourful paper bag, took the money and put it in the till. 'Do you take American Express?' another woman asked. 'Yes, of course!' Sarah smiled, enjoying the bizarre situation.

'Tell me, is it your mission in life to rescue the perishing?' Philippa said when the Americans had gone. 'I'm Philippa Paget, by the way.'

'I am Sarah Vale.'

'Don't suppose you'd be interested in working here?' Philippa narrowed her eyes against the smoke of a fresh cigarette. 'Or perhaps you have family commitments?'

'I had once. Not now. And I couldn't work full time, I have another – job.'

'Could you manage – say three days a week?'

Sarah's heart leapt. 'Yes, three days would suit me fine.'

'Starting tomorrow?'

'Starting right now, if you need me.'

'In that case, the kitchen's through there. I like my coffee strong, with plenty of sugar. You'll find milk in the fridge, a cafetière, and a tin of Lyons Continental blend. I can't stand the instant stuff, despite all those "bean shake" adverts.' Philippa frowned. 'By the way, haven't we met somewhere before? Your face seems familiar.'

'No, I don't think so. I'm sure I'd remember if we had.'

When Sarah returned with the coffee, Philippa was sitting with her leg propped up on a waste-paper bin. 'I fell down those stairs a couple of weeks ago,' she explained. 'Next thing I knew, there I was in hospital with a fractured tibia. Just as well I didn't fall on my head! I live over the shop, you see. What you see here is my little world entire.' She laughed suddenly, her laughter tinged with bitterness. 'Not much to end up with, is it? But who cares? I make the best of things, take life as it comes. Now tell me about yourself.'

'There isn't much to tell.' Sarah poured the coffee.

'In other words, why don't I mind my own bloody business?'

'No, not at all. I'm just an ordinary person . . . '

'Oh no, you are certainly not that, Sarah Vale. There is something about you . . . Well, never mind. This coffee is good, by the way. Bloody June can't make coffee to save her life!'

'June?'

'My so-called assistant, the lazy little cow!' Philippa stubbed out her cigarette. 'My God, with a couple of million unemployed, you'd think anyone in their right senses would be glad of a job these days!'

The smell of the coffee, the intermingled fragrances of herbs, spices, and lavender brought back to Sarah a sudden, vivid memory of the old Georgian vicarage in Gloucestershire, the bowl of pot-pourri on the hall table, sunlight streaming in through the long, many paned windows, making patterns on the threadbare carpet; the grandfather clock in the corner ticking away the hours of her youth and childhood; coming home from church on Sunday mornings to find the house permeated with the scent of pot-pourri and freshly made coffee.

One Sunday morning, in particular, when her father had preached a sermon adjuring his congregation not to leave everything to God, to make the most of their talents

141

and opportunities, to remember that the gift of life was not theirs to squander.

She could not have been more than fifteen years old at the time, but the memory of that Sunday morning had stayed with her all the days of her life, that enchanted moment when she *knew* she was happy – as if a camera had clicked to capture a precise image of her parents standing together in a shaft of sunlight, a yellow labrador wagging its tail, and the woman who came in on Sunday mornings to do the cooking, standing in the kitchen doorway with the coffee things on a tray, because the rector liked a cup of freshly made coffee before luncheon was served.

'What are you thinking?' Philippa asked.

'Oh, nothing in particular.'

For one fragrant moment, the memory had been hers. Now it was gone. But this was the way with memories which conjured up, for a fleeting second, a mood of happiness or despair, destined to fade the moment after, seldom, if ever, to be recaptured.

Philippa said, 'This other – job – of yours? What kind of job? A school teacher? A lollipop lady? An actress? An undercover VAT official? A – detective?'

'No.' Sarah gathered together the coffee mugs, the sugar-basin and spoons. 'I assure you that I am none of those things.'

Washing up in the kitchen, Sarah strove, in vain, to recapture that summer Sunday morning of long ago.

When she returned to the shop, Philippa said quietly, 'Now I remember.'

'Remember – what?'

'Why your face seemed familiar. Your photograph was on the dust jacket of a book I read recently.'

Nicholas Tierney had met the beautiful red-haired Maria Alvarez at a dinner party and dance to celebrate her twentieth birthday. The Gowans, a wealthy middle-aged couple who frequently dined at the Carillon, with whom Maria was staying, had decided upon Nicholas to partner their guest, confident that Maria would find him attractive.

Frances and Jack Gowan, who owned a villa in Spain, had become friendly with Maria's parents during summer visits to Tarragona, a friendship resulting in warm invitations to various members of the Alvarez family to visit England. Indeed, Don Alvarez and his stunningly attractive wife, Dolores, had paid several visits to the Gowans' country estate, near York, had dined at the Carillon, and become acquainted with Sophia Tierney and her nephew. Then Don Alvarez had written an exquisitely courteous letter to the Gowans explaining that his daughter, Maria, wished to visit England, to brush up on the language, and asking if she might be permitted to stay with them for two weeks in July. And so the visit had been arranged.

When the Gowans knew that Maria's birthday would coincide with her visit, Frances Gowan decided to celebrate the event in style. A slim, energetic woman who adored entertaining, she'd had fairy lights strung between the trees, a dance floor laid in the conservatory, and hired a firm of caterers to provide the necessary food and drink – lots of champagne, and a birthday cake to be served later to the young people, the sons and daughters of her many friends, who would begin to arrive after the small, intimate dinner party she had planned for the purpose of introducing Maria to Nicholas.

The Gowans could not have foreseen that their choice of a partner for Maria would end so disastrously.

At first, Frances Gowan had congratulated herself on

the choice of that partner. The red-haired Maria was young and very lovely, Nicholas handsome, charming. The rapport between them was undeniable as they chatted together throughout dinner.

Later, when the dancing was under way, Frances had glanced into the conservatory to see the pair of them, swaying to the music, locked in each other's arms, Maria's head resting against Nicky's shoulder.

The following week, Maria and Nicholas had spent every evening in each other's company, dining, dancing, or theatregoing. Frances assumed that all was well. After all, the girl's parents had met Nicholas, and they had not disapproved when Maria rang them to say she had an escort. Spaniards were sticklers for correctness, as Frances well knew.

She received the shock of her life when Maria returned alone from a visit to Acaster Malbis, sobbing hysterically, and rushed upstairs to her room to begin packing. Entering the room, Frances watched, bewildered, as Maria bundled the contents of drawers and wardrobe on to the bed. 'Darling. What is it? What's wrong?' she asked faintly.

'He make me feel so small, so cheap.' Tears rolled down Maria's cheeks.

'You don't – you can't mean that Nicholas tried to – take advantage of you?'

'Take advantage? I do not know that expression.'

'It means – did he try to – make love to you?'

Maria uttered a burst of hysterical laughter. 'Make love to me? No. I wanted so much that he should make love to me. And what does he say?'

'Come, Maria, you must tell me.' Frances stopped wavering and took control of the situation. 'Sit down, and calm yourself. I want the truth. I want to know exactly what happened. You seemed perfectly happy when Nicholas arrived to take you to Acaster Malbis for lunch.'

Sinking down on the bed, 'I was happy,' Maria said bleakly. 'So very happy, for I think that Nicholas will ask me to be his wife. I do everything in my power to make him love me. Then he laughs and says he is not the marrying kind, and I feel small and cheap. Like the woman of the street, not the daughter of Don Alvarez di Tarragona. Now I wish to return home.'

Oh God, Frances thought, how the hell would she and Jack live down the disgrace of returning a broken wreck of a girl to her aristocratic family? As for Nicholas Tierney, the man was nothing more than a philanderer, and she would tell him so if she came face to face with him again.

Ralph Foster heard the story of Sarah's new-found job with mixed feelings of admiration and dismay. That a writer of her calibre should find it necessary to earn money as a shop assistant seemed appalling to him.

Above all, he regretted the long hours that Sarah would spend away from her typewriter, the breaking of those vital threads of concentration necessary to the completion of her book; to the detriment of her creativity. But when he voiced his opinion, Sarah smiled and said that she would have to work harder in the free time left to her.

'Work all night, you mean?' he said sarcastically.

'If necessary.'

They were sitting in the garden at the time, drinking coffee: Sarah watching bees gathering pollen from the antirrihnums, her feet spread out, lazily moving her toes.

'You see, Ralph, I was cushioned, at first, when I started writing. As the wife of a rich man, I wrote for my own pleasure. Frankly, it would not have mattered a damn had I not been published. But now – well, things are different now.' She stopped waggling her toes. 'I chose to stand on my own two feet, and I must do just that.'

Taking a deep breath, 'I could have tided you over,' Ralph said quietly. 'All you had to do was a-ask.'

'I know.' Stretching out her hand; a gesture of appreciation, 'You have been so good to me, so kind. God knows why.' She smiled, tilting her face to the sun, gathering her thoughts as the bees gathered pollen. 'The thing is, I need to see this – thing – this crisis, this hiatus, call it what you will – through on my own.'

Her eyes filled suddenly with tears, her mouth trembled. 'I can't – mustn't be beaten now! Don't you see, Ralph, that it is up to me to retain my independence, my self respect?'

The touch of her hand on his filled Ralph with a burning desire to hold that hand to his lips, throw caution to the wind and ask her to marry him. But the warning voice of commonsense told him that an admission of love would carry no weight with a woman who was obviously not in love with him, that such an admission might lead to the dissolution of a friendship which meant the world to him. And so, lightly pressing her hand, he schooled himself to say, 'Yes, of course. But never f-forget that I am here if you need me.'

Need. The word ran like fire through Sarah's brain. Oh, God, she thought, to go back in time to that daisied lawn of the old vicarage in Gloucestershire; to stand there, her arms outspread to catch the running, laughing figures of her children close to her heart once more, to feel the warmth of their sturdy young bodies against hers, to hear their voices, high-pitched with excitement, begging her to play games with them, tugging at her hands to draw her into their marvellously enclosed world of make-believe.

Touch was so important, so necessary to the human race. The sublime joy of touching the hands, hair, the lips of a beloved person, betraying an innate need of love and understanding. The light pressure of Ralph's hand, the words he had spoken unleashed a tide of memories. Poor Ralph, who had probably never known, nor desired, close physical contact with any human being.

Chapter Eleven

Suki's pregnancy had come as a shock to Faulkner, so had the degree of hardness he had discerned in her when she'd handed him the ultimatum – get rid of your wife, or else . . .

Difficult to imagine that a rock-hard vein lay beneath that ultra-feminine exterior, her doll-like prettiness, softly curling blonde hair, and those enormous violet-blue eyes of hers.

Now the divorce had been finalized, Suki wanted a church wedding, and her explosion of temper, when he told her that this was out of the question, made his confrontation with Sarah seem highly civilized by comparison. Suki ranted, Suki raved. Finally, Faulkner, in extremis, shouted at her to go ahead, to fix up the wedding in Westminster Abbey for all he cared, or any other bloody Anglican church, if she could persuade any bishop or prelate to marry a divorced man to a woman in her condition.

Suki dissolved into tears at that point, but common sense had prevailed. She had agreed to settle for a registry office ceremony followed by a reception at the Mayfair, an extended honeymoon in Europe, plus a consolation prize of five thousand pounds for her piggy-bank.

She turned up at Marylebone Register Office in a white, chauffeur-driven Rolls-Royce, wearing a white, mini-skirted dress, carrying a bouquet of pink orchids to disguise her bump, her long blonde hair threaded with silver ribbons; eyelashes spiked with black mascara; full, sensuous lips blotted to nothingness with a covering of creme eraser; complexion equally pale by courtesy of Elizabeth Arden's Flawless Finish.

The pressmen and photographers she had invited to record the occasion had a field day as they crowded round her, firing questions, popping flashbulbs.

Piqued by his children's non-appearance at the wedding, awaiting the arrival of the bride, Faulkner felt soured, less than happy that Suki had invited so many friends of her own age group to witness the ceremony – odd looking men with long hair tied back in pony tails, wearing jeans and tight leather jackets, girls with cropped hair, dressed all in black. Black boots, long black skirts, black sweaters hung about with silver chains and cabbalistic crosses – reminiscent of a witches' coven.

Then Suki had turned up looking like a child in the last stages of galloping consumption, misshapen, walking awkwardly, her long legs, beneath the ridiculous pelmet of a skirt, splayed slightly like those of a newly born foal. Tenderness had overwhelmed him. Then, slipping the wedding ring on her finger, he knew triumphantly, that she would grace his home, his table, his bed, as Sarah had never done.

They had driven to the champagne reception in the Mayfair's Crystal Room, holding hands, gazing raptly into each other's eyes – the ageing tycoon in his grey morning suit and pearl tie-pin, and the enceinte madonna clever enough to have made up her mind, in a Paris hotel bedroom, exactly what she wanted from life – a rich, charismatic husband, all the trappings of wealth.

Thank God, she thought, cutting the cake, that Faulkner's children had declined to attend the wedding. Children of any age Suki found boring, particularly babies, who seemed to her nothing more than tubes, imbibing at one end, leaking at the other. But once the bump which had ruined her figure was safely delivered, she would simply pass it on to someone else to take care of.

Drinking champagne, the new Mrs Vale imagined the delight of being slim once more, of driving to town in the rakish white sports car with the number plate SV1 Faulkner had given her as a wedding present, of shopping for new clothes, squandering his money on a completely new wardrobe.

Then, when the bump had been born, she would plan a series of cocktail and dinner parties to impress Faulkner's business associates; urge him on to even greater success; make him take up weight training and jogging to keep himself in trim. The poor darling was getting just a bit thick round the middle, which might have some bearing on that embarrassing problem of his . . .

The honeymoon over, as the weather grew warmer and the unwieldiness of her body began to play havoc with her nerves, Suki had taken to lying on a canopied sun-lounger near the swimming pool, wearing a bath-towel sarong; a tray of drinks, a mobile telephone, a pile of paperback novels, scribbling pad, pen, spray on perfume, sun-tan oil, and her makeup bag, on a low table beside her.

Once established as the new, bona-fide mistress of the Marlborough establishment, Suki had lost no time appointing a cook-housekeeper and a daily cleaner to ensure the smooth running, the dusting and polishing of the house she detested: A. because it was not big or grand enough; B. because she considered Marlborough a boring backwater town; and C. because her life seemed overshadowed by the 'ghost' of the first Mrs Vale.

One day in July, following a succession of long, expensive phone calls to friends in Paris, Rome, and New York, telling them how bored she was, picking up her scribbling pad and pen, Suki scrawled, '*Must find a suitable nanny. Contact London Agency. Arrange interviews. Talk to Faulkner re brilliant idea. Make him see sense*'.

Pushing up her sunglasses to nestle, tiara-like, in her thatch of blonde hair, staring at the shimmering water of the swimming pool, having come up against her husband's mulishness on former occasions, she wondered how difficult it would be to bring him round to the idea of moving to London to live – preferably in one of those magnificent Victorian houses near Hampstead Heath.

Not very difficult, she imagined, if she played her cards right, pulled the right faces, got him a little drunk, managed to persuade him that living closer to the City would spare him the horror of commuting; all those boring traffic snarl ups on the M4.

Feeling suddenly less bored, Suki saw her transition from this inadequate house to that of her imagination as a fait accompli. All she had to do was quirk her little finger and Faulkner would come running, rather than risk a scene at such a delicate stage of her pregnancy.

The kind of house she had set her heart on, spacious and grand, would, Suki imagined, feature in the glossy magazines, with photographs of herself, Faulkner, and the baby, alongside pictures of the sound-proofed nursery complete with a Victorian rocking-horse and a high, Victorian fireguard.

The last item on Suki's scribbled agenda. 'Remind Faulkner to get rid of that red Mini in the garage. What the hell is it still doing there anyway?' At which point the baby dealt her a savage kick in the stomach.

Verity Vale walked quickly along Kensington High Street towards the flat she shared with two other art students, her face set in what was fast becoming an habitual expression of hauteur. She was a tall girl, fashionably slender, quick tempered, spoilt by her father's success, taking for granted that whatever she wanted she would be given. In the past, riding and ballet lessons, her own pony – of which she had quickly tired when it came to feeding and grooming the animal.

The sketchiness of her education had more to do with her lack of erudition than lack of money. Faulkner had shelled out vast sums in school fees and private tuition, to no avail. Whilst her brother Richard soaked up learning like a sponge, Verity had frittered her time away drawing odd, Picasso-style faces on sheets of expensive cartridge paper. And so she had gained admission to the Kensington School of Art to fritter away more of her time in the pursuance of a nebulous career as a fashion designer or an interior decorator. But at least she had not, so far, opted out of art school to fulfil her secondary ambition of becoming a fashion model.

The most traumatic experience of her self-centred young life so far had been her parents' divorce, the feeling of revulsion when she knew that her father had committed the indecency of impregnating a girl scarcely older than herself. How could he have done such a thing?

Brooding on the injustice of life in general, carrying a shopping bag of groceries because it was her turn to do the cooking, she entered a house in Prince's Gardens and hurried upstairs to the top flat, where she emptied her purchases – brown rice, tomato purée, fresh fruit and vegetables – on to the kitchen table.

Finding a saucepan, putting on the rice to cook, she wandered through to the sitting room to stare out of the window at the small oasis of green set in the heart of Kensington, thinking about the divorce, casting her mind back to recall incidents which had not seemed important at the time – Daddy leaving them alone on that holiday in Dorset, for instance. She and Richard had been quite young then, and Mother had explained that their father had been called away unexpectedly for an urgent business appointment, which explanation they had accepted. But, strangely enough, that was the last holiday they had spent together as a family. Thereafter, they had gone to the Gloucestershire vicarage for their summer holidays, but Daddy had never stayed with them.

They must have been quite poor at that time, she supposed, remembering the terraced house in Swindon in which her childhood memories were based. Much later had come the Marlborough house, the paddock, the pony, the swimming pool, the boarding school near Calne which she had loathed and detested, although she had gone home quite often on weekend exeats. But Daddy was seldom at home, and if he was there, Mother and he had seemed like strangers.

Little wonder, Verity thought bitterly. All her mother seemed to care about was tapping away for hours on end at that blasted typewriter of hers. But even as the thought occurred, Verity knew, deep down, that she was being unfair to Sarah, glossing over the hours her mother had spent in the kitchen, preparing and cooking meals for herself and Ricky during the school holidays.

Even so, she was not prepared to forgive Sarah for allowing Suki Mitford to enter into their lives. And because it lay in the nature of the young to blame someone else for their misfortune, Verity blamed her mother for allowing herself to become fat and dowdy to the detriment of her marriage. Taking her father's side initially, because she had always seen herself as Daddy's girl, had thought the sun shone out of her father, Verity's self-centred little world had collapsed about her ears when Sarah had told her that day in the Cedar Cafe, that Faulkner wanted his freedom to marry someone whom she could never – *would* never – accept as a stepmother.

She had, that day, in a fit of pique, put words into her brother's mouth which he had uttered only once, in fun. Her damning, 'Richard agrees with me', had no foundation in fact for the simple reason that the break up of their parents' marriage had not affected him all that deeply. What Richard actually said, when he knew what was about to happen, was, 'Poor old Ma. How rotten to be lumbered with a femme fatale at her time of life. I wonder how she'll cope?'

'Knowing Mother, she won't cope at all,' Verity had replied bitterly, 'she'll just go on being as fat and ineffectual as ever.' Then Richard had said, 'Hang on a minute. Mum may be a bit of a heavyweight, but she is still our mother. Frankly, I'm quite fond of the old girl, so why don't you give your jaw a rest? Or are you being so bitchy cos you've had your nose pushed out of joint with Daddio?'

About that time, Verity recalled, Richard had started dating her flatmate, Leonora, with whom he had swanned off to Greece, in a romantic haze, about the time she had sent Sarah that clipping from a Sunday newspaper.

Frankly, Richard, selfish to the core, could not have cared less about their parents' divorce, Verity realized. Sarah, in his opinion, had done the only sensible thing in conceding the victory to a younger, more attractive woman, in quitting the scene of conflict and making a new start for herself, whilst Verity, soured by bitterness, had felt no regret about the cutting she had sent her mother, no feelings of remorse that she had deeply wounded someone once close and dear to her, just as she had felt no compunction over refusing to attend her father's wedding, or telling him that, from now on, she would never set foot in his house again.

A sputtering sound as the rice boiled over, sent her scurrying back to the kitchen, where she mopped up the spillage, and searched in the freezer compartment of the re-frigerator for a tray of mince to supplement the rice and vegetables. Completely at a loss, frowning, she wondered if the mince would need thawing or not. How the hell was she supposed to know? She hated and detested cooking.

At that moment she remembered a warm kitchen, the smell, not of burnt rice, but of heartwarming beef stew on a cold winter evening, firelight dancing on the walls and ceiling of that poky living room in Swindon, Sarah saying grace.

Suddenly, Verity began to cry, long tendrils of hair falling about her face in a soft golden cloud. The trouble was, she could not understand why she was crying.

Richard had been meaning to write to Sarah, but life had been far too hectic lately with his finals coming up, and falling in love with Verity's flatmate, the lovely, languid

155

Leonora, with whom he spent every minute of his spare time away from his studies.

Leonora's charms had effectively blotted out guilt feelings over his mother. In any case, he imagined that Verity had kept in touch with her. Dark haired, full-lipped, slightly but powerfully built, possessing the exuberance and selfishness of well-heeled youth, his parents' split-up seemed scarcely to worry him. Couples headed for the divorce courts were the norm these days – only there weren't divorce courts as such nowadays, one of his flatmates had told him. One furnished the details and let the solicitors fight it out between themselves. The knowledgeable lad, who seemed au fait about such matters, said that complications arose only when the custody of young children was involved, or endless wrangles over money.

Frankly, Richard had no quarrel with his father, whose wealth guaranteed the continuance of his own lifestyle – trips abroad, designer clothes, flying lessons, the low-slung, high powered sports car Faulkner had given him on his nineteenth birthday – and would guarantee his future, a place on the board of directors of the Vale Computer Company when his education was complete.

The only thing that worried Richard was, would the odious Suki Mitford bleed the old boy white? And, in time to come, inherit the whole bang-shoot? Stupid of Sarah, he considered, to have walked away from the marriage without making damn sure she had her fair share of the cash. But then his mother had never been a realist, and she had rather asked for trouble, puttering about the house in those shapeless garments of hers. And yet he was fond of the old girl, and he really must get in touch with her one of these days, pay her a visit perhaps, cheer her up a bit.

156

He had even gone so far as to consult his diary. Next weekend? No. He was taking Leonora to Oxford. The weekend after? Impossible. Leonora had invited him to Stroud to meet her parents. OK, so he'd write to Sarah, better still, give her a ring. It was then he discovered that he'd lost her phone number. Just as well, perhaps. He wouldn't really know what to say to her. No, he would write to her, except that he hated letter writing, a pastime in which he seldom indulged.

Chapter Twelve

Suki Vale had been delivered of a daughter, a squalling, red-faced bundle which she mischievously threatened to name Pembroke, if Faulkner refused to sign the deeds of the Victorian mansion she had set her heart on.

Having gone through the blood, sweat and tears of his wife's travail in the labour ward, having watched, with a sick feeling in the pit of his stomach, the emergence of the baby's head from the narrow passage between Suki's open thighs, Faulkner knew that he was beaten.

As much as he disliked the idea of moving to Hampstead, he could not bear the thought of having his daughter named after an antique table.

Leaving the hospital to which Suki had been rushed in the early hours of the morning, Faulkner drove to Marlborough High Street where he parked the grey Mercedes before entering the Castle and Ball Hotel, ordering a double brandy, and sitting down at a table in the bar to mull over the events of the past few hours.

Deeply shaken, having witnessed the birth of his child, he concluded that Sarah would never have dreamed of wanting him with her when she gave birth to Richard and Verity. Things had changed now, of course, but he still regarded as a retrograde step the involvement of husbands in the messy business of the labour ward.

Downing a second double brandy, he considered that giving birth was, after all, a woman's function to perform with a certain degree of modesty and mystique.

The brandy must have gone to his head. Suddenly, Faulkner found himself regretting the lost years of his marriage to Sarah. That she had known all along about his affairs had come as a shock to him. He had imagined himself to be so clever in covering his tracks, and he had, quite honestly, forgotten all about his first conquest, Carmen Longstaff, with whom he had slept after leaving his wife and family in Dorset to finish their holiday alone.

The trouble with Sarah, she had been too clinging, allowing him no breathing space, lumbering him with two children before he had had time to begin his climb to success. And yet . . . Oh, what the hell!

Ordering a third brandy, he thought gloomily of the decaying mansion in which he and Suki would rattle round like peas in a drum, along with the housekeeper, the nanny, and the other servants whom Suki regarded as necessary appendages to the household. Christ, he thought bitterly, not only worried about expense but the prospect of Suki's yuppie friends' invasion of the house when it had been refurbished. Then, how would he fit into the picture?

Feeling suddenly old, what if Suki took it into her head to have separate bedrooms in that bloody mausoleum, which he regarded in much the same light as those decaying tombs erected to generations of long dead Victorians in Highgate Cemetery.

She had been up early to get on with *Amabie*, writing the scene of his first meeting with Miriam, the lovely Jewish girl with whom he was destined to fall in love.

The shrilling of the alarm clock which she had set to ring at 7.30 brought Sarah back to reality. Leaving her typewriter, she ran the bath water, made herself a cup of strong black coffee and a slice of toast, bathed, dressed, and hurried downstairs.

Walking towards Coppergate wearing navy slacks, a light cotton tee-shirt, hugging a hand-knitted cardigan about her shoulders, she thought about her overdue telephone bill.

Stopping at a newsagents, she bought a packet of Polo mints. The change from a pound coin would, she hoped, prove sufficient to buy a lunchtime sandwich at Alf's Cafe in Market Street.

She had placed in her shoulder bag a notepad and biro. With a modicum of luck, she might find time to pop round to the library during her lunchbreak, to fit in a little research about York's early Jewish community. Unlikely there had been one in Rosedale. Amabie, she reflected, would have met Miriam in York, possibly at a street market. Lost in thought, engrossed in her characters, working out dialogue, Sarah passed the boutique without noticing, and had to retrace her steps.

'Oh, there you are.' Philippa regarded her coolly, 'I saw you go by a moment ago.'

'Yes. I'm sorry, I . . . '

'Never mind. Let's get on, shall we?'

There was much to learn. Philippa spent the first hour showing Sarah the stockroom, explaining where the hand-thrown pottery, the soft toys, flower pictures, and hand-carved boxes had originated: 'So you won't feel a complete duffer when the customers start asking questions,' Philippa said. 'The scarves are mainly Italian, that white and green pottery comes from Portugal, the le Creuset items are, of course, French. But I'm sure a woman of your intelligence and imagination will have no difficulty weaving a little romance into your sales' talk.' Lighting a cigarette, she perched on a high stool and regarded Sarah thoughtfully. 'What's really behind this job lark?' she enquired, arching her eyebrows, 'Background for your next novel?'

'No, I meant what I said. I really do need a job.'

'But I thought authors had villas in the South of France, penthouse apartments in New York, champagne and caviare for breakfast.'

Sarah laughed. 'I'm sure many of them have – the famous ones, that is.'

'Come on, let's have some coffee before the tourists start flooding in,' Philippa suggested, heaving herself from the stool, clutching her stick with one hand, waving her cigarette holder in the other. 'You'll have to get used to passive smoking, I'm afraid. I've tried stopping, but it's no use. The trouble is, I enjoy it.' She chuckled throatily. 'Besides, it takes my mind off my troubles. Dressing the way I do, helps, too: plastering my face with makeup, and having my hair dyed red; drinking too much whisky and dry ginger. Oh, I have all the vices.' She limped proudly ahead, a colourful figure in her brightly patterned ankle-length skirt, lightweight black bouclé sweater, cerise silk scarf, and masses of dangling beads, bracelets, and chandelier earrings.

'I expect you think me common,' she said defiantly, when Sarah brought the coffee mugs through to the counter.

'No. As a matter of fact I think just the opposite. Sugar?' Sarah smiled.

'Uncommon, you mean?' Philippa spooned a heaped helping of sugar into her coffee. 'A – character?'

'Well, yes.'

'Good. That's the way I intend to be seen. It's quite simple, really. Good psychology. That way, people scarcely notice my age.'

'Does growing old worry you that much?'

'Doesn't it worry you?' Philippa's cerise lipstick left an imprint of her lips on the rim of the mug.

'There are different ways of ageing,' Sarah said.

'There's nothing wrong with my mind, if that's what you're driving at.' Philippa shrugged. 'I'm sorry, it's just that I get a little tired of being a "character" at times. I'd give my eyeteeth to be young again. But they do say that youth is wasted on the young. Take yourself, for example!'

'What do you mean?' Sarah frowned. 'I'm not exactly in the first flush of youth.' She felt suddenly on the defensive.

'No, but you could do a lot more with yourself if you tried. My dear Sarah, I'm paying you a compliment. You're a nice-looking woman; you could be stunning, if you put your mind to it.'

Silently, Sarah took the mugs through to the kitchen, washed them, wiped the tray, and put the milk in the refrigerator, thinking how easy it would be to slip out by the back door, return to her typewriter, to ring Philippa saying that she had changed her mind about the job.

Someone came into the shop at that moment; she heard the sound of voices, Philippa's laughter. Ridiculous to take offence at Pippa's remark, Sarah thought. How could she have known that her words had conjured up a newspaper cutting, a picture of Suki Mitford, blonde, young and glamorous, holding a glass of champagne, standing beside Faulkner at that engagement party, looking up at him with adoring eyes.

Youth had not, apparently, been wasted on the young

in the case of Faulkner's 'girl Friday', Sarah thought with unaccustomed bitterness, remembering the winter evening when her life had shattered suddenly like brittle glass; the searing jealousy she'd experienced of the younger, more attractive woman who had come between herself and the man she had married in the belief that vows, once taken, could not be easily set aside and forgotten.

Squaring her shoulders, Sarah re-entered the shop.

Philippa and the customer were standing together near the shelves of le Creuset ovenware. The customer was the dark-haired man Sarah had first noticed in York Minster, who reminded her of Amabie.

Following that first jolt of recognition, picking up a duster, Sarah turned her back and began dusting a shelf of Capo di Monte figures, listening to his voice, his laughter. Catching sight of him in a mirror, she paused to study his face in detail, the curve of his mouth, lightly tanned complexion, dark hair brushing the white, roll-neck sweater he wore with beige slacks – a lightweight sweater which emphasized the breadth of his shoulders, the powerful chest muscles, the trimness of his physique linked to the kind of grace that belonged to a Spanish bullfighter.

She could almost see him, dressed in the vibrant costume of the toreador, poised, scarlet cape in hand, sword pointed in readiness for the kill, or standing on a cliff top overlooking a turbulent sea, holding in his arms the waif-like figure of a young girl dressed in white, lips unsmiling, eyes burning with a nameless, pent-up desire, a longing for understanding, and freedom. A man whose faith had been shattered suddenly by events beyond his power to control. The face of the man who had once stood beside her, in York Minster, staring into the All Saints' Chapel like a lost soul.

When he had gone, Philippa said, 'Look, Sarah, I'm sorry if I offended you. Actually, I was paying you a compliment. Trying to at any rate, in my muddle-headed way.'

'With the proviso that I might appear more attractive if I cared more about my personal appearance?'

'Why don't you?'

'Frankly, I wouldn't know where to begin. And that's the story of *my* life. Now, shall I go on with the dusting?'

'No. To hell with the dusting! Look here, Sarah Vale, I like you enormously, don't ask me why! You're as prickly as a bloody porcupine! Stop fiddling about with that duster, and listen! I'm – lonely.'

Philippa paused to light a cigarette, frowning, narrowing her eyes against the rising smoke. 'I need someone to cross swords with occasionally. Friendship without a touch of acrimony is like cooking without salt. I say things I don't mean, get people's backs up.'

'Perhaps that's why you're lonely.'

Philippa threw her head back and laughed. 'There! That's the kind of remark I enjoy. My husband and I used to fight like cat and dog. It was marvellous, exciting. I miss the rows, the making up afterwards: Frankly, I miss the presence of a man in my life, the flattery, the cut and thrust of those moments when the battle of the sexes begins, the sizing up, the opening gambits. As one grows older, comes the certain knowledge that love is merely a game, a pastime, unlikely to last. From a woman's viewpoint, the certainty that when everything begins to wag, sag, bag and drag beyond redemption, the best she can hope for is a snappy game of Trivial Pursuit.'

She paused reflectively, 'Take that handsome young devil, Nicholas Tierney, for example.'

'Nicholas Tierney?'

'The man who left the shop ten minutes ago,' Philippa said impatiently. 'Surely you noticed him? Sophia Tierney's nephew. Don't tell me you have never heard of the Carillon Hotel?'

'No, but never mind. Go on. What about him?'

Philippa shrugged. 'Simply that he is the kind of man who makes a woman feel like a woman, however old and decrepit she may be. One hears rumours, of course, but I would give ten years of my life for . . . Oh, never mind what!'

A bevy of laughing tourists entered the shop at that moment, Scottish by their accents, in search of 'wee mindings' to take home with them. 'Nothing too expensive.' They loved the lavender sachets, the 'A Present from York' ashtrays and tea-towels, the hand-carved 'love' spoons, what Philippa Paget regarded as the gimmicky, rubbishy stuff she felt obliged to stock to please her less discerning customers.

Seated behind the counter, in charge of her musky kingdom of sparkling glassware, gilt-framed mirrors, Capo di Monte figures, greeting cards, Italian silk scarves, and gimmickry, she resembled a colourful bird of paradise in an aviary of dunnocks.

Turning, she handed Sarah a bill of sale in respect of the le Creuset ware she had sold to her last serious customer. 'Just pack this lot in a large carton from the stockroom,' she said, 'ready for collection. Nick Tierney will be calling back for them at two o'clock.'

The bill, Sarah noticed, was made out to a Miss Sophia Tierney, the Hotel Carillon.

The Carillon. Nicholas Tierney. Amabie . . . 'One hears rumours, of course, but I would give ten years of my life for . . . Oh, never mind what!'

Rumours? What kind of rumours? Sarah wondered. And what would Philippa give ten years of her life to achieve?

'Simply that he is the kind of man who makes a woman feel like a woman, however old or decrepit she may be . . . '

Catching sight of herself in the full-length stockroom mirror, Sarah saw reflected there someone she scarcely recognized as herself: a stranger, badly dressed, dumpy, worried looking, with tousled hair.

Never a vain woman, she had seldom looked into a full length mirror since her wedding day, when she had seen, in her mother's cheval glass, a slim, bright-eyed girl all in white, shining hair caught back in a curled cluster beneath a flowing veil.

La Carillon, she thought. That meant a peal of bells; carilloner, to chime or to ring, the way the bells of her father's church had rung for her on her wedding day. She saw briefly, in her mind's eye, the daisied lawn across which she had tripped hopefully in her white satin slippers, the masses of spring flowers as she walked down the aisle to make her vows of fidelity to Faulkner Vale.

Dragging a stout cardboard carton and a mass of wrapping paper from an alcove, Sarah wished, desperately, that she had not caught sight of herself in that too revealing mirror.

The sun warm on his face, Nicholas strolled along Coppergate towards St Mary's Square.

At times, the narrow streets of the city seemed claustrophobic, unbearably hot, especially on those bad days when he awoke with the devil on his shoulder. No telling when his dark moods would occur.

Madeleine, a firm believer in astrology, had told him those moods of his were part and parcel of his birthsign, that Geminis were two personalities rolled into one.

How easily she had been able to read his moods, to coax him back to a pleasanter frame of mind. One particularly black day, just after he had left university, when he had said passionately that he wanted to get away from Paris, away from his father's condemnation of him as a failure, a disgrace to the name Tierney, Madeleine had encouraged him to go back to England, and he had known then how deeply the charged atmosphere between himself and his father was affecting her.

And so he had made his home with Sophia, ostensibly to learn hotel management. But he had never seemed capable of buckling down to the hard work involved. Nor had he been all that interested. Frankly, he could not have cared less who did the laundry, paid the wages, polished the silver, and did the washing up. On the credit side, he had discovered a penchant for arranging sight-seeing tours, theatre and nightclub outings for the guests, a natural flair for hosting the dances held in the romantic setting of the great conservatory; had come up with valid suggestions to improve that setting by the addition of coloured spotlights, a glittering witchball, more exotic shrubs and flowers.

He had learned, in time, the names of most of the staff, but not what they actually did for a living – except Michel, the receptionists, the waiters, the barman, and the chambermaids. But the names of the small army of part-time employees who came in to wash windows, cut the grass, and clean out the swimming pool, remained as foreign to him as those of a Japanese football team. In any event, they came and went so quickly, that contingent of part-timers, that it had scarcely seemed worthwhile remembering their names.

Entering Betty's Café, he was shown to a vacant table near a window overlooking Stonegate. Ordering a pot of coffee, he congratulated himself on having concluded the le Creuset deal at slightly more than the usual ten per cent discount: twelve and a half to be precise, because he had exerted his charm on the woman who owned the shop, a flirtatious old biddy whom he rather liked, despite her over-the-top makeup and her mass of dyed red hair.

Perhaps she, too, was lonely, he thought, looking out of the window at the thronged pavements, savouring the feel of summertime in the air, admiring the pretty, slender young girls in their cotton dresses. Possibly the flirtatious old biddy, too, had decided to cock a snook at life, as he had done since the death of Madeleine. And yet . . .

All very well pretending, but the time came, often in the early hours of the morning, after a restless, dream-invaded sleep, with no one there to applaud the performance, when the human spirit was at its lowest ebb, that the naked truth came uppermost, the shattering awareness of one's own follies and failures; the sharp, unbearable pain of loss; the blinding tears, the longing for the return of a beloved being, the dreary contemplation of a future without love.

Foolishly, he had imagined for one brief, illusory moment, that Maria Alvarez might be the one to dispel his isolation, to open his heart to a feeling of warmth, of summertime in the city. Certainly he had been strongly attracted to her, as he had been to many other women since his abortive encounter with Anna Stravinska, but never to the point of total commitment, his views on marriage warped by the failure of his parents' relationship.

Common sense told him that, with the right woman, physical intimacy would present no problem, that somewhere this 'right woman' must exist. But where would he find her? In Paris, Rome, Madrid, New York, San Francisco?

The world was a big place, the need of escape a constant torment at the back of his mind, the reason why he had felt unable to promise Sophia that he would stay at the Carillon for at least one more year.

Chapter Thirteen

Leaving the boutique at one o'clock, heading towards Alf's Cafe, Sarah bumped into Helen, coolly elegant in a pale blue pleated skirt and matching sweater, carrying a laden shopping basket.

'Sarah! How lovely to see you.' Helen smiled warmly. 'Have you time for a coffee, a bite to eat?'

'Why, yes, I – actually, it's my lunch-hour.' No use beating about the bush. 'I've taken a part-time job,' Sarah explained. Catching Helen's look of surprise, 'A matter of keeping the wolf from the door.'

'Come on,' Helen said decisively, taking the initiative, 'I know a quiet little café in Davygate. No use trying Betty's, they'll be rushed off their feet. Mustn't waste your lunchbreak queueing.'

Sarah looked anxious, she thought, pale, and much thinner.

'I've missed your visits to the library,' Helen said, when they were seated at a table in an upstairs room with an oak-beamed ceiling. 'How's the book coming along?'

'I'm not sure,' Sarah confessed. 'My agent feels it has potential, but my publishers are hanging fire, hence the job. Oh, just a ham sandwich and a cup of coffee for me, please,' when the waitress appeared to take their orders.

'Me, too.' Helen wished she dare risk ordering Sarah

a decent meal of quiche and salad, saying that lunch was on her. But no, better not, she decided, recognizing the Emily Brontë pride of the woman.

'You were saying?' Helen prodded gently, when the waitress had gone.

'Simply that things are slow in the publishing world.' Sarah smiled suddenly, her sense of humour coming uppermost. 'Like Mr Micawber, I am hourly expecting something to turn up. Meanwhile, I have to pay my way. I was lucky to find a job at my age, with my lack of qualifications – apart from secretarial work, and I wouldn't go back to taking shorthand for all the tea in China.'

'What does this job of yours entail?' Helen asked, treading warily.

'Dusting, serving, making coffee, so far. This is my first week. Eventually, I imagine I'll get around to changing the window displays, checking stock. Shopwork in general.'

'I see. How many days a week?'

'Three. Tuesdays, Thursdays, and Saturdays. At least that's what Philippa suggested.'

'Philippa?' Helen frowned. 'You don't mean – Philippa Paget?'

'Yes. Why? Do you know her?'

Helen said quietly, with a touch of bitterness, 'I should do. My brother and Philippa were engaged to be married. But that was a long time ago. She treated him shabbily, in my opinion.'

'I'm so sorry. I had no idea.'

'Why should you? It's all in the past. One of those unfortunate affairs that never came to fruition. Quite simply, Philippa – Pippa we called her – met and married someone else, a close friend of Alec's – Roy Paget

– who would have been the best man at their wedding, had things turned out differently.'

Helen drew in a deep breath. 'Not that I was entirely sorry when Pippa turned down my brother in favour of Roy. They never seemed entirely suited. Alec is a reserved kind of person. Frankly, I felt rather relieved when . . . What I mean is, I don't think they'd have been happy together, my brother and Pippa. The trouble is, Alec has never really got over her. But then,' she smiled ruefully, 'I imagine that a larger-than-life character like Philippa Paget might take a little forgetting. At any rate, I dread to think what might have happened had Philippa been called upon to take care of a semi-invalid.'

'A – semi-invalid?'

'Well, yes, Alec's legs were pretty badly injured when a landmine exploded in that Falklands fracas, which is why he's confined to a wheelchair most of the time, though, thankfully, he can still manage to hop along to the bathroom on his own, with the aid of crutches. Otherwise, he might have ended up in some Army home for the chronically disabled. I can't see Pippa coping with that kind of situation.'

Changing the subject, 'Have you heard of the Hotel Carillon?' Sarah asked.

'Yes, of course,' Helen replied, 'Why do you ask?'

'Tell me about it.'

'Well, the Carillon is, I suppose, York's most prestigious hotel, ruled, with a rod of iron, by another larger-than-life character, Sophia Tierney.' Helen smiled reflectively, 'Alec and I went there to celebrate the award of his B.E.M. The food was out of this world, and Madame Sophia sent a bottle of Dom Perignon to our table, with her compliments. Then her nephew asked me to dance.' A wild rose colour stained Helen's cheeks, her eyes sparkled. 'It was like a dream. I hadn't danced for years, but he was so charming, such an excellent dancer – and I *had* drunk a couple of glasses of champagne!' She laughed. 'He made me feel like a queen, and he was wonderful with Alec.'

Sarah insisted on paying her share of the bill. Outside the café, she glanced at her wristwatch. 'I must hurry. It's three minutes to two. Mustn't be late.'

'A word of warning,' Helen said quickly. 'Don't let Pippa make too many demands, or, next thing you know, she'll want to extend your three days to four, then five.'

'Thanks. I'll remember.'

'Same time next week?' Helen called after her.

'Yes. Fine. Must dash now.' Sarah hastened back to the boutique, praying to heaven that she would not bump into Nicholas Tierney on the doorstep. Why, she had no clear idea, except that she looked such a wreck.

But Nicholas had already called to collect his consignment of casseroles, according to Philippa, who seemed slightly put out for some reason. 'Oh, there you are,' she said brusquely. 'I've been frightfully busy. Do you think, in future, that you could bring sandwiches?'

'Work through my lunchbreak, you mean? No, I don't think so.'

'*I* don't have a lunchbreak,' Philippa said crossly.

'Ah, but you are management, I am merely the "sorcerer's apprentice",' Sarah said lightly.

'Touché!' Philippa lit a cigarette. Narrowing her eyes, she said, 'What would you say if I offered you four days' employment instead of three?'

'I would say, thanks, but no thanks.' Sarah smiled to take the sting from her reply. 'You see, I need time for my writing and research. The days we agreed on suit me fine. But you are at liberty to replace me, if you wish. I'll manage somehow.'

'Replace *you*?' Philippa laughed, genuinely amused. 'My dear Sarah, so far as I am concerned, you are irreplaceable! The "sorcerer's apprentice" indeed! Well, the "sorcerer" could do with a mug of hot, strong coffee before the next influx of "wee mindings"!'

'I'm sorry, Frances, but what do you expect me to do about it?' Sophia spoke coolly on the telephone to the overwrought Mrs Gowan. 'Do remember that Nicholas is not a child, and I am not his keeper. What happened between him and Maria Alvarez is none of my business.'

She paused to listen, then said, 'No, he has not confided in me, nor is he likely to do so . . . *What*? I'm sorry, Frances, but I regard that remark as extremely offensive; totally unwarranted.'

With shaking hand, Sophia replaced the receiver. How dare Frances Gowan have referred to Nicholas as a gigolo? The term implying a man of ill repute, a professional dancing partner deriving money from some mistress or other.

Frances Gowan's suggestion was not only derogatory but ludicrous. Even so, Sophia could not help wondering why, despite his long stream of encounters with attractive women, Nicholas had never evinced more than a passing interest in any one of them.

But, of course, she knew why. Because of Madeleine: that illusory yardstick of perfection which made him incapable of falling in love with any woman who did not measure up to her standard.

Madeleine! As much as Sophia had loved her enchanting sister-in-law, she wondered would Nicholas never be rid of his mother's ghostly presence in his life; the haunting fragrance of her white gardenias?

And what of her brother, Clive, about to begin his retirement? Secretly, Sophia had hoped that Clive would return to England once his days in the diplomatic service came to an end, that he would sell the house in the Rue St Hélène; that he and Nicholas would somehow patch up their quarrel and draw closer together. But that pipe-dream was scarcely likely to come to fruition.

A few days ago, in a rare letter to his sister, Clive had stated his intention of remaining in Paris, of returning to the Rue St Hélène subsequent to a brief trip to England to hand in his seal of office, and attend the dinner in his honour as a retiring member of the diplomatic service.

Meanwhile, life for Sarah assumed a pattern of work, and more work. Getting up early to write, she would, on her 'boutique' days, break off to bathe and dress before hurrying to Coppergate to cope with Philippa's quirky personality – far more exhausting than writing. But she needed the money.

She had, from her first wage packet, bought Verity the ammonite pendant, with which she had enclosed a specially chosen birthday card and a letter begging her to write or telephone. There had been no response.

Meanwhile, Sarah's Thursday lunchtime meetings with Helen had become part of her routine, to which she looked forward with pleasure, as a means of release. Never before had Sarah had a close woman friend in whom she could confide, and while she enjoyed, to some extent, her 'cut and thrust' relationship with Philippa Paget, it was to Helen she confessed her fears that *Amabie* might never be published, that she and Verity might never be reconciled, that Richard would drift away from her irrevocably once he took his place on Faulkner's board of directors.

One day, Philippa said casually, 'Did Verity like her necklace?'

'I don't know. I haven't heard from her yet,' Sarah replied, re-arranging the Italian silk scarves. 'But you know how children are, these days!'

'Not really. You see I never had any. I'm not even sure that I wanted any.' Pippa chuckled hoarsely. 'Funny, I've never told anyone before. My husband left me because I refused to get pregnant.' She flicked the ash from her cigarette. 'Why did your husband leave you?'

'Because he got someone else pregnant,' Sarah said coolly, feeling the softness of the scarves in her hands, loving their vibrant colours and design.

'And you would rather not talk about it?'

'There isn't much point, is there?'

'No, I suppose not.' Philippa sighed. 'Except that it does help to let one's hair down occasionally. Which reminds me, why the hell don't you have that mane of yours brought under control?'

'Because it's my hair. I've always worn it long, and I'm used to it this way,' Sarah retorted, thinking here we go again, wishing Philippa would stop needling her about her personal appearance.

'All right, no need to lose your cool. It was merely a suggestion.' Puckering her lips, blowing out a smoke ring. 'Frankly, Sarah, you'd look more attractive with a short haircut. Even better if you wore makeup, and why the hell don't you treat yourself to a few clothes that fit you properly? A decent suit, perhaps? A pair of high-heeled shoes? What's wrong with that?'

'Nothing, except that even if I wanted to change my

176

appearance, I couldn't afford it,' Sarah said bluntly. 'Shoes, suits, makeup, and haircuts, cost money!'

Chancing her luck, Philippa commented, 'Has it ever occurred to you that, had you spent more money on your appearance when you were married to that rich sod, Faulkner Vale, he might never have got another woman pregnant?'

'And has it ever occurred to you, Philippa, that if and when I need your advice, I'll ask for it!'

Sarah heard the ringing of the telephone as she walked upstairs to her flat, lumping her shopping bag, thinking it was bound to be a wrong number.

It had been a long and difficult day, and her feet hurt. Turning her key in the lock, dumping her shopping bag on the rose settee, she picked up the receiver. 'Hello,' she said dully.

'Sarah? Is that you? Where the hell have you been? I've been trying to get in touch with you all day!'

'Freya?'

'Yes, darling, it's me! Now, listen carefully. Are you sitting down, by the way?'

'No, I'm standing near my desk.'

Freya laughed. 'Then you better had sit down – unless you prefer to faint standing up! The fact is, I've had an offer for *Amabie*. Wait for it! The good news is, Foremost are offering a twenty thousand pounds advance!'

'Would you mind repeating that?' Sarah sat down abruptly.

'I knew you'd feel stunned! Isn't it super news? Of course, they want the completed manuscript as soon as possible, but there should be no difficulty about that. The thing is, they love what you've come up with so far!

Well, the advance speaks for itself, doesn't it? Personally, I couldn't be happier. I told them all along that you were a potential bestselling authoress. Now that they have come round to my way of thinking, I foresee a happy future for both of us, my love! Many, many congratulations!' A pause. 'Sarah, are you there? Are you listening?'

'I'm sorry, Freya. Please forgive me, I feel a bit faint!' Hanging up the receiver, head spinning, Sarah stumbled towards the bedroom.

Peeling off her clothes, she got into bed and lay, head buried in the pillows, needing to be alone, to sleep . . . to relax her limbs, to lie diagonally in the double bed she had bought, lumps and all, from a saleroom, when all she could really afford was a Zed-bed or a palliasse.

Falling asleep, she dreamt of a dark-haired man in whose arms she discovered the meaning of love – a glorious amelioration of the senses, beyond the circumference of earthly life.

Wide awake, she dreamed of Paris in the spring, New York in the fall, Switzerland in winter; imagined herself sailing down the Nile to Luxor, travelling to Venice aboard the Orient Express.

In a state of euphoria linked to the lessening of tension, Sarah imagined herself skiing down some mountainside amid glorious alpine scenery. That she had never skied in her life scarcely impinged. She would simply fly like a bird, revelling in the sensation of freedom, catching the scent of the pine trees; the sun warm on her face. Tired of practicalities, she saw herself jetting off to New York; swanning about some country estate a lá Daphne Du Maurier, dogs bounding at her heels; opening village fêtes, telling her chauffeur to call back for her at five o'clock; spending a week at a health farm, emerging slim as a wand. And all the time she knew she was pipe-dreaming. She laughed.

Likely as not, learning how to ski, she would break a leg the first day out; sailing down the Nile, she'd be bitten by mosquitoes; the country estate would never materialize. As for spending an entire week living on celery sticks and carrot juice, the mind boggled. In any case, money could not buy the things she really wanted from life, the love and respect of her children, a return to the happiness of youth.

She could think of a hundred ways in which to spend her hard-earned money, but penury taught prudence. When the contract had been signed, and the cheque from her publishers arrived, less Freya's ten per cent, plus VAT, she would hurry to the building society, present the cheque to the astonished girl behind the counter, withdraw enough cash to indulge in a shopping spree – buy a joint of beef, two new bath-towels; possibly some new clothes. She might even take Philippa's advice and have her hair styled.

Philippa! Pondering her dilemma, Sarah knew that to leave Philippa at the height of the season was unthinkable. Foremost Books wanted *Amabie* as soon as possible, but the manuscript was nearing completion. A few more weeks of concentrated hard work and it would be finished. She saw no reason to upset the balance of her own life, or Philippa's. She would go on working at the boutique until the summertime bonanza was over, then ask Philippa to find a replacement. Meanwhile, she would not mention her windfall to her inquisitive employer.

But she must share her happinesss with someone.

Picking up the telephone, she dialled Ralph's number.

*   *

To Faulkner's relief, Suki had decided to name their daughter Felicity. He had secured the property in Hampstead, the builders had started work, and the house would be ready to move into at the end of September.

To his chagrin, Faulkner had had to admit that removal to a bigger house seemed the only solution to the overcrowding problem. Since the arrival of the baby's nanny – with whom the housekeeper did not see eye to eye – he dreaded returning to Marlborough to find the house in chaos, his peace shattered by the incessant wailing of his infant daughter.

Christ, he thought, coming home one overpoweringly hot evening to the sound of yammering voices from the kitchen, overlaid by the lusty bawling of a hungry baby, the sooner they moved to Hampstead, the better.

Pouring himself a stiff whisky from the cut glass decanter on the drinks table in what Suki termed 'the lounge', which Sarah had referred to as the drawing room, Faulkner regarded, in resentful silence, his new wife as she entered the room wearing her Bruce Oldfield casuals – cream silk culottes, matching shirt, and high-heeled gold sandals – blonde hair swinging loose about her shoulders, her complexion darkened with makeup to emphasize her sun tan.

'Oh, there you are,' she said coolly, 'about time too. Don't forget we have guests for dinner this evening.'

'Guests?'

'Oh, for heaven's sake, darling! I reminded you this morning. Don't you listen to a word I say?'

The baby continued its incessant wailing from the nursery.

'What's the matter with *me*?' Faulkner said heatedly, 'More to the point, what's the matter with Felicity? Why the hell don't you feed her; change her nappy? Surely to God it isn't asking too much that a mother, plus a nanny, should be capable of taking care of one small child?'

'Nanny's preparing her bottle now,' Suki said coldly.

'Bottle? What's wrong with breast-feeding?' Faulkner retaliated angrily. 'Sarah breast-fed Richard and Verity!'

'How dare you mention that woman's name to me?' Turning swiftly on her gold-sandalled feet, Suki stormed out of the room.

Oh God, what had he said, what had he done? Faulkner thought, blaming himself for the row.

Anxious to make up the quarrel, following Suki to the bedroom, he flung his arms about her in a foolish attempt at reconciliation, saying he was sorry, begging her to forgive him for his thoughtless remark about breast-feeding their baby.

'Oh, for heaven's sake, not now!' Impatiently shrugging away from him, Suki unfastened the straps of her sandals, slipped out of her clothes, wrapped herself in a towelling robe, and hurried through to the adjoining bathroom, fuming inwardly as he hung about in the doorway watching her as she stood naked beneath the shower.

'Must you really do that?' she asked icily, knowing that she had this rich, elderly husband of hers exactly where she wanted him, having discovered that the more harshly she treated him, the more slavish he became, the more money he showered on her.

Feeling the warmth of the Badedas scented water on her soft, tanned skin, turning away from his soulful gaze, she thought that tomorrow she would swan up to town to buy more antiques for the Hampstead house, have lunch with Sam Dexter, her exciting, young interior decorator, visit the Bond Street salon where she had her eyelashes dyed and her nails manicured, then squander lots more lovely money on clothes, perfume, and makeup.

The pity of it was that Faulkner was fast becoming a stinking old bore: forever pawing her; wanting to make love to her – accompanied by heavy breathing as he reached his climax. *When* and *if* he reached his climax!

Sam Dexter, on the other hand, well versed in the art of lovemaking, made her feel the way an attractive woman should feel in bed, lazily happy and fulfilled.

Stepping out of the shower, Suki said airily, 'By the way, darling, I'm going to Bristol tomorrow, staying overnight with Meg Somers.'

'Meg Somers?' Faulkner regarded his wife suspiciously. 'Who's she?'

The lie tripped easily, smoothly, from Suki's tongue. 'Darling, don't you remember? She's the person I told you about who used to look after me when I was little.'

'No, I don't remember. In any case, why stay with her?'

'Because it's her birthday – or it will be tomorrow – and I want to take the poor old creature to a show, followed by a slap-up meal, with lots of champagne, in which case I shall not be in a fit state to drive home afterwards.' Suki added, ascerbically, 'What's the matter, don't you trust me?'

That hint of acid in Suki's voice convinced Faulkner that to cross her further might end in her denial of his conjugal rights when the bloody dinner party she had sprung on him was over.

'Of course I trust you,' he murmured, helping her on with her bathrobe, nestling his cheek against her hair, clasping his hands about her slim waist, utterly besotted by her beauty, 'but you will leave me Meg Somer's phone number, won't you, so that I can ring up to say goodnight?'

'That's impossible,' Suki said casually, thrusting his hands aside, 'Meg isn't on the telephone. Now, isn't it about time you started getting ready for dinner?'

'I still can't take it in.' Ralph looked at Sarah across the table with its centrepiece of crimson roses. 'All I c-can say is, c-congratulations. S-success could not have h-happened to a nicer person.' Solemnly raising his glass, 'May *Amabie* take the w-world by storm, and may my friend, Sarah Vale, take her rightful place in the hall of fame!'

'Get buried in Westminster Abbey, you mean?' Sarah laughed, slightly embarrassed. 'Thanks, Ralph, but I'd rather be buried beneath the elm trees of my father's old church in Gloucestershire – the place where I grew up.'

Tears sprang to her eyes. Brushing them away, she smiled apologetically. 'I'm sorry, the truth is I can scarcely take it in myself. But success isn't just money, there are more important things – areas of my life in which I have failed completely.'

Setting down his glass, 'Because of your children, you mean? B-because they haven't kept in t-touch with you?'

'Yes.'

'But now that money – forgive me – is no longer a problem, you c-could meet with them, talk things over.'

'I've thought of it,' Sarah laid down her serviette, 'but they might see me as a fussy, overbearing mother. I couldn't bear that. It's important that they make the first move. In any case, I couldn't go to London until the autumn because of my job.'

'Your job? But surely you'll give that up now?'

'No, that wouldn't be fair to Philippa. I can't leave her in the lurch.'

'No, of course not.' How typical of Sarah to stand by her guns, Ralph thought, knowing he had never loved her more than he did now.

Had she looked up at that moment, she must have read his feelings towards her in his eyes. Just as well, perhaps, that she was looking at the roses in their shallow, silver bowl.

Chapter Fourteen

Clive Tierney returned to Paris with a deep feeling of relief that the formalities of his retirement from the diplomatic service were over and done with.

He had hated the speeches, the presentation dinner in London, attended by shaky facsimiles of himself whose careers had ended a decade ago: had hated even more the up and coming bright young sparks reminiscent of himself forty years ago.

Thankfully, the Simenons had decided to stay on to look after him, despite the windfall of Madeleine's bequest. And yet, seated at one end of the dining table, being waited on by François Simenon, eating the delicious food prepared by his wife, Claudette, Clive viewed his future with dismay.

Robbed of the mainsprings of his existence – his work and Madeleine – he scarcely tasted the food set before him.

'Monsieur is not hungry?' Simenon's voice held a note of reproof as he cleared away the scarcely touched remains of the crème brulée.

'No. Please serve my coffee in the lounge.'

'Of course, Monsieur, just as you wish.'

The pain in Madeleine's limbs had happened quite suddenly. At first she had laughed and said that a woman of her age must expect a touch of rheumatism now and then.

But surely a 'touch of rheumatism' could not account

for her sickness and dizzy spells, the times he had found her in a state of collapse, so weak and faint that she could scarcely crawl?

Looking into the past, Clive remembered that when his wife's condition had worsened to the extent that her doctor had advised a visit to Switzerland to consult an eminent orthopaedic specialist, he had driven her there himself, realizing that a long, involved train journey would prove too tiring; beyond her limited powers of endurance.

They had made the journey in easy stages, staying overnight in Dijon and Lucerne, before travelling to Geneva; to the clinic of a Monsieur Antoine Thiery, at which he and Madeleine would stay until certain tests had been carried out – Madeleine in a private room of the clinic, himself in a chalet in the grounds.

Never would Clive forget that chalet, the long, anxious hours he had spent there in isolation, the sound of lake water lapping against stones: pacing the shore, hands clasped, praying for his wife's recovery – remembering Madeleine as he had always seen her, as the shining star of his existence. An unreachable star, tormenting him with her loveliness, stabbing his heart with jealousy of any other man who came within a mile of her – particularly his son, Nicholas.

As the night wore on, Clive remembered that fraught moment when Antoine Thiery had called him into his office to tell him that Madeleine was suffering from multiple sclerosis – a replacement of normal tissue of the nervous system by fibrous tissue, the hardening of which would inevitably result in a complete loss of mobility.

Typically, Clive had brushed aside that diagnosis as nonsensical. Like a man possessed, he had lined up other specialists in Zurich, Bern and Basle, clutching at straws.

But Madeleine had calmly refused to visit those other specialists, as if she had quietly accepted her fate and intended to deal with it in her own way, on her own terms.

Above all, she said, when they returned to Paris, she did not want her son to know of her illness. As far as Nicholas was concerned, she had a touch of arthritis which made walking difficult.

Helplessly, Clive had witnessed her decline, the deformation of her limbs. Yet never once had Madeleine admitted defeat. When she could no longer visit her dressmaker, her coiffeuse, her beautician or her friends, they came to visit her.

And so, whenever Nicholas had made brief, flying trips to Paris to see his mother, he had found her sitting up in bed, smiling, her hair beautifully coiffed, face skilfully made up, wearing a frothy lace pegnoir, her usual bowl of gardenias on her bedside table, saying what a fraud she felt giving in to a touch of arthritis.

When he had gone, a prisoner of her crippling disability, she would sit at her bedroom window gazing hungrily at the passing parade along the Rue St Hélène, feasting her eyes on a world of which she was no longer a part.

Even in death, her face, soft complexioned as a gardenia petal, hair beautifully arranged, dark eyelashes brushing her cheeks, there had been no visible signs of her long affiliation with pain, those last, desperate moments at the medical centre where her heart had stopped beating.

Sitting beside her bed, Clive had prayed for her recovery, the faintest glimmer of recognition, the merest word of love. He would never forget to his dying day, that during a brief spell of consciousness, her last thoughts had been of Nicholas.

'Don't blame my son,' she murmured weakly. 'The fault was mine. All mine.'

Nicholas. Always Nicholas, Clive thought bitterly. Always 'my son', never 'our son'.

But was Nicholas his son? Or had Madeleine been pregnant at the time of their marriage?

The carriage clock on the mantelpiece chimed two. Aware of the silence, Clive walked alone the avenues of memory, slotting together the jigsaw puzzle of the past, his mind fretted with worry; remembering that the child he had believed to be his, born prematurely, had borne not the slightest resemblance to himself or Madeleine.

If only he knew for certain.

And what about that star-shaped brooch from a 'secret admirer'? Madeleine had refused to divulge the name of that admirer; had simply laughed and said, tormentingly, that it was none of his businesss.

He had handed over that brooch, and the rest of the jewellery from his wife's safe, to M. Renay, after the reading of the will, the day after Madeleine's funeral, when the dapper *avocat* had returned to the house to oversee the removal of the jewels and the paintings Madeleine had willed to Sophia.

The pictures, Renay had told him, would be crated and sent to Mademoiselle Tierney as soon as possible; the jewellery sold at auction later that year, according to Nicholas' instructions.

At least, Clive had known the satisfaction of turning his son out of doors. What Nicholas did with his life from now on was none of his business, nothing whatever to do with him. How dare the young pup have turned up at his mother's funeral unshaven, the worse for drink? How dared he have brought up the matter of conscience?

And yet, sitting with his head in his hands, it was the matter of conscience that most troubled Clive Tierney.

The thought occurred that he was, perhaps, going slowly but surely out of his mind.

The boutique was filled with the usual throng of tourists. The atmosphere, overpoweringly hot and musky, the endless questions fired at her, the length of time the customers took to make up their minds over the simplest purchases, had given Sarah a cracking headache.

Early that morning, she had been struggling with the penultimate chapter of her book; faced with the task of drawing together the threads of the story, thinking that this, perhaps, was the way Emily Brontë had felt writing the penultimate chapter of *Wuthering Heights*.

The middle-aged couple she was serving had embarked on a squabble over a suitable present for the wife's mother. 'If you think I'm paying the earth for one of those Capo di Monte figures to sit on top of your mother's television set, you've got another think coming,' the man said sourly. 'Why don't you buy her a scarf and have done with it?'

'Because Mother never wears a scarf. She loathes scarves, and well you know it,' the wife threw back at him.

Resisting the temptation to walk away and let them get on with their quarrel, Sarah said placatingly, 'May I suggest a compromise? These hand-thrown vases are rather nice.' Ignoring her, the couple continued their argument over the Capo di Monte.

At that moment, Nicholas Tierney entered the shop with a woman in tow. A slender, casually yet smartly dressed American whose cropped blonde hair and skilful makeup belied her age; the puffiness beneath her eyes, her crepey throat, and brown-spotted hands.

'Say, Nick, isn't this just the most darling shop?' the woman enthused in an accent savouring of Savannah, of Scarlett O'Hara in *Gone With the Wind*, of shade trees, plantations, and watermelon vines. 'Why, I declare, it's quite out of this world.'

She was clinging to his arm, Sarah noticed, with scarlet painted fingertips; looking up at him adoringly, and he was smiling down at her as though oblivious of the difference in their ages. But Philippa had told her that Nicholas Tierney possessed the power of making women feel attractive no matter how old or decrepit they may be. Not that this woman appeared decrepit. Like most wealthy American matrons, she looked as if she lived on a diet of orange juice, salads, and vitamin pills, and spent the greater part of her life in a beauty parlour.

Busy coping with a crush of customers at the counter, Philippa signalled to Sarah with her eyes to leave the quarrelsome couple and concentrate on Tierney and his companion. Conscious of her lumpish appearance, the throbbing pain in her head, Sarah stepped forward to serve them, wishing the floor would open, she looked and felt such a wreck. 'May I help you?' she said stiffly.

Tierney smiled charmingly, scarcely looking at her. 'Do you mind if we browse a little first?'

'No, not at all.' Sarah watched as the American woman fluttered from showcase to shelves, exclaiming over this and that, darting flirtatious glances at Nicholas, asking his opinion, behaving like a silly schoolgirl, Sarah thought. But perhaps this was what men liked – being looked at adoringly, made to feel important. Possibly that was why

Faulkner had grown tired of her. Throughout the years of his faithlessness, she had felt it unnecessary to shore up his ego as she had done in the early days of their marriage.

The American woman's browsing resulted in the purchase of a dozen Portuguese plates, several hand-painted Portuguese cockerels, a quantity of silver pendants, rings, and bracelets, and three expensive Capo di Monte figures, which she paid for with her American Express card, by which time Philippa had taken over completely, leaving Sarah to cope with the till and the less important customers. Tierney must be feeling like a cat with a saucer of cream, Sarah thought ungraciously, with two flirtatious women drooling over him. She wondered what he would think if he knew she had used him as a role model for Amabie, and that he was about to die at her hands. The thought provided some satisfaction.

The heatwave had broken suddenly. Rain-swept streets gleamed the colour of pewter that Sunday morning when Sarah laid Amabie to rest. The epilogue was short and simple, in which the present day Miriam visited the churchyard at Lastingham, drawn there by a scarcely understood feeling of destiny.

Sarah could not very well have written: 'I lingered round them under that benign sky . . . wondered how any one could ever imagine unquiet slumbers for the sleepers in that quiet earth'.

Instead she wrote, 'And so Miriam unearthed a few violets, and laid them gently on the grave of a man she had never known. And yet . . . '

Looking out at the rain-soaked garden, balancing the words of the final paragraph in her mind: ' . . . she knew that they were destined to meet in another time, another place,' Sarah wrote. 'Or perhaps they had met, long ago: that meeting swallowed up by the mists of time.

'Winding a strand of ivy about her finger, as a token of remembrance, Miriam walked slowly towards the coach that would take her back to a world as foreign to her as the shores of England, seen through a mist, had once been to Amabie. And throughout that journey back to her own world, she twisted the strand of ivy in remembrance of him'.

The book finished, Sarah lay down her head on her arms, and wept.

Clive's telephone call startled Sophia. She had thought him incapable of emotion. Apparently she was wrong. The man sounded distraught. Recognizing a cri-de-coeur when she heard one, keeping calm for her brother's sake, making no attempt to discover the reason for his call, she said simply, that of course she would come as quickly as possible. Tomorrow, perhaps, or the day after, as soon as the travel arrangements had been made. She would wire him the time and date of her arrival in Paris.

The call ended, she stood near the window looking out at the lights, the traffic streaming along the A19, pondering her best course of action, deciding to say nothing to Nicholas for the time being. Almost dinner time, she would dine with him, as usual; speak to him later.

Receiving his aunt's summons to her apartment, at midnight, he realized that something was wrong.

They had dined together as usual, then she had gone up to her apartment whilst he had visited the kitchen to discuss with Michel next morning's visit to the supermarket.

To Nicky's surprise, he had begun to look forward to these early morning excursions to watch the porters busily unloading the fresh consignments of meat, fish, and vegetables, listening to Michel's reasons for choosing exactly what he wanted for the Carillon – the meat because of its grain and texture, its delicate marbling of fat; the fish for the pinkness of the gills, firmness of the flesh, the brightness of the eyes; the vegetables according to the season of the year. Runner and broad beans, and peas were past their best now, hence his preference for marrows, courgettes, celery, and globe artichokes.

Following his discussion with Michel, who had his own private source of supply of game, poultry and eggs, which he guarded as assiduously as a gaoler in the Tower of London might have guarded Sir Walter Raleigh, Nicholas had gone up to his flat to undress. He had just emerged from the shower when the phone rang and he received the summons to his aunt's apartment.

Quickly thrusting his arms into a towelling bathrobe, his hair still wet, he hurried along the corridor to her drawing room.

Undressed, ready for bed, wearing a Japanese robe embroidered with gold and red dragons, Sophia was standing near the window, looking down at the floodlit garden.

'Tante Sophia! Is anything the matter?' Looking at her concernedly, he noticed the network of lines about her eyes and lips, clearly visible now that she had removed her makeup. She smiled faintly, revealing her still near perfect teeth. 'I am going to Paris,' she said, 'tomorrow if possible.'

'Paris? But why? Why so suddenly?'

'My brother needs me.'

'Is he ill?'

'Not physically. At least he made no mention of illness when he telephoned. Possibly he needs help, at least that is the impression I gained. He sounded overwrought.'

'Father? Overwrought?' Nicholas uttered a mirthless laugh. The idea of his codfish father being overwrought seemed ludicrous. Out of character.

'Whether or not you believe it, and no matter what your feelings may be, he is still my brother,' Sophia said coolly. 'This is a family matter.' More heatedly, 'What is the point or purpose of carrying on this vendetta now that Madeleine has gone? Has it ever occurred to you that if *he* is strong-willed and stubborn, so are you?'

Despite the warmth of the late August night, Sophia shivered suddenly. 'I'm sorry. I called you to ask if you would make the necessary travel arrangements on my behalf.'

'But of course.'

Knowing he was angry, she said, 'I had planned to go to Paris anyway, sooner or later, to visit the cemetery at l'église St Germaine, to take flowers for Madeleine.' Straightening her shoulders, 'The thing is, I must be certain that you will take charge here, make sure that everything runs smoothly during my absence.'

'You don't trust me, is that it?'

'Nicholas! For God's sake! Of course I trust you!'

Turning away, he said, 'I'll get on to the travel agent first thing in the morning. Goodnight, Aunt.'

'Nicholas!'

Turning a deaf ear, he left the apartment.

When he had gone, sinking down in a chair, this was the first time, Sophia thought, they had parted as enemies, not friends. The first time he had failed to award her the accolade of a kiss.

Torn between her love for Nicholas, her duty towards Clive, Sophia did not relish her trip to Paris. Above all, she could scarcely bear the thought of laying flowers on Madeleine's grave.

Clive met her at the Charles de Gaulle Airport. His greeting lacked warmth, although they had not seen each other for almost a year. He looked much thinner, Sophia thought, and his hair had begun to recede from his high forehead.

The car he now drove – a Renault – seemed a come down after the chauffeur-driven embassy Daimler he had sent to meet her in times gone by. Even so, Clive was a splendid driver, and he still dressed formally, correctly, perhaps ridiculously, as an English country gentleman.

Obviously, retirement had merited no lowering of his personal standard. She knew instinctively, that, stranded on a desert island, he would still dress for dinner – the Admirable Crichton syndrome personified.

The house, she thought, seemed curiously empty and lonely, robbed of Madeleine's sparkling presence.

Seated at her dressing table, brushing her hair, Sophia imagined that she heard brisk footsteps coming along the landing outside her room, expected the door to open at any moment to admit the slim, smiling figure of her sister-in-law.

Until this moment, Sophia had never quite realized that Madeleine was gone for ever, that never again would she come under the spell of that warm and vibrant personality.

When the gong sounded, picking up her evening shawl and gold-embroidered purse, Sophia went down to dinner.

The food was excellent. Madame Simenon had obviously gone to town on the menu, wanting to please her. The hors d'oeuvres were delicious, the roast lamb and slightly undercooked vegetables, a delight: the blackberry fool a melt-in-the-mouth concoction. And yet, the excellence of the meal failed to please Clive who picked and poked at each dish in turn, and turned a deaf ear to his sister's attempts at conversation.

Over coffee in the drawing room, Sophia said quietly, 'I came as quickly as I could. Now you appear to have nothing to say to me.'

Jerkily, Clive set down his cup and saucer. 'Not now, Sophia, it is too late, and I am far too tired.'

'Stuff and nonsense! It is barely ten o'clock,' Sophia said briskly. 'It's about Madeleine, isn't it?' she persisted. 'Oh, for God's sake, Clive, stop hiding your head in the sand! You said you wanted to talk to me. I'm here. So why prevaricate?'

'Very well, then, it *is* about Madeleine.' Clive's voice roughened. 'The thought that she may have been unfaithful to me is driving me insane!'

Sophia's brain clamoured a warning.

'You were close to her,' Clive continued hoarsely. 'You know the truth, don't you? Now you must tell me what she told you!'

Firming her lips, despite the thudding of her heart, Sophia said calmly, 'You are wrong, Clive. Madeleine told me nothing of her past life, her personal affairs. Why should she? There was nothing to tell. She was your wife, for God's sake. She bore you a son. Now she is dead. Knowing her as well as I did, I am certain that she was never unfaithful to you at any time after your marriage.'

'But before our marriage? What of that? Was the child Madeleine gave birth to really my son? Or was she already pregnant when she married me?'

Sophia said carefully, 'Madeleine was much younger than you, very beautiful; attractive to other men. But there is no proof whatever that she was unfaithful either before or after your marriage.'

'But there *was* someone,' Clive said bitterly, 'someone who gave her a diamond and sapphire brooch, whose name she would not reveal. When I asked her, she laughed and said it came from a secret admirer.'

'Is that all?' Sophia drew in a deep breath. 'For heaven's sake, Clive, that is the oldest trick in a woman's armoury. She was probably trying to make you jealous because you hadn't been paying enough attention to her. She might well have bought the brooch herself.'

'But she did not. I know, because I went through her cheque book and credit card entries,' Clive admitted.

'You did – *what?*' Rising quickly to her feet, gathering her belongings, staring at her brother, 'And I thought you to be a man of honour,' Sophia said contemptuously. Her hand on the doorknob, 'You'll tell me next that you paid a private detective to spy on Madeleine! Well, did you?'

'No, of course not! How could you believe me capable of such a thing?'

'Talk sense, Clive! You have just admitted that you spied on her in other ways.'

Opening the door for his sister, Clive said stiffly, 'I'm sorry you think me dishonourable. I thought that you, above all people, would understand my feelings. Apparently I was wrong. Good night, Sophia. I might have known that your love for Madeleine would outweigh your loyalty to me.'

'In other words, you think I lied when I told you I knew nothing of Madeleine's past life?'

'More to the point,' Clive said coldly, 'I am quite certain that you lied.'

They breakfasted together on the terrace next morning. Delicately paring fruit with a pearl-handled knife, Clive asked his sister how she intended to pass her time in Paris, intimating, by his tone of voice, that he regretted having asked her to visit him in the first place.

Sophia said calmly, 'No need to worry your head about me, Clive. I shall not require an escort.'

'In that case, please make use of my second car, the Honda. Here are the keys. Now, if you'll excuse me, I have several important letters to write.' Pausing at the French windows, he said, 'Dinner's at seven. I'll see you then.'

Finishing her breakfast, staring at the garden where, long ago, she and Madeleine had played hide and seek with the infant Nicholas, Sophia knew that her refusal to divulge her sister-in-law's affair with Jules Dinard, had driven a further wedge between herself and her brother. But nothing on earth, whatever the cost, would make her betray the trust Madeleine had placed in her that day at Bouvrier's, when she had confessed her love for Dinard; or force her to admit that she, Sophia, believed Dinard to be the father of Madeleine's child.

Driving towards l'église St Germaine, Sophia stopped to buy an armful of white carnations and to drink a cup of coffee – that marvellously bitter-sweet stuff that only born and bred French people know how to make properly, served in thick, gold-rimmed, octagonal cups, topped with bubbles.

From her table she could see a dusty, cobbled square, shuttered houses, a row of old men dozing in the sunshine. Continuing her journey, the scent of flowers filling the car, Sophia saw the road signs – l'église St Germaine two, then one kilometre.

Drawing the car to a halt near the church gate, she walked up the path to the door. Entering the building, she laid the flowers on the pew beside her, and knelt down to pray.

How Nicholas must have hated coming to this place, living through the solemn Mass, his eyes fixed on the narrow coffin containing the shell of the woman who had been all the world to him.

A black-robed priest flitted silently from the vestry. Pausing to genuflect to the Christ figure above the altar, he noticed that the woman kneeling in the second pew was weeping.

When Sophia rose to her feet, the young priest moved forward to speak to her. '*Pardonnez, madame. Vous êtes étranger ici?*' His voice softly compassionate.

'*Oui, monsieur.*' Sophia smiled. Speaking in French, she explained that she had come to visit the grave of her sister-in-law, Madeleine Tierney.

'Ah, yes. Father Pierre has spoken of her. She came here often, before her illness, to visit him, I believe.'

'Did she?' Sophia frowned. 'I had no idea. I assumed that Madame Tierney had broken her ties with this place a long time ago, when she moved to Paris.'

'Oh no, madame. You are mistaken. Father Pierre told me that she came here often, accompanied by an old friend of the family. A man whose name I cannot remember.'

'A Monsieur Jules Dinard, perhaps?' Sophia suggested, her heart hammering against her ribs.

'No, I am quite certain that was not his name. Forgive me, madame, I am a comparative newcomer to this church. As a matter of fact, I arrived on the day of the funeral.' Searching his memory. 'The man whose name escapes me was elderly, very handsome, as I recall, who sat alone during Mass, and was not present at the graveside.'

The young priest continued, 'I remember wondering what had happened to him after the service. He seemed very upset when the cortège arrived. Only natural, I suppose, in the case of an old friend of the family, *n'est ce pas?*'

'Yes.'

'The strange thing is,' the priest went on, 'every day since Madame Tierney's funeral, fresh flowers have arrived to adorn her resting place.'

'Gardenias?' Sophia asked quietly.

'Yes, gardenias,' the priest replied.

Chapter Fifteen

Awaiting Michel one warm autumn morning, Nicholas looked at the sun-washed façade of the Carillon. A remarkably lovely building, it was possessed of a certain style and elegance not always evident in Victorian architecture, he thought, regarding objectively this high, wide and handsome house which had become his second home.

He particularly liked the terrace with its interspaced pots of geraniums and trailing greenery, and the magnificent conservatory with its masses of exotic blooms, which had become a special feature of the hotel.

Cleverly, Sophia had emphasized the anachronistic flavour of the Carillon without altering its essentially Victorian characteristics. And yet, a businesswoman to her fingertips, she had reacted positively to his suggestion of floodlighting the garden and the terrace, of adding an annexe with steam rooms, jacuzzis, and a beauty salon – which she had leased to a qualified beautician, Tonya Beringer, on a salary plus commission basis.

Indeed, Nicholas reflected, his aunt had seemed pleased by his interest, and had shown her appreciation in listening intently to his ideas for spotlighting the conservatory dance floor and bar; and for the wording of the new brochures advertising the Carillon as an hotel with its roots in the past, its heart in the future.

The sun warm on his face, he noticed Tonya Beringer's car enter the driveway.

Crunching the red Metro to a halt on the gravel, switching off the ignition, the girl swung her long slim legs from the driving seat and sauntered towards him, clad in the briefest of mini skirts and a black, figure-hugging sweater, a bulging shoulder-bag hitched carelessly over her left shoulder, self consciously smoothing her hair with her right hand.

Smiling widely to display her enviable teeth, giving Nicholas the full benefit of her sensuous, hip-swinging gait. 'My, you are an early bird,' she said in a pseudo-refined voice – knowing that he was usually up and about early because she had made it her business to find out.

'So are you, come to that.' Her voice grated on his nerves, and yet Nicholas returned her smile, as courtesy demanded, realizing at the same time that this meeting was no chance affair, that Tonya had arrived, in full war-paint, for the purpose of seeing him. It was all so obvious, and he had spent a lifetime running away from the obvious.

His heart ached for Madeleine, the subtle fragrance of her gardenias, a glimpse of her lovely face discerned beneath a pale pink hat brim, the warmth of her smile, the touch of her hand on his.

Glancing at his watch, 'I wonder what has happened to Michel?' Nicholas said. 'I'd better find out. If you'll excuse me.'

Staring after him as he hurried towards the back entrance of the Carillon, Tonya felt as though she had received a slap on the face. How dare he dismiss her so casually after all the time and trouble she had taken to wash her hair and apply her makeup? But perhaps it was just as well, she thought angrily. Everyone on the staff knew about Michel's preference for young, attractive men, and if Tierney was tarred with the same brush, she'd be far better off without him. And yet she could have sworn that Nicholas was perfectly – normal, and she still fancied him like hell. What girl wouldn't? He was so bloody handsome, so – macho. Or was he?

There had been some kind of fuss recently about a Spanish girl. Rumours spread like wildfire at the Carillon, which was how she had come to hear about Michel. Not that he was blatant about his affairs. Whatever he got up to in his private apartment adjoining the kitchen quarters was kept strictly under wraps, and Michel himself was not unattractive to women. Still, men of his ilk very often were. Now here she was, at a loose end, with a couple of hours to kill before her first hair appointment.

Marching back to her car, switching on the ignition, she drove, in high dudgeon, between the gateposts, as Nicholas and Michel emerged from the hotel.

Glancing into her driving mirror, so that was the way of it, she thought, putting two and two together. Those so-called 'affairs' of Tierney's – the Spanish girl, the American woman, and all the rest she had heard about – were a smokescreen to hide his true inclinations.

Thank God she had found out in time. She had more than her fair share of men friends whose sexual motives were clear cut. Even so, driving back to her flat, she smarted under Tierney's indifference.

Catching sight of the car and its occupant, Michel, in a bad temper because he was late and Nicholas had not called him sooner, wrinkled his face in disgust. 'My God, I gave you credit for a little more sense than that.'

'What do you mean?'

'The Beringer girl. She is not your type.'

'You think I don't know that?'

'Then why waste your time? What are you trying to

203

prove?' Michel, who slightly resembled Charles Aznavour, spoke English with the merest trace of an accent, although he would occasionally burst into a torrent of French when things went wrong in the kitchen.

'Prove?' Sitting at the wheel of the Hotel-Carillon-logoed van used for marketing, adjusting his seat-belt, Nicholas frowned. 'What the hell are you driving at?'

'What am I . . . ? Look, *mon ami*, and believe me, I speak as your friend, these trifling affairs of yours are the talk of the hotel. Have you no respect for your aunt's feelings, your own reputation?'

'I see,' engaging first gear, 'so you and Sophia have had your heads together?' Nicholas said scornfully. 'I might have known!' Gravel spurted beneath the tyres as he drove the van recklessly down the drive. 'You are a fine one to talk. What of *your* reputation?' Then, his anger subsiding, 'I'm sorry, Michel. Forgive me. I didn't mean to say that.'

Michel's lips curved in a clownish smile of pain laced with regret. He said quietly, 'You see, *mon ami*, how hard it is to live down one's past? But there was only one person I really loved, and he died in Paris, a long time ago.'

'I'm sorry, Michel. I am truly very sorry.' Nicholas turned the van between the gateposts on to the main road.

Michel twitched his shoulders regretfully, 'I believe you. But I cannot help thinking it is time you came to terms with yourself: your own life – the future. Time you found someone to care for. A nice sensible woman who would make you happy.'

Nicky laughed. 'Thanks for the advice, but I'm not into "sensible" women. In any case, what makes you think I'm not happy as I am?'

'I know you are not. Sophia knows it, too, and that worries her. What is it with you, Nicky? Don't you want to settle down?'

'Mind your own business! I suppose Sophia put you up to this?' Nicholas was driving even more recklessly now: too fast, the devil on his shoulder.

'No, Sophia did not, how you say, "put me up to it", I make it my business because I care for you. Oh, not in the way you may imagine.' Michel uttered a mirthless laugh. 'I know what people say about me. It is a problem I have lived with all my life. But you, *mon ami*, have no such problem to contend with. Now, for God's sake slow down, unless you wish to get to heaven in a hurry!'

Nicky eased his foot on the accelerator. He said bitterly, 'How can you be so sure – about me?' Concentrating hard on the road ahead, 'Would you believe that I have never made love to a woman in my life?'

'*Never? Mon Dieu!* No, that I cannot believe!'

'It happens to be the truth.' Keeping his eyes on the road. 'I tried once, a long time ago . . . '

'And you let one failure . . . one setback . . . No! *C'est impossible!*' Michel interrupted, 'How old were you, for God's sake? Fourteen, fifteen?'

'Eighteen, as a matter of fact.'

'And how old was the girl? Fifteen? Sixteen? And where did this attempted seduction take place, in a haystack?'

'No, Michel, not in a haystack. And she was not a girl but a woman, an actress, thirty-five, maybe even forty. I didn't even care how old at the time. I simply . . . '

'Ah, now I see. Now I understand.' Michel nodded. 'She make you feel small, *n'est ce pas?* She humiliate you? She make you afraid of women? And so you cling more

205

closely to the one woman in the world with whom you can make love with your eyes – the beautiful Madeleine. Forgive me, my friend, but is this not so?'

Carefully choosing his words, 'You seem to forget, Michel, that my mother is – dead,' Nicholas said briefly.

'Ah yes, sadly that is so, but her memory lives on in your heart, *n'est ce pas*? And nowhere can you find a woman to take her place. And so you build up the false image of yourself to cover up your loneliness and fear. You throw out the – how you say – the smokescreen to make every woman believe you are something you are not? Because, I think, the so handsome, the so proud and desirable Nicholas Tierney, cannot live with that sense of failure which is ruining his life!'

'If any other man had said that to me . . . '

'I know, *mon ami*, you would have broken his jaw, flattened his nose.' Michel smiled ruefully as Nicholas shuddered the van to a halt.

'An old friend of the family.'

Kneeling beside Madeleine's grave, Sophia saw that the gardenias placed there were indeed as white and fragrant as only freshly delivered flowers could be, with no hint of browning or staining of the delicate petals.

Sitting back on her heels, Sophia pondered the mystery of the 'old friend of the family' the young priest had mentioned. Possibly Clive would know, but she thought not. As far as she knew, Clive had not even known that Madeleine had come often to St Germaine to visit her father confessor, accompanied by that 'old friend of the family'.

Unwrapping the carnations, her eyes brimming with tears, Sophia laid them gently on the grave, overcome

206

by the thought that the mortal remains of the woman she had loved as a sister lay forever hidden from her sight.

The gravestone bearing the inscription: 'Sacred to the Memory of Madeleine Tierney', gave no indication that this had been the titled wife of a former ambassador, the mother of a beloved son. Just as though Madeleine's life had counted for nothing from the moment the first spadeful of earth had rattled on to her coffin.

But at least someone had loved, and still daily remembered her, and Sophia intended to discover the name of that person.

When Sarah's cheque arrived, she held it as though it might self-destruct like one of those tapes in a spy movie. At the building society, she almost regretted handing it over the counter – rather like giving up a newborn child for adoption, she thought wryly. Then, withdrawing fifty pounds, all that remained of her former bank balance, she felt weak at the knees realizing how close she had come to losing her battle for survival.

The little wad of notes felt warm and comfortable tucked inside a zipped pocket of her shoulder bag. First she treated herself to a pot of coffee at Betty's, and sat near a sun-warmed window looking at the passers-by, dreamily happy and content, planning what she would do with her newly acquired wealth.

Flowers, she decided. She would treat herself to a dazzling bouquet of carnations and long-stemmed roses. And beef. Hmmm, yes, a sizeable joint of topside; purple sprouting broccoli, courgettes, a bottle of Vacqueyras Dom de la Fourmone; invite Ralph and Helen to dinner at her flat. Possibly Philippa, too, and Alec.

But no, better not. Helen had told her that Alec was still in love with Pippa. How Philippa felt about Alec, Sarah had no idea – she had never broached the subject, had not even mentioned that she and Helen were friends. Also, of course, it would be impossible to get Alec's wheelchair up that curving staircase to her flat.

In a relaxed frame of mind, playing with ideas, it occurred to Sarah that she might book a table for the four of them at the Carillon. The possession of money imparted a certain recklessness to one's way of thinking. How curious. She had never felt this way when she was married to Faulkner. But a subtle difference lay in spending one's own money and someone else's. She might have felt differently had she contributed to Faulkner's success following his first extra-marital relationship, but she knew she had not. Wrongly, perhaps, she had entered the enclosed world of her imagination as a veiled protest against Faulkner's betrayal.

For the first time since the divorce, Sarah felt herself to be a person in her own right, capable of standing on her own two feet.

Her happy stream of consciousness continued. Shored up by the thought of her nine thousand pound bank balance, the nine thousand still due to her, plus royalties, Sarah began thinking in terms of buying a car – a red Mini. Why not? Why hadn't she thought of this before? With autumn on the way, the countryside would look its best.

Sipping her coffee, she thought of a September tide of trees awash with golden leaves, the delight of setting forth, alone, on misty September mornings. 'Now, Voyager, sail thou forth to seek and find.'

Now that *Amabie* was finished and on its way to

the copy editor, she must give some thought to her next book. *Amabie* had come to her as a flash of inspiration during that memorable coach trip to Lastingham. A car might lead her to discover more tucked away village churchyards and folk museums. She must buy a map of the area. Rummaging in her bag for jotter and pencil, she started making a list which she headed: 'Transfer five thousand to Lloyds Bank. Ask for cheque book and credit card. Look at second-hand cars. Ask Ralph the name of a decent, reliable firm. Purchase road map. Write Mr Lumsden. Ring Mr Trumble. Write Richard and Verity. Give Philippa a month's notice. Arrange dinner at the Carillon. Buy a decent dress. Have hair cut?'

Not too sure about the latter, she underlined the question mark. So far so good – at least she had begun to think positively at last, to have faith in her own potential as a writer, but the thought of giving Philippa notice without good and sufficient reason, worried her. Still, she must be honest with the woman. Besides, she enjoyed working at the boutique and had come to value Philippa's friendship, her unorthodox outlook on life.

Finishing her coffee, Sarah paid her bill and walked along Stonegate, pausing now and then to look in the shop windows, loving the ancient buildings, hanging flower-baskets, uneven pavements, and that air of other worldliness, of old world charm and beauty held captive in Georgian doors and fanlights, worn steps, and the interiors of shops glimpsed through the bulging glass windows of a bygone age.

Suddenly, on an impulse, why ring Mr Trumble she thought, when she could just as easily see him?

The brass nameplate 'Trumble and Allpress, Estate

Agents, established 1906' glinted in the sunshine of a mellow autumn day. Climbing the stairs, Sarah recalled her initial meeting with Eustace Trumble, the way she had felt on that occasion – a plump, middle-aged woman, as poor as a church mouse, bowed down with worry, attempting to make a new life for herself in a strange city: in need of a home. And what must poor Mr Trumble have thought of her when she had walked into his office to impart the information that she, a writer of historical novels, wanted a self-contained flat, in a Georgian house, to rent? Then, when he had found her the flat she had longed for, she'd had the cheek to tell him that she couldn't really afford it.

Mr Trumble's pleasant-faced secretary was still in attendance. 'Ah, Mrs Vale,' she said, smiling. 'Mr Trumble is free at the moment, if you'd care to go through to his office.'

'My dear Mrs Vale,' Trumble rose to his feet as she entered, 'how nice it is to see you again! Please sit down. There's nothing wrong, I hope.'

'No, not at all.'

'You do – like – the flat?'

'I adore the flat, Mr Trumble. In fact . . . ' The thought came to her as a flash of inspiration, clear cut and decisive. 'I should like to pay a year's rent in advance, if that is agreeable to you, and the Archaeological Trust.'

Thinking about it afterwards, Sarah realized that securing a roof over her head meant more to her than any amount of pipe-dreams, that nothing else, weighed in the balance against security of tenure, mattered a damn. She could do without a car, if necessary, without a new dress, flowers, a joint of beef. She could not do without her home.

Philippa's eyebrows almost disappeared into her fringe of dyed red hair. 'So, you've made it at last, have you?' she said, lighting a cigarette. 'Well, congratulations! Now, I suppose that I had better place an ad in the local paper for a new assistant?'

'You're angry, aren't you?' Sarah asked, pouring the mid-morning coffee. 'You feel I'm letting you down?'

'No.' Puffing hard on her cigarette, 'it's just that I have got used to having you around,' Philippa admitted, 'and I can't imagine what the hell I'll do without you.'

'But we'll still be friends?'

'If you believe that, you are more naive than I thought,' Pippa said ascerbically, pulling a face at the lack of sugar in her cup of coffee. 'Oh sure, you'll pop in now and then, *en passant*, to see how the "old bat" is doing, but we won't be close any more.'

'That's nonsense! You could always invite me round for a snappy game of Trivial Pursuit.' Sarah smiled. 'Or we might go to the theatre occasionally.'

'You've begun to change already,' Philippa remarked.

'In what way?'

'You are too bloody self confident, for one thing.'

'I thought you wanted me to change. Here, have some sugar.' Taking the bull by the horns. 'By the way, do you remember Alec Grayson?'

'Alec?' Philippa looked startled. 'Of course I do. Why? Don't tell me you're interested in him?'

'I've never met him, but I know his sister quite well.'

'Helen? The unimpeachable Helen!'

'That's unfair. She's a very nice person.'

'That's what unimpeachable means, isn't it? Like Caesar's wife, above reproach? And I suppose the "nice"

Helen couldn't wait to tell you that I jilted Alec on the eve of our wedding? Well, why shouldn't she? It's perfectly true.' Phillipa laughed briefly. 'I wasn't an "old bat" then; quite attractive, as a matter of fact.

'Alec and Roy were in the Army together. Friends, though I can't think why. They were as different as chalk and cheese. Exact opposites. Alec wanted commitment, a home, children.'

'And you didn't?'

'No. What I wanted was love, excitement. Sex. Roy offered me everything I wanted on a plate. Now you know what a rotten old tart I really am!'

'Go on,' Sarah said quietly.

'You really want to know?' Philippa frowned, lighting a fresh cigarette. 'All right, then, it was love at first sight. Roy swept me off my feet. I knew, the first time he danced with me, that I wanted him in a way I had never wanted Alec, that he wanted me, too. How can I explain? Alec made me feel old before my time. He was so bloody considerate, forever calling me "dear", offering his arm, helping me down steps. With Roy I felt alive, young, that life was a great, shining adventure waiting to be lived.'

A customer entered the shop at that moment, a small, fluttery woman who bought two greetings cards, a lavender sachet, and a linen tea towel.

'Want to hear the rest of the story?' Philippa said, when the woman had fluttered off with her purchases. 'It's a bit of an anticlimax, really. The story of two people who, when the sexual aspect of the marriage had worn thin, grew to dislike each other intensely.

'When Roy left the Army – long before Alec, I imagine – we bought a bungalow on the outskirts of

York – a place called Acomb, and he landed himself a job as the sales director of a local motor-car company. You know the kind of setup? "We offer the best trade-in prices". By which time he had started niggling on about a family, wanting me to get pregnant. God, it was all so bloody boring, that flaming bungalow, me stuck at home all day. All I needed was a bawling infant and a line of wet washing strung out to dry, I don't think!

'That's when he swanned off with a feisty red-head with two illegitimate children by a former lover. Roy always did have a penchant for redheads!'

'Oh, Philippa, I'm so sorry.'

'No need, I assure you. The last thing I want is pity. After the divorce, I sold the bungalow, took my share of the profit, mortgaged this property, borrowed money from the bank to purchase the stock and fittings, and settled down to earn my own living. Even so,' Philippa sighed, 'I can't help wondering . . . regretting having treated Alec so badly. How is he, by the way? Do you know? I often wish I could see him again, tell him how sorry I am . . . '

Catching sight of herself in a gilt-framed mirror, Philippa remembered when her hair had been naturally red, the colour of autumn leaves, her complexion clear and bright, devoid of heavy makeup.

What had happened to change a young girl into an old harridan? Life, she supposed. Life had happened. Life, the old artificer who knew no pity when it came to turning young flesh into old, dreams to ashes.

Sarah met Helen, as usual, the following Thursday, eager to impart the good news of her cheque, to watch the effect of this latest development on her friend's face.

These weekly meetings had become equally important

to both women. When Helen had done what she termed the 'heavy' shopping, she would leave her Volkswagen Estate in the supermarket car-park, and walk to Davygate to meet Sarah.

Caring for Alec had meant the curtailment of former social activities, to some extent. Not that she minded. Helen enjoyed her brother's company. On warm summer evenings she would work about the garden while he read, or tackled a crossword puzzle. Occasionally, an ex-Army friend of his would come round for a drink and a chat, and Helen would go indoors to bake a few scones or get on with some ironing. Above all, she wished to provide companionship for Alec when she came home in the evening, to make up to him in some small way for the war-time incident which had ruined his life. Now, Sarah's friendship meant a great deal to her – a woman on her own wavelength in whom she could confide.

'Oh, how splendid!' Helen's face glowed when Sarah told her that the long-awaited cheque had, at last, arrived. 'Let's have some wine to celebrate!'

Sarah laughed. 'Why not?' She felt as if this city, a taste of success, and a friendship worth having, had wound shining ribbons of happiness about her heart.

They ordered quiche, salad, jacket potatoes, a carafe of La Flora Blanche.

'Speaking of celebration, would you and Alec be my guests for dinner one evening? I thought – the Carillon. I remembered that you had been there before, and there was no difficulty over Alec's wheelchair.'

'The Carillon? How marvellous,' Helen said enthusiastically. 'Of course we'd love to come. But it's frightfully expensive. Are you quite sure? Sorry, I'd forgotten that you are now a woman of means!' Her eyes twinkled.

'Wait till I tell Alec! He's dying to meet you. I just hope to goodness his dinner jacket fits him. If not, I'll make him buy a new one in honour of the occasion.'

'I'm inviting Ralph Foster, too,' Sarah said, sipping her wine, 'to make up a foursome.' She added, hesitantly, 'I had thought of inviting Philippa, as well, but that could be embarrassing for Alec. I told her we were friends, by the way.'

'Oh? What did she say?'

'She regrets having treated Alec so badly. The truth is, I feel sorry for Philippa. There's a great deal of loneliness and doubt beneath that brash exterior of hers.'

'Did you tell her about Alec? About the – accident?'

'No, and I haven't mentioned the dinner party. I felt I must ask you first. Possibly Alec wouldn't want to see her again after all this time.'

Helen wondered how Alec would react to the idea of meeting Pippa after so many years. Strange that two people, living in the same city, had not come together again if that was what they wanted. Was it a matter of stiff-necked pride that Pippa had never contacted her brother, and vice versa?

Raising her glass, Helen said, 'Here's to *Amabie*, to the future.'

'To the future,' Sarah echoed, tilting her glass.

She felt physically sick as the hairdresser's scissors snipped purposefully into her mass of hair. The man, young and confident, appeared not to have heard when she begged him not to cut it too short. An hour later Sarah emerged from the salon feeling like a flower show chrysanthemum, her hair a mass of upturned petals on the stalk of her vulnerably exposed neck.

215

The flame-coloured silk creation swirled gracefully about her legs as Sarah turned this and that way in front of the dressing-room mirrors. Startled, she saw as a stranger the slim reflection looking back at her, the slimmer waistline, uplifted breasts, and slender thighs of someone who could not possibly be herself.

The saleslady appeared enchanted. 'That is perfect, and the colour's exactly right for you. Now, would you like to try on the jacket?'

Might as well go the whole hog, Sarah thought, remembering Philippa's advice about a suit and high-heeled shoes. She must be mad, but she loved the feeling that she could afford some decent clothes for a change, that she had no reason to feel ashamed of her figure: astonished that she had lost so much weight without really trying. But this was just the beginning . . .

As long as I don't lose sight of myself, the real Sarah Vale, she thought, lying prone on the beauty specialist's couch, her face smothered in a clay mask. But what was so special about the old Sarah Vale whose life had been laced with failure and regret?

And yet there came a time in every woman's life when she must decide for herself whether or not to cling to the remnants of a disappointing past or go forward, with all flags flying, into a hopeful future.

Her relationship with her children having reached an impasse, what had she got to lose in creating a new image? Time to stop being conciliatory, she persuaded herself. She had tried, in vain, to heal the breach between herself and Verity in particular. The time had come to tell them, 'This is the way I am now. A person in my own right. Like me or lump me. The choice is yours.'

There had been something symbolic, she thought, in ceremoniously dumping, in a City of York litter-bin, a carrier-bag containing a pair of slacks, a shapeless sweater, and her old, bulging sandals; in leaving, on the floor of the hairdressing salon, those long strands of hair.

Returning home, Sarah hurried upstairs, not wanting to bump into Ralph before she had had time to get used to her new image, her smartly tailored grey suit, high-heeled court shoes, chrysanthemum hairstyle, and skilfully made-up face.

Hurrying through to the bedroom, dumping her collection of carrier-bags and parcels on the bed, she felt like a child on Christmas morning, opening each one; thrilling anew to the flame silk dinner dress and jacket, the various skirts, cashmere sweaters, gold sandals, the soft leather walking shoes, silk scarves and accessories, the potions, powder, lipsticks, and eyeshadows she had purchased with her Lloyd's cheque card.

How much she had spent on this, her first ever shopping spree, she dare not think, but catching sight of herself in the dressing table mirror, she realized that every penny had been wisely spent. The old, shapeless mess that had been Sarah Vale was gone for ever. A mysterious, yet undeniably more attractive, woman had taken her place.

When the phone rang, Sarah walked through to the other room to answer the call, moving unhurriedly, imbued with a new, exciting sense of style and self-containment.

It was Helen, ringing to say that Alec had raised no objection to meeting Pippa. Indeed, he appeared to be looking forward to seeing her again.

'I'm glad,' Sarah said quietly, 'but Pippa may turn down the invitation. You will warn Alec of that possibility?'

'Is anything the matter?' Helen asked uncertainly. 'You sound – different.'

Sarah laughed. 'I *feel* different! Helen, I've had my hair cut; bought lots of new clothes!'

'That's wonderful – unless you regret the rape of the locks?'

'No, I don't think so.'

'You don't sound too sure.'

'It came as a bit of a shock, that's all, seeing myself as a giraffe-necked woman.'

Helen said, 'By the way, do you mind if we cancel lunch on Thursday? I've booked a hairdo at twelve-thirty. The only time my girl could fit me in.'

'No, of course not. We'll meet at the Carillon, then, at seven-thirty on Friday?'

Minutes later, the phone rang again. This time Freya was on the line, sounding breathless, as if she had been running in the London Marathon.

'Darling,' she enthused, 'your interim cheque has just arrived, but that isn't all! Foremost have sold the paperback rights in *Amabie* for fifteen thousand pounds!'

'Freya, that's – marvellous!'

'Isn't it just? But there's more to come! They have also sold the hardback version to the Americans! There's even talk of a film option, but don't bank on that just yet. The thing is, you are about to become a very rich lady indeed!' A pause, then a worried, 'Sarah, are you there?'

At that moment, Sarah had no idea where she was, on her head or her heels. 'I'm here,' she murmured.

'Oh, good. I thought you'd fainted! Now, listen, darling, if you can come up with a great idea for your next book, and if *Amabie* lives up to expectation, I might just pin down Foremost to an even higher advance next time!' She added anxiously, 'You *are* thinking in terms of another book?'

'Well, yes. But I've scarcely had time to draw breath yet. Unfortunately ideas don't grow on trees.'

'This I know and understand, believe me.' Freya sighed. 'There's nothing tougher than writing a successful follow up novel; proving you're not just a one-off author. Sorry, darling, I'm not being bitchy about your first four books, but *Amabie*'s the front-runner.' A pause, 'I suppose you couldn't write a sequel, *Son of Amabie*?'

'No, I don't think so. I'm sorry, Freya, I do need a little more time . . . '

'Of course you do! I'm not pressuring you,' Freya said apologetically. 'Why don't you take a break? Go away on holiday? Give the old brain cells a rest?'

'I'll think about it.'

'Great! I have faith in you, Sarah. I know you'll come up with something brilliant. Well, 'bye for now. I'll mail your cheque first thing tomorrow.'

'Goodbye, Freya – and thank you for all you've done for me.'

When she had rung off, Sarah stood quietly near the window for a little while. Freya's words, 'You are about to become a very rich lady' she found disturbing rather than comforting. Money, she knew to her cost, was no guarantee of happiness, not if it changed people beyond recognition, as it had changed Faulkner and, to some extent, her children.

Forcibly the thought struck her that she, too, had begun to change so far as her personal appearance was concerned. Was this simply the beginning of more radical changes in her lifestyle, her way of thinking? Already the pressures of hard work and worry had taken their toll of her peace of mind. How would she cope with the pressure of finding a theme for a new novel? And would her writing, robbed of spontaneity, suffer as a result of that pressure?

Leaving the flat, she crossed the road and entered the Minster, in search of the peace of mind she hungered for. More importantly, a sense of balance, a return to the simple beliefs of childhood; that 'still, small voice' of reason and comfort in danger of being lost, forgotten, or ignored in the mounting pressures of her life.

How strange she thought, hearing the curious echo of her own footsteps on the stone floor of the Minster, that however large or small the church may be, the atmosphere was the same; the fragrance of flowers and burning candles; the rich colours of the stained glass, the aura of peace, of stillness, the common denominators which linked this mighty building to the little Norman church down a country lane in Gloucestershire.

Raising her eyes to the glory of the Rose Window, she prayed inwardly that the kernel of love buried deep within her would not wither and die for want of love, and knew how deeply she regretted the loss of love from her life, how much she needed to love and to be loved in return. That money, success, even failure, mattered not at all, compared with the overwhelming power of love.

Chapter Sixteen

Sophia moved forward, smiling, to meet Father Pierre, frail-looking, with white hair, whose hand rested on an ebony walking stick.

'Thank you for seeing me, Father,' she said, as he led the way to his study and invited her to sit down. 'The reason for my visit . . . '

'There is no need to explain. Father Dominic told me. You came to visit Madame Tierney's grave. Also, I think, you expressed interest in learning the identity of a certain friend of the Alberge family who attended the funeral. May I ask why?'

The priest's study felt cold, despite the warmth of the day; it smelled faintly of incense and decay.

'The truth is, I loved Madeleine, but I knew next to nothing about her past life. I was not even aware of her maiden name, Alberge, until you mentioned it.'

The priest's lips parted in a thin smile, 'But surely, there is no mystery about that? Madeleine's husband could have told you?'

'The subject has never arisen.' Sophia felt intensely uncomfortable, aware of the man's air of veiled hostility. 'Living in England, I . . . '

Interrupting her sentence, 'Has it occurred to you that the dead should rest in peace?'

Meeting his eyes, 'Unfortunately, it is often the living who cannot rest.'

Father Pierre sighed deeply. Turning his eyes away, 'You speak in riddles. I do not understand what you want of me. I take it that you are not a Catholic? If you were, you would know that I cannot divulge secrets of the confessional.'

'I never meant you to do so.' Sophia's discomfort mounted, and so did her irritation. 'I am well aware of the duties of your calling. I simply had not imagined that the identity of a friend of my sister-in-law would come under the seal of the confessional. But no matter, I am sorry for having wasted your valuable time.'

Rising to her feet Sophia knew that to attempt further conversation would prove both useless and humiliating.

'Good day, Father.' With a brief nod, she took her leave of him.

Crossing the hall, she heard footsteps. The old servant who had let her in shuffled towards her, a warning finger raised to her lips. 'I could not help overhearing,' she whispered, glancing nervously towards the study door. 'The man you are looking for is le Comte de Vigny. The Château de Vigny lies five kilometres from here. Go now, quickly. I liked Madame Tierney. She was good to me.' She added, 'Father Pierre will warn M. le Comte of your visit. He is cunning, that one, like a fox. I should know. I have been with him a long time. Too long.'

The château stood on rising ground, the roof visible above plantations of trees.

Driving the Honda along a dusty approach road, between banks of rhododendrons, Sophia noticed that the sky had darkened, as though a storm was brewing. Getting out of the car to drag open an iron gate barring the entrance to a more recognizable driveway, she heard a low growl of thunder, felt the first spots of rain on her face.

The drive wound on beneath overhanging trees. The rain was coming down more heavily now, to the background accompaniment of thunder and jagged flashes of lightning. Suddenly, the house became visible; the drive widened to a sweep of gravel bordered with lawns of roughly mown grass and neglected flowerbeds.

Switching off the ignition, Sophia got out of the car and hurried up the steps to the entrance. Tugging the iron bell-pull, she wished that she had brought an umbrella.

Awaiting an answer to her summons, she noticed that the cracked paving stones of the terrace were littered with fallen leaves, the windows grimed over with an accumulation of dust and dirt, the shutters as bleached as dry bones. The bell had pealed eerily, like a death knell. Cold and shivering, Sophia wished that she had let well enough alone, that she had not come to this isolated and disturbing place.

The door was opened by a woman of peasant stock, unsmiling, with a lined face and work-roughened hands, wearing a black, high-collared dress, and an apron. 'You should not have come,' the woman said hoarsely, 'Maria should not have sent you.'

'You were expecting me, then?'

The woman regarded her coldly, 'M. le Comte is resting. He does not welcome visitors.'

'Thank you, Clothilde, that will be all. Please set another place at table. I take it that you will accept my luncheon invitation, Mademoiselle Tierney?'

The man who came forward to greet her was tall, with a mane of white hair swept back from a high forehead and a lean, ascetic face, with piercingly dark brown eyes, who,

223

taking her hand in his, briefly, charmingly, touched her fingertips with his lips. 'And so, Sophia, we meet at last,' he said, in English, speaking the language as fluently as Sophia spoke French, with the merest trace of a foreign accent. 'I offer my apologies for my housekeeper's lack of tact. She does tend to treat me as a recluse at times.' He smiled. 'I am Charles de Vigny. Welcome to my home. Shall we go through to the drawing room? Perhaps you would care for a glass of sherry before luncheon?'

Crossing the hall, Sophia noticed that the walls were hung with family portraits, weaponry, and faded tapestries. Bemusedly, she entered the drawing room with its elaborately carved Italian marble fireplace, in the grate of which smouldered a fire smelling faintly of apple boughs.

Holding her hands to the warmth of the fire, she shivered slightly in her damp clothes, tensed her shoulders as a jagged flash of lightning lit up the room, saw that the windows overlooking the neglected terrace were streaming with rivulets of rain. Perhaps the sherry, offered by her host, would warm her.

De Vigny said, 'Madeleine was very fond of you. She spoke of you often, with great affection, I should not, otherwise, have welcomed your visit.'

Taking a calculated risk, Sophia said quietly, 'Thank you for the gardenias. She wore gardenias the first time we met, at the dinner party to mark her engagement to my brother.'

Charles de Vigny said slowly, 'She also wore them at her first communion. She was just fourteen at the time.'

'Father Dominic told me that you were an old friend of the family.'

'Yes, we were friends, also neighbours, before the

Alberges moved to Paris. Madeleine's father, Paul Alberge, an artist by profession, opened a gallery in the Place l'Opéra. Not a wise move on his part, I'm afraid, but his wife, Arlette, disliked living in the country. I can understand why. She was a beautiful woman, strong willed and ambitious, with a growing daughter whom she wished to marry off as quickly as possible.'

Sophia frowned. 'Marry off? Surely not? I imagined that most mothers would wish to do the exact opposite.'

'Arlette Alberge bore no resemblance to "most mothers", I assure you. She was a neurotic woman, intensely jealous, who wanted always to be the centre of attention.'

'You mean she was jealous of her own daughter?'

'That is putting it mildly. Madeleine, at eighteen, was springtime personified, the most beautiful . . . ' De Vigny's eyes kindled with remembrance. 'Forgive me, I . . . ' He seemed lost for words. 'I could not believe it when I knew that Madeleine had become engaged to a man old enough to be her father – Philippe Joubert – the husband Arlette had chosen for her.'

The housekeeper entered the room at that moment. 'Luncheon is served,' she said stolidly, casting a stony glance at Sophia.

'Thank you, Clothilde.'

The dining room was cold and rain hammered against the windows. When they were seated at the long table, Clothilde brought in bowls of broth, and warm bread rolls. 'This is very good,' Sophia said appreciatively.

'I'm glad you approve.' De Vigny smiled, pouring the wine. 'Tell me, Sophia, why did you really come here?'

Startled, she said, 'Apart from wanting to visit Madeleine's grave, my brother needed me.'

225

'Really?' De Vigny raised his eyebrows in surprise. 'I imagined that the estimable Sir Clive Tierney stood as the Rock of Gibraltar, in need of no one.'

'Did Madeleine tell you that?'

'Of course. I was her confidant, her friend. If she could not come to visit me, she would write letters. Her "outpourings" she called them. She had a way with words. Her thumb-nail sketches of embassy life made fascinating reading: the balls, the parties, the receptions, the clothes she wore. I knew every detail of her wardrobe, her jewels . . .'

'Then I imagine you know who gave her a sapphire and diamond brooch in the shape of a star?' Sophia asked intently. 'Was it Jules Dinard?' A jagged flash of lightning lit the room.

'No, not Dinard.'

'Who, then?'

De Vigny said quietly, 'I gave Madeleine that brooch.' '*You?*'

Clothilde clumped into the room just then to clear away the soup plates and bring in the chicken pot-au-feu, which she served in haughty silence, disapproving of the stranger at her employer's table.

When she had gone, de Vigny said, 'I can see that you are shocked. But hasn't it occurred to you that, despite your love for Madeleine, you scarcely knew her at all? Love, after all, is blind at times. Totally misleading.'

'So it would seem.' Clenching her hands to keep them from shaking, 'I can see one thing quite clearly however, that I made a mistake in coming here today. Now, if you'll excuse me . . . ' Sophia rose to her feet.

'No. Please sit down.' De Vigny spoke softly, tilting his head in a way which reminded her of someone else.

But the fleeting moment of half recognition was gone before she could fully capture its significance. 'I did not intend to shock you. Nor did I mean to imply that your love of Madeleine was not reciprocated. You must believe me when I say that she cared a great deal about you.'

As Sophia sank back in her chair, 'You see, she was a child at heart, and remained so until her dying day,' de Vigny said softly, staring into the past. 'Her first husband, Philippe Joubert, regarded her as a kind of ornament, a possession, something he had bought and paid for, to be displayed alongside his fine pictures, his collection of Chinese jade and eighteenth-century porcelain. But he never really loved her as she deserved to be loved.'

He continued, 'The Joubert house in Paris was a showplace, never a home. Of course, Madeleine possessed everything that money could buy, lovely clothes, fantastic jewels. Everything except – love. Soon she discovered that she meant less to her husband than his string of racehorses, his yacht, his business enterprises, his latest mistress. Need I continue? I have no wish to burden you with unwelcome knowledge, merely to explain why, after Joubert's death, Madeleine turned to Jules Dinard for comfort.' He smiled sadly, 'I suppose she felt that life owed her at least a little happiness.'

Sophia's eyes filled with tears. Feeling suddenly old and tired, she said simply, 'I would have done anything in my power to help her, if only she had trusted me.'

'You did help her,' de Vigny said gently. 'You must believe that. She loved you a great deal, but there were certain facets of her life which she felt unable to divulge to anyone apart from myself and her Father Confessor, Pierre Goudot: her feelings, for instance, when her mother, Arlette, died in a hospital for the mentally deranged, five years after the death of her father, Paul Alberge. Poor Madeleine, how deeply she suffered.'

Now the storm was directly overhead, echoing the tumult of Sophia's quickly beating heart. She said, when the thunder had died away, 'The question remains. Why did Madeleine marry my brother? Obviously, she was not in love with him.'

Fingering the stem of his wineglass, 'What does he believe?' de Vigny asked.

'That Nicholas is not his son! You know the truth about that, don't you? You say she confided in you, therefore she must have told you.'

'Perhaps I do. But what is the point of raking over the past? Madeleine is dead. So far as I am concerned, her secrets died with her.' Again that half familiar turn of the head.

My God, Sophia thought, even the long curve of the cheekbones were the same, the mobile mouth, the expression of the eyes. How could she have been so blind? She was looking at Nicky's face as it might be in years to come, when age had deepened the lines about his eyes and lips and his mane of dark hair had turned white. 'Tell me, M. le Comte,' she said slowly, 'why did you leave the church so suddenly at Madeleine's funeral? Was it because you could not bear to look at your son?'

Briefly, de Vigny covered his face with his hands. 'It's true, isn't it? You *are* Nicky's father?' Sophia said harshly. 'Well, why don't you look at me? Or are you too ashamed? Christ almighty, if you cared for Madeleine, why the hell didn't you marry her? How could you have simply stood by when she married first

Joubert then my brother? You were a rich man, a friend of the family . . . '

Uncovering his face, de Vigny said simply, 'I was also a priest. Now do you understand?'

Shocked beyond belief, Sophia's mind raced with the implication of his words, the horror of his betrayal.

As if he knew what she was thinking, he said in a low voice, 'There could be no question of marriage between us in the beginning. We were both very young. I had entered the priesthood at my father's request. My elder brother, François, was alive then. It was he who would inherit the title, the land, this house. I cared nothing for that. I loved my brother, respected my father.'

He bowed his head, pushing back his hair with long, sensitive fingers, in the grip of an almost unbearable emotion. 'I had always loved Madeleine, and so there was always an inner turmoil between love and duty. How can I possibly explain? I can see now that I should have gone against my father's wishes. If only it had been that simple.' His mouth twisted suddenly with the pain of recollection. 'We had always been a devoutly Catholic family. My father was not a strong man, in no way dictatorial, but kind and gentle. Had he been otherwise, I might have taken pleasure in defiance. The fact remains that I did as he wished. Call me foolish, weak, a coward, if you like. But when I knew that Madeleine had married Philippe Joubert, my feelings convinced me that I had no right whatever to call myself a man of God.'

'Go on,' Sophia said hoarsely.

Clasping his hands, elbows resting on the table, de Vigny continued, 'What happened between Madeleine and me came later, much later, after the deaths of Joubert, my father, and my brother, when I had been granted leave to settle affairs here. That is when Madeleine came to me in need of help.' His voice broke suddenly with emotion. 'The physical expression of my love for her was inevitable. You see, I cared for her more deeply than my conscience, even the vows I had made before God. More than life itself!'

A flash of lightning lit up the room as de Vigny's clenched hands crashed down on the table in a futile gesture of despair. 'You want me to go on? Very well, then. When I knew that Madeleine was going to have a child – our child – I begged her to marry me, to wait until I had been granted dispensation from my vows.'

'Vows which you had already dishonoured,' Sophia said in a voice which seemed scarcely to belong to her.

'Yes, vows which I had already dishonoured.'

'And – Madeleine?'

De Vigny said quietly, 'Madeleine refused to marry me. Nothing I could do or say would make her change her mind. Loving me as much as she did, she could not bear the thought of my disgrace. To seek dispensation from my vows was one thing, to create a scandal quite another.'

'And so she married my brother?' Sophia said bitterly. 'Married him knowing she was pregnant with another man's child. How could she have done such a thing?'

De Vigny leaned back wearily in his chair. 'But you never really believed that Nicholas was his son? Would you have been less shocked had you discovered that Dinard was the father?'

'I don't know! I don't know!' Shakily, Sophia rose to her feet. 'I need time to think!'

Feeling in her handbag for the keys of the Honda, she hurried from the room, across the hall to the front door.

Swiftly following, de Vigny called her name. 'Sophia! Wait! Before you go! Now that you know the truth, what will you do?'

Turning to face him, Sophia said angrily. 'What do you suggest I do? More to the point, what do *you* intend to do? Go on living a lie? What of your son's future? What of your own future, come to that? My God, look at this place! Have you no pride in yourself or your inheritance?' She tugged open the door to stand on the terrace, the rain mingling with her tears.

'Above all things,' de Vigny said simply, 'I cannot let you leave thinking ill of Madeleine. Had your brother been kinder, she would have told him the truth, that she was carrying another man's child. If you could read her letters to me, you would realize how deeply she suffered.

'Sophia, Madeleine *was* a child at heart. A beautiful, unsophisticated child. But surely you must have realized that? The world she inhabited was not a real world at all.'

'I don't know what you mean.'

'Then I'll tell you.' De Vigny smiled faintly, remembering Madeleine, 'The world, to her, was a fairytale place filled with the fairytale people she created from her vivid imagination to shut out the horror of her marriage to Philippe Joubert, the death of her mother in an insane asylum.'

Sophia said hoarsely, 'Are you trying to tell me that Madeleine also was insane?'

'Certainly not. She was, however, a consummately fine actress who played a lifelong role to perfection.'

De Vigny's words took Sophia's mind back in time to Bouvrier's, Madeleine's admission that she would have liked to be an actress – 'Pretending to be someone else'.

'What would you have me do?' Charles smiled sadly, 'Tell my son that the mother he adored lived a lie?'

'I don't know. I can't think straight at the moment.'

'But you will come back, Sophia, before you leave Paris? You will tell me of your decision? Try to forgive me for all the harm I've done?'

'To whom in particular?' Refusing to be swayed by his charm, his looks, his charisma, 'To Madeleine, my brother, or to your son? Unlike you, M. le Comte, I make no promises that cannot be kept.'

Chapter Seventeen

Candlelight gleamed softly on the polished dining table. Silently, Simenon served the two people seated at opposite ends of the table, thinking how different the atmosphere would be if Madame Tierney were alive to lighten the gloom with her bubbling conversation.

It seemed to the servant that the house in the Rue St Hélène had become a morgue since the death of the mistress, that perhaps Claudette was right in saying they should think of retiring from service, find a nice little apartment somewhere, and enjoy their inheritance.

Over coffee, which Simenon served in the drawing room, Sophia thought that Clive looked depressed, a little foolish, perhaps, in his formal evening dress. Irritated by his silence, his formality, she noticed the way he hitched his trousers to preserve the knife-edge creases, before lowering himself into his favourite chair.

When Simenon left the room, she watched the play of firelight on her brother's face, and wondered, as she had often done before, if it was really possible that they had been born of the same mother within twenty minutes of each other: experienced a sudden stab of regret that even when her sibling had turned to her in extremis, she had found nothing comforting to say to him, had, on the contrary, turned on him bitterly, contemptuously, when he confessed to having scrutinized Madeleine's bank statements and credit card entries.

Pouring the coffee, Sophia nursed the secret of her visit to the Château de Vigny, her encounter with le Comte de Vigny. The bitterest blow of all, that Madeleine, whom she had loved, had lived a secret life all her own – remorse and guilt kept hidden behind a smiling façade, a charming, light-hearted persona – and had seldom betrayed, by a word or a glance, the bewildering complexity of her innermost thoughts and emotions.

Leaning forward to receive the cup of coffee Sophia had poured for him, Clive asked her what she had done with her day. Not really interested, speaking to break the drawn out silence between them.

'I drove to St Germaine,' Sophia told him.

Clive's eyelids flickered. 'Were you caught in the storm?'

'No, I was lunching with someone at the time. A Comte Charles de Vigny.'

Clive arched his eyebrows. 'A friend of yours?'

'No. We had never met before.'

Clive said pompously, 'Wasn't that a trifle foolish? Lunching with a stranger?'

'Perhaps,' Sophia conceded, 'but he was very charming, and quite informative. He knew Madeleine as a girl. I wonder you've never heard of him. Didn't Madeleine ever mention his name?'

'No,' Clive said stiffly, 'Madeleine preferred not to talk about her past life.'

'Why not?'

'Really, Sophia!' He rattled down his cup and saucer, annoyed by her questions. 'Madeleine preferred not to dwell on the past, and I respected her wishes.'

'Tell me, Clive,' Sophia said, ignoring the danger signals, 'when you married Madeleine, were you in love with her?'

During the long silence that ensued, Sophia saw reflected in her brother's face a silently fought battle of emotion which touched her deeply. Poor Clive, she thought, how involved his emotions must be that a comparatively simple question could not be answered with an equally simple yes or no.

He said at last, as though the reply had been torn from the depths of his soul, 'I worshipped the ground she walked on.'

'Oh, my dear.' Leaning forward, she clasped his hand, feeling closer to him than she had ever done before. 'And what of your son? What of Nicholas?'

Withdrawing his hand, ashamed of his momentary weakness, assuming his usual mask-like expression of indifference, he said coldly, 'I have no son!' His mouth worked awkwardly, the lips curving in a rictus grimace of pain, 'You know that Nicholas is not my son! Madeleine told you so herself, didn't she? *Didn't* she? I want the truth, Sophia!'

Rising quickly to her feet, standing proud and tall, frightened by the wild look in her brother's eyes, yet determined to speak her mind, 'And when you discover this so-called "truth" you are searching for, what then? Tell me, Clive, what is it you really want? Justification of your treatment of Nicholas, of Madeleine? Or could it be that you are seeking absolution from your own sins of omission?'

'What the hell do you mean?' Eyes blazing, standing up, Clive took a threatening step towards Sophia.

Unflinchingly, she faced her brother. 'You wanted the truth, now you shall have it.' Sophia spoke contemptuously. 'All life long, you have swept the board with your intolerance, your "holier than thou" attitude? When our parents died, did you spare a thought for their suffering? Did you stop to consider what it must have cost them to plunge that car over a cliff? No, all you thought about was yourself; how their deaths would affect your career.'

Driven by a compulsion to speak, to say that which she had kept bottled up for a long time, 'You were kind to me in asking me to share your apartment after our parents died, after the inquest and the funeral, but you offered no crumb of real comfort, we never shared our grief. Or could it be that you felt none?

'When you met and married Madeleine, I thought her influence would change your uncompromising outlook on life. I might have known better. You knew from the start that she was a devout Catholic, that she wanted her child brought up as a Catholic . . . '

'That's enough, Sophia!'

'No, it is not enough. You say you worshipped the ground she walked on, but you made damn sure that the ground she walked on was *your* ground. After all, what was so sacrosanct about your religion? All you have ever done is pay lip-service to a God of love from whose teaching you have apparently learned nothing of compassion or understanding.'

'How dare you?'

'I dare because it's the truth! Now Madeleine is dead, and you have closed your door in the face of her son . . . ' Sophia bit her lip, realizing the implication of her words.

Clive said coldly, 'Exactly. *Her* son. Not mine!'

Knowing she was wasting her breath, Sophia gathered up her evening bag, and shawl. Turning at the door, she said, 'I shall be leaving here tomorrow, quite early. With

236

your permission, I should like to borrow the Honda for a few days. I'll return the car to the garage before I leave Paris.'

Looking back on her life, Sophia thought, as much as she had enjoyed her uphill struggle to create the hotel she had dreamed of, despite all her success in the achievement of that dream, she had, perhaps, lost sight of the simple values of life – marriage and children, grandchildren playing about her skirts. Too late now. In any case, she had never met a man whom she had wished to marry, apart from Michel, who was not the marrying kind.

Michel!

She had fallen in love with him at l'école de cuisine all those years ago, then, one day, taking her hand in his, he had said gently, 'You will never get anywhere with me, you know. All I can ever hope to be is your friend.'

And so, despite her initial heartbreak, Sophia had settled for that. Friendship, when she had wanted him desperately to make love to her, when her every waking moment was filled with thoughts of Michel, despite his fiery temper, his, at times, curt dismissal of her as a stupid Englishwoman who had never learned the facts of life.

Amazingly, their friendship had endured, and Sophia knew that always – always – there would remain a kind of asexual love between them, a deep bond of mutual respect and understanding which somehow outshone physical love.

It occurred to Sophia, as she made ready for bed, that the years had pressed her into a mould, a certain way of thinking no longer valid since the death of Madeleine; her meeting with Charles de Vigny, as if the hitherto important facets of her life had suddenly dissolved like a mist on a summer morning, leaving her vulnerable, afraid, yet blessedly clear sighted.

Tomorrow, or the next day, she decided, she would drive to the Château de Vigny. She had, after all, received an invitation to return there once her mind was made up. But not until she had cast aside her black garments – the clothing of 'Latrodectus Mactans' – the black widow spider of cuisine, as one journalist had described her.

She did not want expensive clothes. Turning her back on smart wool dresses in emerald green and lilac, on neat, dressy suits à la Pierre Cardin, she chose, to the boutique owner's displeasure, simple cotton blouses and matching skirts, marked down to half price in the autumn sale, a soft wool cardigan, and a blue woollen shawl, because the colour reminded her of the Madonna's cloak in a painting by Raphael, and of the blue wool dress Madeleine had worn that day on the Louis Quinze sofa.

That same afternoon, Sophia, feeling liberated, rather like a peasant woman in her light cotton garments, legs bare, wearing espadrilles, walked down to the village of St Thérèse, her fine, greying fair hair, which she normally wore drawn back severely from her face, loose about her shoulders. Possibly she looked ridiculous, mutton dressed as lamb, but she did not care. Neither, apparently, did the people who passed her on the road; farm workers driving wagons of turnips and sugar-beet, a young mother with a baby in a pram, two older women, dressed in black, with lined faces, carrying bunches of flowers, who greeted her in passing: '*Bonjour, madame. Il fait très chaude, n'est ce pas?*'

The Carillon, Sophia thought, sitting at a table in the

small, local estaminet, drinking a glass of Chardonnay, seemed a million lightyears away, and she seemed a different person. It was then she realized, with an overwhelming clarity of vision, that she had grown weary of her old life, her old self.

Glancing down at her feet, dusty from the road, feeling the delicious coolness of a light breeze ruffling her hair from an open window, revelling in the anonymity of her new clothes, she wished she might stay here for ever – buy a small, possibly derelict farmhouse in the heart of the French countryside, a couple of acres of land on which to grow her own vegetables and keep hens – to graze, perhaps, a few mistreated donkeys and horses.

Her imagination also encompassed the restoration of that derelict farmhouse into a home far removed from the stresses and strains of everyday living, in which she might live out the rest of her days in peaceful seclusion. She was, after all, no longer young. How did the words of that song go? 'And the years dwindle down to a precious few . . .'

Arriving at the Château de Vigny, she saw a curling column of smoke rising into the air.

Parking the Honda, getting out of the car, turning a corner of the house, she saw de Vigny, clad in a pair of disreputable corduroy trousers and a crumpled blue shirt, a panama hat pulled down over his eyes, piling weeds on to a bonfire.

'What on earth are you doing?'

'What does it look like?' He pushed back the panama, and laughed.

'Burning rubbish? *You?*'

'As you see, I paid attention to your lecture on

the ethics of good husbandry.' Leaning on his rake, he said, 'Look around you, Sophia. The land as far as you can see belongs to me, as it belonged to generations of de Vignys before me.' He was speaking more seriously now, wrinkling his eyes against the glare of the sun. 'That land has been well cared for by my tenant farmers, administered by a land-agent named Colbert – an excellent man at his job, appointed by my brother François, with whose help and advice he planted the vineyards on the southern slopes, developed the trout farm in the valley, and the afforestation programme over there to the north.'

De Vigny eased his shoulder muscles. 'I am not entirely ignorant of my duties and responsibilities, although the state of the house might indicate otherwise. There were reasons why I wished it to remain as I knew it in – shall we say happier times? Call it an old man's folly if you like, an eccentricity of mine, a desire to keep sacrosanct certain memories of the past.'

'There is no need to explain.'

'I should like to, if you care to listen. My brother was engaged to marry Colbert's daughter, Louise. Had that marriage taken place, if there had been children, my own life, and Madeleine's, might have been very different.'

'What happened to prevent that marriage?' Unconsciously, Sophia had moved closer to de Vigny, wanting to hear more, beginning to see him in a different light, no longer hostile towards him.

'François and Louise were killed in a car crash on the Route Nationale,' de Vigny said simply. 'The month was August, the time of the great trek south to the Riviera. They were on their way to spend a holiday in Nice.'

'Oh, how dreadful!'

'Yes, it was. Very dreadful . . . Then I was granted

compassionate leave to settle affairs here. The rest you know.' He paused briefly, in the grip of a strong emotion, his face betraying the depth of that emotion. 'Afterwards, my one thought was to escape from the world.' A smile softened his features. 'I thought I had done just that – until . . . ' The smile deepened . . . 'until Thor, the hammer of the gods, came to exact retribution.'

'Not at all, I simply came to tell you . . . '

'Please, not now! May we leave that till later? I am so hungry I could eat a horse. Unfortunately, Clothilde sent word this morning that her husband is ill. I cannot, therefore, offer you a cooked lunch, but there's a cold chicken in the larder, and I *can* offer you a glass of wine.'

Leading the way to the kitchen, pausing on the threshold, 'By the way,' de Vigny asked, 'what happened to change the formidable "Woman in Black" into the facsimile of a French peasant? Not that I am complaining, you understand? I like your new, softer persona.' He smiled. 'You should always wear your hair that way, it suits you.'

'Here, let me!' Shrugging aside the compliments, bustling towards the pantry, bringing forth the chicken, setting it down on the table, Sophia began slicing off thick chunks of breast: making a thick white sauce to which she added grated blue cheese, herbs, and a soupçon of white wine, sleeves rolled up to her elbows, doing what came naturally, creating a Cordon Bleu dish from leftover scraps, moving easily about the kitchen, finding the ingredients she needed to complete the meal – potatoes which she quickly sautéed in piping hot fat, florets of cauliflower, finely diced carrots, and sticks of chopped celery which she flung into fast boiling water; stale breadrolls which she split, spread with butter and grated garlic, then slipped into the oven to warm.

'This is marvellous, simply glorious,' Charles said appreciatively.

'You'll be telling me next that I've missed my way, that I should have been a cook,' Sophia said sarcastically, watching the man eating the food she had prepared for him, thinking how much he had changed since their last meeting. Now he, too, looked like a peasant, and the hot sun had burned his face and hands.

'Well,' glancing at her watch.

'You are not thinking of leaving?'

'I'll see to the washing up first.' Getting up, she carried her own plate to the sink; turned on the tap.

'But I want you to stay. We have things to discuss. A room has been prepared. I asked Clothilde to make up the bed in readiness for your return.'

'Perhaps that is why she decided to keep away,' Sophia suggested, swishing suds into the water, looking out at the neglected vegetable garden.

'You haven't answered my question. Will you stay as a guest under my roof? Stay as long as you wish.'

'To cook for you?' she asked, tongue in cheek: 'Help with the garden?'

He smiled. 'If it would please you to do so, it would certainly please me to have you here.'

Glancing up at him as he came towards her carrying dishes to the sink, she saw Nicky's smile, his way of walking, proudly, gracefully, every muscle coordinated, and knew why Madeleine had loved de Vigny.

Plunging the plates into the hot water, 'I'm sorry,' Sophia said, turning her head away, 'I can't stay here. Besides, it's high time I went home, back to the Carillon.'

'Where you will slip back into your role as the "Woman in Black"?'

'But of course. I, too, have responsibilities.' Sophia spoke more sharply than she had intended.

'And yet I think that you are not averse to your role as a French peasant?'

'No. But one cannot go through life play-acting.'

De Vigny said thoughtfully, 'Has it ever occurred to you that the "Woman in Black" is the play-actor, the peasant woman the reality?'

'You don't begin to understand!' Stacking the plates on the draining board, Sophia felt suddenly irritated, at a disadvantage.

She couldn't think why. She simply wished the man a thousand miles away.

Looking at Sophia, Charles recalled the pleasure of watching her moving about the kitchen, preparing and cooking lunch: the delight of scrubbing soil from his hands at the kitchen sink; realized that seldom, if ever before, had he known the simple joy of coming indoors from hard physical labour to sprawl his aching limbs beneath a homely table, to taste wine as he had never tasted wine before – sweet and warm upon his tongue.

He said, hesitantly, 'Please, Sophia, I wish very much that you should stay on for a little while longer. If not under this roof, at a small farmhouse of mine, on the estate. No, please, I beg of you, do not refuse, do not say no until you have looked at it.'

'Very well, if you insist.'

Enchanted, Sophia saw the low, beamed ceiling of the main room, running the length of the house, a wide stone fireplace; deeply embrasured windows overlooking an orchard littered with wind-fall apples.

They had walked from the château through deep, cool woods splashed with autumn tints, to where the pantiled farmhouse roof was visible through the trees. And yet no signs of a farmyard were in evidence. De Vigny explained that his tenant farmers nowadays preferred up to date houses within easy reach of schools and hospitals, and who could blame them?

'My estate manager wanted me to bulldoze the house,' Charles said, as they entered, 'but I decided to let it to those in need of spiritual sanctuary – writers, artists, poets, or whomever.'

'I see.' A feeling of peace washed over Sophia.

'Well, what do you think?'

She knew what he meant. 'Yes, I'd like to stay here,' she said softly.

'Good. I'll telephone Colbert, ask him to see to things, send in someone to clean and dust; bring in food, clear the hearth; lay a fire. The last occupants moved out only yesterday, I believe.'

'The people who stay here, do you ever come into contact with them?' Sophia asked, as they made their way back through the woods.

'No, but that is an understood thing. These woods are private.' Charles held out his hand to help Sophia across a rough patch of ground. 'Naturally, this embargo does not apply to you.'

'I should hope not! After all, "Thor, the hammer of the gods!"' She laughed.

'That was meant as a joke.'

'I know.' She rested momentarily, her back against a tree, to regain her breath.

'I thought we might dine together this evening,' de Vigny suggested. 'I will light a fire in my sitting room.'

They ate a simple meal of bread, cheese and fruit, in the kitchen, then de Vigny led the way to the room in which they had first drunk wine together.

He had brought up champagne from the cellar, and lit a myriad candles set in silver gilt candelabrum. How different the room looked now, Sophia thought, holding her hands to the blazing log fire. De Vigny seemed different too. She had begun to glimpse the real man behind the slightly arrogant façade, a man capable of warmth and laughter, of physically hard labour, of kindness and consideration.

She thought, watching him uncork and pour the wine, how readily he had understood that she could not accept his invitation to stay at the château, and so he had offered the compromise of the farmhouse without question. *Tout comprendre c'est tout pardonner.*

At first she had made no allowance for the man's suffering, his state of mind over the mistakes and failures of the past. Yet he must have suffered deeply, as Madeleine had done.

Crossing the room, he handed Sophia a glass of champagne. 'Let us drink a toast,' he said. 'To the good things of life – acceptance of those things we cannot change, the courage to change the things we cannot accept, and the wisdom to realize the difference. Santé.'

Raising her glass in response, she said softly, 'I have reached the conclusion that the past is best buried and forgotten.'

'Thank you, Sophia.' Gratefully, Charles raised her hand to his lips.

Chapter Eighteen

Parking the Mercedes in the gravelled drive, Faulkner
Vale paused to look up at the house, disliking intensely the
montage of bay windows; mansard roof, and clinging ivy.

Now the bills had started flooding in for the altera-
tions, decoration and furnishings of what he thought of
as the 'monstrosity', Faulkner's passive acceptance of his
wife's folly had changed to sullen fury over her mindless
extravagance.

Entering the house, he flung his briefcase on the circular
hall table. The centrepiece of stuffed birds beneath domed
glass he saw as barbaric, suffocatingly ugly. Glowering at
the red-carpeted stairs complete with gimmicky brass rods,
he felt that he had strayed on to the film set of a Victorian
melodrama.

Resisting a strong urge to liberate the stuffed birds
with a blow of his fist, he padded upstairs in search
of Suki. Approaching the first landing window, looking
out at the garden, he viewed with distaste the disfigured
statuary lurking in between banks of laurel and rhododen-
dron bushes, which Suki regarded as 'quaint', Faulkner as
ridiculous.

The master bedroom contained a massive Victorian
bed, wardrobes and dressing table, a velvet-covered chaise-
longue, and bedside tables draped ankle length with
green sprigged material to match the heavily lined and
be-tasselled curtains.

The door leading to the en-suite bathroom stood open. He heard the sound of running water, and caught a whiff of expensive bath-oil. Seconds later, Suki emerged damp and warm from her ablutions, eyebrows raised when she saw him standing there. 'I didn't hear you come in,' she said, towelling her hair – as if he had no business to be there, he thought bitterly.

'I do happen to live here,' he reminded her, watching darkly as, draping herself on the dressing table stool, she began a hairbrush attack on her tangled locks.

'In one of our moods, are we?' Catching his eye through the mirror, she said, 'What is it this time? Something specific, or just another fit of the sulks?'

'Something very specific. Money!'

'Oh, *that*!' Suki looked bored.

'Money which you appear to think grows on trees.'

'And doesn't it?' Turning, she puckered her lips, pulling her little girl face which he had once found so devastating. Then, meeting his hostile stare, abandoning her playful pose, 'Oh my God, not again,' she muttered, throwing down the brush. 'Frankly, I'm getting more than a little fed up with your meanness.'

'*Meanness!*' His cheeks empurpled with rage. 'We'll see about that! I'm warning you, Suki, if this extravagance continues, I shall cancel your credit cards, and advise the bank not to honour any more of your cheques!'

Springing to her feet like a tigress. 'You wouldn't dare,' she spat at him. 'Of all the mean, contemptible tricks! Well, try that with me, and you'll end up sleeping in your study! I mean what I say.'

And this was the crux of the matter, Faulkner thought bitterly, the hold Suki had on him. Sex for money. Christ, what a fool he'd been. One wrong word, one trifling disagreement, and out into the open came the constantly wielded sword of her sexuality, the threat of her withdrawal from the marriage bed, the loss of what, in Victorian times, had been termed 'conjugal rights'. A term well in keeping with this bloody mausoleum he now inhabited, not as the master but a slave tied to his wife's insatiable appetite for money. Money to spend on clothes, when every built-in cupboard and wardrobe was already full to overflowing with her dresses, suits, shoes, hats, and furs – furs which even the richest women jibbed at wearing these days because of the cruelty connotation. Not that Suki cared a damn about that, her argument being that she had not actually shot the wretched animals herself.

Moreover, she had begun, recently, to jet to New York, Paris, or Madrid, if she felt like it, to visit her friends, leaving their child in the care of the nanny who now occupied a suite of rooms in the soundproofed nursery wing. If he raised any objection to her globe-trotting, she said sweetly, 'But, darling, I'll be back in a few days. Besides, I know the cleverest little dressmaker,' in New York, Paris, or wherever, which Faulkner knew, to his cost, to be true, when the bills for her spending sprees landed on his desk.

This time her bluff would not work. Drawing on his business acumen, seeing this marriage as a deal that had gone badly wrong, Faulkner knew he had the whip hand. His better judgement had been warped by his aberration in letting Suki twist him round her little finger, in allowing her to talk him into buying this house, in relegating his personal belongings, his Lowry paintings and the furniture from the Marlborough house to a back room because, she had explained, all that modern stuff would be out of keeping with the rest of the house. He said grimly,

'There is no question of sleeping in the study. Tonight, because I choose to do so, I shall sleep at my club. In the meanwhile, I expect you to give serious thought to your position as my wife, and your financial situation. You might also remember that I gave up a great deal to marry you . . . '

Furiously interrupting, she said, '*What* did you give up? Go on, tell me, I'd really like to know. No, don't bother. I'll tell *you* – a frump of a wife you hadn't slept with for years. I haven't forgotten, if you have, all those bloody pathetic details you told me in Paris about your private life with what's her name? Oh yes, Sarah!' Suki laughed scornfully, 'God, how you went on about her and those boring children of yours. Well, if that's what breast-feeding does . . . ' She stopped speaking abruptly, knowing she had gone too far. 'Oh, for God's sake, darling. All this because I wanted a home of our own, because I want to look nice for you . . . '

'You call this a home?' Faulkner looked with distaste at the heavy, ornate furniture, the caparisoned bedside tables, the overpowering Victorian wardrobes, and the elaborate window drapes, remembering what this room alone had cost him in terms of hard cash.

Goaded by his sarcasm, she said, 'Well, it's a damn sight better than that common or garden brick box in Marlborough where there was scarcely room to swing a cat!' Then, less forcibly, 'Faulkner, where are you going?'

'I have already told you. To my club.'

Turning away, Faulkner walked out of the room, hurried downstairs, picked up his briefcase from the hall table, and then, with malice aforethought, striking the case of stuffed birds with the flat of his hand, he heard the satisfying tinkle of broken glass as he stalked out to the car, switched on the ignition, and drove away from the house he detested, to his club in Mayfair.

The publication date of *Amabie* had been set for the third week in May, Freya told Sarah on the phone. 'That means maximum sales with summer looming on the horizon, plus the publicity campaign Foremost are planning: television appearances, broadcasts, book-signing sessions, and so on. Darling, isn't it thrilling?'

'Thrilling? It's – *horrifying*!'

'Nuts! Sit back and enjoy it! You are to receive VIP treatment, and about time too! Final details haven't been worked out yet, but there's to be a launch party at the Mayfair. Oh, by the way, is your passport up to date?'

'Passport? No, I'm afraid not.' Remembering that Faulkner had never invited her to accompany him on his trips abroad – for obvious reasons, she said, 'I let it expire some time ago. Why do you ask?'

'Because, come the summer, you'll be jetting off to New York for a series of chat-show interviews to coincide with the publication of *Amabie* in the States!' Thinking of Sarah as a fat, untidy lady, Freya paused briefly to frame her words 'Look, love, when you've applied for a new passport, why not think in terms of a really good wardrobe? I know you don't care two hoots about – dressing up, and why should you? But our American chums prefer English authors to look the part. You know, the tweed suit, sweater and pearls syndrome? But not to worry about the face and hair, they'll give you the works beforehand, and I'll be there to make sure they give you a list of likely questions before you face the cameras.'

'Is all this strictly necessary?' Sarah's heart quailed.

Freya drew in a deep breath, 'Look at it this way,'

she said persuasively, 'here is the chance to become an internationally known writer, a household name – and, God knows, you deserve that kind of success. Possibly *Amabie* is just a one-off, but I don't think so. You have great talent, Sarah.' Another deep breath. 'Heaven alone knows how you managed to make a novel about a medieval glassblower work on so many different levels, to create the greatest romantic hero since Heathcliff, those chilling St Bartholomew's Day riot scenes, and the kind of mystery reminiscent of *The Name of the Rose*, but you did it, so why not advertise the fact?'

'It's not as simple as all that,' Sarah demurred.

'All I'm saying,' Freya continued, 'if you play your cards right, one of these days you could have everything you've ever wanted – you name it. Just imagine meeting the élite of the publishing world, becoming well known.' An anxious pause. 'By the way, you *are* getting to work on your next novel? *Sarah?*'

'Well, yes and no. That is, I have the germ of an idea . . .'

'Tell me.'

'There's nothing much to tell, I'm afraid, except I've discovered there was a cholera epidemic in York . . .'

'A *cholera* epidemic!' Freya said disbelievingly. 'Sorry, darling, but are you *sure*? I mean, who the hell would want to read a book about a cholera epidemic?'

'Come to think of it, who the hell would want to read a book about a medieval glassblower?' Sarah reminded her.

Hanging up the receiver, she viewed the future with misgiving. Writing a bestselling novel was one thing, facing television cameras, jetting off to New York to come up against a barrage of questions from a string of breezy, confident chat-show hosts, quite another. She would never be able to bare her soul in public, and she knew it.

Flopping on to the rose velvet settee, she failed to imagine herself sitting at a window overlooking Central Park, lost amid a sea of skyscrapers, meeting the élite of the publishing world. In the event, what would she find to say to them?

As for the prospect of a life of luxury, she could imagine nothing more boring, more soul destroying, than sunning herself, day long, on a balcony overlooking an eternally blue sea. She was just an ordinary woman who happened to enjoy writing. And what was the use of a solo performance, with no one to share her success?

The row between Michel and his sous-chef blew up over a comparatively minor incident. Both men were quick tempered. Soon the row had escalated into a fight of savage intensity. Nicholas arrived on the scene to find them locked together like wrestlers, Michel, the slighter of the two getting the worst of the struggle. Then the sous-chef picked up a knife, and there was murder in his eyes.

'Enough!' Wrestling the potentially lethal weapon from the man's grasp, 'Now, get out before I call the police.' When he had slunk away, muttering abuse, 'Are you all right, Michel?' Nicky asked anxiously.

'Get back to work,' Michel directed the kitchen helpers who had gathered to watch the fight. Eyes blazing, he said, 'As for you, Nicholas, how dare you interfere in my kitchen?'

'For God's sake, Michel! The man was about to knife you!'

'*Merde!* Sophia would never have interfered in such a way! Now, leave me alone. I have work to do!'

'If that's your attitude!' Turning away, his own temper rising, Nicholas went upstairs to the dining room, wondering where the hell Sophia had got to. She had been away for over a week now without a word of explanation, not so much as a phone call or a letter, leaving him to cope with a series of crises which he had not known how to handle. This, the latest, was the final straw. Damn this bloody hotel!

He had better ring up Paris, find out what was going on, how much longer his aunt intended staying away. Was she doing this deliberately? Chucking him in at the deep end to find out how he would cope during her absence? But what if he couldn't get hold of Sophia? What if his father answered the phone?

The scene with Michel had undermined his self-confidence – what little he had. Michel, whom he had thought of as a friend, an ally. Badly shaken, Nicholas wondered if the staff saw him as a poor substitute for Sophia, if they were laughing at him behind his back?

The dining room was full, as usual, the hotel guests sitting there in ignorance of the kitchen drama which had taken place below stairs, that two of the chambermaids had not appeared on duty that morning, and the central heating system had gone on the blink, resulting in a series of complaints, all of which had fallen on his shoulders.

The head waiter coughed discreetly at his elbow. 'We have a party of five coming in this evening. A celebratory occasion, I believe. May I suggest table six?'

Was the man being helpful, patronizing, or impertinent? Difficult to tell. 'Yes, table six would seem all right to me,' Nicholas conceded, aware that the maître, who knew far more about seating arrangements than he did, had, most probably, already issued orders to his team of waiters. 'A celebratory occasion, you say? In that case, better send a bottle of wine to the table with the compliments of the management.'

'Of course, sir.' Another discreet cough, 'Madame Tierney usually orders a Chardonnay or Sauvignon on such occasions. Which would you prefer?'

'Neither!' To hell with all this, Nicholas decided. To hell with everything! Since he was in charge, carrying the can for Sophia, 'Let's make it a bottle of Dom Perignon, shall we?'

The surprised, slightly pained expression on the head waiter's face did him a power of good.

Applying her makeup, Sarah wondered what Ralph would say when she went downstairs to await the arrival of the taxi. Stepping into her flame silk dress, feeling the soft folds of material swirling about her legs, picking up her evening bag, it might have been kinder, she considered, if she had warned him beforehand that she had had her hair cut.

Ralph, she assumed correctly, was the old-fashioned type of man who disliked changes. Too late now. Closing the door of the flat, she half wished that she could stick her hair back on, that she had worn her 'Dog Toby' dress with the frilled collar: for his sake, not hers.

Fiddling with his bow-tie, Ralph wished he felt less awkward in his evening clothes.

Brushing what remained of his hair, practising his deep breathing exercises, he wondered if Sarah would appear in the green dress with the frilled collar and cuffs. Not that he cared a jot what she wore.

Everything he had done, these past few months, had

been done for her sake. His lengthy sessions with his speech therapist, for instance; mowing the grass of the walled garden, weeding the herbaceous borders; 'Feeling out of sight for the ends of Being and ideal Grace . . . '

When the bell rang, he hastened to open the door and stood on the threshold in stunned silence, totally unprepared for the new-look Sarah.

He realized, of course, that she had lost weight, but her old camouflage of bulky sweaters and generously cut slacks had concealed her dramatically scaled-down proportions. And what on earth had she done to her hair, her face?

'Well, do you approve?'

'You look – lovely.'

'But you don't really approve, do you?' Sarah smiled sadly. 'I'm sorry. I didn't mean to shock you. It was meant to be a surprise, hopefully a pleasant surprise.'

'You don't begin to understand, d-do you?'

'Understand – what?'

Tossing caution to the wind, feeling suddenly liberated, uncaring of his speech impediment, his thinning hair and weak eyesight, Ralph knew that his moment of truth had arrived – that it was now or never. He said desperately, 'I l-love you. I think I l-loved you from the moment I saw you, Sarah, I . . . '

His courage almost deserted him. His words, 'Will you marry me?' came in little more than a whisper.

The taxi arrived at that moment . . .

'For heaven's sake, Alec, calm down! Try to relax. I expect Pippa is feeling just as nervous as you are!'

Helen Grayson groaned as her brother swung his motorized wheelchair around abruptly for the umpteenth time – equivalent to the pacing of a normally mobile man.

'I doubt that!' Alec smiled grimly. 'You know, as well as I do, Pippa's propensity for taking command of any given situation. Frankly, Helen, I'd far rather you went to this bloody dinner without me. I don't think I can face it, after all.'

'Face meeting Pippa again, you mean? But what about Sarah? What about me?'

'Have you stopped to consider that it is your future which most deeply concerns me?' Alec said softly, facing his sister.

'I think I understand what you mean.' Helen's eyes filled suddenly with tears. Turning her head away, staring into a mirror, patting her hair into place, 'But this is *your* life, Alec, as well as mine. Do you think that I would stand in the way of your happiness if you and Pippa came together again?'

'But if, by some miracle, that happened, where would you go? What would you do? Face facts, my dear. You, Pippa, and I could never live together under the same roof. It's true, isn't it, that you have never entirely forgiven her for marrying Roy Paget instead of me?'

'No, you are quite right, I have never forgiven Pippa for that. But you needn't worry about me, Alec. In fact,' Helen turned away from the mirror, smiling faintly, 'I might be quite pleased to get rid of you. So put *that* in your pipe and smoke it!' She picked up her evening bag, 'So are you coming to Sarah's party, or not?'

Alec smiled ruefully, 'Of course I am! What are we waiting for? Let's go!'

Closing the boutique, Philippa went upstairs to get ready for Sarah's celebration party. Riddled with nervous tension at the thought of meeting Alec again, she poured herself a stiff scotch which she sipped slowly while running the bath water.

When the bath was ready – a mass of foaming Badedas bubbles – she slipped into it, and lay there, her hair tied up, Mammy fashion, in a pink silk Italian headscarf, a second glass of scotch in front of her on the soap rack.

Possibly she had done wrong in accepting Sarah's invitation to her celebratory party. Downing her second drink, wallowing in the warm, scented water, Philippa realized that the last time she had seen Alec she had been a slender young girl with naturally auburn hair, thinking that the world owed her a living.

But what the hell? Time changed everyone. No need to worry. Even Liz Taylor and Oprah Winfrey were having trouble with their weight these days. She would simply sail into the Carillon as large as life in her new multi-coloured evening dress, wearing her flashiest ear-rings, plenty of mascara and lipstick, her freshly dyed hair brushed out, back-combed, and well lacquered, not giving a damn what anyone, especially Alec, thought of her.

Rising like Venus from the foam, she poured herself a third drink which she placed on the dressing table, and swallowed in quick gulps as she applied her makeup . . . first a layer of her favourite tan foundation cream, pressed into the pale puffy areas around her eyes with a piece of damp cotton wool, then her mascara, taking care not to blink her eyes until it had dried.

Downing a fourth scotch, she wondered if this was the way artists felt creating a masterpiece on canvas; seeing in the mirror her face as a smooth, youthful, sun-kissed oval. Thank God she had never taken to wearing glasses.

Pressing in quantities of dark powder, brushing off the

surplus with a Boots' complexion brush, she wondered if Alec wore glasses, if he had ever, or always worn glasses? Perhaps he had worn glasses and she had never noticed. He seemed the kind of man who might have worn glasses, she considered, even as a young man. But perhaps he hadn't, because how could a young man, with glasses, ever have passed an Army examination? Had her husband, Roy Paget, worn glasses? She simply could not remember. The world seemed to be floating away from her in a blissful haze of forgetfulness.

Now for the eyebrow pencil. Whoops! Careful, old girl! Mustn't make one eyebrow darker than the other.

When the taxi she had ordered arrived, Philippa went downstairs clinging carefully to the banister, reeking of her favourite perfume, a colourful Spanish shawl thrown about her shoulders, earrings dangling, feeling amazingly light-headed and carefree; more than ready for her encounter with her old flame, Alec Grayson.

Possibly, Sarah thought afterwards, she should feel grateful to Philippa for ruining her celebration party. She had realized, of course, that Pippa was drunk the minute she crossed the threshold. Helen and Alec, herself and Ralph had been in the conservatory bar when Philippa made her entrance, looking rather like an elderly Spanish whore.

Sarah's heart sank. Helen and Alec exchanged glances. Ralph looked up in dismay as the bizarrely dressed figure of Philippa approached the table, walking very carefully, the way inebriates toe chalk lines to prove themselves still capable of self control, he thought, sunk in gloom because he had so badly mistimed his proposal of marriage. Why the hell hadn't he waited and chosen a more propitious moment? To make matters worse, Sarah had not uttered a word in the taxi and when they had arrived at the Carillon, Helen and Alec were waiting in the reception area.

Following the introductions, they had gone through to the bar for pre-dinner drinks, and been handed menus, and so there had been no chance for a quiet word with Sarah who was talking animatedly to Helen and her brother. Too animatedly, Ralph conjectured, as if to cover her embarrassment.

Studying the menu, Sarah thought, I never dreamt, I never guessed . . . The old feeling of camaraderie with Ralph had gone the moment he uttered the fatal words, 'I love you.' In one fleeting second it seemed that her life had swung off balance. All along, she had based their friendship firmly on her belief that, with Ralph, she was safe from emotional entanglement, believing, as she had, that love and marriage were the last things on his mind. To have her safe, devoted friend change into a potential husband had been more than she could handle. Whatever she might have said to him, in the back seat of the taxi, would have sounded ridiculous, and so she had kept silent, worried sick about what she would say to him, in the fullness of time, when she would have to break it to him gently that she had never seen him in the light of a lover, much less a husband.

Oh God, why did life have to be so complicated?

But that was just the beginning of the evening. Worse was to come. Philippa was to come!

Catching sight of Alec, Pippa weaved forward to embrace him. Throwing her arms about his neck from behind, leaning forward, almost overwhelming him with her perfume, she planted a kiss on his cheek, grimaced as the back of his wheelchair dug into her bosom, frowningly realized why he had not risen to his feet to greet her,

259

thinking muzzily, Christ almighty, old rockin' chair's got him! Sarah might have warned me – at the same time crying merrily, 'Hi, Helen. Long time no see!'

'Philippa, may I introduce my – friend and neighbour – Ralph Foster?', Sarah said desperately, wondering if she had committed a social gaffe, if the woman should be introduced to the male? Not that Pippa seemed to care one way or the other.

Rising to his feet to shake hands, this could not be Sarah's employer, Ralph thought. The woman was as tight as a tick. He could smell the whisky on her breath from where he was standing. 'So pleased to meetcher,' Philippa gushed. Then, turning her attention to Sarah, 'Hey, what the hell have you done to yourself? You look shensational! Everyone, doesn't Sarah look shensational?' Sinking down in a basket chair, 'Are we having pre-whatsit drinkie poohs?' Gaily snapping her fingers to attract a waiter's attention, 'Hey, garçon, bring me a large whisky and ginger.'

'We were just about to order,' Helen said, tight lipped. 'Perhaps you'd care to look at the menu?'

Smiling beatifically, '*You* order for me, Alec,' Pippa insisted. 'After all, you know what I like, don't you?' She regarded him fondly. 'Did you know, Mr – er – Ralph, that Alec and I were once engaged to be married?'

Startled, 'No, I didn't know that,' Ralph replied, jerked from his reverie over Sarah and his mistimed proposal of marriage.

'Well, we were, weren't we, Alec?' Philippa sighed deeply. 'It was all my fault that we didn't make it to the altar, but I was young then. Young and foolish . . . '

Oh, God, Sarah thought.

★   ★   ★

Philippa insisted on guiding Alec's wheelchair into the dining room, although he could have managed perfectly well, even better, on his own. By this time she was in full spate, saying silly things, being flirtatious with Alec, to his embarrassment, too tipsy to realize that she was being objectionable.

People looked up in mild surprise, some in annoyance, as the 'Voice' entered the normally dignified atmosphere of the Alexandra Room. Sarah thought wildly of the lady in Rupert Brooke's poem who came and 'quacked' beside him in the wood, ruining his contemplation of the evening sky, breaking into his solitude, and saw Nicholas Tierney at the far side of the room. Briefly, their eyes met before Sarah looked away, wishing she had never dreamed up the evening, especially not placed either Philippa or Alec in what she might have realized would be a difficult situation. But then, she had not for one moment imagined that Philippa would behave in such a spectacular manner.

The first course passed uneventfully. By that time, Philippa had taken a seat next to Alec, and a diversion had been caused by the arrival of the champagne. The room was warm. Music had begun to drift through from the conservatory. Sarah breathed a sigh of relief. Alec was charming, a calming influence on Pippa, possessed of a sense of humour, patience and understanding.

When Nicholas came to the table to have a word with Alec in particular, whom he obviously admired, and to ask if everything was to their liking, Philippa butted into the conversation. Anxious to establish her proprietorial rights so far as Alec was concerned, clutching his hand, she managed, somehow, to knock over the table-lamp and a glass of claret at the same time.

Sarah saw, as if in slow motion, a stream of red

dripping from the ruined tablecloth on to Helen's dress, heard Helen's sharp intake of breath as the stain on her skirt widened and deepened.

'Oh, Helen, I'm so sorry . . . '

Rising hurriedly to her feet, 'Not to worry, Sarah, it isn't a Zandra Rhodes' creation, just something I picked up in Debenham's winter sale.'

'Even so . . . '

Philippa burst into tears.

Alec looked like a drowning man.

'Please, take my serviette, H-Helen.' Ralph waded manfully into the breach.

'Thank you.' Helen began dabbing ineffectually at her skirt with the proffered napkin. Taking control of the situation, Nicholas signalled a waiter to change the ruined tablecloth, and led the weeping Philippa from the room, closely followed by Sarah, who, holding herself responsible for the debacle, suggested that she should take Pippa home by taxi, and stay with her until she had slept off her hangover.

'That's entirely up to you,' Nicholas said, his arm supportively round Pippa's waist, 'but mightn't it be better to let her stay here overnight? One of the chambermaids will take care of her. After all, why spoil your celebration?'

'That's very kind of you.'

'Not at all.' What an attractive woman, Nicholas thought.

'I blew it! I really blew it, didn't I, Sarah?' Philippa moaned between hiccups and floods of tears. 'My big chance, and I blew it!'

'Not to worry,' Nicholas said consolingly, 'you'll feel better after a good night's sleep.' Smiling at Sarah, 'Would you mind ringing for the elevator? I have my hands rather full at the moment, I'm afraid!' Referring to the fact that Philippa had now clasped her arms about his neck in a stranglehold and refused to let go, rather like a drowning woman clinging to a life-raft.

And that, Sarah thought afterwards, was the beginning of her strange, at times abortive love affair with Nicholas Tierney; that moment when their eyes met as she rang for the elevator, when after the chambermaid arrived to take charge of Philippa, alone with Nicholas in the hotel foyer, she knew that their meeting sooner or later had been inevitable. A foregone conclusion.

Nicholas could not have explained to anyone just then his desire to hold Sarah in his arms. He strove to remember the words of a poem learned long ago – 'desolate and sick of an old passion. I have been faithful to thee, Cynara, in my fashion.' 'Sick of an old passion'? He had never met this woman before, and yet he felt he knew her, as though they had met somewhere before, a long time ago, in another place. 'Please dance with me,' he said urgently, taking her hand. Then, feeling its unresistant warmth in his, he led her towards the source of the music.

They moved together as one person amid an oasis of greenery, with shining, coloured spotlights reflected in the maplewood floor. They were so close that she could feel his heartbeat. They had the floor to themselves. Guests had not yet begun to drift through from the dining room. The tune, 'Edelweiss', recalled student dances long ago. Sarah smiled dreamily, pushing to the back of her mind that she should have gone back to her table. But dancing with Nicholas had been too strong a temptation to resist.

Looking down, he noticed the warm curve of her

cheeks, tender mouth and softly curling hair – the colour of wheat at harvest time touched by the autumn sun. Why had they never met before? Why the celebration party? He wanted to know more about her.

'We *have* met before,' she told him, in reply to his first question.

'Have we?' Frowning slightly, he said, 'Are you sure?' Racking his brain to remember, 'I felt we had, but . . . It must have been a long time ago.'

'Not really. We met at Philippa's boutique this summer. You came in with an American lady. I asked if I could help you, or if you were browsing.'

'I remember the American – an hotel guest. That's all, I'm afraid. I must have been wearing dark glasses to have missed seeing you.'

'The shop was busy at the time.'

'Even so.'

'My hair was longer then.'

'I'm sorry, I don't understand!'

'It's quite simple. I needed a job, Pippa gave me one. I was in the shop on another occasion – when you came in to order some le Creuset casseroles.'

'You'll think me awfully dense, but I still don't get it. Your name *is* Sarah Vale, isn't it? I mean, Philippa called you Sarah, and table six was booked in the name of a Mrs Sarah Vale. This much I know. I saw your name on the list my head waiter shoved under my nose, so it didn't take a Sherlock Holmes to work that one out.' Smiling, he led her into a series of gentle turns. 'So what are you celebrating? A wedding anniversary? An – engagement?'

'No, the publication of – rather the acceptance of a book I wrote recently,' Sarah said, reluctantly, wishing that he had not asked that particular question, wishing, at the same time, that the music would never end, that they could go on dancing like this for ever, his arm firm about her waist, their fingers intertwined. But, in her experience, nothing lasted for ever, especially not happiness. Happiness was nothing more than a series of stepping-stones in life which one remembered with joy . . . As she would remember this dance-floor, this music, the coloured spotlights, the scent of hot-house blooms, the trio of musicians – pianist, saxophonist and drummer – on the spotlit dais at the far end of the room. And to think she had once believed that the magic of first love could never be recaptured or reprised. Or was it simply that she had never been in love before? Certainly the way she felt now bore no resemblance to the way she had felt, as a young girl, lightly stepping across a daisy-starred lawn in a white wedding dress.

When the music stopped, still holding her hand, Nicholas said, 'We shall meet again soon.' Looking into her eyes, 'Strange, isn't it?'

'What is?'

'This feeling I have that we somehow – belong together. I can't explain. Sarah, please tell me, am I making sense? Have you that feeling, too?'

'Perhaps. I don't know. I don't think so.' Was this his particular 'line', she wondered, clinging to her core of common sense, refusing to be swept off her feet, realizing that he must be at least six or seven years younger than her, taking fright suddenly because life had taught her to mistrust her feelings when it came to the question of love.

After all, what *was* love? At best, a heightening of emotion which had no basis in reality – rather like Christmas Day – so many gifts beneath the Christmas tree, all brightly packaged and tied with tinselled ribbons.

Afterwards, putting out the tree, and the crumpled wrapping paper for the dustbinmen to collect.

'If you should change your mind, I'll be in the Minster, on Sunday, at noon,' Nicholas said quietly, 'near the All Saints' Chapel.'

Chapter Nineteen

Returning to her guests, Sarah explained that Philippa was staying overnight at the hotel. Helen had been to the cloakroom to dry her ruined dress as best she could, and made light of the incident, but Sarah knew that she was upset, and so, despite his gallant attempts at conversation, was Alec – while Ralph appeared as the knight in 'La Belle Dame Sans Merci', 'alone and palely loitering'.

That he would bring up the subject of his proposal when he asked her to dance with him, was inevitable, Sarah knew, but she could scarcely refuse his invitation. Her heart sank at his opening gambit, 'Please, Sarah, we have to t-talk.' Then, because he was her kind friend and neighbour, placing her hand on his shoulder, she said gently, 'I'm sorry, Ralph. I never dreamt that you. . . ' How could she put it without wounding him too deeply? '. . . cared for me as more than a friend.'

His hands felt clammy. He held her stiffly, unnaturally, in the manner of one who regards dancing as a penance rather than a pleasure, which was perfectly true. Ralph, who possessed no sense of rhythm, danced, as he talked – haltingly, somewhat jerkily, consciously trying to avoid stepping on his partner's feet.

Striving valiantly to keep in time with the music of the quickstep, he said, 'I r-realize I s-should have w-waited . . . ' (Oh, God, he must remember to breathe properly.)

'I chose the wrong t-time, the w-wrong place, but I meant what I s-said.'

'I never doubted that for a moment.'

'You see, we have so much in c-common . . . ' His eagerness to explain brought beads of perspiration to his forehead. 'I think that we c-could be happy together. I w-want to take c-care of you. Protect you.'

Haunted by the music of a waltz, 'Protect me? From what? Life?'

'I'm s-sorry, I don't understand.'

Sarah could not have put into words, at that moment, the feeling that she had just begun to live, that what she had once thought of as living had been little more than the tuning of instruments before a concerto; that the way she had felt a few minutes – or could it have been several lifetimes ago – was, perhaps, the way Miriam had felt when she scratched the name 'Amabie' on the wall of her prison.

'Sarah! Are you all right?'

'Oh yes, of course. I'm sorry, Ralph, just a bit tired, that's all.'

He said, disappointedly, 'I s-suppose I realized all along that you d-didn't really care for me. But I s-shall keep on hoping that you'll c-change your mind.'

That was the trouble, Sarah realized. She *did* care a great deal for Ralph Foster.

Alec thought that Pippa had not changed much at all. She was still her own worst enemy. He remembered that she had been very drunk indeed the day she told him that their wedding was off. But at least she had been honest with him, and it was this streak of honesty he had most admired, the quality of earthiness which had kept her memory fresh and alive in his heart.

He had jibbed at her guiding his invalid chair into the dining room. Her well-meant gesture had undermined his carefully erected barrier of self-sufficiency, his pretence that he didn't mind having had his bloody right leg amputated below the knee. Of course he minded! He also minded that Philippa had made a fool of herself in a roomfull of strangers, that his crippling disabilities had made it impossible to lead her from the room, as he would have done had not his blasted wheelchair got in the way.

Helen thought despairingly, Alec is still in love with Philippa. No matter how badly she behaved, the old feeling was still there. Despite all her attempts to create a loving home atmosphere for her brother, and in spite of his gratitude for all the meals she had cooked for him, all the shirts she had ironed, the countless times she had hurried home from the library to keep him company, she had known all along that he was deeply unhappy, hiding his true feelings behind a smokescreen of light-hearted banter and amiability, rather than admit how much he hated being a cripple.

The thought occurred that if, some day in the not too distant future, Pippa and Alec came together in a positive way, her own life would be drastically altered. Alec was right in saying that no way could the three of them live under the same roof, which meant that she would have to find a place of her own, to make the best of her life as a lonely spinster. If only, like Sarah, she might discover a kindly neighbour such as Ralph Foster to invite her down for a meal occasionally . . .

Obviously, Sarah was in love, Helen thought as she and Ralph came back to the table. The faraway, reflective look in her eyes, the ambience about her – as though she was haloed in light – could mean only one thing. But with whom was she in love? Surely not Ralph Foster, who despite his niceness, was scarcely capable of invoking such a glow.

And then the sensitive Helen, putting two and two together, knew the answer. Nicholas Tierney – a man towards whom she had also felt strongly attracted on the occasion of Alec's award celebration dinner – with whom she had felt so strong a rapport that she had felt certain, afterwards, he would telephone her, invite her to dinner, lunch, or whatever. Of course, she should have known better. And yet . . .

Now, she wondered, should she warn Sarah that Tierney's stock-in trade as host to the countless, unattached women with whom he came in contact on the spotlit dance floor, meant less than nothing to a man seemingly incapable of forming a deep, lasting relationship with any woman. No, of course not! She would simply keep on reiterating that she did not care tuppence about her ruined dress, keep on smiling, clinging to that smile as a smokescreen against her deep-seated dread of the future.

Thinking about Sarah as he talked easily to other guests, Nicholas remembered her warmth, the feeling he'd experienced, dancing with her, that he had come close to some source of life-giving water. Her eyes, blue and direct, held no hint of the archness he disliked in women. For this reason alone he would have felt attracted to her, but beyond that lay a feeling of Kismet, that they had met somewhere before – at a time of stress, even danger. Ridiculous, of course, and yet holding her in his arms, he had felt even more strongly the powerful undercurrent of an age-old attraction, so that when the dance ended, he had known that he must see her again: that their meeting again would be inevitable in any case, whether pre-arranged or not.

Sophia telephoned from Heathrow the following day to say that she would arrive in York at four-thirty.

Dressed once more in black, her hair drawn back in a French pleat, no one looking at the outwardly composed English lady seated near the window of a First Class compartment, her eyes closed, could have guessed what was going on in her mind.

On the flight from the Charles de Gaulle Airport, she had relived memories of Indian summer days in the sun. Days of blissfully uncomplicated freedom, of waking in the early hours of the morning to the chattering of birds in an orchard of apple trees whose boughs arabesqued in graceful curves to the sweet smelling grass. A woman who, limber and fit, had walked from the red-roofed farmhouse where she had slept like a child, through the deep, cool woods bordering the garden of the Château de Vigny, to find Charles busy pruning the long-neglected rose bushes, hoeing weeds, trundling garden lumber to a smouldering bonfire.

Later, Sophia remembered, they would discuss the question of food, then drive together to tucked away villages, to shop – a faceless couple so far as the inhabitants were concerned – unknowing and uncaring that the tall, sunburnt man wearing a panama hat was le Comte de Vigny, his companion in her sloppy espadrilles and peasant clothing, the formidable owner of an internationally famous hotel.

As the train sped northward, memories of candle-lit evenings invaded Sophia's mind, and one evening in particular when Charles had talked about his son, and she had realized the depth of his despair that he had never known the joy of seeing the boy grow up. A man who had lived, vicariously, his son's life through the letters and photographs Madeleine had sent him.

Spitted on the horns of a dilemma, he had desperately wanted to meet his son, to spend some time with him, but that was an impossibility. Alone in the château, he had spent a near lifetime of regret fretting over his failures as a man, a priest, and a father, and, he admitted to Sophia, the question of his son's inheritance.

'You mean the de Vigny title, the house, the land?' That Nicholas was the undoubted heir to the de Vigny fortune had never even crossed Sophia's mind. Startled, she said, 'But how could that be achieved?'

'Without breaking my promise to Madeleine?' Charles had smiled enigmatically. 'There is one way,' he said quietly.

'I don't understand.'

'I am asking you to marry me, Sophia.'

Nicholas parked the Daimler in the station forecourt, studied the indicator board, and crossed the footbridge to Platform 5.

Meeting Sophia, he knew there was something different about her. Obviously her holiday had done her good. He had been afraid, recalling the coolness between them on the eve of her departure for Paris, that her greeting might reflect that coolness. Instead, she kissed him warmly and talked, inconsequentially, about her journey.

In the car, as a matter of courtesy, he asked after his father's health. A difficult question, Sophia thought, fastening her seat-belt. 'Clive is not well,' she said. 'Retirement does not suit him. He has too much time on his hands; too much time to brood.'

'About what?' Nicholas filtered the Daimler into the line of traffic flowing towards Lendel Bridge.

'I think that Madeleine's death has affected him deeply.'

'Really? You do surprise me. Or could it be that he is finding it hard to live with his conscience after all?'

'Perhaps,' Sophia conceded.

'You must have had a fairly boring time of it, then, coping with his moods.' Nicholas's voice was tinged with the bitterness which came uppermost whenever he spoke about his father.

'I didn't stay with him for very long.' Sophia kept her eyes on the traffic lights.

'Oh? As bad as all that?' Turning into St Leonard's Crescent, passing the Theatre Royal, Nicholas glanced briefly at his aunt, sensing a mystery.

'Let us say that I aired certain opinions, and leave it at that, shall we? Now, tell me, how are things at the Carillon?'

Nicholas said resignedly, 'Certain opinions have been aired there also, I'm afraid.'

'Meaning what, exactly?'

'Michel and I had – words.' He smiled ruefully. 'I'm sorry, Aunt, I did my best. Apparently my best was not good enough.'

Michel and Sophia talked together, much later, in his apartment, after dinner had been served, when the night porter came on duty to set the early morning tea trays.

The reins were once again in her hands, she realized,

as pouring her a glass of wine, 'It is good to have you back, Sophia,' Michel said fondly.

She regarded him thoughtfully, this man with whom she had once been hopelessly in love, wondering what had happened to all the passion she had once felt for him. She could see quite clearly now that fate had been kind in dismissing her dreams of an in-depth love affair, even marriage, with the irascible Frenchman.

Fondling the stem of her wine glass, 'Tell me, what is really troubling you?' Sophia asked.

With a shrug of the shoulders, he said, 'Perhaps I am beginning to feel my age. I take it that Nicholas has told you what happened?'

'Yes. But why the anger . . . ?'

'That you, of all people, should need to ask,' Michel interrupted explosively. 'I could not bear the humiliation! Being made to look a fool in front of my staff!' Spreading his hands, he resembled the joker in a pack of playing cards.

'There must be more to it than that!' Sophia said calmly. 'Face facts, Michel. The man was about to knife you. He might have done so had Nicholas not stepped in when he did.'

'You think I don't know that?' Michel's face crumpled. 'It is the realization that I am no longer in control that makes me think that it is time to go home, back to France.'

'Are you saying that you wish to dissolve our partnership, after all these years?' Startled, Sophia put down her wine, untasted. Rising quickly to her feet, placing a hand on his arm. 'You are just tired, that's all, in need of a rest.'

'Yes, I am tired. Very tired, in mind and body.'

Clasping Sophia's hand, 'We have been the good friends for a very long time, you and I, *n'est ce pas*? We have built up something – *très* important.' Lapsing suddenly into his own language, 'Now I wish to live a little before I die, to read all the books I have never had time to read before; to travel! Would you believe that I have never been to Italy, Switzerland, or Greece? Have never seen the glories of Rome or Florence? A mountain glacier; the Acropolis?' He smiled ruefully, 'But I shall not leave until you have found someone to replace me.'

'Replace *you*?' Sophia's eyes filled with tears. Glimpsing, momentarily, the man she had once been in love with, with a faint stirring of an old passion, she said softly, truthfully, 'But *you*, Michel, are irreplaceable.' Then, moving slowly towards the door, 'Even so, you must live your life as you see fit.'

'Sophia!' Swiftly crossing to her side, 'Just one thing more. I am sorry that I could never give you the love you deserved. You know the reason why that was not possible. You should have married, *ma chèrie*: had children of your own to care for.'

Standing at the window of her apartment overlooking the floodlit lawns, watching the constant ebb and flow of traffic beyond the boundary wall, Sophia knew that she had reached a watershed in her life, saw the crumbling of her tiny empire of soft beds and hot bathwater, of perfectly cooked food, of music and dancing, her role as 'The Woman in Black'. But what of Nicholas?

She had turned down de Vigny's proposal of marriage, knowing that he was not in love with her, unable to face the convoluted business of legally drawn up documents to establish her nephew's right of inheritance through herself.

Robbed of joy in believing that their relationship was based on more than a possible marriage of convenience, she had wondered, as she said goodbye to him, if de Vigny had seen her, from the beginning, as a sacrificial lamb? An easy means of escape from an untenable situation?

If so, she had given her heart to no purpose. Fool that she was, she had imagined that the time they had spent together meant more to him than the stitching up of a marriage contract. Apparently she was wrong. And yet Charles had seemed desolate when she turned down his proposal. Well why not? It must have come as a shock to him that an ageing spinster had not jumped at the chance of marriage; a solution of the problem of Nicky's inheritance.

How carefully he must have worked out the scheme beforehand, Sophia thought bitterly. Perhaps, even as he had watched her moving about his kitchen, preparing a meal from a few leftovers, when he had tucked his hand into her elbow on their shopping expeditions, had applied a glimmering taper to the drawing-room candles, and poured champagne into her glass, he had been thinking that here was a woman to be wooed for the sake of his son's inheritance. And yet . . .

Clear sightedly, Sophia had come to a different conclusion. And this plan of hers she believed to be the only way in which to resolve the dilemma.

Chapter Twenty

Summoning Nicholas to her private drawing room, Sophia broke the news of Michel's retirement as a forerunner of her plan of action, knowing what his immediate reaction would be. Being cruel to be kind, she considered, relying on her own judgement. Poor Nicky. But he would thank her in the long run. At least, she hoped so.

'Michel retiring?' Nicholas said disbelievingly, facing his aunt. 'Because of me?' Running his fingers wearily through his hair, he said, 'God, what a mess!'

'You mustn't blame yourself,' Sophia said consolingly. 'He is not getting any younger. A cliché, perhaps, but an irrevocable fact of life. None of us can go on for ever. Michel simply feels the time has come to – how shall I put it? To make up the arrears of living.'

Sophia had hung, and spotlighted, the paintings Madeleine had bequeathed to her, on the walls of her drawing room, lovely, simple paintings of France, depicting poppied cornfields, grape-bloomed vineyards, tall poplar trees beneath a sunlit sky: the Ile de la Cité by night. France, where her heart lay, would always lie from now on, alongside her memories of an Indian summer.

She said quietly, 'I told you that I had not stayed long with my brother. We quarrelled rather bitterly, I'm afraid. I left Paris because I needed to be alone, to think, to get my life into perspective.'

'Oh?' Puzzled by Sophia's sudden switch of subjects

– from Michel to his father. 'And did you succeed?'

'Yes.' She turned to look intently at the paintings. 'I've always loved France. I spent a number of years there, you know, before my brother married Madeleine? But Paris was too hot, the Rue St Hélène too full of memories.'

'I can imagine,' Nicholas said, puzzled by his aunt's curious behaviour – almost as if she had taken temporary leave of her senses.

Sitting down, knotting her fingers together in her lap, 'Clive offered me the use of his car,' Sophia continued, 'and so I went – gypsying.'

'Gypsying?' Nicholas felt inclined to laugh. But she seemed quite serious.

'I mean that literally. I bought myself some colourful clothes, a pair of espadrilles, let my hair down, and went bare-legged.' She smiled. 'Are you shocked?'

'Shocked? No, of course not. A bit surprised, that's all.' Returning her smile, 'I have never thought of you as the nomad type. And how did you feel?'

'Liberated! Alive! It was wonderful to meander along, eating when I felt hungry. And then I discovered a little farmhouse – a kind of spiritual retreat – a long way off the beaten track.'

'You lived *en famille*?'

'No, I stayed there alone. The peace was indescribable. There was no telephone. My bedroom overlooked an orchard. I slept like a child.'

'Sounds idyllic.'

'It was. The owner told me that he lets the place to those in need of sanctuary – mainly writers, poets, painters.'

'The owner?'

Sophia's fingers tightened imperceptibly, 'A Comte

278

de Vigny. He explained that the house had been due for demolition. The farmyard and outbuildings had already been cleared away, but he decided to keep the main building, to let the woods encroach. We met occasionally. I found him to be a quiet man, charming and cultured.'

'Really?' Why was Sophia telling him all this? Nicholas wondered.

As if reading his thoughts, she said softly, 'I should like you to spend a little time there. Knowing what you have been through recently . . . You need rest, my darling. Peace.'

On the point of brushing aside the idea as nonsensical, something in Sophia's face, the expression in her eyes, the curious tension about her, made Nicholas realize that this was very important to her, in no way the whim of an elderly maiden aunt fussily concerned about his welfare. More of a cri-de-coeur. And, 'Peace,' he murmured, as though he had seldom heard the word before and scarcely understood its meaning, knowing that the past months *had* taken their toll.

Attempting to come to terms with Madeleine's death, his father's rejection, pushing aside his weariness of mind and body had been an exhausting battle of will over circumstance, of uneasy sleep and involved nightmares in which he had found himself lost in a fog – searching for Madeleine, hearing her voice, her footsteps, her laughter, yet unable to find her.

Perhaps his aunt was right in saying that he was in need of spiritual sanctuary. Peace, Nicholas thought.

A wise woman, Sophia.

Saturday.

Awaking early, Sarah wandered through to the kitchen

to make coffee. Strangely disorientated, mug in hand, she stared out of the sitting-room window at the Minster carpark, the gates as yet unlocked. Pale September sunlight gilded the cobblestones, a scattering of autumn leaves drifted down from the trees.

She missed Amabie, the discipline of writing. She disliked the unaccustomed neatness of her desk, her covered typewriter, and missed the challenge involved in finding the right words to bring her ideas to fruition. Now her brain seemed stultified with worry: the prospect of facing television cameras and chat-show hosts, of jetting off to America next summer. (The arrival of her passport had triggered a new wave of anxiety on that score.)

She felt that some crisis was looming, far more enervating and nerve-racking than writing a book to a deadline. Perhaps her altered relationship with Ralph lay at the root of her misgivings, or her brief encounter with Nicholas Tierney. Even Helen's ruined dress, and Philippa's spectacularly bad behaviour had assumed gigantic proportions.

Bathed and dressed, she went shopping, dreading that Ralph might ring up with a dinner invitation. Pushing a supermarket trolley, she found herself rehearsing excuses, unable to bear the thought of having to make conversation, of steering him away from the subject of marriage.

Putting away her groceries, when the phone rang, she half decided to let it ring, but what use would that be? Sooner or later she would have to face the inevitable. A sense of relief washed over her when she heard Helen's voice and just as quickly vanished when Helen said, 'Look, Sarah, I must talk to you. Could we meet on Monday or Tuesday?'

'Is anything the matter? You sound upset.'

'Well, yes. But I can't discuss it on the phone. Alec's

in the next room. Tuesday, then? The Davygate restaurant?'

Oh, God. More trouble!

But the real crisis was yet to come – due to arrive on the four o'clock train from King's Cross.

She had changed into a blue woollen housecoat, switched on a Brahms' piano concerto and settled down on the rose settee to listen, when the front doorbell rang. Who on earth . . . ?

The man seemed impatient. Sarah could not see his face, just his outline. It was dark outside. But the moment he spoke – she knew. 'I must have rung the wrong bell.' No hint of an apology. But then, Faulkner seldom apologized for his actions. 'It's Mrs Vale I wish to see.'

'You had better come in, then.' Heart hammering, a terrible thought occurred. 'The children. Has something happened to the children?' she cried, imagining Richard stretched out on a mortuary slab; Verity in the intensive care unit of some vast London hospital. Why else should Faulkner have come, if not to impart bad news?

'Sarah?' In the lighted hallway, Faulkner stared at her in disbelief. 'What the hell have you done to yourself?'

'Never mind me!' She pressed her hand to her lips. 'For God's sake, tell me about the children!'

'For heaven's sake, calm down. There's nothing wrong with them, as far as I know.'

'Then why are you here?' She felt bewildered, badly shaken, slightly sick.

'I want to talk to you.'

'What about?'

'Not here. I take it you have a room?'

'A – room?' Nothing he said seemed to make sense.

'Where do you live? Upstairs?' He seemed irritated, Sarah thought, speaking to her as if she were a child, a not very bright one at that. Did he imagine that she lived in a garret? How dare he arrive on her doorstep without a by your leave, and begin his bullying tactics as if he was still married to her? But he was right about one thing, conversation was scarcely possible in a draughty hall with the front door standing wide open. 'Close the door,' she said, 'and come with me.' Refusing to be intimidated. 'In here.'

The look on his face when he walked into the sitting room afforded her some amusement. He looked stunned, to put it mildly. He felt as stunned as he looked. How the hell had she managed all this – a woman on her beam-ends, as poor as a church mouse?

He had come to York expecting to find her in some seedy bedsit with a sink and a cooker screened off by a cretonne curtain, fatter and dowdier than before, a shapeless bundle in slacks and sloppy sweater, pathetically pleased to see him, being brave, or trying to, then having to admit that she had done wrong in refusing his generous offer of financial help. But the woman facing him in her own drawing room, as slim as a wand, was as far removed from his imaginings as cheddar from camembert, chianti from champagne.

An astute assessor of good living, that certain aura denoting financial stability, he noticed the flowers scattered about the room – not simply bunches of dahlias or Michaelmas daisies stuck haphazardly into vases to brighten up the place, but gracefully and strategically placed arrangements – pink roses and carnations – in white jardinières, to enhance the symmetry of the room, the white panelling and tall windows, the fireplace: a background befitting a beautiful woman. And Sarah *was* beautiful, far lovelier now than she had been on their wedding day. And not only beautiful, but elegant. Elegant and prickly.

Shifting ground, Faulkner trod more warily. The new Sarah seemed to him as an unexploded bomb with a tricky device mechanism, in need of careful handling. He felt at a disadvantage. Thinking to rescue the perishing, instead he had come up against a person he scarcely recognized, the kind of woman he found exciting – slim, attractive. He had scarcely expected the bonus of beauty thrown in.

He said, 'I should have telephoned first, asked your permission to come. The fact is, I acted on impulse.'

Still unsure what he was driving at, she said, 'You'd better take your coat off.' Sarah felt like Alice in Wonderland – a story she had always detested. At least he had changed his blustering tactics. Vaguely, she wondered why. If only she could think clearly. Why had he come? And why, after all this time, should she find his presence disturbing?

She noticed, with distaste, the casual way he threw his coat carelessly over the back of a chair and planted himself firmly on her mother's settee; noticed his hand-made Italian leather shoes, grey suit, silk shirt, and gold Rolex watch, his appearance of having been rubbed down with olive oil or suntan lotion. Why was it, she wondered, that rich men, growing old, grew silkier and glossier as time went by? Exuded wealth from their pores, seemed to walk in an aura of Havana cigars and expensive after-shave lotion; conjured up visions of sleek cars, business luncheons, and hide suitcases? Above all, she disliked his proprietorial air, as if he had every right to be here, to interrupt her quiet enjoyment of a Brahms' piano concerto.

She said, 'I take it you'd like a drink? There's a bottle of wine in the refrigerator.'

'Oh? Need any help?'

'No thanks. I can manage to uncork a bottle of wine on my own.'

He said, sniffing the bouquet, 'Vacqueyras Domaine?' He had always prided himself on his 'nose'.

'I don't know. I didn't read the label.'

Faulkner laughed. 'My dear girl, you should pay attention to these things, develop a palate to tie in with your new lifestyle.'

'I no longer drink Bristol cream sherry, if that's what you mean.'

'Oh, come now, Sarah. You've obviously done quite well for yourself . . . '

'Have you seen the children?' she asked, determined to keep to essentials.

'Not recently, no.' Resentful of her interruption. 'But Richard will be joining the firm in the new year. That much has been settled.'

'And Verity?'

'What about Verity?' Irritated by Sarah's insistence. 'She's still at the Kensington School of Art, according to Richard; still living with two of her fellow students. You needn't worry, I have given her all the financial help she needs to continue her studies, to squander on clothes and holidays. And I happen to know that she swanned off to Greece during the summer vacations.' He sounded resentful.

'Needn't worry!' Sarah drew in a sharp breath. 'Of course I worry about her! You mean to say that you have made no attempt to see her?'

'No, not since she made it perfectly apparent that she did not want to see me.' Getting up, Faulkner paced, glass in hand, towards the windows. Glancing at Sarah's desk, 'Still writing, I see.' Unable to resist a dig about her work, which he had never regarded as more than a footling pastime, 'Isn't it about time you came up with a bestseller?'

'That is not important. About Verity . . . '

Crossing to the fireplace, resting an arm on the mantelpiece, 'That is why I decided to come,' Faulkner said, 'to talk about the children; their future. Especially Verity's. The girl is obviously unsettled.' He paused to frame his words, 'The truth is, so am I.'

'*You?*' Sarah looked at him disbelievingly. 'I don't understand.'

Faulkner shrugged his shoulders. 'Not very pleasant to admit, but my marriage to Suki is over.' He spoke bitterly. 'That she married me for money became apparent early on. My own fault, I suppose. I indulged her every whim: would have gone on doing so, I imagine, until I discovered that she was having an affair.'

'And you find that hard to accept? You, of all people?'

'No need to rub it in!'

'Look, Faulkner, I'm sorry you're in trouble,' Sarah spoke more kindly. 'But what can I do about it? I am no longer a part of your life.'

'That could be changed.'

'In what way – changed?' Again the feeling of disorientation, as if nothing he said made sense.

'You're an intelligent woman. Is there any need to spell it out? I am asking you to make a home for me, Sarah, and the children, to let bygones be bygones.'

'You are not serious?' She felt inclined to laugh. 'But that's ludicrous!'

'You find it amusing that I have come all this way to heal

the breach between us? To put forward a proposition for the good of all concerned? Frankly, Sarah, your attitude amazes me.' He was on his high horse now.

'Heal the breach? You speak as if we had had a lovers' tiff! We are divorced, for heaven's sake! You wanted your freedom to remarry! Now you have a new wife, *and* a child. What of them? Especially the child. You say that your wife is having an affair. Are you certain of that? You haven't been married five minutes. Now, here you are, having fallen at the first hurdle, speaking of yet another divorce. To make matters worse, you apparently expect me to pick up the pieces; provide a shoulder to cry on; make a "home" for you, whatever that may mean. Are you looking for a housekeeper? Is that it? If so, you've come to the wrong place. I suggest you try an employment agency.'

'Stop babbling, Sarah, and listen to me!' He was being masterful now, intent on getting his own way, coolly weighing up his best approach. 'Our divorce was a mistake. It should never have happened. You said you wanted it, too, but I don't believe that. You had a great deal of freedom, a car, a lovely home, the children's affection. We had our ups and downs, of course, what married couples have not?' Here came the great confession. 'I did not realize until it was too late, how much our life together meant to me.' Faulkner appeared to mean what he said, and perhaps he did, Sarah thought. But, knowing the way his mind worked, there must be a catch somewhere.

She said, slowly, 'So what you are really saying is, that you want to pick up where we left off?'

'That is precisely what I mean! Verity in particular has been hurt by all this. The girl needs stability!'

How typical of Faulkner, Sarah thought angrily. Turning the tables had always been a trick of his; making others feel guilty. 'Things might have been different had you stayed closer instead of rushing off without discussing the children's future,' he said. 'I did ask you, the night you left so abruptly, to smooth their path a little. But no, you wouldn't listen. All you had to do was tell them that we had agreed to part amicably . . . '

'And did you really imagine that they might just not have noticed a blonde, pregnant stepmother? Oh, really, Faulkner. Talk sense!'

'That was uncalled for.'

'I'm sorry. But this patching up of our marriage? Do you really imagine it would work? I am not the same person. I have made a new life for myself.'

'That is precisely the reason why I think it *would* work, because you *are* different.' He felt, triumphantly, that he had struck the right note at last. 'You look marvellous, Sarah. Every credit due to you for that. I can't think how you managed to survive, but I'm sure Verity and Richard would feel proud of your efforts.'

'But you didn't know, when you came all this way to "heal the breach", that I *had* managed to survive; that I looked "marvellous", as you put it,' Sarah reminded him. 'You expected to find me living in one room. And yet you were prepared to have me back, warts and all. Why, Faulkner? It doesn't make sense. Why me?'

'I thought I'd explained all that!' Damn the woman. Why the uncomfortable feeling that she would ferret out the truth sooner or later? he thought irritably.

'Women have never been a problem with you,' Sarah continued. 'If, as you say, your marriage to Suki is over, why come all this way to persuade someone you expected to find living in a bedsit, presumably every bit as fat and dowdy as before, to come back to you, when you might, more reasonably have turned to one of your old flames?'

'You are being very cruel, Sarah, totally unreasonable. Hasn't it occurred to you that I, too, might have changed; that I also need stability, a settled home life, a woman capable of understanding?'

'Understanding of – what? That you are feeling your age, perhaps?' Sarah frowned slightly, sensing an underlying reason for all this. 'You're not – ill, are you?'

A dull flush mounted Faulkner's cheeks, linking the network of thread veins. He said, pompously, 'There seems little point in continuing this conversation.' Glancing at his wrist-watch, he said, 'There's a train due in half an hour. I had planned to stay overnight. We might have had dinner together, but I see that you are in no mood for sensible conversation!'

Picking up his coat, he continued, 'I am disappointed, Sarah, that you have so lightly dismissed all I have said to you.'

'You're wrong. I haven't dismissed anything yet,' Sarah broke in, 'Above all,' she confessed, 'I have missed the children. It has been my dearest wish that they would come to see me. I have not tried to shut them out of my life. There has always been an open invitation to visit. And surely you can see that, if I did come back to you, there would have to be a new set of rules? Complete honesty between us. And I don't think that you have been honest with me tonight.'

'But you will give some thought to my proposal?'

'How could I do otherwise?' But Sarah knew, when he had gone, that she would lie awake, churning over in her mind all that had passed between them, and she was right.

At four o'clock in the morning, she got up to make herself a cup of tea, and sat down on the rose settee to drink it, wishing she could think more clearly, somehow distance herself from the here and now. Escape, as Miriam had escaped from her prison . . .

Sunday.

Entering the Minster by the great West door, looking up at the roof bosses portraying scenes in the life of Christ and his mother Mary, and at the Five Sisters' window with its geometric patterns of grey and green grisaille glass, thinking of Amabie, Sarah walked slowly towards the All Saints' Chapel.

Chapter Twenty-one

Helen had arrived at the restaurant when Sarah came in. She had ordered a carafe of wine and was sitting at the table, sipping a glass, looking pale and tired.

'Am I late?' Sarah slipped into the seat opposite. Helen shook her head, 'No, I came early, to get away from the house.'

'Have you changed your day off?'

'I'm on holiday. I usually take a week in autumn, just to potter. Alec and I sometimes spend a few days at Scarborough. But not this time.' She sounded bitter.

'What's wrong, Helen?'

'Give you three guesses.'

'Philippa?'

'Got it in one!' Helen's eyes filled with tears. 'I'm sorry.' She opened her bag to find a handkerchief. 'It's just that Alec is behaving like a lunatic. Oh God, why are men such fools?'

'You can't mean that he . . . '

'That's exactly what I mean!' Anticipating the question, Helen supplied the answer in that same bitter tone of voice. 'He's besotted by her. One would imagine that a man would be put off by a woman who turned up drunk at a dinner party looking like a Spanish galleon in full rig, making a damned nuisance of herself. But not Alec! My altruistic brother has actually started blaming himself for her bad behaviour! It's "poor Pippa this, poor Pippa that", until I could scream.'

'Calm down, Helen! Has Philippa been in touch with him?'

'In touch? My God, she hasn't given him a minute's peace! It started on Saturday, after, presumably, she'd recovered from her hangover. I was at work at the time. He told me later that she had come to the house to apologize. We had a somewhat heated argument, I'm afraid. That's why I rang you. I felt I'd go mad if I didn't talk to someone.'

When the waitress came, Sarah ordered for both of them. When she had gone, she said, 'So what happened?'

Helen uttered a brief, mirthless laugh, 'Huh! The romance is on again! She's on the phone to him every five minutes, and Alec is mooning about like a lovesick teenager.' Drying her eyes. 'I can't bear it. That's why we quarrelled. I told him he was mad to even contemplate getting involved again at his age.' Her mouth trembled. 'I thought I could handle it. I was wrong. Of course he accused me of being jealous, and I am! Jealous that he thinks more about Pippa than he does about me.'

When the waitress brought the food, Helen looked at it as if it would choke her. Edging the plate aside, she said, 'Sarah, what *am* I to do?'

Sarah shrugged helplessly. 'There's nothing much you can do. You'll have to be strong-minded enough to start thinking about your own future.' Stretching out her hand in sympathy, understanding Helen's feelings, 'Look, love, why not go to Scarborough for a few days?'

'Leave Alec at the mercy of that – harpy?' Helen looked stunned. 'That's the last advice I expected you to offer.'

'It's the best advice I *can* give you. Anything you do or say in opposition will aggravate the situation. Come on, Helen, you know that's true. Here, have my hanky, yours is wet through.' She gave Helen's fingers a squeeze of encouragement, 'And when you get back from Scarborough, go to my flat. I'll leave the keys with Ralph.'

'Why? Where will you be?'

'I'm taking a holiday myself, as it happens. I meant to tell you in any case.' This was going to be difficult. Should she tell Helen that she was going away with Nicholas, or not? How would Helen react? Poor Helen who seemed off the idea of romance at the moment. Only one way to find out. Ridiculous to feel guilty. Lots of unmarried couples went on holiday together, Sarah thought. Even so, she did feel guilty. The words, 'Nicholas Tierney has asked me to go to France with him,' were difficult to say.

'What? You mean . . . ?' No doubt about Helen's reaction. She was shocked. More than shocked – antagonistic. 'But you *can't*! You *mustn't*! Don't be a fool, Sarah! You don't know what you'd be letting yourself in for!'

'Perhaps you are right. Possibly I am asking for trouble,' Sarah admitted. 'All I know is, I'd spend a lifetime of regret not finding out for myself.'

'Are you – in love with him?'

'Let us say I'm deeply attracted. More than that I can't say at the moment. Oh, I know there's more to love than physical attraction, but I think,' Sarah spoke softly, ruefully, 'that being with someone is the only way to find out.' She paused, 'Please try to understand.'

Helen said bitterly, 'Perhaps I'm just a frustrated old maid jealous of other people's happiness. I'm sorry, I had no right to criticize, to say what I did. It's just that everything seems to be going wrong.' She bit her lip,

'Funny, I've always seen myself as a fairly competent, well-adjusted person. I imagined that Alec and I would keep on jogging along together as we have done since we started living together.'

Crumpling the clean hanky, 'You want the truth? I was glad when that happened, glad when he was invalided out of the Army. I've never said this before, I was too ashamed. It was just so good to be – needed.' She turned her head aside, fighting to keep from crying. 'Now you know what a selfish beast I really am.'

'Please don't, Helen. That's not true, and you know it,' Sarah spoke gently.

'Yes it is! The reason I reacted so violently just now . . . because I wished like hell that I was in your shoes!' Her eyes wet with tears, looking at Sarah, attempting a smile, 'I wished it was me and not you that Nicholas Tierney had asked to go away with him!'

'I had no idea . . . ' Sarah's heart sank. 'Helen, believe me, had I known how you felt about him, I would never have . . . ' Her mind started working overtime. Perhaps it was not too late to cancel her ferry ticket, to ring Nicholas, tell him she had changed her mind.

As though reading her thoughts, Helen said, 'Pass up this chance, and you'll not only never forgive yourself, *I* shall never forgive you! Nicholas never gave me so much as a second glance.'

'Helen!'

'It's the gospel truth!' Helen's smile reached her eyes. Clasping Sarah's hand, she said simply, 'And – thank you.'

'For what?'

'For – being my friend!' Lifting her wineglass, 'Let's drink a toast, shall we? "To friendship".'

Sarah knew she must see Ralph. A phone call would not do. She could not go away without telling him the truth.

His face lit up when he saw her. 'Come in. I've just made some coffee.' Entering his flat, she remembered that first time when, tired and dusty from the removal, he had given her food, warmth and companionship. If only one could choose and keep the most important facets of a relationship, in this case the uncomplicated friendship and understanding which had meant so much to her. But nothing remained static or uncomplicated when emotions became involved. Difficult to tell a man, I want your friendship, not your love. But this, in essence, was what she had come to tell him, quietly, with tenderness and sincerity.

Sophia had arranged, with Colbert, by telephone, to have food and wine delivered to the farmhouse in readiness for her nephew's arrival. A business transaction pure and simple, between herself and de Vigny's agent. The farmhouse was to let, she wished to rent it. Never at any stage had she considered involving Charles in the transaction. As a matter of course, Colbert would inform de Vigny that the house had been rented to a Mr Nicholas Tierney. Sophia was adamant on that point. The arrangements she was making were on *his* behalf, not hers. Colbert understood perfectly. He would see to everything personally.

Nicky's announcement at dinner next evening, that he was not going alone to France, startled Sophia. 'But I thought you wanted peace and quiet!' Damnation, she thought, seeing the ruination of her carefully laid plans to bring Nicholas and de Vigny together.

'The person I am taking with me is scarcely likely

to cause a breach of the peace,' he said with a hint of amusement. 'After all, you did tell me that the place provides spiritual sanctuary for writers and their ilk, and Sarah Vale happens to be a writer.'

'Sarah Vale?' The name rang a bell. 'You mean the woman who wrote *Lawrence*?' Sophia's face cleared. She had read *Lawrence*, a novel of extraordinary power and perception. A woman capable of such writing, such clarity of vision, might be the answer to a prayer. The cover blurb and the photograph of Sarah – that of a somewhat overweight person, the daughter of a country parson – convinced Sophia that she had better ring up Colbert the first thing tomorrow morning to have the spare room made ready.

Nicholas called for Sarah at seven o'clock on the morning of their departure. The day held a promise of warmth and sunshine, once the early morning mist had cleared. The sky lightened as they drove to Hull to board the ferry. The sea reminded Sarah of Wedgwood blue porcelain. Sunlight glancing on the water appeared as a path of gold leading to a limitless horizon.

For the first time in his life, Nicholas felt at ease with a woman. Standing beside her at the ship's rail, the breeze ruffling his hair, he told her that he had been born in France, that his mother was French, his father a retired English diplomat, living in Paris.

'And your mother?'

'She died recently, I'm afraid.'

'I'm sorry,' Instinctively, Sarah realized what it had cost him to speak of his mother's death. Touched by his confidence, she laid her hand gently on his, and looked up at him, seeing his face in profile as she had done, once before, near the All Saints' Chapel in York Minster. This man who seemed to her the reincarnation of Amabie, especially now, standing at a ship's rail, looking out to sea, his mane of dark hair blown back by the wind.

Following the customs' check, they began the drive through Belgium to France. Bypassing Paris, Nicholas headed the Daimler towards Troyes, then branched off on a series of minor roads in the direction of Fontainebleau.

Over lunch at a village bistro, Sarah told him that she had never been to France before, only to Italy – to Florence – years ago, with a party of girls from her office, before she was married.

'I've never been to Florence,' Nicholas said, pouring her a glass of wine. 'Arguably the loveliest city on earth. What did you think of it?'

'Frankly, I loathed it,' Sarah admitted. 'The streets were so narrow, so hot, chock-a-block with tourists, I could scarcely breathe.'

'A bit like York at the height of the summer season?' Nicholas suggested, with a smile.

'Yes, exactly like that.' She laughed. 'Moreover, I didn't get a wink of sleep. There was this melon-stall under my bedroom window. I had no idea that Italians were so fond of melons! The vendor was still shouting them his wares at three o'clock in the morning!' Pausing to take a sip of wine, she said, 'I never want to see another melon again as long as I live!'

They came to the farmhouse in the woods as to a caravanserai after their long journey. And this seemed an enchanted world to Sarah, this low-beamed building set amid firebrand trees burning with the gold, crimson and scarlet of a breathtakingly beautiful Indian summer.

Putting a match to the fire, Nicholas thought that Sophia had been right about this place. It *was* peaceful, as if the generations of people who had lived beneath this roof had left behind something of their warmth and simplicity, a sense of continuity and purpose.

When the fire had begun to burn, he went through to the kitchen to find Sarah sorting through the boxes of groceries on the kitchen table – a massive, scrubbed wooden structure, lit by an overhead oil lamp, round which, in days gone by, the farmer and his family would have gathered at mealtimes. It was a room still redolent with the scent of herbs, cooking, coffee, and Gauloises cigarettes.

Thankfully, whoever was responsible for the farmhouse had lit a fire in the Aga.

'Here, let me help!'

'I'm afraid dinner will be a bit of a makeshift affair,' Sarah said, putting tinned food into a cupboard.

'Not to worry! Anything will do! I've had enough rich food to last a lifetime!'

'In that case, how about omelettes?'

'Great! Fine with me!' Nicholas grinned. Then, 'Speaking of cases, I'd better take the luggage upstairs to our rooms . . . '

Rooms, Sarah thought, cracking eggs into a bowl. Obviously, then, she and Nicholas would not be sleeping together. Was she pleased or sorry? Difficult to decide which, tired after her long journey; a stranger in a strange place. But why rush fences? This was just the beginning . . . If she and Nicholas were destined to become lovers, she would far rather it happened naturally, in the fullness of time, a coming together born of a mutual desire – without which physical union meant little or nothing.

After supper they went through to the living room to sit by the fire, aware of the solitude, the silence broken by the crackling of the logs, the faint night sounds beyond the windows, the barking of a fox, the tapping of a branch against the glass. Sarah shivered.

'Are you cold?' Nicky asked.

'No, just tired. It has been a long day.'

'You're not sorry you came?'

'Of course not.'

'I'm tired, too. I suppose we may as well have an early night.' Standing up, he stretched his arms, eased his shoulder muscles. Turning to see to the fire, he said, 'Lord, I haven't gone to bed this early in years. Must be the country air. There, that should do it.' He turned to pick up his cigarette case and lighter. 'Oh, dammit. I meant to bring something to read.'

'I've brought a manuscript copy of my book, if that would do.'

'Really? Sure you don't mind?'

'Not at all, though it needs some revision. I thought I might work on it while we're here.'

They went upstairs together, Sarah leading the way. Delving into her suitcase, she handed him the manuscript.

'Thanks. Quite a blockbuster. How many pages?'

'Around four hundred. I forget exactly how many.' Ridiculous to feel so nervously aware of his presence in her room. Lovemaking was obviously the last thing on his mind, yet she sensed that he, too, felt uneasy as he stood near the door, holding the manuscript, and said 'Goodnight, Sarah. Sleep well.'

Closing the door of his room, why the hell hadn't

he kissed her goodnight? he thought angrily. But if he had, what then? Holding her in his arms, he would have wanted to make love to her. To what end, what purpose?

This kind of situation had arisen too many times before during his lifetime – the initial feeling of desire succeeded by his failure to reach a physical climax – those failures linked to his first abortive relationship with Anna Stravinska, more deeply to his fear of total commitment to any woman, however desirable she may be.

Switching off his lamp, he lay sleepless until the early hours of the morning, deeply conscious that Sarah might also be awake. Just a feeling he had. Tiredness was no guarantee of sleep as he knew only too well, not when the mind remained in top gear. Ridiculous that two adult people should lie in separate beds when the attraction between them was so powerful. All he had to do was cross the landing to Sarah's room to put an end to the impasse. He could not do it. Instead, relighting the lamp, he picked up the manuscript and began reading.

Chapter Twenty-two

Up at daybreak, he was stoking the Aga when Sarah came down, concentrating on the task in hand. He had made a pot of coffee, opened the back door to the scents of the countryside, but the devil was on his shoulder. The darker side of his Gemini personality had come uppermost, a feeling of depression brought about by sleeplessness and self disgust.

Yesterday he had felt happier than he had done for years, serenely confident in Sarah's company. All that had changed now to a deep introspection about his future, linked to the failures of the past. He knew the mood would pass in time. Madeleine would have told him to go away by himself for a while until he felt better.

Madeleine. An hour's drive would take him to l'église St Germaine. How Sarah would take his absence on their first day at the cottage, he could not imagine. Possibly she would feel hurt. Even worse, he imagined, if he stayed with her in his present mood.

She knew the moment she saw him that something was wrong. Sensing his restlessness, she wondered if he regretted asking her to come away with him, a feeling borne out when he told her that he would be leaving her on her own for a while. 'I hope you don't mind,' he added. 'I'll be back before dark.'

Inured to disappointments, to keeping her feelings in check, carrying the coffee cups to the sink, she said,

'Don't worry, I'll find plenty to do.' Running the hot water, swishing liquid into the washing-up bowl, pretending not to mind, 'I'll explore the garden, take a walk in the woods.'

Ashamed of his churlishness, wishing he could explain that his need of solitude was no fault of hers, knowing that he could not begin to explain anything at the moment, he said, 'Quite sure you won't mind being alone?'

'Of course not. I'm used to it. The occupational hazard of a writer.' Nothing on earth would have made her show how much she minded.

When he had gone, she wandered into the garden. The farmhouse had come so close to demolition that the orchard and the kitchen garden had been allowed to run wild. Parsley, mint and thyme grew in thick clumps alongside the crazed paths leading to a sagging greenhouse, fallen apples littered the unmown orchard grass.

Here and there she came across discarded relics of an old way of life – a broken shopping basket in which enterprising birds had built their nest, a cracked and pitted enamel jug, a handful of clothes pegs, a clay pipe – conjuring up visions of the people to whom these objects had once belonged.

Sarah imagined the farmer's wife, a sturdy French peasant woman, pegging out her washing to dry; gathering a basketful of herbs and vegetables for the family supper; her husband and sons coming in from their days's work to wash the dirt from their hands before sitting round the table to eat the food the woman had prepared for them, a heartwarming stew, perhaps, or chicken pot-au-feu. Simple, nourishing food to satisfy appetites sharpened by fresh air and toil.

There was a fresh chicken in the larder, vegetables,

wine, garlic. Going indoors, Sarah decided to cook chicken pot-au-feu for the evening meal, and set about her preparations, peeling the vegetables, crushing garlic, finding a strong iron pan.

Cleaning and jointing the chicken, she thought about Faulkner's dramatic reappearance in her life, his startling proposition that she should go back to him for the sake of the children. But as what? His wife, housekeeper, more ludicrously – his mistress?

Perhaps she had been wrong in dismissing the idea of returning to her old life, in turning down Ralph's offer of marriage. Coming away with Nicholas had seemed an escape from her problems. Now, here she was, alone, faced with the inescapable knowledge that he was not in love with her. Perhaps Helen had been right in saying she didn't know what she'd be letting herself in for. Poor Helen whose vivid imagination had probably conjured up scenes of unbridled passion, Sarah thought. Certainly the last thing she had imagined was being left alone.

Driving to St Germaine, Nicholas stopped on the way to buy flowers from a wayside stall – bitter-scented white chrysanthemums and purple Michaelmas daisies, wishing the flowers were not so commonplace. The blossoms of springtime were more in keeping with Madeleine's charming, light-hearted personality – daffodils and plumy white lilac. But this was autumn, not spring.

He had no wish to enter the church, to recall that agonizing moment when Madeleine's coffin was carried in and he had seen the cold, withdrawn expression on his father's face. Instead, he walked slowly to the place where his mother lay buried, head bowed, afraid, almost, to look at the grave, feeling the hot, useless tears welling up.

Sarah had not asked where he was going. Perhaps he should have told her. Certainly he could not have borne her to come with him, to witness his lack of control. Possibly he was wrong not to have told her. Reading the first chapters of *Amabie*, he had been struck by her power of perception, her ability to enter the minds of her characters. Amabie had stepped from the pages as a living being, so strong a character that he could scarcely believe he had not been patterned on a living person. Himself, perhaps. But that was not possible. And yet the man bore an uncanny resemblance to himself.

How strange. Laying the flowers on his mother's grave, Sarah and Madeleine seemed linked in his mind in some indefinable way. Suddenly, he felt more at peace. Comforted. Aware that he was not alone after all. It was then he saw the spray of gardenias near the headstone, and wondered who they were from. Picking up the flowers, catching their fragrance, remembering Madeleine in the full bloom of her beauty, he felt her presence; the indestructible power of love in the air about him. Love. The only thing in life worth having.

Leaving the chicken to simmer, her writer's mind alive and questing, Sarah walked in the woods, a wonderland of colour, the paths carpeted with fallen leaves of red and gold.

Lost in thought, she heard the cooing of wood pigeons, the flapping of their wings as they rose and took flight, disturbed by some sound or other. Then she heard the cracking of twigs, and saw a tall man coming down the path towards her. 'You must be from the cottage,' he said. 'I am Charles de Vigny.'

'Sarah Vale. I hope I'm not trespassing?'

'Not at all. On the contrary, it is I who am trespassing on your privacy.' Under normal circumstances, he would not have ventured near the farm cottage, but the urge to see his son had proved too strong a temptation to resist when his agent had told him the house had been let to Nicholas and his female companion. 'Tell me, is everything to your satisfaction?'

'Oh, yes. It's a wonderful place. So remote, so peaceful.' Sarah brushed a fallen leaf from her hair. 'Are you the agent?'

De Vigny smiled. 'I'm sorry, I hadn't realized . . . I suppose, strictly speaking, that I am your landlord.'

'Oh, lord! You must forgive me, I had no idea. Perhaps you'd care to have tea with me?'

An attractive woman, de Vigny considered as they walked to the house together, sensibly dressed for the country in a tweed skirt, green sweater, and flat-heeled shoes. He wondered if she and his son were lovers. If so, Nicholas showed good taste. But where was Nicholas?

'Would you mind coming through to the kitchen? It's warmer there.' Sarah led the way. 'My friend will light the sitting room fire later, when he returns. He – he's gone out for the day.'

'Leaving you on your own? Doesn't that worry you?'

'Not really. Why should it?' What an odd question, Sarah thought, fetching the cups and saucers, opening a packet of biscuits, unless de Vigny imagined . . . Flushing slightly, she said, 'We are both free agents. Merely friends.'

'My apologies, Miss Vale. I did not mean to imply . . . '

Pouring boiling water on the tea-bags, 'No need to apologize. And I am Mrs Vale, by the way.'

So his son and this attractive older woman were not

lovers? A pity. He wondered if Sarah Vale minded that Nicholas was not her lover, and decided this might well be so. Despite her attractiveness, the bloom was missing – that special bloom which lights up a woman when she knows she is loved. The look in her eyes when she spoke of her 'friend', had convinced Charles that she was almost certainly in love with Nicky.

Had Madeleine been right, then, in worrying that their son seemed incapable of falling in love? 'Always,' she had written, 'the senseless flirtations, never a sense of purpose or commitment. I have often wondered if he is frightened of women; incapable of making love'.

Drinking tea, Sarah asked de Vigny about the farmhouse and the people who had lived there. 'My agent would know,' Charles told her. 'He will have the records in his office. I'll ask him to look them up for you.' He smiled, 'Why? Are you thinking of writing a book on the subject?'

'Perhaps. That's one of the reasons I came here, to find the subject of a new novel.'

'How intriguing! Tell me more.' Soon they were talking as friends about English and French literature, with Sarah getting up now and then to see how the chicken was doing.

Impulsively she suggested, when he rose to his feet, that he should stay for supper. De Vigny declined the invitation. 'Nothing would give me more pleasure, but my housekeeper is expecting me.'

Turning at the door, he said, 'On the other hand, perhaps you and your friend would care to dine with me tomorrow evening? Shall we say seven o'clock?'

Explaining that it would be preferable to drive to the house rather than risk the woods after dark, he thanked her for the tea, and walked back the way he had come.

An hour later, busy in the kitchen, Sarah heard the arrival of the Daimler.

Nicholas seemed distant at first. Soon the warmth of the kitchen and the effects of the dry white Mouton Cadet he had opened to accompany the pot-au-feu, seemed to lessen his tension. The great arc of the oil lamp above the table accentuated the tired lines about his eyes and mouth.

Glancing across at him, this was the troubled man she had first seen in York Minster, Sarah thought, not the man she had danced with at the Carillon, or the man who had stood beside her near the ship's rail. Not the smiling companion of yesterday, nor one who bore the slightest resemblance to the man she had seen talking to a stringy blonde girl in Betty's Cafe, playing escort to an elderly American, and that dazzling redhead at Acaster Malbis.

If only she could come close enough to find out what was troubling him. But experience had taught her never to pry. She simply knew that he had touched her heart as no man had done before.

He had lit the living-room fire when he returned. Now it was burning brightly, casting flickering shadows on walls and ceiling. Some of the old furniture had been left where it was – a huge oak dresser occupying the space of one wall, for instance, because it would never have fitted into a modern house.

The hearth, of wide stone slabs, and the chimney-breast, reminded Sarah of *Wuthering Heights*. The long, chintz-covered settee in front of the fireplace was flanked with matching armchairs. De Vigny, or his agent, had obviously considered the comfort of their guests, she thought, nestling in a corner of the settee, tucking up her legs.

When Nicholas came in with the coffee, she told him about her meeting with Charles de Vigny, and his dinner invitation.

'What was he like?'

'Very tall, distinguished looking. Charming.'

Pouring the coffee, 'I imagined that so distinguished a person would not have taken the trouble to call on his tenants,' Nicholas said. 'A French nobleman, no less.'

'What do you mean?'

'He has a title. Le Comte de Vigny.'

Sarah laughed. 'And to think I mistook him for the agent, and gave him tea in the kitchen.'

About to sit down, suddenly Nicky remembered that he had left a present for Sarah on the back seat of the car. 'I'll be back in a second. I've got something for you.' He went out to the car, returning moments later with an armful of flowers. 'With my apologies for leaving you on your own today,' he said, placing them on her lap.

Surprised and delighted, 'Oh, thank you. Chrysanthemums! They're lovely.'

'I bought them at a wayside stall on my way to l'église St Germaine,' he told her. 'I went there to visit my mother's grave.'

So that was the reason. Even so, instinct warned Sarah not to pursue the subject. She said, untucking her legs, 'I'll put them in water. There'll be a vase in the kitchen, I expect.'

'I'd better light the lamps.'

'No. Please don't. I much prefer firelight. In any case, the kitchen lamp's still on. I can find my way.'

There were several stone jugs in the pantry, Sarah discovered. Choosing two of them, filling them with water, she arranged the flowers. Returning to the living room, carrying the jugs, she saw that Nicholas was lying back in one of the armchairs, long legs resting on the hearth, his head against a cushion, eyes half closed.

'Tired?' she asked quietly, placing one jug of flowers on the dresser, the other on the low table near his chair, where he had put the tray of coffee, glasses, and a fresh bottle of wine.

'A little.' Opening his eyes, he looked up at her. Unlike most women, she had not jumped in with questions about his visit to the cemetery. For this reason he felt able to tell her about it, and about Madeleine; and about his relationship with his father.

The floodgates open, speaking jerkily at first, pausing to open the wine, holding the glass in his hands, staring into the fire, he confessed his hatred of his father whose coldness had so deeply affected his own life, and Madeleine's.

'There are times when I wonder if I have inherited his inability to show affection,' he said bitterly.

'I'm sure that's not true.'

'But then, you don't really know me. I feel . . . God, how can I explain?' He shivered. 'As if I were two people rolled into one. Madeleine told me that Gemini people often are, but it's more than that. It's as if there were some kind of barrier inside me, holding me in check: the fear that I may someday lose the part of me that is Madeleine, that I shall become more and more like my father.'

She left him still sitting near the fire, knowing there was

nothing more to be said for the time being. Nothing that would help. Lighting a lamp, she went up to her room, and lay in bed listening intently for the sound of his footsteps on the stairs. None came.

She must have fallen asleep then, for she dreamt that she was walking along the corridor of a strange house, opening doors to look into empty rooms, feeling the way she had felt as a child when, late for school, she had found the playground empty, and entered the building to find that lessons were already in progress, the other children sitting at their desks.

Awaking from her dream, she wondered if the sound she had heard was part of that dream, or reality. Feeling that something was wrong, she got out of bed and put on her dressing gown.

The broad, uncarpeted landing led to an open staircase. Her hand on the banister, she could see, from where she was standing, the faint glow of the living-room fire. Going down a step or two, she saw Nicholas sitting in the arm-chair, shoulders hunched, head buried in his hands.

Hearing the rustle of her gown, he looked up, rubbing the back of a hand across his face, as if bemused. 'Sorry, I didn't mean to disturb you.' He smiled awkwardly, shaking his head as if to clear his muddled thoughts. 'I had this bloody awful nightmare . . . '

Glancing at the clock, she saw that it was almost twenty past one. The room was cold now that the fire had almost gone out. Quickly crossing towards him, she threw a handful of kindling on to the ashes, waited until the twigs had taken hold, then carefully put on a couple of logs. 'You must be frozen. I'll make some coffee,' she said, going through to the kitchen, taking with her the tray with the empty cups, noticing that the wine bottle was empty, the ashtray filled with half-smoked cigarettes.

'I fell asleep in the chair,' he said, when she came back with fresh coffee. Handing him a cup, she knelt down in front of the hearth. The fire was burning strongly now. He said, 'I dreamt about my father. I was on the landing outside his room. I knew my mother was inside that room. I could hear her crying, calling out to me. Calling my name over and over again.' He shivered. 'When I tried to go to her, my father barred the way, and all the time I could hear Madeleine's voice begging me to help her . . . Then I saw her. Oh, Christ!' The cup he was holding fell to the hearth and broke into pieces.

'Don't! Please, don't!' Turning away from the fire to kneel at his feet, she put her arms about him. 'It was just a dream. Nothing to worry about. Nightmares can seem very real, very dreadful. I know. Try to put it out of your mind.'

'I wish to God I could. But it wasn't just a dream, these things really happened.' He shook his head impatiently. 'You don't understand. How could you?' Staring into the past, speaking in a low voice, 'As a child, I would get out of bed, stand outside my parents' room. I knew my father hated me. Children sense such things. Whenever he was there in the house, Madeleine was different, afraid of showing me too much affection. There were always closed doors when my father was there, shutting me away from Madeleine . . . '

He drew in a shuddering breath, 'He did not even warn me that she was desperately ill. When I arrived in Paris, she was already dead. Her body was lying in state in the house when I got there. Then came the closing of another door when my father told me I was no longer welcome under his roof.'

310

'I wish I knew what to say. How to help you.' Sarah slipped her hands into his, her face upturned, eyes tender.

With a deep sigh, Nicholas bent forward to kiss her, very gently at first – the merest touch of lips on hers. Then his arms were about her, his lips more demanding. She could feel the hammering of his heart, the strength of his arms as he crushed her closer to him.

Holding Sarah, he experienced a momentary release from the horror of his nightmare. Desperately in need of warmth, of a physical contact with another human being, of reassurance and love, he clung to her as he had never clung to a woman before, knowing that this was someone he could trust, remembering the sense of comfort he had felt at l'église St Germaine, his identification of Sarah with Madeleine, not because of physical similarity, but something far deeper – a kind of spiritual grace and integrity.

Then came the feeling he dreaded, the deep-seated dread of failure, the erection of the mental barrier of self doubt beyond which he could not pass, just as, in his nightmare, and so often in reality, he had come up against the doors his father had closed in his face.

Knowing that he cared too much for Sarah to subject her to humiliation, his failure as a lover, his pride deeply entrenched, he did what he had so often done before, in similar situations, but this time with a very real regret. No laughter.

Releasing her from his embrace, he stood up. Taking her hands, he drew her gently to her feet. 'Forgive me,' he said.

'For what?' Sarah's own pride stood in the way. Not for the world would she have given tongue to her thoughts at that moment. Why ask, 'Because you are not in love with me?' Transparently, he was not. After all, she had literally

311

placed herself in his hands. But never again. Sick at heart, deeply ashamed, knowing how much she had wanted him to make love to her, she left him standing near the fire and went upstairs to her room.

Watching her go, remembering the touch of her lips on his, the way he had felt holding her body close to his, that sublime, initial feeling of release, that overwhelming upsurge of passion he'd experienced before his mental torment began, he wished himself the son of a peasant farmer, dull of intellect, his days ruled by the simple pattern of the changing seasons, of toil and tiredness, returning home from a day's work, his father's hand warm on his shoulder, earning approval for a job well done.

Chapter Twenty-three

Charles de Vigny stood on the steps to welcome his guests. All day he had waited for this moment – meeting his son face to face.

'Sarah, how lovely you look. And you must be Nicholas. Forgive the familiarity. Please, call me Charles.' He led the way to the drawing room. 'Sit near the fire. Now, what will you have to drink?'

So this was his son. Scarcely able to take his eyes off Nicholas, de Vigny remembered the night he had been conceived – the night Madeleine had come to the château, as to a place of spiritual sanctuary, an unhappy, bewildered woman, alone in the world, devastated by the deaths of her parents, also that of her husband, Philippe Joubert, whose cruelty towards her she had never understood.

How lovely Madeleine had looked that night, and how vulnerable. She had driven from Paris in such reckless haste, Charles remembered, pouring wine for his guests, that she had not even thought to wear a coat, despite the pouring rain, and arrived soaking wet, explaining breathlessly that the car had run out of petrol halfway up the drive, and she had walked the rest of the way.

Madeleine had knelt by the fire in this very room, he recalled, offering the wine. He could almost see her now, a waif-like figure in her black dress, her wet hair loose about her shoulders, looking up at him as he warned her not to catch cold, saying huskily, 'Would it really matter if I caught pneumonia and died?'

'Of course it would matter!'

There had been servants in the house at that time. He had told one of them to run a hot bath for Madame Joubert, another to light a fire in one of the guest rooms, and to place hot-water bottles in the bed.

Later, when the servants had retired, he had gone to her room to make sure she was warm enough . . .

Recalling his duties as host, offering his guests more wine, de Vigny pushed to the back of his mind his disturbing memories of that night, long gone, when, blinded by his love for Madeleine, nothing else in the world had mattered – not his vows nor his conscience – only Madeleine.

Now, here was their son, the child they had created together that rainy October night, long ago, when the priest had assumed the role of a lover; that child grown to manhood.

Proud that he had passed on something of his own colouring and physique to his son – nevertheless his charm of manner, his smile, his fascination, were all Madeleine's, de Vigny thought. And yet he seemed strained, ill at ease. Charles wondered why.

The conversation turned to Sophia's visit to the farmhouse, the good her holiday had done her. 'I have never seen her looking so fit,' Nicholas said. 'In fact, I've never known her take a holiday before. Her life revolves around the Carillon.'

When the housekeeper came in to announce that dinner was ready – not Clothilde but a more efficient woman who had taken her place – Charles ushered his guests to the dining room. Madame Frontenac had set the table with

314

sparkling glassware and well-polished cutlery, and bustled in with a tureen of soup which she served quickly, piping hot, while her husband, whose duties included helping his wife in the kitchen and dining room, brought in the wine de Vigny had chosen to accompany the meal.

By the flickering light of the candles gracing the long table, how alike Nicholas and Charles were, Sarah thought. Odd, the resemblance had not struck her yesterday when he came to the cottage to drink tea in the kitchen. Now she could not help noticing, not only the likeness, but the way he looked at Nicholas: his expression of – what? Pride, interest, anticipation?

The meal was well cooked, the wine excellent. Conversation hinged on the de Vigny estate; the trout farm, the afforestation programme. Then Charles mentioned that Colbert had found the farm documents Sarah wanted, and suggested a tour of the estate next day. A picnic lunch, perhaps, followed by a visit to the trout farm and his agent's office to pick up the papers.

Over coffee in the drawing room, de Vigny turned the conversation to the Carillon, asking Nicholas about his role in the running of the hotel.

'I've never been quite sure about that,' Nicholas said ruefully. 'I went into it in a dilettante way, to fill in time until I decided what I wanted to do with my life. So I have more or less drifted with the tide. My father was a diplomat, embassy life exciting. I liked the coming and going and the Carillon offered the same kind of atmosphere. I enjoyed planning entertainment, acting as host,' he spoke self deprecatingly, 'putting the icing on the cake, with no idea what had gone into the baking of the cake.'

'When I was young,' Charles said thoughtfully, fingering the stem of his wineglass, 'my father wanted me

315

to enter the church. I did what was expected of me, but I knew almost from the start that I was not cut out for the priesthood.' His voice deepened. In the grip of scarcely concealed emotion, he continued, 'When I sought dispensation from my vows, I had to live with the guilt of what I had done. Changing direction is not always easy, yet there are times when it is necessary, even vital to do so.'

A strange undercurrent of meaning seemed to flow beneath his confession, an intensity of feeling directed towards Nicholas, Sarah thought, as though de Vigny knew him well and cared deeply about his future, which seemed odd, since they had never met before.

The day that followed would remain in Sarah's memory as one of the happiest she had ever known, despite its ending.

Charles arrived at ten o'clock, driving a Volkswagen estate, the back of which contained a picnic hamper, rugs, and a black labrador called Rufus, a recent addition to his household, Charles explained.

The weather was perfect, the countryside at its loveliest, bathed in the warmth of this seemingly endless Indian summer. The arable land, shorn of its harvest of grain, lay amber-coloured in the sun, the horizon was misted with a shimmering heat-haze: trees in their glory of autumn tints appeared as blobs of crimson and gold on an artist's palette; earth lay umber in their shadows; the landscape was dotted with the little communities of farms, houses and school buildings; seagulls followed in the wake of a tractor, the driver of which Charles acknowledged with a smile and a wave of the hand.

Then the scenery began to change as the great dark

swathes of the pine forests shadowed the road on either side, and the hard, baked surface of the track ahead, littered with pine-cones, into which de Vigny had nosed the car, petered out suddenly.

Switching off the ignition, 'I hope you are feeling energetic,' Charles said. 'It's quite a climb to the top, but the view from there is worth the effort.'

The forest, cool and green rose about them, the peace stirred merely by their footsteps and the joyful barking of the dog as they found sticks for him to fetch, and he bounded ahead of them on the stiff, upward path between the trees. Stretching out his hand, Nicholas helped Sarah over the rougher patches, and they laughed, completely at ease with each other, and with de Vigny who led the procession, striding along with remarkable vigour.

Imperceptibly at first, the trees began to thin out. Then suddenly they were in the glare of the sun once more, standing on a high plateau. Sarah caught her breath. The transition from cool greenness to the shimmering heat of the day was almost *too* sudden. De Vigny laughed, 'I know what you are thinking. Now, tell me if you think the climb was worth it.' He extended his arms to encompass the view, and she wondered if this was the way the young priest had looked standing at some resplendent altar, eyes aglow, head thrown back, an expression of intense joy on his face. Scarcely likely, since he had turned his back on the church. Or possibly this was the kind of altar for which he had been searching all along, an altar not clothed in embroidered linen, rich in gold-plate, with glimmering candles, and the smell of incense, but one of grass and trees, and the resinous scent of the pine forest.

'It's – wonderful!' Sarah could not have explained, at that moment, the feeling she had that this was a turning point in her life, as though she had reached some pinnacle of happiness she would remember for ever, with Nicholas beside her, holding her hand, and the dog crouched, panting, on the wind-ruffled grass.

Returning to the car, they got out the hamper, spread rugs on the ground and ate hungrily of the veal and ham pie, crusty bread, cheese and pâté that Charles had provided. They fed the dog titbits, poured water for him into a red plastic bowl, laughed at his antics and ruffled his silky black coat. They drank coffee from earthenware kitchen mugs and relished the strong reviving taste of it after their long, hard climb.

Looking at Nicholas, sitting with his back to a tree, making a fuss of Rufus, Sarah glimpsed a different side of his personality, one she had never seen before, and which she liked far better than the rest. Gone was the haunted stranger of York Minster, gone the man in whose arms she had danced that night at the Carillon, the introspective, nightmare-ridden Nicholas whose complexities stood between them as a barrier, and of whom she felt slightly afraid, uncertain, ill at ease, overwhelmed by his stronger personality; he was a man possessed of the power to shatter her self-confidence by a look or a word. The thought occurred that slimness was no guarantee of increased self-confidence, not if there was still an anxious, fat lady hidden deep inside. But now he was smiling, totally relaxed, the tired lines about his eyes no longer visible, as if the hard exercise, the sunshine, and the laughter, had sent fresh blood surging through his veins, and the sorrows and failures of the past had ceased to exist. With Ralph Foster, she thought, she would know a quiet, uneventful kind of happiness. Possibly boredom.

With Nicholas, uncertainty, unpredictability.

The picnic things cleared away, Charles turned the car and drove them to the trout farm in the valley, where his agent, Maurice Colbert, elderly, balding, wearing gold-rimmed spectacles, a white open-neck shirt over lightweight slacks, and a colourful, Noel Coward type cravat in lieu of a tie, came out of his office to greet them, eager to explain the way the farm was stocked and run, pointing out the various stages of development, speaking quickly in his own language so that Sarah missed most of what he was saying. Not that she minded. It was good just to enjoy the sunshine; to watch Nicholas; for the first time to see him in the company of other men, thinking that this, perhaps, was what he needed to balance his life, that there had possibly been far too many women to cosset and protect him, to cater to his ego. What a pity that he had never known the love and comradeship of his father.

The tour over, Colbert made tea for them in his office, and gave Sarah the farm records she had requested. Of course, how stupid of her, she might have realized they would be in French, that she would not be able to make head or tail of them.

Nicholas laughed, 'Not to worry, I'll translate them for you!'

Returning to the cottage, at least their long day in the fresh air had eased the strain between them, Sarah thought.

Yesterday had been hard to live through, as though the events of the early hours stood as an insurmountable barrier between them – events which neither of them had referred to. Equally, laughter seemed to have dried up at source, along with easy, natural conversation. Although

Nicholas had driven her to a nearby village, to shop, and they had wandered round the market square together, buying fruit and fresh vegetables, bread and honey, they had been stiffly formal with each other.

Today, they had laughed in the sun, linked hands. She had felt warm and alive again. How wrong she had been to let her pride stand in the way of a closer understanding of Nicky's problems. How different things might have been had she stayed with him the other morning; asked him why he was sorry; given him a chance to explain. In the light of this new day, she saw clearly that the barrier between them had been of her own making. If only she *had* stayed.

'Tired?' he asked.

'Yes, I am rather.'

'Why not have a bath?' he suggested. 'I'll light the fire and see to the meal. Cold chicken OK?'

'Cold chicken sounds wonderful!'

Lying supine in deep, scented water, closing her eyes, Sarah heard the comforting sound of the fire being lit in the room below; the bumping of a basket of logs, the raking out of dead ashes. And this was the crowning happiness of her day, this feeling of a new beginning – being given a second chance.

Towelling herself dry, she slipped into a warm, bouclé housecoat, brushed her hair, applied a little makeup, and went downstairs.

A second chance, she thought. This time, pray God, she would not fail, as she had done before, to make him realize how much she loved him.

He was standing near the fire, thoughtfully watching the flames flicking the apple boughs he had brought in from the shed. 'Nicky,' she said softly.

At the sound of her voice, he looked up at her, an

expression of longing in his eyes. Moving quickly forward, drawing her into his arms, 'Sarah,' he murmured, 'Oh, Sarah . . . '

'Now it's my turn to say, "I'm sorry" . . . '

'No, it was my fault, not yours!' Frowning suddenly, he said, 'Someone's coming! Who on earth . . . ?'

The twin beams of a car's headlights raked the ceiling. They heard the crunch of tyres on the gravel, footsteps, an urgent rapping on the front door. Then Charles de Vigny entered the room, breathing heavily.

'Forgive my intrusion,' he said briefly, 'but it is bad news, I'm afraid. Sophia telephoned a few minutes ago to say that her brother has been taken to the medical centre in Paris. She wants you to go there at once, Nicholas. He is seriously ill.'

Chapter Twenty-four

Looking at Nicholas, Sarah saw the colour drain away from his face.

Moments ago, she had believed they were on the verge of a new understanding. Now, reading the cold expression in his eyes, she knew that he had retreated once more behind his self-imposed barrier of bitterness towards his father. Even now, when the man may be dying.

De Vigny said, 'Sophia has arranged a flight from Teesside Airport. She asked me to tell you that she will meet you at the hospital as soon as possible.'

Sarah and Charles exchanged worried glances as, silently, grim-faced, Nicholas went upstairs to pack an overnight bag.

'I think that you had better go to him,' de Vigny suggested. And, 'Yes,' Sarah replied uncertainly.

Entering Nicky's room, she saw that he was bundling his shaving gear, dressing gown, pyjamas, haphazardly into a zippered hold-all.

'My father,' he said bitterly, 'the despoiler of other people's happiness!'

'Please, *don't*!'

'Don't – what?'

'Give yourself reason for regret.' Laying her hand on his arm, 'After all, he *is* your father.'

Nicholas said abruptly, 'Look, Sarah, I know you

mean well, but the last thing I need, right now, is a penny lecture from a parson's daughter!'

'In that case, there's nothing more to be said, is there?' Turning away, she hurried from the room, feeling as if she had received a blow on the face.

Later, when the rear lights of the Daimler had disappeared into the darkness, Charles said briskly, 'And now, my dear, you are coming home with me.'

'That's very kind of you, but I couldn't possibly . . . '

'Nonsense! I insist!'

Clive Tierney had suffered a massive stroke. Simenon had discovered him lying at the foot of the stairs when he had gone through to the dining room to clear the breakfast things; he had quickly sent for an ambulance and later telephoned the Carillon.

'I'll come as quickly as possible,' Sophia said, reacting coolly in this emergency as she had done in all the other crises she had been called upon to cope with throughout her life.

Her flight landed at Charles de Gaulle Airport shortly after midnight. Arriving at the medical centre, she found Nicholas, grey-faced, in one of the waiting rooms, and knew instinctively that she was too late. 'Nicky,' she said softly, as he hurried towards her, hands outstretched, 'when – when did it happen?'

'About an hour ago. There was nothing to be done. He never regained consciousness.'

Sophia took charge of the situation. Nicholas seemed curiously detached, disinclined, at first, to stay at the Rue St Hélène, although M. Renay, the attorney, had imparted the news that Sir Clive had left everything to his son. Indeed, Sir Clive had made a new will a matter of a few days ago. An act of prescience, Renay suggested, recalling their last meeting, his client's fretful desire to settle his affairs, as if he knew that his days were numbered and wished to set his mind at ease: 'To make up for my sins of omission,' Clive had said enigmatically.

Gathering the reins firmly in her hands, seated at Clive's desk, it was Sophia who got in touch with the minister of the Anglican church, and her brother's successor at the embassy, who drew up lists of guests to be invited back to the house for a simple buffet luncheon after the funeral, who ordered flowers, planned menus and instructed the servants, wishing, irritably, that Nicholas would at least show some interest in the proceedings instead of wandering about the house like a ghost.

The Indian summer had broken at last. On the day of the funeral, torrential rain poured down from a leaden sky: gutters, choked with fallen leaves, overflowed into bubbling streams, slowing traffic, surprising the population of a city whose lives had become geared to warmth and sunshine. Initially, Sophia had discussed with Nicholas the possibility of taking her brother's body back to England for burial, an idea which he wearily rejected. 'My father chose to live in France,' Nicky said. 'I think he would have wanted to be buried here.'

Representatives of the diplomatic service, M. Renay, the Simenons, and many of Madeleine's friends attended the service, and huddled round the graveside beneath a mushrooming of black umbrellas.

Standing proudly erect, keeping a tight rein on her emotions, Sophia wept inwardly for the waste of a human life, that of a man who had never learned the secret of happiness, how to laugh, love and show forgiveness. It distressed her to think that their last words had been spoken in anger, that death had robbed her of the chance of making amends. But perhaps the elegiac praises of the Anglican minister, uttered from the pulpit with forcefulness and conviction, were best remembered, the failures of Clive's life forgiven and forgotten. He would have been pleased, she thought, to be eulogized as 'one who never turned his back but marched breast forward, an upholder of justice and moral values, an English gentleman of the highest order.'

If only she knew what was going on in Nicky's mind. Could it be that Clive's death had hit him harder than she thought? He appeared to be in a state of shock, waging a silent, exhausting battle within himself. But there were important matters to be discussed. Somehow she must get through to him. She had the feeling that his future depended on it.

When the informal buffet was over and the guests had drifted away, Sophia ordered tea in the little room which had been Madeleine's boudoir. Nicholas was standing near the window staring out at the rain, his back towards her. 'Thank you, Simenon,' Sophia said, when the man came in with the tray, 'it has been a long, tiring day for all of us, especially your wife. Please tell her to make dinner as simple as possible. We'll have something cold left over from the buffet.'

When he had gone, 'Come and drink your tea, Nicky,' she said. 'It is time we talked about the future.'

'What is there to talk about?' Moodily, he turned away from the window.

'A great deal, I'd have thought. You have scarcely spoken two sentences to me these past few days.'

'I'm sorry, Aunt. I've had a lot on my mind.'

'That is perfectly obvious. We both have. Sudden death is not easy to cope with.' Sophia's mouth trembled suddenly. 'I wish now that Clive and I had not quarrelled. I shall never forgive myself . . . I know he was a difficult man, but . . .'

'Difficult? Is that how you saw him?' Nicky said forcefully. 'He was a monster! As a child I was frightened to death of him; as a boy I grew to loathe him. As a man I hated him for his harshness, his bloody – incorruptibility, his self-righteousness; the way he tried to crush Madeleine's spirit! Why the hell did he marry her in the first place? He never loved her!'

'That's where you're wrong,' Sophia said quietly. 'He worshipped the ground she walked on. He told me so himself, and I had no reason to doubt his word.'

'Then why did he make her life, and mine, such a misery?' Nicky demanded hoarsely, pacing the room.

Sophia's moment of truth had arrived. 'Because he was jealous of you. Because he knew that you were not his son!'

'Not his son? What the hell do you mean?'

Bowing her head, 'I never meant to tell you. Please, sit down and listen. Listen and try to understand . . .

'You and Clive had one thing in common, your love for Madeleine.' Raising her head, her eyes bright with tears, she said, 'Unfortunately for poor Madeleine, you made the mistake of placing her on a pedestal, never seeing her as she really was, a human being like the rest of us.

'How hard it must have been for her to assume the role of a plaster saint, too afraid of shattering the image you had created for her to admit that she, too, was vulnerable, capable of making mistakes.'

Sophia smiled sadly, 'You're shocked, aren't you? Shocked that Madeleine was not a plaster saint after all, but a flesh and blood woman who once had a love affair, so deep, so passionate, that it remained with her for the rest of her life, even though she spent the rest of her life trying to cover up the truth.'

'If what you say is true,' Nicholas said hoarsely, disbelievingly, 'then – who . . . ?'

De Vigny's translation of the farm documents had revealed no dramatic events on which to hang a plot. In any case, Sarah had never felt less like writing.

She had closed the door of the farm cottage with a deep feeling of regret that the Aga would go out for lack of re-fuelling, the living-room fire would sink to ashes, and the flowers Nicholas had given her would fade and die for lack of water.

It all seemed such a waste – a waste of love, and life, and hope.

She had not wanted to come to the château, but Charles had been so insistent, so kind, that, too tired to argue, she had simply packed her things and placed herself in his hands.

'I'm so sorry this had to happen,' Charles said, after Nicholas had gone, 'but you must stay with me for as long as you wish.'

Next day, he had shown her over the house from attics to cellars, and she had glimpsed something of the past glory in the vast, echoing rooms. The ballroom in particular, with its gilded rococo panelling and dusty chandeliers, dust-sheeted furniture and French windows opening on to a wrought-iron balcony overlooking the broad sweep of the valley below.

'In my grandfather's time,' Charles said, standing beside her on the balcony, 'a bevy of aunts and uncles occupied what he termed "grace and favour apartments". The house was alive then with music and laughter.' He smiled reminiscently, a little sadly. 'I would often stand here, as a boy, watching the arrival of weekend guests. What exciting times those were. Every room in the house would be filled with flowers. Of course we had servants in those days, before the outbreak of war.

'One of my great treats was helping the old gardener to bring in the greenery at Christmas – great fir boughs which I would help decorate with silver paint. François and I had great times together, playing hide and seek. I often wish . . .'

'What do you wish?'

'That François had lived, married, had children and grandchildren to carry on the title. It was never meant to be mine.' Standing there, proudly erect, his head thrown back. 'How different my life would have been if my brother had lived.'

Suddenly, at that moment, the jigsaw pieces slotted together, in Sarah's mind, to form a complete picture. Things which had puzzled her became overwhelmingly clear.

Turning to look at her, 'You have guessed the truth, haven't you?' Charles said simply.

'Yes, I think so. I half guessed that first night, at dinner. But I couldn't be sure.'

Drawing in a deep breath, 'Tell me, Sarah, are you in love with my son?' de Vigny asked quietly.

Shaken by his confrontation with Sophia, when she had gone up to her room, Nicholas went through to the kitchen to tell Madame Simenon not to bother about food for himself, to prepare a tray for his aunt, then take the rest of the evening off. It was then the housekeeper told him that she and her husband would be leaving as soon as he engaged other staff to replace them.

'I am sorry, M. Nicholas,' she said, 'we stayed on after Madame Tierney's death from a sense of loyalty to your father. But now . . . You understand, Monsieur? We wish to retire from service, to spend more time with our grandchildren.'

'Of course. Thank you for telling me.' He walked slowly upstairs to Madeleine's room, remembering the way he used to carry the glass bowl of gardenias to her bedside table.

So many memories . . . Memories of Madeleine, of this house, each room with its ghosts. Sophia had seen as bloody-mindedness his reluctance to return here after the death of her brother, and he had felt unable to explain why he had not wanted to come. He would never again enter the drawing room, scene of his mother's lying in state, without recalling the darkness lit by flickering candles, the sickly scent of the flowers surrounding her coffin, his bitter sense of pain and outrage that she had slipped away from him without a final word of goodbye.

In the adjoining dressing room, opening doors, Nicholas saw Clive's clothes neatly arrayed on hangers, and ran his fingers over the immaculately tailored suit he had worn the last time he had seen him in this house – the day his father had closed the door in his face. Except that Clive Tierney was not his father . . .

The man who had worn these clothes had played no part in his conception. To understand all is to forgive all. Gently closing the wardrobe, he remembered Clive as he had last seen him, a worn out, shrunken old man on the verge of death, and knew that this was the way he would always remember him – the kindest way he could remember him, without bitterness.

Returning to his mother's room, he picked up the leather-bound diary which had remained faithfully dusted but otherwise untouched since her death. Turning over the pages, glancing briefly at the entries, he saw that most of them referred to dressmaking and hair appointments, written in a shaky hand which he scarcely recognized as Madeleine's.

About to close the book, he noticed that something had been written on the last page: 'Poor Clive,' he read. 'My fault, not his. I could not face those other specialists. Have begged him not to let N. know. Clive angry. He thinks it time N. faced up to the truth about my illness. I do not want this. I shall go on pretending . . . '

The last entry, almost illegible: 'Time running out. No more letters to C. If only I could see him once more. Wish Sophia were here. She will know what to do when the time comes . . . Pray God my son will find it in his heart to forgive me . . . I love him so much.'

Guessing that Sophia would still be awake, Nicholas crossed the landing to her room. Strange to think that she was not and never had been his aunt. The thought took some getting used to. He felt as though his life had suddenly swung off balance. Now he must talk to her in more depth. The fact that Charles de Vigny was his father had scarcely sunk in at the time of her revelation. Then, quietly, and with great dignity, she had made her apologies, and left him alone in Madeleine's boudoir.

She was sitting up in bed, wearing the Japanese

kimono with the gold embroidered dragons. 'I had to come,' he said softly.

'I thought you might. Sit down. Here, beside me,' she patted the eiderdown.

'I have asked Claudette to bring your supper on a tray.'

'That was kind of you, but I'm not hungry.'

'They are leaving, by the way, the Simenons.'

'Yes, I half expected they would come to that decision.'

'Talking of decisions . . . ' Holding Sophia's hand, 'I have decided to sell this house.'

'Have you, my dear?'

'You are not surprised?'

'I should have been more surprised had you decided to keep it.'

'May I ask why?'

'It has outlived its purpose.' She smiled sadly. 'One cannot go on living with ghosts.' She tightened her clasp on his hand. 'The past is over and done with. That is the reason why I have decided to sell the Carillon.'

'Sell . . . ?' Abruptly Nicky got to his feet. Startled by her announcement, gripping the bed-rail, he said, 'But you can't! It's your life!'

'It was my life. Not now.' She looked at him standing there, his face dark with concern. 'It might have been different had I someone to hand it on to. But facts must be faced. I know that your heart has never been in it, my dear. In any case, I wouldn't want to stay on without Michel.'

Her eyes filled with tears. 'I was very much in love with him once, a long time ago,' she said. 'I knew, of course, that he was not in love with me and never could be, but that made no difference to my feelings. One has no jurisdiction over love, I find. One cannot choose who

331

to love and who not to love. Would it were that simple.'

'I'm sorry, Aunt. I never knew.'

'There is something else you do not know.' Sophia's lips trembled, 'Your father, Charles de Vigny, asked me to marry him.'

Nicholas looked at her bemusedly, 'And you refused?'

Sophia drew in a deep breath. Blinking back the tears, she said, 'It was really a business proposition. I'd rather not go into that now.'

'I see. And if it had not been a business proposition?'

The faintest semblance of a smile. 'I would have said Yes.'

De Vigny's question, 'Are you in love with my son?' startled Sarah.

'Yes,' she said slowly, 'but he is obviously not in love with me.'

'Are you quite sure about that?'

Looking across the valley, thinking that the bright Indian summer was over now, feeling a hint of coldness in the air, shivering slightly, she said, 'I think so. A woman always knows when a man is not in love with her. Perhaps I fell in love with a figment of my imagination.'

'You are cold. Forgive me. Come, let us go down to the fire.'

In the drawing room, he made Sarah sit down in the wing chair drawn up near the hearth. Pouring her a glass of wine, he said grimly, 'This is all my fault.' Remembering Sophia, 'I should have told Nicholas the truth when Madeleine died.'

God, what a fool he'd been, how blind, how stupid to believe that Sophia would have married him for the reasons he had given her. Why hadn't he told her he loved her? 'A woman always knows when a man is not in love with her.' But perhaps Sarah was wrong about that. Perhaps a woman did not know when a man was in love with her because the man had not the courage to say so, to *make* her believe it.

He had never felt more joyfully relaxed and hopeful. Leaving Paris early, heading the Daimler in the direction of the château, Nicholas experienced a thrill of pleasure at the thought of seeing Sarah again, and of meeting with Charles de Vigny. Smiling as he drove, he wondered what he would say to him – 'Hello, Charles,' or, simply, 'Father'? He had no doubt whatever what he would say to Sarah – 'I love you.'

In a matter of days, his whole life had changed. Gone were the churning self-doubts, his inability to make decisions regarding his future.

Last night, Sophia had warned him that Charles might expect him to stay on in France, to make his home at the château, to learn about the administration of the de Vigny estate. Not that the prospect seemed unpleasant to him. He loved France, would spend as much time with his father as possible, getting to know him better. Hopefully, he might persuade Charles to lease him the farm cottage as a pied-à-terre for himself and Sarah, a place they could go to whenever they had time to spare – Sarah from her writing, he from his role as the new owner of the Carillon.

Concentrating on the road ahead, his decision to take over the Carillon would, he realized, entail a great deal of hard work and commitment.

Commitment. The warmth and strength derived from the thought that he had, at last, felt able to make a solid commitment to one course of action ran through his veins like fire. The thought of making a lifetime's commitment to one woman set his pulse racing with the desire to hold Sarah in his arms, to bring her to the realization that she was the one woman in the world for him.

He had known, last night, when Sophia told him that she was leaving the Carillon, that he could not let it go to strangers who might alter it beyond recognition – all that had been built up over the years with so much loving care and attention. But even more strongly had come the realization that this was his home. Not the house in the Rue St Hélène, nor the Château de Vigny, but the rambling Victorian mansion standing, like the Rock of Gibraltar, on the outskirts of the City of York with its glorious Minster, grey city walls, and narrow twisting streets, where his formative years had been spent. Not always happy years, but rich years; part of the tapestry of his life which he could never bear to part with.

Nearing his destination, he was filled with a kind of nervous apprehension as he saw the great dark belt of the pine forest adumbrated against the skyline, and the palely glimmering tanks of the trout farm in the valley. He would drive straight to the cottage, he thought. With luck Sarah might be there, busy in the kitchen, or in the orchard; or possibly in her room getting on with the revision of *Amabie*.

Sweeping the car to a halt, he hurried to the front door, expecting to find it open. It was locked. Peering through the living-room window, he saw that the fire was out, the flowers he had given Sarah on his return from l'église St Germaine, drooping listlessly for lack of attention.

Of course, what a fool he was. De Vigny would never have allowed her to stay on alone at the farmhouse. He would have insisted on her staying at the château.

Driving quickly between the banks of rhododendrons leading up to the house, he remembered, with a feeling of self disgust, his curt dismissal of her the night he went to Paris. How could he have been so insensitive? She must have been hurt, even angry. All he wanted was the chance to explain that the man he was then bore no resemblance to the man he was now.

Parking the car in the drive, he hurried, two steps at a time, to the front door, and rang the bell.

'Oh, M. Tierney,' the housekeeper's husband said when he answered the door, 'if you have come to see M. le Comte, I regret that he is not at home. He and Madame Vale left first thing this morning, for Paris.'

'Paris? Did he say why?'

'Simply that he had some urgent personal matter to attend to after he had seen Madame Vale to the airport.'

'The – airport?'

'Yes, Monsieur. Madame has gone back to England.'

Chapter Twenty-five

Sarah had been right in thinking that he had not been totally honest with her, Faulkner thought bitterly. Not that he had lied exactly. He had simply withheld one vital piece of information, the symptoms of which were becoming increasingly obvious, not to say embarrassing.

On honeymoon with Suki, he had blamed his slowness of response to their foreplay as fatigue pure and simple. In any case, he had scarcely expected a woman in her condition to indulge in the pastime of arousal. Or possibly his lack of interest in love-making had had to do with his bride's appearance: bloated, to put it mildly.

Pregnant women, supposedly at their most beautiful in the process of fulfilling their most important function in life, had never seemed so to him. Furthermore, he had aroused Suki's contempt by his frequent visits to the bathroom.

'For Christ's sake, Faulkner, what the hell's the matter with you?' Suki had snapped at him accusingly. 'You're spending more time in that bloody bathroom than you are in bed! Well, all I can say, you'd better see your doctor when you get home. Tell him to give you some "waterwork" pills!'

To be told by his physician that frequent visits to the loo were not uncommon in a man of his age, had scarcely comforted Faulkner, who saw as a threat to his sexual prowess the hinted at prostate-gland surgery which may be necessary if the prescribed course of tablets failed to work.

The tablets had not worked. It was then that the spectre of enforced celibacy, plus the slamming of the door in his face as Suki had marched down the front steps to enter a waiting taxi, had persuaded him to turn to Sarah in his hour of need.

Moreover, the end of his marriage to Suki had come with a pyrotechnic display of fireworks reminiscent of a Chinese New Year celebration. Made as angry as a hornet when she had discovered her case of stuffed birds shattered beyond repair and by Faulkner's high-handed departure to his club, fuming at his threat to cancel her credit card accounts, she had telephoned Sam Dexter, whose advice had been both simple and direct: 'Leave the silly old bastard!'

'How the hell can I?'

'Quite easily, I'd have thought. Pack an overnight bag, come round to my place, and we'll take it from there.'

'What about the baby?'

Dexter sighed impatiently. '*What* about the baby? Bring it if you must, but personally I'd far rather you left it where it is – unless you'd feel cheated. Frankly, my love, I have never quite seen you in the light of motherhood incarnate, so why not let the father assume responsibility?' He laughed suddenly, 'Know what? I've often thought that the divorce rate would drop dramatically if wives left their kids for the husband to look after! Why any woman should want to tote around her mistakes for the rest of her natural is beyond me. Must have something to do with the umbilical cord – a form of emotional strangulation if ever there was one.'

He paused to light a cigarette. 'By the way, I'm flying to America next week to face-lift a client's house on Long Island. If you want to make the trip, I'd rather you came unencumbered. OK?'

Faulkner scarcely knew what had hit him. Arriving home, expecting to find his wife in a chastened frame of mind after his night at the club, he had gone up to their bedroom to find Suki emptying drawers, and flinging the contents of her wardrobes on the bed.

Staring in amazement, he said, 'What the hell do you think you are doing?'

'What does it look like? I'm leaving!' Facing him squarely, Suki resembled Queen Boudicca about to plough the knives of her chariot wheels into human flesh. *His* flesh!

'*Leaving?*' (Where had he heard those words before?)

'Don't tell me you're surprised!' Contemptuously, 'You walked out on me last night. Now the boot's on the other foot! What a fine bloody catch you turned out to be! Here!' Raking in her handbag, she flung a handful of letters and hotel bills at his feet. 'Show these to your bloody solicitor! Divorce me! I should care! Well, go on, pick them up! Gloat over them! Fumble over them! That's about all you're good for, isn't it? *Fumbling!*'

Angry, shocked beyond belief, he said, 'But you can't just walk out like this! What about Felicity?'

Snapping the catch of her jewel-case, 'From now on she is your responsibility,' she told him succinctly, marching downstairs. 'I suggest *you* try breast-feeding her!'

At first, Verity had frostily declined her father's telephone invitation to have lunch with him at the Savoy Grill, until she knew that his marriage to the odious Suki Mitford was over and done with, and that Richard had also been invited to attend what appeared to be a family reunion celebration, when she had felt it her duty to reconsider the invitation, if only to speak her mind on the subject.

Richard, as usual, was unashamedly hungry, charming, outgoing, and indifferent to his parent's problems. His attitude clearly indicated: 'So the blonde bimbo finally came to her senses? Why all the hassle?' More important, by far, the menu. He hoped to heaven that his order of lobster mayonnaise would consist of something more substantial than a little claw-meat resting on four spaced out asparagus tips. 'You were saying, Father?' he asked brightly, wishing he had plumped for the Steak Diane.

'Simply that I hope you and Verity will give due consideration to my proposal,' Faulkner reiterated, nettled by his son's inattention, his apparent disinterest in anything apart from the menu.

'Oh, what proposal was that?' Richard asked cheerfully.

Verity said, disapprovingly, 'If you had been listening, you'd have heard Daddy say that he would like us to move into his new house.'

'What? You mean the "mausoleum"?' Richard bunched up his eyebrows. 'For heaven's sake why, Father? I thought you hated the place.'

'Daddy says we can have our own apartments,' Verity told her ill-mannered sibling, thinking it might be rather nice to get away from the cramped flat she shared with her fellow students: regarding more kindly her errant father now that he had come to his senses.

'Oh, really? Great! Why not?' Richard enthused, hedging his bets: ordering Steak Diane in addition to the lobster mayonnaise, thinking that if the 'old boy' was so desperate for company, he might as well move into the 'mausoleum' with the lovely, languid Leonora. Truth to tell, he was fed up with his shared flat in Holland Park, in which close encounters of the sexual kind were scarcely possible. One never knew, for instance, when the bedroom door would burst open to admit some fool intent on finding a clean pair of socks.

Sarah's flight from Paris had landed at Heathrow an hour ago. Passing through customs, she telephoned Freya to say she was in London, and could they meet somewhere for lunch?

'But of course, darling! How wonderful,' Freya enthused. 'I have a contract for you to sign, and a cheque to deliver. Shall we say the Savoy Grill at one o'clock? I'll ring up right now. Book a table.'

Arriving ahead of time, Sarah thought how odd it all seemed. A matter of a few months ago, she could scarcely afford a ham sandwich at Alf's Cafe, now here she was on the threshold of possibly the most famous restaurant in London.

Glancing round the room, her heart missed a beat. It couldn't be! In that moment of recognition of Faulkner, Richard and Verity sitting together, apparently on the best of terms, Sarah's immediate reaction was to run away, but her feet seemed soldered to the floor.

How lovely Verity looked, and how grown up, wearing a medley of softly draped garments of the kind worn by fashion models on the pages of *Vogue*, so understated it wasn't true, apart from the cost of the designer labels; the kind of garments that flowed as limpidly as a summer stream. But her daughter could not very well have turned up at the Savoy Grill wearing knee-shredded jeans and a Marks and Spencer's sweater, Sarah thought, longing to hold the girl in her arms, as she longed to hold her son, Richard. But not Faulkner!

With a sudden clarity of vision, Sarah knew that her marriage to Faulkner Vale, all her memories of her past life with him were best laid to rest and forgotten. She could never again become a part of his life, even for the sake of their children. She had outgrown him, as, possibly, their children had outgrown her. But she had to be sure about that. Taking her courage in both hands, she walked across the room to their table. 'Hello,' she said simply.

'Look, darling, you've simply got to stop crying,' Freya said, handing Sarah a tissue across a snack-bar table at King's Cross Station. 'So what the hell does it matter that we're lunching here instead of the Savoy? The main thing is, you did what was necessary for your peace of mind.' She added wickedly, with a typical flash of Cockney humour, 'Just wish I'd been a fly in the soup, that's all, when those kids of yours clapped eyes on you! No wonder they were gob-smacked! Truth to tell, I felt more than a little taken aback myself when I caught my first glimpse of the new-look Sarah Vale! So what actually happened?'

'They didn't know me; didn't even recognize me at first,' Sarah confessed, drying her eyes.

Sitting back in her chair, looking rather like a Mexican bandit in a multi-coloured poncho worn over black velvet slacks, 'But what did they actually say when they had stopped being surprised?' Freya asked. Knowing the history of Sarah's rejection by her children and that glossy, womanizing ex-husband of hers, she hoped that she had entered the arena with all flags flying, as befitted a woman who had carved out a new life for herself without the help and support of any one of them. Above all, she hoped that

Sarah would not allow sentimentality to blind her to her children's selfishness.

Recalling the moment when she walked towards that table in the Savoy Grill, the sinking feeling in the pit of her stomach when she said, 'Hello', and saw the blank expression in Verity's eyes as she turned her head to look at her, Sarah thought that this had been the worst experience of her life so far. Then Faulkner and Richard had got up as a matter of courtesy, and Faulkner had said, disbelievingly, 'Sarah, what are you doing here?'

It was then, and only then, that Richard and Verity had recognized her and begun to react to their mother's reappearance in their lives. First came Richard's slow-dawning smile of approval. Always the more gregarious and demonstrative of her offspring, 'Hey, Ma, what have you done to yourself?' he enthused. 'You look sensational!' Snapping his fingers at a passing waiter, he said, 'Lay another place, will you?'

'No, please, that won't be necessary. I'm meeting someone.' How she had remained calm and smiling, Sarah scarcely knew. Verity's cheeks had turned very pale, she noticed, and her hands were clenched into fists, the knuckles showing white, as if in the grip of some strong emotion which she scarcely knew how to handle. It was then Sarah saw, with an upsurge of happiness, that the girl was wearing the ammonite pendant, and said, gently, 'Oh, I'm so pleased you received your birthday present. I wasn't sure if you'd like it.'

Verity said hoarsely, 'I meant to write to you, to thank you. It's just that . . . ' Her eyes filled with tears. 'Oh, Mother, I'm sorry . . . '

'Not to worry!' Mother. Verity had actually called her Mother.

Then Freya had appeared on the threshold, an outrageously bizarre figure in her Mexican poncho and wide-brimmed black hat, and Sarah had said, 'I must go now. But you will keep in touch? Come to visit me?'

'Sure thing, Ma,' Richard said brightly. And, 'If you still want me,' Verity said softly, her eyes brimming with tears.

'Want you? Oh, Verity, you'll never know how much.'

Taking Sarah's elbow, walking with her a few paces, speaking in a low voice, 'The children are coming to live with me,' Faulkner said confidentially. 'They'll have their own rooms. It *is* a very large house.' Taking everything for granted, as usual. 'You can have your own rooms, too, if you like – for the time being at any rate.' He added, magnanimously, 'You can bring your own furniture, if you wish.'

'Goodbye, Faulkner,' she said quietly.

'Goodbye? What the hell do you mean – goodbye?'

She smiled sadly. 'Don't you see? It's all over between us! It was over between us a long time ago! I think from the moment I found that initialled handkerchief under my pillow.'

'Sarah!' But she was not listening. Crossing towards Freya, 'Please, don't ask questions, just drive me to King's Cross! Just get me out of here! *Please*, Freya!'

'Sure thing, honey-bun,' Freya said gaily, 'The food here's not much cop anyway. Give me a British Rail sandwich any day of the week!'

Dear, unorthodox Freya.

Now, all Sarah wanted was to go home. Back to York, the safety of her own four walls, her view of the Minster from her sitting-room window. Home . . .

343

So this was the house that Madeleine had described so graphically in her letters. Walking the garden path, Charles felt he knew every tree, every shrub, each room, as intimately as his own hand; the tesselated hall with its curving staircase, the Venetian mirror reflecting the half-moon table, the spotlit paintings, delicately fashioned Louis Quinze sofas in the drawing room. He could almost imagine the faithful Simenon crossing the hall to answer the doorbell, shrugging on his black alpaca jacket as he came to answer the summons.

'Good afternoon, Monsieur.'

Charles smiled, the man was so exactly as Madeleine had described him. 'I should like to see M. Nicholas Tierney,' he said.

'M. Nicholas is not here, sir. He left early this morning. But Mademoiselle Tierney is at home.'

'Then perhaps you would give her my card.'

'Certainly, if you would care to wait in the drawing room.'

Minutes later, Sophia came in, looking pale and drawn, Charles thought, unable to tell if she was pleased to see him or not. 'Hello, Charles,' she said gravely.

'My dear Sophia . . . '

'Please sit down. I hardly expected to see you here.'

'I had to come. But first, tell me, how is Sir Clive?'

'My brother is – dead.' Sophia spoke calmly. 'I arrived at the medical centre too late to see him alive. Not that he would have known me. He never regained consciousness.'

'I am sorry. Please accept my condolences.'

'Thank you.' Keeping a tight rein on her emotions. 'But why have you come? Simenon told me you came to see Nicky. May I ask why?'

344

Looking directly at Sophia, 'To tell him the truth,' de Vigny said simply.

'Then you've had a wasted journey. He already knows. *I* told him.' Her self control wavered. 'Well, fools rush in, as the saying goes.'

'So it would seem.' His eyes held hers. 'Behold then, the greatest fool in Christendom!' Rising to his feet, crossing towards her, sweeping aside formality, pulling her to her feet, holding her hands, he said, 'I asked you to be my wife for one reason, and one reason only, because I could not bear the thought of spending the rest of my life without you.' Smiling down at her. 'I love you, Sophia.'

Resting her head against his shoulder, too tired to swim against the tide any more, how did the last verse of that song go? Sophia wondered hazily. Ah, yes, 'And these few precious years I'll share with you. These vintage years I'll share with you'.

Coming home, Sarah saw the grey stone city walls, the leaning gravestones of the cholera cemetery. But the subject of her next book, already teasing her mind, would be not about death, but life. Life and love. A contemporary novel, set in France, with flashbacks to the First and Second World Wars. A family saga. The main character a woman writer in search of love. A novel, possibly, with a sad ending, when the woman realized that the man she loved was not in love with her.

The sitting room lamps had been switched on. The undrawn curtains revealed a wedge of turquoise blue sky, a star or two, the glow of the Minster flood-lights.

It was that busy time of evening when people came home from work to kick off their shoes and switch on the television.

Dumping her luggage, 'Helen,' Sarah called, 'I'm home!'

Helen emerged from the bathroom, clad in a bath-sheet, obviously startled. 'Sarah! I had no idea! I thought you'd be away much longer!'

'Is anything the matter?'

'No, of course not . . . That is, Ralph and I are going to the Theatre Royal to see *Gaslight*.'

'And you thought I'd mind? Is that it?'

'Well, naturally. After all, Ralph is your friend, not mine!' The pinkness of Helen's cheeks betrayed her agitation that, in accepting Ralph's invitation, she had committed a crime against friendship. 'I'm sorry, Sarah, it's just that he asked me, and I said yes.'

'Then hadn't you better hurry and get dressed?'

'But what about you?' Helen said worriedly, 'You look exhausted. What – happened?'

'Nothing happened.' Sarah smiled briefly. 'Nothing at all.'

As the plane lifted from the runway, Nicholas saw, far below, the sprawling city of Paris, a mass of twinkling lights, bathed in the lilac mist of an autumn twilight, swirling away in the encroaching darkness.

Paris, the city he would forever think of as Madeleine's. Not that the memory of Madeleine could hurt him now, as it used to. For Madeleine had loved and been loved in return; had known the passion and power of an overwhelming love affair. For this he felt intensely grateful, that her loveliness had not gone to waste, that the

346

memory of that love had remained with her all the days of her life, that she had faced death serenely, without fear, because of the sustaining power of love.

Love.

Nothing happened. Nothing at all. But Sarah knew that something *had* happened.

In time to come, the pattern of the past days would emerge much clearer, much stronger. In time, the pain of an abortive love affair would pass. God willing, she would remember only the good things. Above all, that she was still capable of loving, of feeling happiness as well as pain.

A thin, light rain was falling as she walked across to the Minster. The city seemed half asleep at this hour of the morning, the streets silent and empty now that the summertime was over. She felt, as closely as a heartbeat, the enveloping charm of this place she had come to love so much. This city which had been her refuge and inspiration ever since that cold February night when she had walked out of the station to find shelter beneath the roof of the Perivale Guest House.

And what of Nicholas?

Entering the Minster, walking slowly towards the All Saints' Chapel, he would stay on in France, she thought, live in the Château de Vigny, turn his face to the future, make a new life for himself far distanced from the old. One day, perhaps, he would find someone to love, a woman with whom he would share his life, a woman capable of making him happy.

If only she had been that woman.

*   *   *

Instinctively, he had known where to find her. Coming in from the rain, he saw her standing near the All Saints' Chapel.

Treading softly, he moved slowly towards her.

THE END